Chapel Springs Survival

by Ane Mulligan

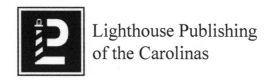

Lighthouse Publishing
of the Carolinas

CHAPEL SPRINGS SURVIVAL BY ANE MULLIGAN
Published by Lighthouse Publishing of the Carolinas
2333 Barton Oaks Dr., Raleigh, NC, 27614

ISBN: 978-1-941103-58-6
Cover design by Ken Raney: www.kenraney.com
Interior design by Karthick Srinivasan
Original artwork by Terence Mulligan

Available in print from your local bookstore, online, or from the publisher at:
www.lighthousepublishingofthecarolinas.com

For more information on this book and the author visit: www.anemulligan.com

This is a work of fiction. Names, characters, and incidents are all products of the author's imagination or are used for fictional purposes. Any mentioned brand names, places, and trade marks remain the property of their respective owners, bear no association with the author or the publisher, and are used for fictional purposes only.

Brought to you by the creative team at Lighthouse Publishing of the Carolinas:
Susan Price, Brian Cross, and Eddie Jones.

Library of Congress Cataloging-in-Publication Data
Mulligan, Ane
Chapel Springs Survival / Ane Mulligan 1st ed.

Printed in the United States of America

Praise for *Chapel Springs Survival*

Buckle up for another bumpy and funny ride with the ladies of Chapel Springs. Characters are funny, caring and just want to do the right thing for the community, with unexpected and humorous results. Mulligan has written a wonderful contemporary novel that tickles the funny bone.

~**RT Book Reviews,** 4 Stars

Pour yourself a tall glass of sweet tea and head out onto the porch with this richly woven tale of life in a small, but suddenly booming southern town. Mulligan's characters are warm and engaging, not to mention delightfully human, as they struggle to navigate problems both big and small, proving in the end that nothing is impossible when we hold tight to faith and keep our hearts open.

~**Barbara Davis**
Author of *Summer at Hideaway Key*

With her trademark wit and Southern charm, Ane Mulligan takes us on another trip to the idyllic town of Chapel Springs. With Claire Bennett and her zany crew of friends and family, Mulligan spins an endearing tale of how far we'll go for those we love, and the ones we hope will love us in return.

~**Jennifer AlLee**
Carol Award Finalist and Best-Selling Author

In her entertaining follow-up to *Chapel Springs Revival*, Ane Mulligan brings us back into Claire Bennett's ever-bustling life. There are enough challenges and conflicts here to keep Claire constantly on her toes, and you'll love her for her vulnerability and strong perseverance against withering odds. Claire may not always get it right, but she tries so hard, you just know she and Chapel Springs are sure to survive.

~**Trish Perry**
Author of *Better Than Chocolate*

Fans of Ane Mulligan's *Chapel Springs* novels will be delighted once again to spend time in this quintessential little town in Georgia with its colorful coterie of friends, family, and lovable souls. In *Chapel Springs Survival* Mulligan introduces us to a bevy of issues surrounding the expanding tourist town and pits protagonist Claire Bennett against a surprise family member who she must learn to forgive, and ultimately love—even if the girl is best described as a *prickly cactus*!

~**Kellie Coates Gilbert**
Author of *A Woman of Fortune*
(Library Journal's Best Book of 2014)

Spirited author Ane Mulligan has written a cheeky sequel in *Chapel Springs Survival*. Mulligan delivers page-turning plot twists and relatable characters in this second installment of life in the charming and unpredictable town of Chapel Springs. This is a highly recommended read.

~**Sandra D. Bricker**
Author of Live-Out-Proud fiction,
including the *Jessie Stanton* series and *Moments of Truth*

I so love Ane Mulligan's stories. My bet is that you will too!

~**Eva Marie Everson**
Best-selling, award-winning author of *Five Brides*

Reading the *Chapel Springs* series is like coming home to the place you wish you were from, to the friends you know and love.

~**Gina Holmes**
Best-selling, award-winning author of
Crossing Oceans and *Driftwood Tides*

Chapel Springs Survival is a delight to read! Ane Mulligan is a master storyteller with a humor that catches you from behind and tickles your heart. I found myself chuckling out loud at its quirky characters and loving the dynamics of this small town exploding at the seams!

~**Dineen Miller**
Multi-published and award-winning author

"Friendship has no survival value; rather it is one of those things which gives value to survival."

- *C.S. Lewis*

Dedication

To my dear daughter-in-law, Zully Mulligan. You made our son happy, and our hearts are filled with gratitude and love. And of course, the precious grandsons you added to our lives helped, too. You're the daughter of my heart, and I love you.

Acknowledgements

This book was such fun to write since it involved Mama's retribution. So very special thanks go to our eldest son, Michael, and his wife, Zully, for allowing me to tell their story. In this book, it was *much* embellished, as our real story had no conflict. We loved Zully from the moment we met her.

As always, a gazillion thanks to my critique partners Michelle Griep and Lisa Ludwig. You hold my feet to the fire. I couldn't have done this or any other work without you. You're worth your weight in coffee and chocolate!

I could never miss thanking Ginger Aster, my wonderful beta reader. You catch my mistakes and plot holes and make sure I correct them. I rely on you, my friend. A road trip is in our future!

It's not easy to fully express my thanks to Sandra Bishop, my wonderful award-winning agent. We were friends first, sharing many an evening after ACFW conferences. That makes for a great relationship. Thank you for believing in me, hanging in there when God said, "Not yet," and continuing to pray for me and be a friend. You're the best!

To the team at Lighthouse Publishing of the Carolinas: thank you! An extra dose of thanks to Susan Price, my wonderful editor! I knew you were special when it turned out you know Portuguese. Talk about God-coincidences. I'm looking forward to working with you again.

Thanks to the members of ACFW for allowing me to ask lots of questions. Y'all are the best!

To my husband, thank you for your support and your incredible paintings for my covers! I love you. To our son, Chef Greg, thank you for keeping us fed while I lived in Chapel Springs.

Last but most, my undying thankfulness to my Heavenly Father for always whispering to my heart.

Chapter 1

Like a shot pinball, Claire Bennett pinged against, around and between hordes of straw hats, bikinis, and plaid shorts. All along Sandy Shores Drive, shoulder-to-shoulder throngs of people crowded the sidewalk and spilled into the avenue. A party atmosphere—with noise level to match—permeated the quiet morning and their once peaceful village.

What had they done? When she and her friends envisioned the revitalization of Chapel Springs, it was a nice, controlled rise in tourist trade—not this craziness.

One bruised elbow later, Claire reached the door of her art gallery, *The Painted Loon*, and turned her key in the lock. A heavy hand grasped her shoulder. Her heart skipped a beat. Was she about to be robbed?

Hold on. In broad daylight? With this crowd watching? She may not be the brightest color on the palette, but she did possess a little common sense. Her gaze traveled up the beefy arm to a scraggly-bearded face with beady eyes. A rolled red bandana wrapped around his forehead held back salt-and-pepper hair. Beside him stood a bleached-blonde motorcycle mama, dressed in a halter-top and the skimpiest shorts Claire had ever seen. Strings hung from their ragged edges and drew attention to the lumpy cellulite dotting the back of her thighs. Who was this woman trying to kid? She was fifty if she was a day.

"You're the loon lady," Motor-mama said. "We want to see your pots." They tried to shoulder their way into the gallery, but Claire stood her ground.

"I'm sorry, we aren't open yet. Please come back at ten." She threw the deadbolt, pulled down the window shade, then leaned her back against the door and drew in air. The familiar scent of lemon oil-rubbed wood with the underlying twang of turpentine surrounded her like a security blanket.

After rattling the door handle a few times, the couple retreated. Claire released her breath in a whoosh as she slipped into the back workroom, where she and her gallery-partner-slash-best friend, Patsy Kowalski, created their art. And, Claire had to admit, a problem for Chapel Springs. The review they received last year—Patsy for her paintings and Claire for pottery—had put them on the art world's radar.

Between that and the town's cleanup campaign, Chapel Springs attracted half the population east of the Mississippi. Then Rod Campbell, Nashville's newest country heartthrob, strolled into *The Painted Loon* one day and bought some artwork. He told a Hollywood producer about them, and the producer told one of his starlets, who was an art collector.

Now Chapel Springs was filled with stargazers. Their quiet little village by the lake had become *the* trendy place to visit in north Georgia. Oh sure, Chapel Lake was the best summer vacation spot in the state, with its tournament fishing, beautiful beaches, and fabulous hiking trails. Naturally, the town's merchants wanted to increase the tourist trade.

Because Claire had come up with the revitalization plan, the mayor blamed her for the ensuing problems. And problems were plentiful. College kids decided their little village was the perfect party town. Aside from their noise and litter, *and* traffic congestion on the main road through town, Chapel Springs didn't have enough rentable living space for more than a couple hundred overnighters.

Claire's sigh came all the way from her toes. Apparently, that lack of foresight was also her fault, along with the wild parties in Warm Springs Park. However, their cantankerous popinjay of a mayor sure took credit for the financial gains.

Peeking out the back door, she found the coast clear and sprinted for *Dee's 'n' Doughs*. One of Dee's apple fritters and fortifying high-test coffee would go down good. Then Claire and her friends, all local entrepreneurs, could strategize a way to survive this pickle.

She slipped into the bakery's rear entrance and was immediately plunged into gastronomic delight by the heady aroma of sugar and spice. It made her want to lick the air. Dee stood next to a large industrial mixer, pouring milk into its stainless steel bowl. Claire waved but between concentration and the noise of its motor, Dee didn't look up. However, her new assistant, Trisha, who was elbow deep in a huge batch of some wonderful concoction, did look up and frowned. With the back of her wrist, she rubbed the side of her nose, leaving a trail of flour.

Claire waggled her fingers as she passed by. "I'm avoiding the foot traffic out front."

"Well, just don't touch anything."

Sheesh. Even a newcomer knew her infamous reputation for calamity. She had hoped being elected to the town council would have brought her a modicum of respect. But no such luck. She was still the town's favorite joke. If Henderson's hadn't had a Halon fire alarm system in the cooking school, it wouldn't have been a big story.

Maybe if she ran for council chairwoman she could change her persona—become a purveyor of wisdom instead of a diva of disaster. Pondering that thought, she scurried through the double swinging doors into the front.

A din louder than Dee's giant mixer rolled over her. Van Gogh's ear! The hordes had invaded *Dee's 'n' Doughs*, too. And they all chattered at once like monkeys in a jungle. She started toward the bay window when a hand rose above the crowd and waved at her—from the opposite side of the room.

"Over here, Claire."

The vacationers had commandeered her favorite spot too, relegating her friends to a smaller table in a dark corner. Maybe it was for the best. They could talk unobserved back there. She grabbed a cup of coffee and a warm apple fritter, then joined Patsy and Lydia Smith, who owned the Chapel Lake Spa. Except she wasn't Lydia Smith any longer. She was now Lydia Sanders. At least she didn't have to throw away anything monogrammed.

Claire hip-bumped the closest chair, moving it so she could sit.

"Ouch."

"Oh, my, I'm so sorry, Lacey." Embarrassed not to have noticed her, Claire patted her friend's shoulder and tried to hang her Minnie Mouse tote bag on the back of the chair at the same time. Her fritter and coffee tipped precariously. Patsy made a grab for them before she spilled everything all over Lacey's shoulder.

"Thanks, girlfriend." Claire couldn't count the times Patsy saved her from mortification. The first, if she remembered correctly, was when they were four and Claire tried to make grilled cheese sandwiches in the toaster.

She planted her backside in the seat. "So, what do y'all think of this ... this crush of humanity?"

Lydia craned her neck to look at the mob crowding the bakery. Her shiny, dark brown bob swayed, brushing her jaw line. "I'm surprised they're still here. Once school started, I thought we'd get our little village back." Her fluid voice and slow Alabama drawl charmed even Southerners. She and her sister, Lacey, both had that sweet Alabama accent, but somehow Lydia's was more pronounced.

"This is way more than any of us expected." Patsy tore off a corner of Claire's fritter. She claimed it was her duty to help Claire avoid gaining weight. "I figured when August was behind us, they'd leave. It's September and they're still here."

For the first time in her life, Claire wished the temperature would drop. Then again—"It'll be leaf peepers next," she grumbled around a mouthful of fritter. "All I can say is I'm thankful we don't have a ski resort."

Lydia swatted Claire's hand. "Don't say that out loud. Mayor Felix will find out and want one."

"Did you hear the McMillans put their house on the market yesterday?" Patsy's forehead wrinkled beneath her bangs. "And they're not the only ones."

"Really?" Claire ripped open a packet of raw sugar and stirred its contents into her coffee. She wasn't surprised about the McMillans, since Bev filed for a divorce, but—"Who else?"

"The Lees, the Chapmans, and a couple of others. The Greins moved last week."

With so much congestion in the streets and the park, Claire hadn't been taking long walks like usual. It was one way she kept up on everyone, but she never saw the for sale signs. Her twenty-one-year-old twin daughters would be devastated. The Grein kids were among Megan and Melissa's, closest friends. This wasn't good, and Felix Riley would try to blame her for that, too. "What can we do? Anyone have a good idea?"

Patsy shook her head. When she started to chew her bottom lip, Claire knew something was up. That was Patsy's "I've got a problem" M.O. But when she sighed on top of the lip-chew, a sick feeling dropped like lead into Claire's stomach. "What? What's wrong?"

"Last night Nathan made a few choice noises about all this."

"What do you mean 'noises'?"

"For one, he said if he wanted a loud, congested town he'd move to New York. At least there he could make more money."

Claire recoiled like she'd been slapped. She didn't know what she'd do if Pat-a-cake moved away. They grew up together, suffered through acne together, raised their babies together. Her chest constricted. Nobody knew her like Patsy did. Tears stung the back of Claire's eyes. "Pat-a-cake, he's not serious is he?" Her fritter lost its flavor.

"He ordered home delivery of the New York Times so he can look at the classifieds." Patsy tormented the artist's callus on her right middle knuckle. Whoa, she was scared.

Claire could maybe put up with losing a few old friends and neighbors, but not Patsy and Nathan. Why, Nathan was her Joel's best buddy, and Patsy was like a sister. This was serious. They had to do something—but what?

The bells on the front door rang with a jocular jingle. A man entered the bakery wearing nothing more than a Speedo and a sombrero, and he was at least fifty pounds over the Speedo limit.

That was the last straw for Claire. Between Patsy's possible move and this sight, she crossed her eyes and pushed the covered apple fritter to the middle of the table. "I think I just lost my appetite."

Lydia giggled behind her hand. "If my husband had worn one of those on our honeymoon, I'd have cut it up and buried the evidence."

Claire could see her doing it, too. Lydia was a true steel magnolia. Which reminded her—"How was the honeymoon? I sure wish you had gotten home sooner. I needed you at the town council meeting."

There were issues on which the mayor and Claire retained opposite views, to say the least. The pleasure she got over his near apoplexy when she won the open seat on the town council had been worth the aggravation of campaigning. Felix Riley would skin the bark off his mother's Sweet gum tree if he thought it would line his pockets, and he knew she'd be watching him closely. He'd have some wild scheme to fix this mess without losing any revenues. She knew that man and didn't trust him one iota.

"Virginia Beach was fantastic." Lydia swirled a plastic stir stick around in her cup.

Her mind was obviously not here, because her cup was empty. So was it just Virginia Beach or the new hubby? "Do tell? What hap—"

Patsy's foot connected with Claire's left ankle. "Ow! What?"

She glared at Patsy, who raised one eyebrow at her and gave her "the look."

"Oh, right." Claire had made a vow to guard her tongue against blurting out whatever popped into her mind. Most times, the darn thing seemed to work on its own before she could stop it, though. Leave it to Patsy to remind her to engage her filter—another reason for her not to move.

Claire returned a wry grimace to her grinning friends. "Sorry."

"Why did you want me at the council meeting?"

Lydia was obviously ignoring Claire's intended question about her new hubby. Okay, she'd find out later anyway.

"I needed reinforcements. Patsy had a showing in Atlanta and couldn't be there, and Dee's kids had soccer practice. For one thing ..." She paused, wanting the gravity of her impending announcement to sink in. "Felix has appointed his brother to oversee the springs' restoration."

Patsy choked on her coffee. Even Lacey's eyes bugged and her mouth dropped open. Only Lydia didn't react, but she hadn't lived in Chapel Springs long enough to know the mayor's brother well, so Claire forgave her faux pas.

Patsy grabbed a napkin and wiped her chin. "Dale Riley hasn't got enough brains to give himself a headache. How's he supposed to come up with an idea?"

Claire nearly spewed the mouthful of java she'd just gulped. "Why, Patsy, that was downright merciful. I'm not sure he deserves the compliment."

Patsy and Lacey both giggled, but Lydia tipped her head to the side as if a different perspective might make this conversation less confusing.

Before Claire could explain, the door burst open, its bells jangling wildly, and the devil himself—uh, Dale Riley—shuffled in.

"Whatever tidbit he's heard," Patsy said, "it's burning a hole in his tongue."

In Chapel Springs, there were three forms of communication: telephone, telegraph and tell Dale. He and his brother had determined their sole purpose on earth was to humiliate Claire—that and think up schemes to make money. Armed by caffeine, she pushed her empty coffee cup aside.

"I'm ready for him."

He spied them quickly enough and aimed his get-along right for their table. But instead of taking a bead on Claire, his usual target, he grabbed a chair from a neighboring table, scooted it in between her and Lacey, and plopped himself down. With his back to Claire. She didn't know whether to be insulted or relieved.

Dale leaned close to Lacey. She leaned close to her sister. Tension as thick as the frosting on one of Dee's cinnamon buns spread between them. His eyebrows rose to his nonexistent hairline. Did he think that made him look like he had something more than a baldpate? Except for two small tufts on either side, he had more hair growing out his nose than on his head.

He pulled on his ear. "I hear Jake fired his Looziana chef at The Krill Grill. Why'd he do that? Ain't nobody can cook seafood like a "N'awlins" chef. You watch. The place'll die in a week." He sat back, a self-satisfied smirk on his round pink face.

Lacey blinked then shrugged.

Dale squinted his beady eyes. "Din' cha know about it?"

Claire wanted to slap him upside the head. He'd badger a corpse if he thought he could get a rise out of it. "Give it a rest, Dale."

He turned and speared her with a leer. "You thinkin' of applying, Claire? That would cinch Jake's failure—if 'n ya didn't burn the place down first." He snorted a cackling laugh.

She refused to satisfy him with a response and returned as cold a stare as she could muster with her blood boiling. He chortled at his own joke and returned his attention to Lacey.

"So, didn't ya know?"

"Of course I did. Jake knows what he's doing. And the new chef is way better. His jambalaya is to die for."

Bless her heart, saying that much was quite a stretch for Lacey, but the result was worth it. Dale deflated like a sinking soufflé. Whatever trouble he was trying to stir up, Lacey stole his spoon.

He recovered quickly enough, though. Looking past her to Lydia, he turned on the charm. No matter what Claire thought of him, she had to admire his gumption. Still a bachelor at sixty-four, he never gave up hope of finding a bride. She'd give up her next sale to know what was going on inside his head right now.

"You're the one they's callin' the 'widow on the hill,' ain't cha?" He propped his elbow on the table and leaned his jaw on it, staring moon-eyed at Lydia.

Now it was her turn to lean back and send the rest of the women gathered around the table a silent plea for help. "Uh, not—"

"Don't you have a job to go to?" Claire asked him.

"Nope." He never took his eyes off Lydia. "I quit."

Most likely got fired.

"Bagging groceries at Lunn's ain't my idea of a career." Dale grinned at Lydia, who leaned back a little more.

So, Claire's weren't the only produce he'd squashed or bruised.

"I'm goin' into gee-logical restoration. After I fix the springs, I'll move onto bigger things like inveramen ... uh ... envirymen ... uh, that green stuff." He glared at Claire. "And I don't mean collards." He rose and hitched his britches. "I'll get me a big career. One fittin' to support a wife in style." He winked at Lydia but didn't wait for a response. At the coffee bar, he poured a to-go cup and left.

Gasping for breath between giggles, Patsy wiped her eyes. "I just can't get a handle on Dale with a wife or what she would actually be like."

Neither could Claire. "He seems to have pinned his hopes on our 'widow on the hill.'" She steered a wink in Lydia's direction.

"He's not serious is he?" Her voice rose to a squeak. "He's joking, right?"

"You might want to get caller ID." Claire picked at the rolled edge of her paper coffee cup. "When Dale gets an idea, it sticks in his nooks and crannies, and it looks like he's got his sights set square on you."

"But I'm married now."

Claire chuckled. "Dale doesn't know that. He left before you could tell him." And she couldn't wait to see his face when he found out.

"I need a refill." Lydia hurried to the coffee bar.

Claire stuffed her napkin into her now empty cup. "While she gets more caffeine, do you have any ideas to corral the crowds?"

"Not really. Too bad these folks can't spread themselves around," Patsy said. "Why aren't there more towns on the lake? Other than Pineridge and Scarlet's Ferry on the south shore, Chapel Springs is the only village with a beach and lake access."

"The terrain doesn't allow for it without destroying too much of the forest or excavating into the lake." Claire brushed stray crumbs off the table. "The twins did a report on it in high school."

Lydia returned with her cup steaming. "What am I going to do about Dale?" She wrinkled her nose when she said his name.

Claire couldn't help herself. It was too delicious. "Invite him to dinner and let Graham open the door."

Lydia's eyes sparkled over the top of her cup as she took a sip. "That would be fun, but it's not really nice."

"Neither is Dale. Now, tell us about the honeymoon."

"But without the details," Patsy said.

Lydia's slow smile revealed perfect teeth and the promise of a romantic tale. Claire and Patsy scooted in close. They were all about romance. It wasn't but a few months ago during the town revival, that they had launched their own Operation Marriage Revival and were still giddy over its success. However, at one point during the process, Claire suspected Lydia of trying to steal Patsy's Nathan. When they discovered she'd simply hired him to be the spa's accountant, they were mortified. It took a couple of weeks before they got over the chagrin and became close friends with Lydia. She, bless her heart, had forgiven them—even laughed at them, saying she was flattered, in a way.

"You're one of us now, so no holding back," Claire said.

Lydia's romance had been a whirlwind, and she surprised them all by tying the knot at a Sunday morning church service. She'd said other than her sister, Lacey, they were all the family she had.

Claire rested her chin on her fists. "Details, woman, all of them."

A deep rose colored her cheeks. She took another drink then rotated her bracelet. "Graham is such a romantic man. So different from Sam, who was military through and through. He's tenderhearted and thoughtful. We had a condo instead of a hotel, and he got up early each morning before I was awake and—" Again, she stirred her now half-empty cup.

Claire nudged Patsy and tilted her head toward Lydia, and grinned.

"—Brought me back a magnolia with my breakfast and the newspaper."

"That's so sweet. He's been a widower for a long time hasn't he?" Patsy asked.

"Yes, over twenty years. He ..." her eyes flitted to Lacey for half a heartbeat. "He lost his first wife in a convenience store robbery. It was very sad. His children were young—five and six. That colored his outlook I have to say. He's very protective when we're out in public."

"I think it would make a wonderful play." Lacey's soft voice caught them all off guard.

Lydia frowned at her. "I don't think that's a good idea at all. Graham wouldn't be pleased one bitty bit."

Lacey waved her argument away. "I'm not going to write it. I'm just saying it would make a good script." She scooted her chair back. "I've got to get on to the bank. See y'all."

Chapter 2

When had Wes started his slide into hermitude? Claire sat at her potter's wheel, hand hovering above the switch, trying to pinpoint an exact date but couldn't. It had been a gradual descent into silence. She wanted to shake him out of it, but how, when she didn't know what it was? He didn't seem angry. Just the opposite. Could it be—?

"New technique?" Patsy elbowed Claire's shoulder.

"What?"

"Staring at that lump of clay until it obediently forms itself into a pitcher."

"Oh." She looked up. "I'm worried about Wes." The youngest of her five kids and the only one left in the nest.

"What's wrong?"

"He's not talking."

"Wesley? The schmoozer?" Patsy moved back to her easel. "He could get a fence post to converse."

"Not anymore. He comes in and goes straight upstairs. We see him at dinner only long enough for him to wolf down his food, then he's gone again. To his room. I can't figure it out." She tossed the drying clay into a bag for rewetting and reached into the barrel for a new chunk.

Patsy picked up a fan brush and dabbed it against her palette. "Chase went through that." She swept a band of blue across the canvas.

Chase? "Did you find out why?"

She mingled some green paint with the blue, feathering the edges. Claire loved watching her pull three dimensions from a flat canvas. She tried painting once, but hers remained flat. She needed clay to form dimensions.

"He met some kids from Pineridge when he played soccer on the high school travel team. He knew we wouldn't approve of them, so he kept quiet. To jump to the punch line, he started smoking pot. And drinking."

Talk about flabbergasted. Drugs? That was a hard stretch. Was Wes into drugs? Clay squeezed between Claire's fingers. "I can't believe it. Not your Chase. Why didn't you ever tell me?"

Patsy dunked her brush into a jar, and stirred so hard the turpenoid sloshed over the edge. Wiping her hands on a towel, she sighed. "I don't know, Claire. Pride, maybe? I just didn't want to admit my son used drugs."

That didn't surprise her. Patsy always tried to ignore problems— bury them. Not Claire. She wanted to dig 'em up and get rid of them. She centered the softened clay on the wheel and flipped the switch. As the wheel turned faster, she smoothed the shape upward. "What did you do?"

A better question, what should she do? Keeping her eyes on the clay, she pulled it up and out as it spun on the wheel, smoothing the sides. Could she search Wes's room? She moistened her fingertips in the bucket.

"After we found the evidence in his room, Nathan sat him down and gave him a choice—he could stop what he was doing and straighten up or go to military school."

Chase would have been some sergeant's supper. He had Patsy's gentle nature. That's why it was so hard to imagine him pulling such shenanigans. "Obviously, I know which he chose. But what did he say?"

"He seemed relieved. Said he'd gotten himself in with some strong personality types and didn't know how to get out. It wasn't long before he was back to his normal self."

Claire's thoughts spiraled with the rhythm of the wheel and the porcelain clay beneath her hands. Wes wasn't easily swayed, but then, what did she know of his college friends? The clay rose and rounded beneath her hands, taking the shape of the pitcher's bowl. If only she could work out a solution to her problems as easily. The thought of Wes on drugs frightened her. Maybe—

She took her eyes off the clay to glance at Patsy. "Do you think I should search Wes's room?"

"I don't know, Claire. He's almost twenty. Chase was only fifteen."

Nineteen. Wes was still nineteen and the thought of drugs left her bumfuzzled. She wet the clay again and slid her left thumb into its center forming a depression. As it hollowed, she used one hand to smooth the inside. Wes left for classes at nine and didn't return most days until dinnertime. She moved her right hand to the outside of the clay and pulled, drawing the top edges up for the pitcher's neck. Sneaking into his room at noon wouldn't hurt. Subterfuge didn't bother her one bitty bit, if she had a good reason, like when she spied on Lydia and Nathan.

But what if she got caught? Wes would hate her. Her hands began to shake. The pitcher leaned off center and wobbled. She pushed, but it was too late. It flopped over, resembling a dying goose.

Armed with still warm-from-the-dryer-laundry as an excuse, Claire first tapped on the door to Wes's room, then cracked it open and peered inside. She knew he was still at school, but peeking into his personal space still felt like an intrusion. On his bed, the quilt lay rumpled and partially puddled on the floor where he'd flung it back when he awoke.

She pushed the door wide and went in, controlling the urge to straighten the bedding. A pile of dirty clothes lay beside his hamper. He was so like his dad. She had to find a basketball hoop to attach to their hampers. Maybe then, they'd at least try to get their laundry inside.

Setting the laundry basket on his bed, she craned her neck toward the desk. It was messy, too. They'd always told the kids their rooms were their private spaces. As long as they didn't leave food lying around and they vacuumed once a week, she and Joel didn't insist they keep them neat. Megan and Wes were their sloppy kiddos. The other three preferred to be organized. Claire still couldn't figure out whose pool that gene came from.

She stared at the computer. Last year, Wes actually forked out his own money to buy it. He needed more time than the family computer allowed, so he said, and he wanted to work in the quiet of his room. With the added homework in college, she hadn't blinked an eye. It seemed reasonable, and it was his own money, something Wes rarely spent. The kid saved nearly every penny he'd ever earned.

With all the time he logged on his computer, she'd been looking forward to seeing the results in his grades this semester. She moved closer to his desk. An envelope corner poked out from underneath a pile of papers—economics spreadsheets it looked like. How did he manage to understand those things? She touched the envelope's corner, sliding it further out from under the papers. The return address appeared, at least a portion of it. It was from UGA. His grades.

Pride swelled up within her. She only finished two years of college and Joel never went. They wanted their kids to get degrees. Charlie and Adriana graduated—Adrianna with honors. The twins were in their senior year, and Wes was now a sophomore. Claire couldn't wait to bask in the glow of his good grades. She snatched up the envelope.

A door slammed downstairs. She froze. Footsteps thumped on the stairway. She stuffed the envelope back underneath the papers, heart hammering against her ribs. Running on her tippy toes, she spied the laundry basket. Oh no!

She turned and bent to grab it on the run, but her foot caught in the blasted pool of bedding on the floor. She stumbled sideways. Unable to stop her momentum, she whirly birded her arms, trying to catch her balance but couldn't get her feet beneath her bottom. It felt like slow motion until she crashed into the doorjamb. Pain exploded in her right shoulder, and she fell into the hallway.

"Claire?" A pair of brown Docksiders materialized by her nose. Thankfully, they were the ones she'd gotten Joel for his birthday and not Wes's more ragged ones. She lifted her head and peered up at him.

He eyed her with his "what have you been up to" look. "I heard thumping. What have you been up to?"

Told you.

He reached down, and took her left arm, helping her up.

"You okay? Nothing broken?"

"I don't think so." She rotated her shoulder. "I'm okay, but I'm glad it's getting cooler. I'll have to wear long sleeves until the bruises fade."

Joel shook his head and pursed his lips, trying not to smile. "It's a good thing your mom didn't name you Grace."

"Be careful, mister, or I'll tell everyone you slugged me."

He gently rubbed the redness on her shoulder. "What were you doing in there?"

She brushed invisible dust from her jeans. She'd heard discretion was the better part of valor, but in this case she decided confession made more sense. "I've been so concerned about Wes—his change from chatter bug to zip-lip."

"You're not alone. I've worried about it a lot." He turned her around, checking for broken bones sticking out or something.

"Why didn't you tell me?" she asked over her shoulder.

"I didn't want *you* worried." He ended his inspection with her facing him again. "So, did you find anything?"

"No. Well, I didn't search a lot. I found his grades envelope and was about to take a look when you slammed the door and scared the living daylights out of me. And why are you home?"

Joel had never looked so sheepish. He actually toed the carpet.

"To do what you were doing."

She couldn't help herself. She laughed. "I'm glad we're both worried. No wait, I mean I'm glad we're thinking together. I think. So ... you want to go see his grades?" She took his hand and started into Wes's room, but Joel hung back, pulling from her grasp.

"Slow up there, babe. I hate to invade his privacy." He held up a hand to stop her protest. "I know. It's what I came home to do." He took a deep breath and blew it out, then leaned against the wall. "Everything in me wants to trust Wes—wait for him to talk to us."

She rummaged for the right words. "What if it's too late?" She whispered—like the walls were going to tell on her. "What if he's gotten into drugs?"

The color drained from Joel's face. He crossed the hallway to Wes's door and sniffed. Nodding once, he turned her. "There's no pot."

She already knew that. "But what if—"

Joel took her hand and led her downstairs. "Tonight at dinner, we'll talk to him together. Ask him to show us his grades. After all, we're paying for his education. We deserve to see the fruits. We'll decide what to do by what he shows us. Now how about some lunch?"

Together. She loved that word. Joel had changed so much in the past few months. Before, he would have said *he* was paying for the kids' education. At the bottom of the stairs, she paused and put her arms around his neck. "Have I told you how much I love you?"

His gray/blue eyes turned smoky and his voice husky. Other than the bit of silver at his temples and a few crow's feet around his eyes, he still looked as young as when they graduated from high school. He encircled her waist and squeezed. "You better be careful or we won't get anything to eat." His kiss devoured her lips then he planted one on the tip of her nose. "Come on, woman, feed your man."

Building BLTs side-by-side in the kitchen—as side-by-side as they could get with Shiloh, their two-hundred-thirty-pound mastiff, nosing between them, waiting for falling tidbits—she marveled how God had answered her prayers for a revived marriage. Still, while they were together in so many ways, the one that mattered most to her hadn't happened.

Chapter 3

Rays from the rising sun streamed in the kitchen window, and bathed Lydia in its light. She tapped her finger against the tongs in time with the bacon's popping and spitting. Finding the rhythm, she hummed a random tune. Cooking for someone again—instead of just for herself—was a joy, but having that person be her husband filled her with contentment. She sent a silent thank-you heavenward.

Keeping one eye on the hallway from the bedrooms, she cracked and slid two eggs into the bacon grease. Graham liked over easy and if she had her timing down, she'd slide them out of the pan as he entered the room. When they bought this house, she wasn't sure she liked the kitchen open to the living spaces. If there were dishes in the sink and a mess on the counter, she wanted them hidden. But she loved it now. The layout kept her connected with Graham as she cooked. And this morning, she had exciting news.

A moment later, he appeared from the hallway, his tie and suit coat slung over his shoulder. He laid those on a chair in the great room and came up behind her, putting his arms around her waist. When he kissed her neck, shivers snaked up her spine.

"Good morning."

She moved the pan off the burner, slid his eggs onto a plate, and then turned in his arms. His mouth covered hers and sent her heart into outer space, making her feel like a teenager again. Her lips felt lonely when he ended the kiss. "I wish we didn't have to get back to reality, but I suppose it's inevitable."

Graham poured them both coffee, and she brought their breakfast to the table. After he asked the blessing, he dove into his breakfast like a starving man.

"Are your eggs okay?"

"Perfect." He sopped up yolk with his toast.

"I checked my email while you were in the shower. You'll never guess who I had a message from."

"Who?"

"That TV reality show, *Losing*."

Graham's fork stopped halfway to his mouth, his head cocked to one side. "What did they want?"

She leaned forward and tried to contain her excitement. "They want to use my spa for next year or the following year's show." She could almost see his mind working as he looked at her.

"But how did they know about you?"

"When we revitalized Chapel Springs, it drew the media, but then Claire and Patsy had a wildly successful review in an art magazine. That brought some celebrity art collectors. Once they discovered the springs and the spa, they liked what they found and have returned. Someone must have told the show's producer. He visited us about a month ago, but I didn't know who he was at the time."

"That's amazing, hushpuppy." He spread strawberry jam on his toast. "Did you say yes?"

"Not yet. That's what I wanted to talk to you about. The spa needs some expansion for it to happen. But that's not all. We need more housing accommodations in town."

"I thought you said last night that your friends are working on it."

Lydia stirred a spoonful of stevia into her coffee. "Claire's on the town council, and she'll address it at the next meeting. If they can come up with an answer, then I can accept the show's offer. But it will mean investing some money in the spa now."

How would he take that? They hadn't talked much about money before they got married. There were a lot of things they hadn't discussed, but she brushed that aside. He was a banker. Of course he understood investing to make money.

"That shouldn't be a problem. You could probably get an equity loan."

Now she could show him what a good manager she'd been of her money. "I've been saving for future expansion since I opened for business, so I won't need too much. I have the plans already and it's not going to be terribly expensive."

His eyebrows danced and his eyes lit with, what she hoped, was pleasure and admiration. "It appears I married one smart businesswoman."

Her cheeks grew warm and she reveled in the compliment. Her late husband thought she didn't have a brain in her head. He wouldn't even let her balance her own checkbook. But Patsy's Nathan was her accountant, and he taught her a lot. At first, it had been hard since she'd never worked with money, but in time, it seemed she had more aptitude than she realized.

She reached over and squeezed his hand. "Your appreciation means so much to me, Graham."

"Sweetheart, one of the things that drew me to you was your intelligent conversation. You have no idea how many women think men like brainless beauty. Every available single man is overrun with women after a meal ticket."

Their first meeting had been at Virginia Beach, and they talked about a book they both were reading. He opened the conversation, and they'd had a lively debate over the author's qualifications to write it. She couldn't help but laugh. "So it was my brain not my body you fell in love with?"

"You came as a package deal, love bug."

"You always know exactly what to say, and I love you for it."

He polished off the last of his toast. "You know, with the interest rates as low as they are right now, you might want to put your money in a bank CD and take out an equity loan. There are some tax advantages to that."

She weighed his advice. "I'd like to see the numbers, but I'm sure you're right."

He rose. "I'm only going in for part of the day. I'll be home around two."

After sliding his tie under his collar, he knotted it and slipped on his jacket. His Adam's apple bobbed beneath her hands as she straightened his tie, and his golden brown eyes crinkled when he smiled at her, nearly disappearing. Her heart swelled and her pulse fluttered as he held her gaze. Lydia never thought she'd find love again. When he bent his head and kissed her, it made her heart race and her stomach turn flip-flops, but when he groaned with desire—for her—her knees grew weak.

He ended their kiss. "I wish we had another week to honeymoon, but as Chapel Springs S&L's new branch manager, it wouldn't look too good if I'm late." His arms loosened their hold but didn't let go. "How about I take you out to dinner tonight? We can try out Jake's new chef."

"That sounds wonderful." When he finally released her and she shut the door behind him, she wandered back to the kitchen. Like an automaton, she rinsed their plates and loaded them into the dishwasher. Graham was the man of her dreams, romantic, supportive, and spontaneous. Sam—God rest his soul—had been military-rigid in his schedules. Everything always had to have an order to it. Even his death was orderly. She closed the dishwasher and attacked the cast iron frying pan by hand.

Lydia never fit into Sam's image of a wife. But what had he expected? She was eighteen when they married, and if she were honest, their union was her escape from the farm and raising her sister. He was a decent man, though. He never abused her, but she knew she was a disappointment to him.

In the bedroom, Lydia made their bed. The tangled sheets were a testament to their lovemaking. She couldn't help comparing Graham to Sam, the only other man she'd ever known. With him, the act was one-sided. He never took time to know her. She had no idea it could be like this. On their wedding night, Graham took joy in learning what gave her pleasure. He *wanted* to please her. She'd always wondered what the big deal was about it. A grin as wide as the Gulf stretched her lips. Now she knew.

Lydia entered the spa at ten o'clock. Olympia, her massage therapist, greeted her before taking her next client to a room down the hallway. Originally from Spain, the clients—and Lydia—loved the European flavor Olympia gave to the spa.

"I glad you're back. How was the *luna de miel*—how you say? Honey on the moon?"

Lydia chuckled. "Honeymoon. It was wonderful, thank you."

"Thaz good. When Lester and I married, we not have honeymoon. We work instead."

"But you eventually took one, didn't you?"

Olympia clicked her tongue and wiggled her eyebrows. "*Si*, and a *mucho* good one." She disappeared into a massage room, giggling.

Lydia greeted a couple of clients then went to her office, where she spent the next few hours answering emails and getting the next batch of bills ready to be paid by Nathan. Patsy's husband was a good accountant and hiring him had been a smart decision. It freed her up to see to her clients.

With the bills ready and in a manila envelope bearing Nathan's name, Lydia looked over the notes her daughter left for her. Morgan did a good job managing things in her absence. She worked at the bank prior to Lydia opening the spa, but left a couple of months ago to work with her. After all, Morgan would inherit this someday, so it was good she learn the business. She almost had enough hours now for her esthetician license.

Lydia left her office and found her daughter observing one of the estheticians do a mud wrap. She remembered when Claire got one, and she had to quickly back out of the room before she started laughing. Wrapped up like a mummy, Claire had decided to use the waiting time to spy on Lydia and catch her seducing Patsy's husband. She'd never forget her friend falling into the spa's office, covered in mud, the wrappings sliding down around her knees. Or Claire's mortification on learning Nathan was only the spa's CPA.

Poor Claire. Her intentions were so good, but her methods always got her in trouble. Still, Lydia couldn't have a more loyal friend. Claire and Patsy had welcomed her to Chapel Springs and taken her into their circle. She was no longer the newcomer.

By noon, Lydia finished what she came to do, shut down the computer, and hurried home. She changed her mind about going out. She wanted to fix supper for Graham and have a romantic evening. Humming an old love song, she went through her recipe book for something special. She found one for grilled salmon topped with tomato slices and fresh basil. The picture looked delicious. After checking the freezer and the pantry to be sure she had everything, she pulled the fish out to defrost, then went to refresh her makeup. Graham should be home soon.

The door opened as she swiped on some mascara. A final glance in the mirror revealed her light touch with makeup. It didn't appear she had any on. Exactly the image she wanted. She winked at her reflection and hurried down the hallway to greet her husband. When the door came in sight, she came to a screeching halt.

Graham had his arm around the shoulders of a young man. Did she have enough for a third for supper? Who was he? She moved her eyes from the stranger to her husband, raising one eyebrow in question.

"Hushpuppy, let me introduce my son, Kenny."

Graham's pride in his son was obvious, and Lydia smiled as she held out her hand. She just wished he'd told her his son was coming for a visit. "Kenny, welcome to our home."

She glanced at Graham again, waiting for an explanation. Why had he kept the visit a secret? Kenny's smile was warm as he gripped her hand, but his eyes ... they didn't reveal anything about him. It was like they were open but closed. She chided herself for being simply jealous of Graham's time. And that wasn't nice.

"Kenny surprised me in the driveway. I had no idea he planned a visit. It turns out he arrived here last week, while we were on our honeymoon. He's been working for Joel Bennett at the marina."

Working? Did that mean he now lived here? In Chapel Springs? She searched his eyes. Something wasn't right. At the same time, she berated herself for being suspicious. "Where are you staying, Kenny?"

He glanced at his dad then back at her. "Uh, I've been sleeping in my car. There aren't any rooms available in town."

Graham clapped him on the back. "Well, we can't have that, son. You'll stay here for as long as you're visiting. Let's go sit down and you can tell me how things are going. And why you're working at the marina."

Yes, Lydia would like to know that as well. "While you two talk, I need to see to a couple of things for supper."

"Supper?" Kenny grinned. "I haven't heard it called that since I was in grade school."

Graham led Kenny to the sofa. From the kitchen, Lydia could watch them. And listen.

"Lydia was raised on a farm in Alabama, son. Now, tell me what brings you here."

Kenny flashed a huge smile at Lydia. "I wanted to meet my new stepmother and ... well, to be honest, Dad, I got laid off." He dropped his gaze to his clenched hands between his knees. "I don't have enough savings to keep me going much longer."

Oh dear. Did that mean ...

She met Graham's eyes. How could she deny the request there? This was his son. If it were Morgan, she'd want her here. She turned her gaze back, a smile firmly in place. "Kenny, we have plenty of room. There's an apartment in the finished basement. You may use it." She just hoped he planned on paying some rent. He was tall and had definitely not missed many meals, judging by his waistline. It hung over his belt a little too much.

"Thanks, Lydia. I appreciate it a lot. I know you two need your space. I won't be in the way. I promise."

Her heart warmed to him a little more. At least, he recognized the situation. And Graham's appreciation was written all over his face. Yes, she'd made the right decision. She hoped. Graham turned on the golf channel and they watched TV while she worked in the kitchen.

So much for cuddling on the couch with her husband.

Chapter 4

The tantalizing aroma of meat in the backyard smoker greeted Claire as she came downstairs after cleaning up from work. Joel's head was deep inside the refrigerator when she entered the kitchen. He emerged with his arms loaded with salad fixings and sweet potatoes.

He was the cook in the family. She burned hard boiled eggs, and her experience with cooking classes was less than laudable, if one listened to local scuttlebutt. Somehow that whole fiasco got turned around to be her fault. She knew better. That chef had it in for her from the moment she walked into the classroom. Somebody probably tipped him off.

She'd like to cook. Really. She would—if she could without incident. But recipes read wonky to her. Thankfully, she and Joel had worked it out. He loved to cook. He would have gone to culinary school and become a chef if his daddy hadn't refused. Said it was a namby-pamby girly profession. Obviously he never watched those barbeque wars or *Iron Chef*. No matter. She benefitted and their kids didn't have to suffer her cooking.

A sweet potato tumbled from his arms. Claire caught it before it hit the floor and set it on the counter. "What are we having?"

"I decided if we're going to talk to Wes I ought to fix his favorite— smoked pork loin."

"Good thinking." Her Joel may not have a college degree, but he had more horse sense than a professor. "What should I do?"

He gave her a soft kiss and dumped his armload on the countertop. "The salad. You make the best in Georgia. I'll fix sweet tater fries."

"I'm nothin' if not a good chopper." She cut a garlic clove and rubbed it around the inside of a wooden salad bowl. "Have you figured out how we're going to approach the subject of grades?" After tossing the clove in the sink, she tore the lettuce and dropped it in the bowl.

"Straight out. As soon as his mouth is full of meat, I'll ask him for his grades."

"I hope he doesn't choke."

Joel chuckled. "Not Wes. Even if they aren't good, he's always been open with us. I expect an honest answer."

She sliced and slid tomato wedges in with the lettuce, then diced a couple of celery ribs, while Joel went outside to check on the meat. Wes's honesty had better still be intact. She'd never questioned the kids' honor after they were four years old. Prior to that, little lies were to be expected. She stopped chopping. Except Wes. She couldn't remember a time that kid had ever lied to them.

She halved an avocado, whacked its pit with the knife, and popped it from the fruit. Now, she wasn't so sure about his honesty. She wanted to believe him. With the avocado's cool, slick meat against her hand, she diced then added it, along with some blackberries, sliced almonds, and crumbled feta cheese to the salad. She hated secrets and this not knowing.

She slid the salad bowl in the fridge, threw baby spring peas into the steamer pot, then got busy peeling the sweet potatoes for Joel.

Speaking of secrets—

"How's Graham's son working out?"

Joel stopped stirring the glaze for the ribs. "He's a good worker, almost too good. You know what I mean?"

"Not really."

"Maybe it's just my imagination. He's friendly with everyone, so I don't have any complaints." Joel eyed the peeled taters. "Thanks, babe." He checked the temperature of the peanut oil in the fryer, adjusting it slightly. "Nathan stopped by the store this afternoon to pay for his boat slip." He dropped the fries into the basket, the oil popping and crackling as they submerged. "Has Patsy said anything to you about him? He seemed distracted."

"He's more than that. He's talking about moving to New York City."

"What?" Joel set down the bottle of oil so hard it splattered out the top and onto the counter. "Nathan would fit in there about as well as a mountain goat in Iowa. Did Patsy say why?"

She grabbed a paper towel and wiped up the oil. "According to

Nathan, if he wanted this much noise and congestion he might as well live in New York City, where at least he could make money."

"That's insane. He wouldn't last a week."

"Neither would Patsy." She washed and dried her hands and sat down at the table. "Joel, what are we going to do? They're our closest friends."

He checked the oil again and lowered the basket of fries, set the timer, then joined her. "It's gotten crazy around here, that's for sure. I nearly lost a launch today. Poor guy couldn't get a break in the traffic to back his boat into the ramp lane. I had to get out in the middle of the road to create one for him."

She traced a knot on the wooden table. "Do you have any ideas about what to do? We don't want to lose the business, but we've got to control it somehow."

"Not yet." With his thumb and index finger, he rubbed his nose. "Well, that's not completely true. I have a couple of ideas but no way of implementing them."

"Like what?" She leaned back against the banquette. If her Joel came up with a fix, she wouldn't catch so much flak from Felix. Shiloh sat on the floor next to her and put his big head in her lap to get his ears scratched.

"I was thinking the vacant lots next to *The Happy Hooker* could be turned into a parking lot. Then we could close the village to all but residential permit driving."

"But what about getting their luggage to the inns or taking their purchases back to their rooms?" Shiloh raised his head and banged it on the table, making their coffee cups jump. "Poor baby." She rubbed his offended head.

"Got that covered, too. We'd get one or two of those shuttle-tram things. There'd still be transportation but no congestion. And no cruising on Sandy Shores Drive."

It was a workable idea, but—

She frowned. "Felix wouldn't like spending the money on buying trams. And who would drive them?"

"During the summer, high school kids, maybe a retiree during the school months. I don't know. That's one of the problems with the idea. That and who owns the land next to *The Happy Hooker*?"

"Still, it's a logical fix, Joel. I'm going to present it at the next council meeting."

27

"Hold off, Claire. First, we need to be sure the town could purchase the land." The timer dinged for the fries. "I'll get the meat; you pull the fries and call Wes. Come on, Shiloh, let's go outside, boy."

She lifted the basket out of the fryer and set it to drain then called up the stairs for Wes. After hearing his muffled, "Coming," she went back to the kitchen and set out knives and forks. Her hand trembled as she filled three glasses of water. Though it was their son who would be on the hot seat, Claire's stomach quaked.

Wes slid onto the banquette bench as she set their drinks on the table. Shiloh took up his place underneath at their feet. Claire kept the blessing short. Joel no longer blew an exasperated sigh over saying grace and even bowed his head, but she didn't take advantage. At "amen" both he and Wes dug in.

"Oh, boy, my favorite. Thanks, Pop." He shoved a gargantuan forkful of meat into his mouth and closed his eyes in ecstasy.

Claire pushed her peas around her plate. When Joel didn't say anything, she tapped his ankle with her foot, and he returned a small "not now" shake of his head. Her stomach rivaled an erupting volcano, and the peas she'd forked fell back to her plate. He'd better say something soon before she blurted out that they—okay she—had been snooping in his room.

Joel, the master of timing, bided his. Claire's leg started to bounce. She picked up her knife and attacked a piece of tenderloin, but it slipped and peas shot off her plate. They rolled across the table. Wes grinned around a mouthful of pork, and using his thumb and middle finger, shot them back at her.

"Stop that!" She tried not to laugh, but with a passel of peas flying at her, she couldn't help it. She cupped her hand on the table as a goal.

Joel stuffed a couple of fries in his mouth, watching as he chewed. "I need to hire a helper."

Where did that come from? A pea shot past her goal. He was sidetracking the issue of Wes. She frowned at him.

"I called the *Chapel Lake Weekly Voice* to place an ad. Raelene said her nephew might want it."

Wes's laughter died. He swallowed the mouthful of chewed pork. "Why didn't you ask me?"

"You're in school during the hours I need someone."

Claire's eyes flew from her husband to their son and back again. Joel usually had some method to his lackadaisical back-door approach.

More times than she could count he'd trapped her into admitting a blunder.

"I could change up my schedule. Maybe drop a class." His cheeks mottled. That only happened when he got emotional. Her mother-heart hurt within her.

Joel set his fork and knife across his plate and rested his forearms on the table. "Why would you want to do that?"

"Pop ... Mom ... I ..." He blew out a large breath, his cheeks puffing with the force.

Joel cut to the chase. "What's going on, son?"

"I'm not doing so well in school."

"What? You're mumbling. Tell me straight, Wes."

Her man-cub's Adam's apple bobbed.

Joel scowled. "I'm fixing to jerk a knot in your tail."

"My grades arrived. I knew they wouldn't be A's or B's, but ..."

"After dinner, bring them down. Your mother and I would like to see them."

Wes pushed his plate away. "Okay, but you won't like it."

Dinner was over. She hated this. But they had to find out what the problem was, and she hoped it was only the schoolwork. Being a mom was tough. She slipped a chunk of meat off her plate and held it out for Shiloh.

"Why's that?" Joel asked.

"I'm not any good at this. College isn't what I want to do." He raised his head and looked at his dad. His eyes were bright with moisture. He cleared his throat. "I can't focus when all I want to do is be at the marina, working with you. In the family business."

She had to give Wes points for that one. His dad swelled up with pride, and he couldn't hide the pleasure he felt. She couldn't sit there another minute and not say anything.

"Honey, you didn't have trouble in high school. You had a B average. So why is this so much harder?"

"There's a ton of pressure and competition but not a lot of help." His shoulders slumped. "I've tried, Mom, but my heart just isn't in it."

Her dream of all five kids finishing college flew out the window she'd left open over the sink.

Joel bump-punched him on the shoulder. "Yeah? Like the old man, huh? I like that."

"Joel! Aren't you going to encourage him to stay in school?"

29

He failed at looking sheepish. "I could really use the help, and I can start training him to take over."

She shot him her "I'm gonna kill you" glare. "And you're planning on retiring when? You're only forty-eight and we aren't the Rockefellers."

"Claire, I'm not going to force Wes to stay in college if he doesn't want to."

"It's more than just not wanting to." Wes reached across the corner of the table and put his hand over hers. "Ma, my dream has always been to work at the marina with Pop. I'm good at the finance part and the inventory control. Those were the only classes I got good grades in. But to finish college, I had to take all these other ones I hate and don't understand."

Excitement built in his voice as he looked at his dad. "You know I have some ideas that might help expand our business, too. Come on, Pop. Pull the ad. Let me have the job." He glanced at Claire. "I'll prove to you that I'll be a better employee than a student. Besides," he turned puppy dog eyes on her. "Don't you want me to live my dream? That's what you always said when we were little."

What defense did a mom have in the face of that argument? While he and Joel high-fived each other and began to discuss details, she caught a glimpse of the old Wes—the kid who chased his dreams.

Still, something in his arguments seemed calculated. Practiced, like lines prepared for a speech.

Chapter 5

"Come on, Momma. Let's take a walk." Melissa held her sweater as Claire tried to slide her arms into the sleeves. With her daughter being the same height, the left glided in okay, but the right one snagged. She poked and re-poked her hand, searching for the armhole, even rotating a quarter-circle to gain success. No good. She turned once more. Then again—and ended up back facing Melissa.

"Stop!" Giggling, Melissa grabbed her shoulders, stopped the crazy twisting, and slipped the sleeve over Claire's hand.

"You could have done that in the beginning and saved me some aggravation."

"Aw, that wouldn't have been any fun." Her lips twitched as she attempted to stifle her laughter. Melissa slipped the leash on Shiloh, who performed a happy dance at the prospect of a walk.

"You're as bad as your twin." Claire closed the door behind them and they set off at a brisk pace. "Speaking of Megan, how come she didn't ride home with you?"

"She had a date tonight."

"And you don't? I thought you were seeing Craig—somebody."

Melissa shrugged. "By mutual decision, we stopped dating and are now just friends."

Claire stopped and caught her hand. "Honey?" She swallowed the lump of sorrow, rising in her throat at the sight of 'Lissa's sad little smile. "Sweetheart, you need to get over Billy." The twerp broke her heart when he refused to attend church with her or even discuss the possibility of God's existence. Melissa's faith was the most important thing in her life.

"I know. I am. It's just taking time."

Too long, if anyone cared to ask Claire.

They strolled along Pine Drive, enjoying the morning's quiet. Shiloh sniffed every bush and tree along the way and accepted the pats of passing neighbors with kingly aplomb. At the end of the block, they took the left fork along Cottage Lane. Claire loved the long row of adorable bungalows. Their owner, Glen Tabor, had painted each one a different color, making it a rainbow lane. They faced the road so their back porches overlooked the lake. A car stood in every driveway.

"I've never seen all the cottages rented after the season," Melissa said. "I can't get over how people are still here. I wonder who they all are."

Good question. Claire studied the front of the peach cottage. "I really don't know. This was so much more than we ever expected."

"You sound down, Mama. What's wrong?"

Since Claire's nemesis, the mayor, was Billy's daddy, she hated to tell Melissa, but her little tenderhearted daughter wouldn't relent until she spilled her guts. "Felix thinks the revival idea was solely mine. Add to that all the people looking for celebrities, and well, he blames me for the congestion, noise, and whatever else he can think of."

Having the audacity to laugh, Melissa clapped her hand over her mouth. Claire fixed her with the stink-eye, but she laughed harder. "That's so oxymoronic," she managed to sputter between giggles. "He and the town are raking in money, so what's his beef?"

"He never learned the principle of 'the buck stops here.' So each complaint has to have a fall guy. Guess I'm his favorite." Why she had to be so lucky she didn't know.

They cut through a vacant lot to Sandy Shores, strolling past the backside of the cottages. Under the morning sun, diamond sparkles glinted off the lake. Shiloh tugged on his leash, but Melissa made him heel.

"The loons will be returning soon. Shiloh's looking for them, too, aren't you, boy?" Claire patted the mastiff's huge head.

"That's one thing I really miss at school." Melissa used her hand to shield her eyes from the sun and looked out over the lake. "Their mournful calls are part of the wallpaper of home."

Claire picked a dandelion and blew its dust, watching the bits twirl in the air. Of all her chicks, this one was probably the most like her in the way she felt things. Then again, her twin, Megan, had Claire's tendency to plow ahead, never stopping to consider all the consequences. If only she could shape each of them like she did the clay, then each could have the perfect balance.

"Hey, there's the loon lady!" The couple from yesterday waved from one of the cottages.

'Lissa burst out laughing. "Oh, Momma. Loon Lady?"

That girl giggled all too easily. Claire waved at them and relayed the incident to Melissa as they walked. Her chortles made Claire see the events in a new light, and she had to admit it was amusing.

Most of the bungalows' residents were enjoying late morning coffee out on their porches. Colorful pots of pansies sat on the railings, their color changing with each bungalow. She didn't know pansies came in so many different colors. The pots—Melissa pointed to them in delight—were from Claire's whimsy line. For an old bachelor, Glen had picked well. Loons, a bigmouth bass, raccoons, a lazy possum, bullfrogs, and more all held pansies. It dawned on her he'd chosen each for the cottage's name.

Claire and Melissa waved to those who called out helloes. At least they were a friendly bunch. One woman lifted her coffee mug, pointing at it. What? She wanted a refill? Oh—it was one of Claire's mugs. She winked at 'Lissa and shared a mother-daughter giggle. She only started making Chapel Lake mugs this summer. Everyone liked a vacation souvenir, and one that proved useful was even better. She smiled and waved back.

A little boy ran up with a piece of toast and gave it to Shiloh, who rewarded him with a sloppy kiss. Claire pulled a rag from her pocket and wiped the boy's face. "That was a wet thank you wasn't it?" Giggling, he ran back to his mother.

As they approached *The Painted Loon,* Melissa finally told her why she had come home. "You and Aunt Patsy have gotten so busy, you need an assistant."

Claire knew that. Patsy—all the kids called her aunt as her chicks did Claire—and she had already talked about hiring someone. She stopped and faced her daughter.

"You're not thinking of dropping out of school, are you?" Not another one. She couldn't take another one.

Melissa shook her head. "Our roommate wants to be a potter. She's good, Momma."

Claire opened the door to the gallery, and a discordant symphony of voices rolled over them. Patsy had a long line waiting to pay for their purchases. Claire sent Melissa to take Shiloh home, and she took over the register. Five minutes later, 'Lissa was back and relieved Claire so she could help the other browsers. For two solid hours, they didn't have a break. Things finally slowed at noon. Claire closed the door, putting up the "back at 1:00 PM" sign, and the three headed to *Dee's 'n' Doughs* for lunch.

Dee started serving sandwiches that summer when the crowds demanded them, and the locals were just as thrilled. *Dee's 'n' Doughs* was their favorite hangout. After ordering, they found a secluded table. The minute Patsy and Claire had their mouths full, Melissa attacked.

"Aunt Patsy, you and Momma obviously need help. One of my roommates, Nicole, is going to have to quit school. Her dad lost his job, and they can't afford it. She doesn't have enough scholarship money to cover any more." She took a quick breath. "She's a wonderful girl, and she wants to be a potter, and since y'all need help, maybe you could hire her." She stopped and took a large bite of her sandwich.

Claire almost laughed at how 'Lissa timed her bite to allow them to think. She glanced at Patsy, whose amused and indulgent smile spoke her answer. If Melissa made the request, it was a done deal. Claire just hoped—

She fixed her daughter with a steady stare. "Is this Nicole truly as good as you say? Did you tell her—and I know you've already spoken to her about this—that she'd have to run the register and do menial tasks, like dusting and sweeping up after clients?"

Melissa grinned around her sandwich. "Yes, ma'am. She knows that, but she's hoping you'll *teach* her stuff, too. She's willing to take minimum wage or less to get the exposure to you."

Claire licked a crumb from the corner of her mouth. "Me? Why?"

Patsy and Melissa stared at her like she'd dyed her hair purple and pierced her tongue. "Oh, yeah." It was easy to forget she was a newly minted, national award-winning artist when she still cleaned toilets and washed dirty underwear.

"Pat-a-cake, what do you think?"

"I think Melissa's a life saver. I haven't completed a new painting since mid-July. I'm running out of inventory."

Claire mentally tallied what she had in the storeroom and came up woefully short. "Me, too. Okay, 'Lissa. Tell Miss Nicole she has a job. How soon can she get here?"

"Monday." She slurped on her straw, drawing from the bottom of her cup.

"Good. Now, will you help us this afternoon and tomorrow?"

"Sure for ten bucks an hour." Demure, she slurped again as Patsy and Claire cracked up. That kid. She always got what she wanted, but she was so tenderhearted and always wanted to please. Claire couldn't remember her ever getting into trouble. Not at all like her twin sister, Megan.

Or her brother Wes. Claire sighed.

Back in the workroom of the gallery, Patsy and Claire got busy. Her small whimsical vases had sold out and she had a backlog of orders. Since she still had a few of the larger pots, she'd concentrate on the small ones and some bowls.

After pulling a hunk of clay from the barrel, she worked it on the table to make it more pliable before centering it on the wheel head. When it was ready, she flipped on the power and settled her foot on the pedal, slowly depressing it to start the wheel spinning. This one would be a flared bowl—autumn colors she decided.

"Claire?"

"Hmm?" Claire dipped her fingers in the bucket at her knee.

"Has Melissa shown you her latest painting?"

Claire slowed the wheel. "She did. Does she show as much promise as I think she does?"

"Oh, yeah. She got all your artistic genes and soaked in all I had to give her, too." Patsy's excitement caught Claire by surprise. She knew 'Lissa was good, but—

"In fact, I think she'll outshine us both."

The wheel had stopped. She lowered her foot again, carefully holding the clay. "I'd hoped when she was little, that she'd want to be a potter."

"I'm sorry, Claire."

Silly girl. She felt guilty. They both were saps for the guilt factor. "Don't be. I got over it long ago." And she had. Sort of. Okay, not really, but she wasn't jealous of Pat-a-cake. She loved her like a sister. Maybe it niggled because Wes wanted to work with his dad, and Claire felt left out.

She started the wheel spinning faster. Why did she let herself think that way? She wasn't left out of anything. Besides, Melissa would be here, working at the gallery too, once she finished art school. At least she would get her degree and not drop out.

The clay beneath Claire's hands flared and undulated. As its sides rose and widened, she slowed the wheel and pulled at the edges. There was a tiny imperfection in the form, a slight unevenness to the curves. Exactly what she wanted. Not enough for an untrained eye to see, but an acknowledgement to the Master Potter.

Patsy turned on some classical music, and they worked all afternoon in peace. Claire turned out four bowls, half a dozen mugs, and two whimsy vases. After she stretched out the kinks in her arms and back, she put the pieces on the drying shelves. She'd fire them in a few days when they were completely dry. They cleaned up and turned out the lights in back. Melissa turned the closed sign outward on the front door.

"By the way, Momma, Wes called. He said Dale Riley is coming over after dinner."

Suspicion raised the hair on Claire's neck. Wherever he or Felix went, trouble followed. "Whatever for?"

"Wes is giving him computer lessons."

Wes and Dale and a computer? Van Gogh's ear—that spelled trouble no matter how one looked at it.

Chapter 6

Joel and Melissa finished loading the dishwasher while Claire wiped down the kitchen counters. The doorbell rang. Shiloh barked and Wes galloped down the stairs to let in Dale, who raised a hand toward the kitchen doorway as he followed Wes.

"I'm taking me some com-pewter lessons from Wes," he tossed over his shoulder as he tramped upstairs. "Gonna be a World Wide Web surfer."

Putting clothes on a corncob didn't make it a baby doll. Dale was a conniver not a techie. Coupling him with a keyboard could easily reopen the late unpleasantness between the states.

"Let it go, babe," Joel whispered in her ear. "He's harmless enough."

Claire scowled. "So's a rat snake, until it gets in the chicken house."

"Forget him. It's time we leave, and you need to focus your thoughts on the town council."

"Dale is one of the issues." She planted her fists on her hips. "Did I tell you Felix appointed him to oversee the restoration on the springs?"

Joel gaped and stared up the now empty stairs. It was a rare thing for her husband not to have a snappy comeback, but that news rendered him speechless. He slowly shook his head.

She patted his shoulder. "We all had that reaction."

After telling Melissa they were leaving, Claire reminded her not to let Shiloh into the backyard or he'd jump the fence and follow them. The mastiff didn't like being left behind. He took it as a personal affront. "If you go out tonight, give him a couple of treats and put him in the laundry room. Then turn the dryer on." The hum soothed the big baby.

Claire grabbed a light jacket and they headed to the council meeting.

She enjoyed walking. Unless they went outside Chapel Springs, most residents walked everywhere. The bank, where town meetings were held in the second floor community room, was only a half-mile away. It was one of those bonuses of living in a small village—not to mention the benefit to her thighs.

But if Patsy moved away ... that would be like snuffing out a candle. The glow would be gone. The weight of the problem rode heavy on Claire's heart, grieving her. She reached for Joel's hand, entwining their fingers. She wasn't alone in this. He would miss Nathan, too. Those two had been buddies since junior high school.

The sun hung low above the treetops in the evening sky, sending long shadows over the landscape. Indian summer—when the night air turned crisp but the days remained warm. The leaf peepers would soon arrive by the busload. At least they didn't require housing. They only stayed for a couple of hours. A blue jay squawked a warning in the trees above them. With so many people in town all the time, would the birds leave the village, too?

Tom Fowler turned the corner and joined them. He'd been her ally in the town revival program. She wondered where the pharmacist stood now.

Joel loosed his hand from hers and raised it in greeting. "Evening, Tom."

"Joel. Claire." He knocked the ashes out of his pipe and slid it into his shirt pocket as he joined them. "I've been hearing rumblings around town."

She and Joel shared a glance. "Like what?"

"Scuttlebutt has it that our mayor and his brother have cooked up some harebrained scheme to rectify our housing problem."

At "harebrained" Claire knew Tom was on their side. She reached over and slipped an arm through Tom's and one through Joel's, so they formed an impassable trio on the sidewalk. "Joel has a good idea to control traffic, and I'm working on one for the housing." It was true on Joel's part, but while she strained for an idea, technically she was no closer to one than she was to becoming a decent cook.

They'd reached the bank and had no time for Tom to question her more. Thank goodness. She needed her best friend to brainstorm. Joel opened the door, and still racking her brain for an idea, she stepped inside.

Whoa. Claire froze with her hand on her jacket zipper.

By the size of the crowd in the room, those rumblings Tom heard were loud. Each one of the forty or so chairs held a jacket or a handbag. A few people Claire didn't recognize were already seated. Who could they be? Reporters? Normally, only a handful of people came to these meetings and rarely any media. Most of their local business was too mundane for press coverage. Two women sporting suntans that only came from hours at the beach, sat drinking coffee and whispering. They didn't look like members of the press, but they weren't locals either. Claire knew everybody in Chapel Springs. So, who were they and why were they here?

Joel caught her arm. "You're staring. Mingle."

"What? Oh. I'm looking for Patsy. Do you see her?" Claire searched the room. Joel said she depended on her too much. Maybe she did, but Pat-a-cake was her best friend, and after her sister, CeeCee, died when they were fourteen, Patsy slipped into her place as sister/confidant. It was Patsy who helped her grieve and push past survivor's guilt.

Happy Drayton grabbed Joel to help set up more chairs. While they worked, Claire buried her worry in determination by eavesdropping on a few conversations. She wanted to gain a feel for which direction the wind blew, but it was hard to tell. People kept their voices low.

The town's problem had become a hot issue. If they did nothing, the money would continue to flow in, but the Chapel Springs they all knew and loved could be lost. They'd have to change the ordinances, or arrest those who camped in the park. She could see the headlines now. That would dry up revenues faster than Moses did the Red Sea. It wa—

Campers. Campgrounds! Cora Lee Rice had let some of the college kids camp in her property. Maybe they could build a campground. It would help some, anyway. Claire searched the room for the old gal, but she wasn't there. Miss Cora Lee never missed a council meeting. Claire hoped she was all right.

She edged closer to Warren Jenkins, Felix's sidekick. His movie store, *Front Row Seat*, had to be doing a brisk business. Some people were never happy, though. He griped to his wife, Gloria, about having to buy DVDs to replace the outdated videos he held onto for so long. Would he slide out from under Felix's influence? Nah. Never happen. Turning away, she bumped smack into Eileen Carlson.

"Sorry." Claire didn't have to wonder which side she was on. Eileen and Felix had been sweet on each other for donkey's years. It made life a little awkward with Eileen's shop, *Halls of Time*, right next to the gallery. Felix made a habit of stopping in the gallery to annoy Claire after schmoozing with his main squeeze.

Eileen checked the pie she carried and smiled. "No damage."

Claire sniffed. "Apple?"

"Dutch."

Eileen's pies rivaled Dee's. Claire followed her to the table where coffee and other goodies awaited. She cut a piece for Claire and watched her savor it.

Always a sap for Dutch apple pie—the cinnamon, the snap of sweet tart apples, and the crumbles on top with bits of sugar frosting, Claire moaned her pleasure.

"It's fabulous as always."

Leaving Eileen blushing over the compliment, Claire took her seat at the council table, setting her pie in front of her. The chairs, arranged along one side and the two ends, faced the audience. Open bottles of water stood at each place along with small piles of candy. She took a swig of water and set the bottle next to her plate. The others drifted to their places. Nancy Vaughn, owner of Claire's favorite dress shop *Sunspots*, took a seat next to her.

"I hope you have an idea that will corral the mayor, Claire."

"I'm working on som—"

"Let's get started." Boone Clark's deep voice, accompanied by an overzealous bang of his gavel, made her jump. Her knee bumped the table, and three bottles of water bounced and fell over. Faye jumped to her feet, shaking the water off her skirt. Claire snatched up her pie plate and tried to avoid the mess as it pooled in the middle. She was thankful the old tables sank in the middle and kept most of the water contained.

Felix chortled. "Well, we know Claire's here."

She glared at him. Would the world stop on its axis if he ever let a chance go by without pointing out her mishaps? Nancy grabbed a handful of paper towels from the center of the table and mopped up the mess. She frowned at Boone.

"You needn't bang that thing so loud. None of us is deaf." She winked at Claire. "At least we weren't."

The council president and editor of the *Weekly Voice* had the grace to look contrite. His enthusiasm was commendable even if his exuberance deafened them. This was only his third meeting, and she knew he was anxious to make changes, one of them being the town elections.

Claire liked Boone, but why would he want to change their

traditions? Chapel Springs chartered in July of 1903. Elections were held in May and the seat assumed July first. No one but Boone ever questioned having them at a different date from the state and federal. Besides, they went with the town's fiscal year. It made perfect sense in her mind.

"Claire." Nancy nudged her and whispered. "Check out that couple at the back. Think they're press?"

She glanced up from mopping the table. A man and woman, sitting in the back row, had their heads together. Claire didn't see a lanyard on either of them. Usually, the press wore their credentials hanging around their necks for all to see.

"I can't tell. I don't recognize them, though. They aren't from here."

Boone cleared his throat. "Are you ladies about finished?"

"It's all yours, Boone," Nancy said and deposited the sopping paper towels in a wastebasket. With the mess cleaned up, they took their seats again.

"Ellie, please read the minutes of last month's meeting."

Why did they have to do that? Claire finger-pressed a crease between the violet and green stripes in her skirt. They all attended the last meeting. They needed to get moving. That was the problem—they all wanted to study this and look over that. The town needed action but not the kind Felix proposed. She took a bite of her pie. A solid plan to retain the essence of Chapel Springs, that's what they needed. One that—

"All those in favor say aye."

In favor of what? Nancy nudged her and tilted her head toward Ellie. Oh. The minutes. "Aye." She chewed the last bite of her pie and used the back of the fork to press any crumbs onto the tines, then slipped those in her mouth.

"Any old business?" Boone asked. Claire dropped the fork and her hand shot up. He dipped his head to examine her over his glasses. "Claire? Do you have something?"

She put her hand down and swallowed. "Yes. It's come to my attention that our mayor," she nodded at Felix, "has appointed his brother, Dale, to oversee the springs' restoration. I'd like to ask what qualifications Dale has for this job? We weren't shown a résumé."

Felix glared at her. "Didn't want another outsider coming in here like that professor *you* hired."

"Nepotism doesn't replace qualified, Felix." She refused to back down. Dale couldn't work his way out of a wet paper bag. "At least the professor knew geology. His ego problem didn't change the outcome of the findings."

"My brother can oversee a team."

"How will he know if they're doing things right?" Tom pointed his unlit pipe at the mayor. "The job needs a qualified engineer. Dale not only lacks the necessary engineering degree, he lacks *any* higher education. He's simply not qualified."

Claire could have hugged Tom. She tossed him a chocolate kiss from the pile in front of her.

Felix huffed. "I've got to get him employed some way. You want to hire him?" Tom shook his head. "Anyone else?" Not a single hand raised, not even Warren's. Felix spread his hands. "What am I supposed to do with him?"

Claire almost felt sorry for the mayor. Dale arrived back in town six months ago with his worldly possessions in a single suitcase. He'd spent his life in the Army but never rose above the rank of Staff Sergeant. She'd heard stories about his schemes and how, working for the supply sergeant, he provided extra food rations to his buddies—for a price.

"Why not put him to work at Flavors?" Doc asked. Leave it to him to point out the obvious. Doc Benson, Patsy's dad, always said what everyone else was thinking but afraid to say.

"He'd eat all the ice cream," Felix said with a scowl.

Tom chewed the end of his mustache. "Tell you what, I'll give him a chance making deliveries for me. Just get someone else to oversee the restoration."

Pots o' paint, what was Tom thinking? He was a pharmacist. That meant Dale would be delivering prescriptions. Doc's jaw dropped and Claire groaned, envisioning ninety-three-year-old Hannah Potterfield getting Sam Tucker's Viagra instead of her allergy cream while Nellie Neugent got Sally Sampson's Prozac instead of cholesterol medicine.

Chapter 7

"Claire," Boone said. "You did a good job with the diagnosis of the springs' problem, so will you chair the restorations committee?"

Me? She gawked at him at the end of the council table. He must respect her to have suggested that. Her pride, wounded over the spilled water, recovered. She glanced at Joel, sitting in the second row shaking his head. "Too busy," he mouthed.

Okay, he might be right. Her life was crazy right now with trying to replenish her gallery and watch over Wes. And there was the housing issue ...

On the other hand, if she succeeded in overseeing the project, she just might stop being the town's favorite joke. And she couldn't get out of it gracefully, right? After all, it wasn't like they had to start this week.

"I'll be glad to." She kept her gaze trained on Boone even after she saw Joel gesturing frantically from the corner of her eye. She'd hear about it later. *Lord, I hope I did the right thing.*

"If no one has any other old business, we'll move on." Boone perused the agenda in front of him. "Felix? You asked to address the council."

Felix cleared his throat, stood, and smoothed his tie, which rode high on his belly. At his signal, Warren retrieved an easel and carried it to the front of the room.

Tom leaned toward her. "Here it comes," he whispered.

Felix, with typical pompousness, adjusted the easel so both the council and audience could view the large sketchpad resting on it. Oh, bother. He acted like this was a done deal. Was he in for a surprise.

"I'd like to present a proposal that Muldoon Investments Group,

Inc. brought to me." He took a dramatic pause and surveyed the room. Probably making sure all eyes were on him. Claire rolled hers. "They are proposing to build a high-rise hotel right here in Chapel Springs, on the beach at Chapel Lake."

He flipped the page on the easel to reveal a Miami-type monstrosity with palm trees that flanked a pillared entrance and high-glassed stairwells that stretched several floors. Indignation rose in Claire's throat like the Chattahoochee River when the dam released its water. Angry voices escalated throughout the room. Felix startled, put his hand on his chest, and a wounded expression on his face. The man deserved an Oscar.

Boone banged his gavel. "Quiet! Felix has the floor. We'll hear him out."

"Thank you, Boone. This could save our town." He used a laser pointer to indicate the various parts of the complex. The laser was bright—a fancy model with several settings. Claire hoped it would set fire to his drawings. "We have to have more housing. Due to the lack of foresight of certain unnamed persons, my office is getting complaints from residents about people partying all night and a few about campers in their front yards. Warm Springs Park is filled with their trash."

Unnamed persons? Why didn't he just say her name? The puffed up—

"Do any of y'all have an answer?" He turned to Claire. "You started this mess with your 'we gotta revitalize the town' business."

She clamped her lips together. The fact was she didn't have an answer. But any comment she made he'd turn against her. Besides, Joel said the campground would be a tourniquet at best. They needed something more substantial.

"I didn't think so." He turned to the council with his chest puffed out like a blowfish. "This hotel will have four hundred and twelve rooms. It will house all the tourists the town can hold. Think of the revenues it could bring in with weddings and corporate meetings. Now, any questions?"

Why would some company want to come to sleepy Chapel Springs for a meeting? Then again, their employees wouldn't have much else to distract them, other than fishing. Although, North Carolina wasn't far and it had casinos.

Claire raised her hand. Felix stared at her for a moment, his eyes narrowed. "All right, Claire. What is it?"

She bit her tongue against what she would've liked to say. "Where do you propose to build this monstrosity?"

"The land to the north of Ollie Katz's house is unoccupied. It's the last available plot in Chapel Springs with lakefront property, and this group wants lakefront. We don't want them building in another town, do we?"

"Yes." Claire clapped her hand over her mouth. "I mean no. I mean we don't want them building a big hotel at all." She stood up. "This would destroy the feel of Chapel Springs, y'all. Right now, we're Mayberry, USA. Mitford. That's what people love about Chapel Springs. That,"— she gestured to the display—"is Miami. We don't want a big fancy hotel in our village, forcing local residents to move away. If that happens, we lose the heart of Chapel Springs."

She looked at each of the council members in turn. "Faye, like me you were born and raised right here in town. So were you, Tom." She turned and smiled fondly at Patsy's daddy. "Doc, your great-grandparents and Miss Cora Lee's homesteaded in these mountains. Both your families have been here for generations. Yet, your own daughter—" She stopped and had to swallow rising tears. Her voice closed to a whisper. "She may move away if things don't quiet down."

Claire sank into her chair. Nancy slipped a comforting arm over her shoulders. From his seat, Joel glared at Felix. His scowl warmed Claire's heart. He was her champion. She sent up a quick prayer of thanks, and as she did, determination replaced desolation.

Felix planted his fists on his hips. "Well, do you have a better idea?"

Claire reflected his glare right back at him. "I'm working on one. We all are." With a little time, they'd come up with ... with ... something.

Doc Benson lumbered to his feet. The dignity of age and wisdom clung to him like an elder statesman. Claire adored him. Patsy's daddy was her hero, having helped her out of a few peccadilloes, like when one of her large turkey vases fell and clobbered that art critic.

He stepped to the microphone and removed his spectacles. After pulling his handkerchief from his back pocket, he wiped the lenses with care, all the while watching the folks who sat waiting. Finally, he settled his gaze on Felix. "Who owns that land?"

"The Newlanders."

"Didn't Howie move away? I haven't seen him in years."

No one had. There was a time when she'd been friends with Howie, but that was when they were in grade school. She never could understand his disdain for Chapel Springs.

"His great-granny still lives here." Felix glowered at Doc. "She's the legal owner."

Doc scratched the back of his head. "That may be, but she's in her nineties and living at Magnolia Manor. Howie has her power of attorney."

Felix tugged at his collar. His eyes flitted to the audience. Claire followed his gaze, along with Doc. Two men stared back at him from the doorway. Felix shrugged. Could they be part of that Muldoon Group?

"Mayor," Doc said, turning back to Felix. "Why don't we shelve this for now? No sense riling up everybody until you've had a chance to talk to Howie. He might say no." Cheers erupted and Doc sat back down.

"Say no?" The tip of Felix's nose turned red. "Why would Howie say no to a boatload of money?"

The prospect turned Claire's blood cold. She shivered and pulled her jacket over her shoulders. Howie had always talked big schemes for making money. He left Chapel Springs like his tail was on fire, heading for a big city to make his fortune, but the last time Claire saw him, at his daddy's funeral, he didn't look like any millionaire.

Glancing at Joel, she sent a silent plea for help. He winked, making her smile. Surely, together, if they could get to him first, she and Joel could convince Howie not to sell. She sucked in her lower lip and began to plot her strategy.

Felix returned to his seat, and the council addressed their other business. When Boone called for any more new business, Joel asked to address the council. When Boone nodded, her husband made his way to the microphone, stopping once to shake hands with Happy.

"I have a proposal for the traffic situation, and," he nodded at Felix, "it would provide the perfect job for your brother."

She couldn't help smiling. Her husband was brilliant. He may not have a college degree, but he had street smarts—common sense. She sat a little straighter.

"There's vacant land next to *The Happy Hooker*."

Felix jumped up. "We can't build the hotel there. It isn't big enough."

"I know that. Hear me out."

Boone banged his gavel. "Sit down, Mayor. Let Joel have his turn. Then you can answer."

Felix resumed his seat with a grumble.

Joel nodded to Boone. "Thank you, Mr. Chairman. As I was saying,

Happy owns that vacant lot, and he agreed to this. What I'm proposing is parking for visitors just outside the main town. Year-round residents would be issued a window permit to drive in town, but tourists and summer residents would have to park in the lot."

Protests rose from the people Claire hadn't recognized and now realized were summer residents.

"What about getting groceries to our houses? You expect us to walk?" a voice from the back of the room cried.

Joel raised his hand. "No, not at all. My proposal also employs two trams with the ability to add an additional car. They would be in constant movement around the village and outlying homes. Trust me, folks. Happy and I have done our homework on this. The furthest house belonging to summer residents is only three miles from the center of Chapel Springs. With two trams, the longest anyone would wait would be about ten minutes." He zeroed in on Felix. "Dale could be one of the drivers."

Felix stood. Always tight with the town's money, Claire knew he'd hate to spend a buck, even for a good thing. "And who is going to pay for these trams?"

Joel shared a grin with Claire. They had the mayor on this one. She nearly chortled as he answered Felix.

"Happy said he'd be glad to finance it. Of course that means he'll collect the revenues, which will be considerable."

"Not so fast," Felix argued. "I want to see numbers. It may be better if the town bought the land from Happy. After all, it's a benefit for Chapel Springs."

Boone tapped his gavel. "Why don't you and Happy put this on paper, Joel, and bring it by my office. Then Felix and I will go over it and make a recommendation to the council next month."

Joel agreed and the meeting ended.

Joel leaned against the kitchen counter as Claire performed one of the small culinary duties she could do well. She set the bag of popcorn in the microwave, programmed the time for precisely two minutes and thirty-four seconds, and hit start.

"With all you have going, why did you tell Boone you'd oversee the springs restoration?" he asked.

She crossed the floor and slipped into his arms, resting her head against his chest. "I don't know. Yes, I do." She leaned back and looked up at him. "For once, I'd like to prove I can do something without any disasters."

Joel tightened his arms around her. "Oh, my sweet Clairey-girl, don't you know everyone adores you just the way you are? You're the sunshine in Chapel Springs. Sure, you get into trouble, but it's the fun kind. We wouldn't have you any other way." He bent his head and kissed her.

The microwave dinged and Wes's footsteps clomped down the stairs. He must have smelled the popcorn. Nothing else pulled him away from that computer these days. So much for romance. Joel kissed the tip of her nose and broke the embrace.

She pulled out the swollen bag, dumped the popcorn into a bowl, and handed it to Joel to take to the family room. He chomped on a handful as he left the kitchen. She tossed another bag in the microwave for Wes. He could eat the entire thing on his own.

"That one for me?" He opened the cupboard and pulled out another bowl while the microwave hummed and the first kernels popped.

"It is." Taking advantage of the wait, she asked, "What are you up to tonight? Going out?" She hoped a new love interest might get him back into life again. The corn popping increased.

"Nope. I'm getting ready to take a short vacation before I start working for dad." The microwave dinged. He dumped the contents into the bowl and walked into the family room, leaving her in the kitchen with her mouth hanging open.

Vacation? The kid sure knew how to drop bombs. She clamped her mouth shut and followed him.

After handing a glass of sweet iced tea to Joel, she sat beside him. Wes sprawled on the loveseat and stuffed a handful of popcorn into his mouth. On the coffee table lay a brochure for Virginia Beach. She glanced at Joel. He lifted one shoulder, looking as mystified as she felt. After he munched for a moment, he turned the sound off on the TV.

"Son, what is this about?" He cocked his head toward the brochure.

"I'm going to go on a little vacation. Once I start working with you, there won't be any time."

They waited, but Wes chomped another mouthful of popcorn, his eyes on the silent TV. Joel chewed and watched him. Claire watched them both. How could her husband be so patient? First the kid dropped out of college and now he wanted to take a vacation. She fidgeted and bumped her knee against Joel's, giving him a "do something" look. But he either didn't catch her meaning or didn't want to.

The moment Wes swallowed, Claire took advantage of his empty mouth. "And how do you plan to pay for this? You may have dropped out of school, but we're still paying for the twins and don't have any extra cash for a vacation. Your dad and I haven't taken one in years."

His smile spread, revealing a couple of popcorn shells between his teeth.

"It's all paid for, Ma. It won't cost you and Dad a thing."

Joel frowned and handed the bowl to Claire. "How's that?"

Wes wiped his hands down his jeans legs. She wished he wouldn't do that, the grease was hard to get out.

"Last year in my economics class, we set up accounts with a pretend brokerage house. I did so well at choosing investments, that I got a real account with an actual online broker."

Could he do that? Did Joel know about it? She glanced at him, but by his gaping mouth and wide eyes, she guessed not. "What did you use to invest?"

"First I took my savings account—"

"Oh, no, Wes. Not the money your grandma left you? Honey, that was supposed to be a nest egg to help you buy a home someday."

"Ma, calm down. I only used a thousand of that to open the account. I've been investing everything I've made working weekends. I think I have a gift for knowing when to buy and sell." He swaggered in his seat. "I've got a little over twenty-seven thousand dollars now."

What? Claire was proud of him, but that seemed so risky. Still, it was an amazing feat when most not-quite-twenty-year-olds were buying cars and going to parties, not thinking about saving money.

Joel beamed at him. "I think I should turn over my little investment account to you, son."

"I'd love to, Dad. I'm really good at it."

"That's an understatement. You've made an unbelievable amount in a short time, and in a down economy. Can you explain your ideas?"

"Sure. Let me get my iPad."

IPad? Claire stared at him. "When did you get that?"

"That's the only money I've spent out of my earnings, so I could stay on top of the market all the time." He galloped up the stairs.

Claire shook her head. This kid never should have dropped out of school. "Joel, I still don't understand why with his brains, he doesn't like college. It mystifies me."

"Not all kids are cut out for formal education. What matters is that he's happy, and he isn't dependent on other people to support him. You can't say he's lazy."

No, she couldn't. But the shifts in his personality had her befuddled. Tonight, he was like his old self, communicative and enthusiastic. But tomorrow, would he go back into seclusion? She glanced at the brochure on the table. What was in Virginia Beach? Was it just the beach or something else? Wes had never gone anywhere alone before, and the question that nagged her was why now?

Joel picked up the pamphlet. "Maybe we should think about taking a vacation. What do you say?"

"You mean go when he's there?"

"No, that wouldn't be right. I just mean maybe we should plan to go somewhere. Like you said, we haven't taken a vacation in years and never gone alone, at least not since our honeymoon."

Had it been that long? "Who are you?" She snuggled closer. "I'm not sure my husband would appreciate me going away with you. He's rather stodgy about things like that."

He snorted but gave her a sheepish grin. "I keep remembering I almost lost you because I took you for granted. I don't intend to let that happen again."

Her Joel had really changed, and she hoped she had as well. Stretching her neck, she kissed his cheek. "Too bad Wes is getting that blasted iPad. When he gets done showing you his brilliance, why don't you join me upstairs?" She wiggled her eyebrows at him, hoping she looked sexy and not like Groucho Marx.

Chapter 8

Lydia smoothed a thin layer of night cream onto her scrubbed clean face. The floor beneath her feet vibrated from Kenny's stereo going full blast. It was eleven eighteen, time for quiet. She dropped the jar's lid on the bathroom rug when she tried to screw it back on. "Oh, of all the—" She peeked around the door into the bedroom where Graham sat on the side of the bed. "Honey, will you tell Kenny to turn that thing down? We won't be able to sleep with that racket." Not to mention it killed any romantic inclinations. Just having him in the house put a damper on their intimacy.

"He'll turn it down soon. And look." He opened a drawer and pulled out a small plastic container. "I bought us earplugs. No more problem."

No more problem? What was he thinking? She clamped her lips shut while she struggled to speak calmly. "Sugar, I don't want to wear ear plugs. I don't like them."

He set the little box on the counter, crossed the room, and pulled her into his arms. "I want him to feel at home, hushpuppy. He's been through a lot lately and needs to get his feet back under him. Then we'll have our home to ourselves again."

She hoped so. This was not what she signed up for. She wanted her romantic husband back. "Fine, but can you at least ask him to lower the volume some? For me?" She slid her arms around his neck and kissed him.

"You get into bed and I'll go and talk to him."

One more toe-curling kiss and he left the bedroom. She turned back the covers and climbed beneath them. Through the floor, she heard the volume go down a little, but not enough to stop the bass reverberating through the floor joists—and her chest.

Lydia sighed. Kenny had been here a week now, and her refrigerator showed it. She needed to shop for groceries again tomorrow. She rolled over, fighting the heaviness in her eyes and wishing Graham would hurry.

A loud cymbal crash jerked her awake. She reached over, but Graham's side of the bed was empty. The digital clock read one a.m. Through the floor register, she could hear them, laughing. There ought to be a law against grown kids moving in when their parents were newlyweds. She was too tired to even chuckle at the irony of her thought. Punching her pillow, she turned on her side and tried to go back to sleep.

Bleary-eyed from fatigue, Lydia poured her third cup of coffee from Dee's pot of dark roast, added a squirt of mocha flavoring, and rejoined her friends. She wondered if Joel paid Kenny enough to allow him to get an apartment. What if he could share with Claire's son, Wes, if he moved into one?

"How's Kenny doing at the marina? Has Joel said anything?"

Claire cast a glance at Patsy, who gave a tiny nod.

Lydia straightened in her chair. What was that about? "Claire, if Kenny's done something, I need to know. His presence in our house isn't helping Graham and me. I'm hoping he's doing well enough to move into an apartment."

"He hasn't done a thing wrong. He's a good worker."

Lydia waited, but Claire didn't say anything more. "I heard a 'but' in there," she prompted.

"Well, to be honest, there is. He's almost too good a worker. Joel said he felt like it was calculated. I think he's just not used to an over-achiever." Claire fiddled with her earring. "That's what I think it is. After all, he got laid off in a down economy. He wants to keep this job." She patted Lydia's hand. "Don't worry."

Maybe Claire was right. "Do you suppose Wes might want a roommate to share expenses? I'm anxious for Kenny to get out on his own."

"Wes hasn't said anything about moving out. If he does, I'll ask him to talk to Kenny as soon as he gets back from his vacation. He went to Virginia Beach for a few days."

Patsy touched Lydia's shoulder. "Be sure you tell Graham exactly how you feel. Keeping those things from each other will lead to problems. I know, remember."

"I'm trying to, but it's hard without sounding like a shrew. It's like Claire says, Kenny's in a tough spot, and I want to love him." She gazed into the sympathetic eyes of her friends and shrugged. "He's Graham's son. It's just ... well, it seems like Kenny knows exactly which buttons to push on his dad to get what he wants. Not only is he living with us, but—" She debated whether to say it, but Claire and Patsy gave good advice. "I saw Graham give him money this morning."

"How old is Kenny?" Patsy asked.

"Twenty-five."

"Maybe Graham needs to say no."

Lydia stirred her coffee and sighed. "It seems he has a bit of a problem doing that."

Lydia had just set Graham's dinner in front of him when Kenny limped into the house. Had he gotten hurt? She set her own plate on the table as Graham jumped up.

"Son, what happened?" He helped Kenny into a chair.

"It's an old injury that's acting up, Dad."

Graham frowned. "What old injury?"

Lydia got him a glass of water and pulled his plate from the oven's warming drawer. "Would you like some aspirin or ibuprofen?"

"Thanks, Lydia. You're so good to me."

"What old injury, Kenny?"

At Graham's insistent voice, Kenny slumped a bit in the chair. "Remember the motorcycle you bought me, Dad?"

"Of course I remember it. What about it?"

"The wheel locked up and it threw me off. I broke my leg and hip, and when I stand on concrete for a long time, they start hurting something awful. And I have to stand all day at the marina. On concrete floors."

"When did this happen and why didn't you ever tell me about it?"

"You were out of the country then, working for that bank in Dubai. Besides, it wasn't like it was life threatening or anything. Karen took care of me."

Lydia glanced between the two. Who was Karen? A girlfriend? Graham seemed to know because he nodded.

Kenny looked away from his dad to her, his eyes pleading for understanding. "I had to quit working at the marina. I don't want to get hooked on some strong narcotic just to handle the pain."

Lydia watched as a layer of guilt settled over her husband like a mantle. He hunched over his plate under the weight of it. She understood guilt, having carried her share of it over Lacey. It took a few years, but she finally saw it for what it was—a wasted emotion. Or perhaps misplaced was a better word. She had cast hers off, realizing it wasn't beneficial.

Now, she saw with clarity the relationship between her husband and his son. And she didn't dare say a word. This did not bode well for their fledgling marriage—not if Kenny stayed with them for any length of time.

Graham reached out and squeezed Kenny's shoulder. "That's a wise decision, son. If you can avoid that, you'll be ahead of the game. There're other jobs here in town." His gaze fixed on Lydia.

She had to appear happy to help, and she was. Especially if it would get her stepson to stand on his own. "The restaurants are—"

"No, that takes being on his feet all day."

"Oh, right. What about looking in Pineridge? Most of the jobs here in Chapel Springs are retail or restaurant. There's the grocery store, of course. Maybe—Kenny, didn't you say you studied accounting? They might be looking for somebody to do the accounting."

Kenny stared at his clasped hands between his knees. "I tried there when I first arrived. Mr. Kowalski does their books."

That made sense. "I think Pineridge has more opportunities for you. It's a bigger town with more corporate jobs."

"I'd rather be closer to you and dad."

She could appreciate his desire, but Pineridge was a short drive, twenty minutes max. Was he sincere about this? She studied him as he ate. He hadn't had a mother since he was a little boy. He could have been antagonistic to her like some kids were when their parent remarried, but he'd accepted her readily. True, Graham had spoiled Kenny, but it didn't mean her stepson was rotten. He simply needed a strong influence.

"I'll check around tomorrow, Kenny. I'm sure between my friends and your dad's contacts at work, we'll hear of something. Now, let's finish dinner before it gets cold."

Graham squeezed her fingers beneath the table then lifted a forkful of mashed potatoes. Kenny followed suit.

"Wow, this is great mash, Lydia. Dad, you married a terrific cook."

Her husband's smile and wink reinforced her decision. She'd help

Kenny all she could. While they ate, she did a mental walk of Chapel Springs. *Chapel Lake Inn* used Nathan to do their accounting. On the other side of the spa was the drugstore, but Kenny wasn't a pharmacist. *Flavors*, owned by Felix, wouldn't have anything other than serving ice cream and it involved standing.

The next three shops were the boutique, the gift shop, and the used bookstore. All retail jobs. She envisioned crossing the side street and continuing her mental walk down Sandy Shores Drive as she took a bite of croissant. She passed Claire and Patsy's art gallery, dismissed the antique shop, but stopped for a second and considered the bakery. But Dee also used Nathan for her accountant. Hey, would he need an assistant? No, he wanted more business if he was considering a move to New York. That left the hobby shop, the marina—which Kenny already quit—and the bait shop. No, unless he wanted to drive the tram the town had talked about gettin', there wasn't a thing for him in Chapel Springs.

Chapter 9

Claire lifted her newest pieces from the cavern of her kiln. Her breath caught. Like the tide of sunset, greens swirled in waves, blending into brilliant turquoise then disappeared into the truest orange she'd ever achieved. It was exactly—no, it was more than she'd hoped for. That was the wonder, the magic in being a potter. The color she applied would change in the second firing, and she never knew for sure, until the process was finished, what she'd have. After turning the large serving bowl around to check its coloration, she set it on the counter.

If only Wes would comply with her manipulations like the clay—not that she would actually manipulate him—just direct him in the right way. She sighed and lifted out a pitcher, inspecting the depth and translucency of its colors. If Wes listened to her, he'd be much happier, she was sure of it. After all, she had years on him in the life experience department. Did God feel that way about his children? Setting the piece down, she checked it for fatal flaws. Did God feel that way about *her* when she messed up?

"Sorry," she whispered, knowing she must frustrate the fire out of him. "Thanks for not giving up on me."

The bells on the gallery door jangled. Out of habit, she checked her watch. The *Painted Loon* wasn't open yet, and Patsy was in Pineridge getting a haircut at her daughter's salon, so who could it be? Claire went to the door. A waif of a girl stood waiting to be let in, one hand on the bell cord, ready to pull it again. When she saw Claire through the glass, she folded her hands in front of her, and her eyebrows disappeared beneath sparrow-brown bangs. A braid hung over one shoulder, its tip touching her waist, and a large purple canvas tote rested on the boardwalk beside her. Could this be—?

She opened the door. "Nicole?"

As the girl's face split into a smile, her eyes all but disappeared, making her look like a pixie.

"Ah'm so excited to be here, Mrs. Bennett. Melissa has told me so much about y'all. Not that she needed to. I've followed your career. I love your work. Your colors and form are so innovative." She stopped and took a breath, her cheeks a deep rosy red.

The girl's drawl rivaled Lydia's. Claire hoped it was just nerves making her a chatterbox and she wasn't like Charlie's mother-in-law, Zoe, who could talk the hind legs off a donkey. Still, this diminutive Southern belle followed her work. *My, my, my.*

"Come in, come in. I wasn't expecting you until a little later." She stepped to the side as Nicole entered, then relocked the door.

"I know I'm early. I was too anxious to get here to wait another minute." She set her tote on the floor and turned in a circle, her eyes wide as she took in the displays. She stepped over to Claire's whimsy vase display—her gaze locked on the raccoon—and stretched out a hand, staring, then withdrew it.

"That is so life-like. I hope I can do something that good one day."

The wonder in her voice was good for Claire's ego, boosting it skyward. "I'm glad you like it. I've always loved these funny creatures." She turned the raccoon a tick to the right, showing more of its personality. Since this was her new assistant and not a customer, it was time to get to know her. "Let's go in the workroom where we can talk. Is that your portfolio I see sticking out of your tote?"

"Yes, ma'am. Melissa said I should bring it." Suddenly she looked uncertain. "Was that okay?"

"Lissa's right. I'll want to see it, but first, let's get acquainted. Then I'll tell you what I expect and we'll see if that sounds okay to you."

Nicole followed her to the workroom. "Oh, I'll do whatever I need to—even scrub toilets—if it means I can learn from you. You're the best there is, Mrs. Bennett."

She smiled and smoothed the hair at her neckline. "Call me Claire, dear, and thank you. Now, tell me about you."

"You mean my art experience?"

Claire waved dismissively. "Later." More importantly, she wanted to know if Nicole was a good prospect for Wes. "I want to know you, first.

Tell me about your family."

Nicole's eyes grew soft with affection. That was a good sign. "I have one brother and two sisters."

A large family—just like ours. Things were getting better. Claire sat back and crossed her legs.

"My dad's a civil engineer and my mom stayed at home until we all were in school. Then she went back to teaching art history at the high school."

So her love of art was inborn. Even better. "Did you like school?"

A small line appeared between Nicole's brows. "Not really. I mean, I loved art classes and English, but math was beyond me. Not simple math. I mean algebra. Letters are not numbers, y'all know what I mean?"

"I do, but you'd be surprised what you end up using those formulas for. Like mixing colors. There are definite formulas for certain shades."

"Oh, I never thought of that."

This was a good place to introduce Wes to her. At least the idea of him. "I have a son who's the opposite. He's great with math, but not so much with English."

Nicole's expression was guarded as she stared at Claire.

Alrighty then, so maybe her timing was off. She pointed to the portfolio that rested against Nicole's knee. "How about showing me your work? And tell me what you've learned so far."

While Claire leafed through Nicole's photo collection of school projects, she listened to the girl talk about her classes and learning to work with the various clays. She grew more animated and her eyes sparkled. She couldn't fake that. Art was in her soul. It excited Claire and gave her new purpose. She made her decision.

"I'm going to teach you all I know." And introduce her to Wes. Claire's mind whirled. Since Melissa wanted to paint instead of being a potter, how wonderful to have a potter for a daughter-in-law. Claire couldn't wait for her son to come home from Virginia Beach.

"Here's what I have planned. We'll meet here a couple of hours each day before the gallery opens. From your portfolio, I can see your form is good, but your colors are unimaginative." She smiled at Nicole to soften the criticism. "I mean they're fine for a student, but I'll teach you techniques for creating new colorations and help you learn to stretch yourself as an artist. Then when the gallery opens, you'll work the front. Later in the day, you can have time in the workroom to experiment. How does that sound?"

Nicole's elf-eyes sparkled. "I know Melissa told you my dad lost his job and I had to quit school. I didn't know what I was going to do until 'Lissa suggested this." Moisture gathered in the corners of her eyes. "I don't know how to thank you." Her voice squeaked on the last words.

"Just do a good job and learn well." And rescue her son from whatever ails him. "That will be thanks enough. Shall we get you oriented to the gallery?"

With her knuckles, Nicole wiped the corners of her eyes. "I'm ready." She followed Claire back into the gallery and stopped in front of Patsy's "Summer morning" painting. "This is beautiful. Who's the artist?"

"All these are Patsy Kowalski's work. She's my gallery partner."

"Is that Melissa's Aunt Patsy? I thought that was your sister." Nicole scrunched her mouth. "I think I'm confused."

"She's my best friend and as close as a sister. We grew up together, and the kids have known her all their lives." After showing her around the displays, Claire explained the cost book. "You'll need to learn the prices of things." She handed over the book. "You can study it in the afternoons, but keep it behind the counter. You want a client to fall in love with the piece before they know the cost."

Nicole's reverence reminded Claire of herself as a young art student, wondering if she had what it took to make it as a potter. Her heart embraced the girl, and she was glad Melissa had asked her to mentor Nicole.

The rest of the morning was spent teaching Nicole how to use the register and learning the inventory. After they opened and customers began to flow in, Claire stayed at Nicole's shoulder, teaching and observing. She was a fast learner, which filled Claire with confidence.

When Patsy returned from her haircut, she met Nicole and took over teaching her about her paintings. Claire slipped over to *Dee's 'n' Doughs* to pick up sandwiches. Nicole took hers up front to eat behind the register when she was free. Patsy and Claire settled in the workroom.

"I like your haircut. Did Deva take it a little shorter than usual? It's cute." The length was mid-ear and gave her face a lift. "You look younger."

Patsy's hand went to her hair, fluffing the bangs. "Thanks. It was an experiment, but I love the results. I saw a woman with hers like this in New York." She finished her sandwich, wadded up the wrapper, and tossed it in the trash. As she moved to her easel, she slid on the large shirt she always wore when painting. "So, do you think Nicole will work out?"

Claire wrapped the other half of her sandwich and put it in the small fridge. "Definitely. She has the passion it takes to succeed. She's a cute girl, isn't she?" If only Wes could see that. He didn't see anything lately except his computer screen.

A balled up piece of paper hit her on the head.

"Hey, I asked you a question."

She did? "What?"

"I asked how long do you think ... oh never mind." Patsy shook her head and picked up a filbert brush. "What are you thinking about that you didn't hear me?"

"Wes. I'm anxious for him to get back home and meet Nicole. I'm hoping he'll appreciate her, too. I think she's just right for him."

"Claire, you hardly know this girl. How can you know that?"

"I asked her all about herself. Besides, 'Lissa knows her well. They were roommates."

"Maybe so, but she never suggested her brother date her, did she."

"Well, no, I don't think so, but—"

"So why are you? You've never tried to be a matchmaker before. Why now?"

"He needs something to make him think straight. He spends all his time up in his room behind a computer." Claire pulled a hunk of clay from the barrel and started to work it between her hands.

Patsy cackled. "And you think a girlfriend would make him think *straight*? Oh, that's rich." She snorted and spread a swath of orange to the sky on her canvas.

"Yeah, I guess you're right. But something has to wake him up. He quit school, Patsy. He wants to work with Joel."

"Finally. I was wondering how long it would take him to figure that out."

The clay thu-whumped onto the floor. "You knew he wanted to quit?"

"Sugar, that boy has lake water in his veins. Have you watched him closely when he's at the marina or in the store? He's in his element."

Claire picked up the clay and cut off the part that touched the floor. Any dirt or dust particles could cause it to crack in the kiln. "But what about school? He's so bright." She threw the contaminated blob in the trash, then pulled out more clay to make up for what she cut off. "I want him to graduate, not waste his mind on boats and fishing."

Patsy laid down her brush. "I love you, girlfriend, but you're dead wrong here. You're blind to his gifts."

"Oh, really?" Claire knew her own son best. Didn't she? "What do you think those gifts are?"

"Wes is so good with Joel's customers. He knows the lake's moods, and he's the best safety instructor around." She swabbed her brush against the palette. "He never wanted to go to college in the first place."

"He *told* you that or are you guessing?"

Patsy's eyes held her you-better-listen look. "He told me. The same way my kids told you things." Then she smirked.

Oh. Right. Her kids *did* tell her things they didn't tell their mom. "Okay, okay. But it still doesn't solve everything. He hasn't stopped secluding himself in his room all the time. I don't understand it."

"What does Joel say?"

Claire snorted. "He's so chuffed over Wes wanting to be his partner, he's blown it off, thinks it's over. But it isn't." A knot of worry took up residence in her stomach, and its mate throbbed between her eyes.

"Mrs. Bennett?" Nicole's voice interrupted them.

"Nicole, please call me Claire."

"Right. I'm sorry. Claire, there's a man up here who wants to talk to you. He won't let me help him. I tried to tell him you were busy, but he said you'd want to hear what he has to say. He said to tell you his name is Riley."

Felix or Dale? She groaned. Either way, her day was ruined, and since neither would give up, she wiped her hands on a rag. "Okay. Tell him I'll be right there."

A dozen people wandered the gallery. Claire found Dale among them, making comments about her vases.

"Whooey, you shoulda seen Claire wrastle the raccoon that inspired this one," he chortled. "That ole coon got the best of her, it surely did."

Claire closed her eyes and counted to ten. For the first time in her life, she wished Felix were here instead of his brother. Felix may be a curmudgeon and give her a load of grief, but he at least didn't tell tales like Dale. That raccoon was Happy's pet, and it stole her watch, but that didn't mean it got the best of her. No way. She'd grabbed its tail and wrestled the watch back. Just because the coon chomped on her tennis shoe and took out the laces didn't mean it had won.

She flashed a quick smile at the shoppers and grabbed Dale's elbow. "Don't believe a word he says." She dragged him toward the workroom. "You wanted to see me?"

Dale extracted his elbow, stopping in the doorway. He planted his feet, refusing to go further, and looked at his arm. "You got mud on me!" His voice squeaked with accusation and his hands shook.

"It's clay, not mud." She found the offending clay on the side of her hand. "And it won't stain."

"It's still mud. Get me a rag to get it off. Quick!"

Dale was almost crying. Was he afraid of mud—mysophobic? What a boon. It was a discovery she could add to her arsenal. She pulled a rag out of her pocket and handed it to him. After ridding himself of the clay, he glared at her. Then an evil glint came into his eye. Claire retreated a step.

Dale glanced into the gallery then back at her. "Guess who I saw a couple o' weeks ago in the post office in Pineridge getting a passport?"

She should care? "Dale, I'm really busy. I can't imagine why I'd want to know that." She headed back to the workroom.

"Even if it was your son Wesley?" His voice followed her, loud enough for the entire gallery to hear.

And it stopped her cold.

Her Wesley? She turned around and stormed back to Dale. "Get in here." She reached to pull him into the workroom, but he lifted his elbow away and walked into the gallery. He stopped near the entrance and turned his head, glancing over his shoulder as he opened the door.

"Yep, he surely did. Got hisself a passport. Tried to hide from me when he caught sight of me."

That's not unusual, most people did. "That's not a crime, Dale. Wes is a big boy. If he needs a passport, what's the big deal?"

Dale grinned. "If it was all above board, why was he in Pineridge instead of the Chapel Springs Post Office?"

His cackle rang in Claire's ears even after the door shut. A few people in the gallery stared at her. Gathering her wits, she smiled and rolled her eyes. "Every town has a chin-wagger. Y'all just met our rumormonger. Now, how may I help you?"

Her calm exterior didn't match her insides. Her heart pounded against her ribs, and her stomach churned, sending a load of heartburn up her esophagus. Why did Wes need a passport? Virginia Beach might be less than two hundred miles from Washington, D.C., but that didn't make it a foreign country.

What was her son up to?

Chapter 10

Claire was glad. Really. Ecstatic even. Joel had come to church this morning without so much as an attempted excuse—a first. And Pastor Seth's sermon was so good, too. Now, she had a glimmer of hope that one day Joel would believe. But it wouldn't be today. He went to sleep after the opening hymn. At least he had the grace to look embarrassed as he shook Seth's hand when they exited. Seth gripped Joel's arm and pulled him close, whispering. Though his grin was sheepish, her husband looked relieved.

He slipped his hands into his pockets as they walked home. They ambled along in comfortable silence for a few minutes. The sun, having done its job of mellowing the crisp air to the corner of cool and warm, flaunted itself by glinting off the mica in the sidewalk.

"Why didn't you elbow me?"

Claire stumbled on a sidewalk crack. "I was listening to the sermon, not watching you." Actually, it *had* been kind of funny. "What did Seth whisper to you?"

Joel cleared his throat and looked straight ahead. "He said if I hadn't awakened Miss Cora Lee with my snoring, she would have disturbed everyone with hers."

A giggle she couldn't hold back bubbled up. "I didn't know whether to laugh or be mad. But when Miss Cora Lee snorted awake and glared at you, the irony of the situation tickled my funny bone and I couldn't be mad."

"Does she always snore in church?"

"Only when she and her pals stay up too late, playing Yahtzee. We usually ignore her. But with you—" Another giggle sneaked out her nose.

One side of Joel's mouth hitched. "I'm really sorry, babe. I hope you weren't too embarrassed."

Was she? "Maybe a bit, but that's my problem, not yours. I decided I love you more than I was embarrassed. Besides,"—the vision of Miss Cora Lee's indignant scowl made her chuckle—"it really was too funny for words. Like a Mr. Bean sketch."

"I promise I'll be better next week."

Her breath caught. Next week? In the back of her mind, she'd hoped but wasn't sure he would. "Then you won't stop coming?"

"I promised you." He gently shoulder bumped her. "But you better promise to wake me if I fall asleep again."

She bumped him back. "Deal. Have you met Lydia's new husband yet? You weren't with me the Sunday they got married." His expression blank, she knew he hadn't. "Refresher course. She met him at the beach. It was a whirlwind courtship, and Seth married them at the end of the regular service."

"Why? Didn't Lydia want a proper wedding?"

"She said other than Lacey, we're her family. Her sister was slow to accept Graham, though, from what I can read between the lines."

"Why should Lacey care?"

"I don't know for sure. Lydia said they weren't close as kids. She had to help raise Lacey. But I know there's more to their story."

"Leave it alone, Claire."

She fanned her hand on her chest. "Whatever do you mean, sir?"

"Ha! Don't play the innocent Southern belle with me. You jump right in the middle of everything, especially when it comes to your friends. Remember what a former U.S. president said, 'Read my lips.' Leave it alone."

Not at all bothered by him, she laughed as they strolled up the front walk. The house, which sat close to the street, welcomed her. She loved the old place, but the front flower beds were looking a bit forlorn. "We need to plant new fall flowers before it's too late. Want to go to the nursery after lunch?"

Joel looked at the dying annuals as if he'd never seen them. "Why didn't I see how bad these looked?"

"Because they aren't fish?"

Joel crossed his eyes at her like he used to when they were in high school. He always made her laugh then and it still worked.

"I'm kidding. It's probably for the same reason I ignored them. Too busy or too used to them. They were gorgeous for Charlie and Sandi's wedding reception, but I don't think we've touched them since."

"Do you think people would talk if we put plastic ones in?" Joel unlocked the front door. Claire swatted him as she passed, then bent to pat Shiloh, who bounded up to greet them.

"I'll pull Sunday dinner out while you change." In the kitchen, she lifted the marinated skirt steak from the refrigerator and laid it on a plate for Joel to do whatever he was going to do with it. After consulting his list again, she laid out the rest of their dinner ingredients next to the steak. Looked like fajitas. Yum. Her mouth watered.

Strolling the nursery's display of fall annuals, Claire inhaled the sweet fragrance of a tea olive and with it, a memory from her childhood. She must have been about four. Patsy's mother had tea olive growing in her garden, but the blossoms were so tiny, they went unnoticed by Claire. When she asked what smelled so good, Patsy's mom told her it was her garden fairy. Claire and Patsy spent days looking in vain for the pixie.

"Mums in front of the azaleas and rhododendrons will add some nice color to the house." She swept her arm like a game show hostess at the aisles of blooms. "What else?"

Joel pointed to a mountain marigold. "Those look good, and what would you say to a new dogwood tree for the front yard?"

She nearly melted in a pool of goo right there on the nursery's cement floor. Joel was talking her love language. He hated yard work, so for him to suggest planting a tree was a sacrifice. "You remembered!"

He actually scuffed his foot and blushed. "Aw, well ..."

Claire leaned closer and kissed his cheek. He frowned and stepped away. She snickered, and he grinned. She puckered up again.

"I'll go get a cart," he said and loped off before she could kiss him again. The man was so predictable.

After they loaded all the plants and the tree in the bed of the pickup, they headed home. Joel looked in the rearview mirror. "Too bad Wes isn't home to help us."

Claire smacked her forehead. "I can't believe I forgot to tell you this. On Friday, Dale came into the gallery—"

"Dale? In the gallery? That's a first. What did he want—a big bowl to hold gossip?"

"Ha. He came to dish some." She turned her head to keep an eye on the tree in the truck bed as they turned a corner. "Easy, big guy, the tree looks green."

Joel barked a laugh but eased off the gas. "So what did Gossip Goober say?"

"Gossip Goober? Is that what y'all call him?" Claire chuckled. The name suited. Then she sobered, thinking of other names that would better suit, like Devious Dale. "There's something about that man that dills my pickle."

"I've often wondered if he doesn't wear stupid like a vest."

"What do you mean?"

Joel checked the rearview mirror, turned on the blinker, and changed lanes. "I'm not sure, but there's something about him I don't trust. He acts like he's stupid, but just because a chicken has wings doesn't mean it can fly."

She stared at the ribbon of road disappearing beneath them. "He said he saw Wes at the main Pineridge post office filling out a passport application."

Joel looked at her like she'd said she was pregnant. "Now why in Sam Hill would he need a passport?"

"My question exactly."

"You don't have any idea?"

"None. Zilch. Nada."

Joel kept his eyes on the road. She could virtually see the wheels turning in his head as fast as the ones on the car. The tree bent as if it remembered Hurricane Katrina. "Honey, slow down. The poor dogwood is waving at you."

"Wes is twenty next month. We were married when we were twenty. He's a man."

Where was he heading with that? "All true, but is he as mature as you were at twenty? You'd been on your own for a couple of years by then. Wes hasn't."

They pulled into the driveway. He shut off the engine, still gripping the steering wheel with both hands, and turned to her. "He'll tell us when he's ready." He held his hand up to stop her protest. "No, don't argue this one, babe. I know you hate not knowing everything, but you have to trust him."

She clamped her mouth shut. There was no use arguing, the subject was closed. He'd only get mad if she pressed. But where was he really on this? Did he have misgivings like she did? If Wes had always kept his own counsel, she wouldn't worry so much. But until now, the kid had been completely open with them and asked their opinions. That was what had her so mystified. She didn't know her own son anymore, and she didn't like it one bitty bit.

"While I unload everything, why don't you bring us some sweet tea?" Joel set an azalea on the lawn then came up beside her as she plucked her tote from the front seat. He glanced up the street then put his arms around her. "I know this is hard for you, honey bunch, but trust me. And trust Wes. We raised him right."

His nearly public display of affection touched her more than his words. Joel was such a private man that to hug her, even in their own front yard, was a stretch. Her heart lightened somewhat.

In the kitchen, she poured sweet tea into two glasses filled with ice and shot up a prayer for God to watch over her son—and help her keep her mouth shut.

They spent the afternoon in "sweet and sweat" as Great-aunt Lola used to call days of working hard with the one you loved. That always tickled Claire, since her late great-aunt never broke a sweat.

Shiloh sunbathed as they planted, occasionally going to sniff in a newly dug hole. When they finished, the yard was beautiful again. She could visualize it in the spring when the azaleas and rhododendrons turned the yard into a sea of pink, magenta, lavender, and white blooms. For now, it was a palette of gold, burgundy, orange, and yellow mums, set off by a white frame of cotton flowers. Claire pulled off her gloves, bent her leg, and whacked them against her heel, knocking off any stray bits of dirt. "Good job, pardner."

Joel, dirt-streaked from chin to cheek, looked over the yard and nodded. He bumped fists with her. "We do good work, babe. After we clean up, how about we run to *Jake's Rib Cage* for supper?"

Claire woke to the sun spilling in the window and not feeling rested at all. Something woke her in the middle of the night, disturbing her sleep. She'd lain awake, listening but never heard anything. That was when she felt the air pressure changing, bringing on a headache. She'd slipped out of bed, taken a decongestant and two Advil, but didn't get back to sleep until close to dawn.

She still had the headache. With one arm over her eyes, she stretched the other across Joel's side of the bed.

He must have gotten up already.

Brilliant deduction, Watson, since his side of the bed was empty. What time was it? The aroma of coffee slipped into the bedroom on cat's feet, enticing her to roll over and put her own on the floor. For the first time in years, it *felt* like a Monday.

Joel walked into the bedroom with a steaming mug of caffeine for her, and Shiloh carried the newspaper. "Ah, you're awake. I wasn't sure whether to bring coffee or call the coroner."

She squinted at him. "Ha ha." She reached for the mug. "I feel like I've been rode hard and put away wet." She took the paper from the dog, pulled a tissue from the box, and wiped dog drool from the wrapper. She laid it beside her on the bed. She'd read it in a bit.

He kissed her forehead. "I'm sorry. Why don't you go back to sleep and I'll tell Patsy you won't be in today?"

"Can't. Nicole still needs training. I'll be okay, it's nothing more Advil," she picked up the bottle from the nightstand and poured out two, "and caffeine won't help."

"Well, if you're okay, I need to run. See you later."

She waved a limp hand at him with her eyes shut, waiting for the pills to take effect. When the pounding subsided, she took her shower and went to the gallery. A phone call from Joel came at eleven—she'd checked her watch. Wes was at the marina. He'd come home last night. That must have been what woke her.

Joel said she couldn't ask Wes about the passport, but that didn't mean she couldn't try to ferret it out of him with subtleties. With her mind on her son, the day passed in a series of minor mishaps. A little boy, who reminded her of Wes at that age, knocked over one of her whimsy vases. He looked up at her with fear-filled eyes. His young mother felt so badly she didn't have the heart to charge her. The day went downhill from there. The new coloration formula she tried failed and the piece had to be destroyed. A teapot cracked in the kiln and everyone knew a broken teapot leaked.

At three-thirty, Patsy shooed her out. "Go home, girlfriend. Nicole and I can handle things here. Tomorrow will be better."

"Thanks. I hope so."

As she walked home, Claire realized she didn't ask Patsy to say a prayer for her. She could have used it, too. Somehow, she had to figure out how to find out why Wes needed a passport.

Claire took a bite of the rainbow trout Wes caught and Joel cooked. Covered with a light lemon butter sauce, it melted in her mouth. The kitchen banquette seemed so large with just the three of them. Well, four if she counted Shiloh. He sat at the end of the table, waiting patiently for his tidbits. She looked forward to the day when grandchildren began to fill up the empty spaces, tossing the big dog bits from their plates. In her mind, she could hear their giggles now.

Joel had surprised her when he called her from the marina and told her Wes was there. Why didn't he let them know he was coming home? And Joel said he hadn't shared anything about his stay at the beach.

"Another roll?" She handed the basket to Joel. His mouth full, he nodded, took one, then passed it to Wes.

"Thanks, Ma."

"So," she glanced at Joel. His eyes said go ahead. "How was your trip?"

"Nithe." Wes swallowed. "Sorry. It was good. The hotel was nice."

"Where'd you stay?" She tried for nonchalance. Did it work? She peeked sidelong at her son. His head was bent over his plate, his face hidden.

"A small mom and pop place. I don't remember the name." When he raised his head, he didn't make eye contact, and she knew without a doubt, he was hiding something.

She glanced at Joel, but he was no help. He ate calmly as if nothing was wrong, having already decided Wes was old enough to keep his own counsel. Mid-stab of a piece of meat, she paused. Maybe Joel thought Wes would tell him in private later when they were at work—a guy thing. She put the bite in her mouth and chewed.

"I'm going to move out as soon as I find an apartment."

Claire gasped and choked on the meat. Wes jumped up and pounded her on the back. Shiloh yelped and ran in circles, barking. Eyes watering and coughing, she tried to get Wes to stop. She wasn't really choking, just nearly. She waved him off and drew a breath, then patted the dog, who stuck his nose in her face to see if she was all right. "I'm fine, boy."

Reaching from his seat, Joel rubbed her back, intent on her breathing. "You should really give us a warning, son."

"Sorry. I wasn't sure how to say it, so I just said it."

"Now that we know your mother is still breathing, why are you moving out and why now?"

Wes laid his knife and fork across his plate and slouched against the back of the banquette. "It's time, that's all. If I'd gone away to college, I wouldn't be living at home anymore." He drained his water glass and stood. "Ma, you want to help me look for an apartment?"

She blinked, still stuck back on move out. "Uh, sure."

He smiled. "Great. Now, I've got Dale coming over for another lesson in HTML."

Chapter 11

Claire stood on the corner of Main Street and Sandy Shores Drive. Too early for the tourists to be out, her view was unobstructed. Up and down the boardwalk, the changes they'd made to the town last week brought it back to life again. They'd exchanged summer geraniums for pansies and poppies for fall mums, matching the colors to the window awnings at the individual shops. The bright colors, fresh paint, and flowers fluttering helloes in the breeze—it felt like a welcome-home hug, if she'd have been gone.

Yes, Chapel Springs was a kaleidoscope. It made her smile how across from the shops, the lake sparkled as if trying to compete. Her smile faded. What made the village like a warm embrace to its residents also brought that overabundance of tourists. She *had* to keep Patsy and Nathan from moving away. But how could they keep the tourist trade without the tourists?

Her mind churning, she strode into *Dee's 'n' Doughs*. Patsy, Lydia and Lacey were already seated and deep in conversation. She waved then poured a cup of dark roast coffee, inhaling its invigorating aroma. After selecting a blueberry bagel, she slipped it into the toaster and doctored her coffee. Her bagel popped up. Hot. She juggled a moment to keep from burning her fingers. When it had cooled slightly, she slathered it with cream cheese, gathered her things, and joined her friends.

"It was nice to see you and Graham in church yesterday, Lydia."

Blushing, Lydia's gaze flitted to her sister then back to Claire. "It's the only alone time we've had lately."

"Alone in a church full of people?"

"Alone without Kenny."

Claire took a bite of her bagel and glanced at Lacey to gauge her reaction, but she lifted her cup and sipped, hiding most of her face in its depths. Then, she set the cup down with a thunk and rose.

"I need to get going. Claire, I have something to ask you. I'll call you later."

Claire stared at her retreating back. "All righty then." She glanced at Lydia. "What was that about?"

"I have no idea what's going on inside that mind of hers anymore." Lydia shook her head. "She doesn't like Kenny one bit. And it took her a while to warm up to Graham. I'm not sure why."

Graham. Claire couldn't imagine why someone would name their kid after a cracker. "It's probably a case of jealousy."

Patsy frowned. "What makes you think that?"

Claire shrugged one shoulder. "Something in the way her expression changed when Lydia blushed. I'm sure she's jealous."

"Could be. We're so far apart in age, almost ten years, and when we were kids, I really resented her." Lydia took a swallow of her coffee. "Daddy left us when Mama got pregnant with Lacey. He just couldn't deal with being so tied down. I worshiped him, so naturally I blamed her. Then ... " Lydia stopped and folded her napkin. After a moment, she said, "I know it was Daddy's immaturity, but by the time I realized that, we were adults, and Lacey and I hadn't spoken for years."

That was so sad. Claire was grateful her kids were close to one another. There was more to this, though. Something Lydia didn't say. "So how did you repair your relationship?"

"A few years after Sam died, I missed having family around. With Morgan in Chapel Springs, I moved here and didn't give Lacey a chance to ignore me any longer. That and a groveling apology finally won her over. We mended that fence and put it behind us."

Patsy reached across Claire and squeezed Lydia's hand. "That's why she's jealous. She's afraid of losing you again."

Thank you, Patsy for a perfect segue. Claire brushed bagel crumbs from her hands. "Speaking of losing, last night Wes told us he wants to move out."

"And?" Patsy asked.

"What do you mean and? He doesn't need to move out. He's got a perfectly good room at home."

"He's the last chick in your nest, Claire. It's time."

No way. She glared at Patsy. "I thought you'd be on my side."

"I am. We both are, aren't we, Lydia? Look Claire, you raised that boy right. Now trust him."

"That's what Joel says."

"And he's right. Besides, an empty nest isn't that bad." Patsy's eyes twinkled with merriment.

"I'm not old enough. I'm—"

Van Gogh's ear. She was fast closing in on forty-eight. When did that happen? Glancing between Lydia and Patsy, she grimaced. "I guess I am." She stuck out her lower lip. She didn't want to be old enough for her nest to be emptied.

Patsy laughed and nudged her with her foot. "I have a suggestion for you, O Elderly One."

"And what would that be, She-Who-is-Two-Months-Older-Than-Me?"

"Don't let him know you're having problems with it. Seriously, help him find his apartment and then help him decorate it. Think of it as another bonding moment."

"How come you're always right? It's unnatural." Glaring, Claire took another bite of bagel to keep from admitting anything else.

Lydia glanced at her watch. "I've got to go. We're slammed today."

"Did you hire a new massage therapist yet?" Patsy asked.

"I did, and we're still booked solid. No complaints, though. By the way, I've had plans drawn up for adding another floor of bedrooms at the spa. That way, I can include weight loss and house those guests who book the three and five-day packages."

"That's a great idea, Lydia." Claire brightened. This was one smart cookie. The Eislers over at *Chapel Lake Inn* could learn a thing or two from her.

Lydia rose and waved. "See you tomorrow."

Claire waggled her fingers at her and wadded up her napkin. "Time for us to head to work, too. I wish Lydia wasn't quite so busy, I'd love to have a spa day again."

"You can always make an appointment, you know."

"That's not as much fun as spontaneity. Which reminds me, I guess I'm leaving early—to help Wes look at apartments."

Claire's son handed her a folded newspaper with a half dozen ads circled. "We're meeting Haley Jones at the ReMax office."

She barely glanced at the ads. "A realtor? To rent an apartment?"

"That's how it's done, Ma."

Where Wes picked up calling her "Ma" she didn't know, but she loved the affectionate way he said it. It meant he was happy with her. "Guess that shows you how long it's been since your daddy and I looked for one."

At the ReMax office, they switched to Haley's SUV. Claire took the back seat where she could observe Haley and Wes as they drove to the first apartment. The realtor looked familiar to Claire, but she couldn't bring a connection to mind. She settled back against the plush, leather seat, determined not to insert her opinion unless Wes asked for it.

Chapel Springs didn't have any apartment buildings, so they headed to Pineridge. Didn't the McMillans' house have a basement apartment in it? Come to think of it, Vince recently turned his basement into a rental apartment.

"Wes, did you ask your Uncle Vince about his basement apartment?"

"Uh, no, but I suppose I could check with him. That's not really what I want, though, and I thought he already rented it."

"Wes needs to be around young people," Haley said.

Well, thank you Billy Sunday. Where does she come off telling her what Wes needs? Haley wasn't old enough to have a grown child. Claire clamped her lips together and folded her arms across her chest.

Wes shook his head. "I don't want a party scene, though."

"You don't? Why not?"

"I just don't."

Score one for Wes. He didn't have to explain himself to any realtor. Her kid had her good sense. Okay, his dad's good sense, but whoever's, she relaxed.

"All right, we'll scratch the first one on the list then and move to number two." A couple of minutes later, Haley turned the SUV into a complex near the center of Pineridge. "This is a two bedroom, two bath like you asked for. It has a balcony big enough for a grill and table. You can walk to stores and restaurants."

Two bedrooms? What did Wes need two for, not to mention two bathrooms? "Are you thinking of getting a roommate?" Oops, Claire broke her own promise of not asking him questions. Rats.

"It's a possibility. What's the rent on this one?"

"Everything I'm going to show you falls between five fifty and nine hundred a month," Haley said.

"I want to stay close to the lower end."

Smart kid. She only hoped he didn't jump at the first one they saw.

By six o'clock, Claire was hungry and her feet hurt, but she lost her worry about Wes choosing the first apartment. They looked at seven. No, eight. Then he told the realtor he'd make a decision and call her. Haley tried to push him into a choice, but before Claire could tell her to back off, Wes quietly told her he'd call her. On the way home, they discussed the pros and cons of each.

"I'm proud of you, son."

"Why's that? You don't have to wipe my nose anymore?"

She swatted his arm. "You're more level headed than I realized." She swallowed a lump that made a sudden appearance in her throat. "You grew up when I wasn't looking."

Wes reached over and put his hand on her shoulder, giving it a light squeeze. "Thanks, Ma. I appreciate you going with me. And thanks for your input. I wouldn't have thought about laundry inside the apartment, but that would make life easier." He grinned. "Probably easier on you, too, since I wouldn't need to bring it home to do."

"There's that." Although, it would at least keep him coming home. "Once you decide which apartment you want, come by the gallery and we'll pick out a couple of pieces to decorate it with. You know Aunt Patsy will want to give you a painting." She waited a beat. "You can meet Nicole, too."

"Thanks. I'd love to have some stuff of yours and a painting."

She waited. Nothing but silence. They were almost home. "I want you to meet my new assistant, too."

"I heard you, but I'm not interested, Ma."

Feigning innocence, she made her voice light. "Not interested in meeting an employee of mine?"

"I know you, Ma. You could have been a Yenta."

Claire frowned. Brussels sprouts ... she'd been found out. This called for a new battle plan.

By Friday, Claire breezed into *The Painted Loon* with a plan in the making. She should have realized Wes was just like all men. They needed a push when it came to love. In the workroom, she dropped her tote on the desk portion of the counter that ran around three walls of the room, and put her sandwich—she had a couple more pounds to lose, so Dee's was out for a week or two—in the mini-fridge.

"Nicole?"

"Over here, Claire." Nicole's voice floated from behind the open kiln. "Ohh."

Uh-oh.

"That doesn't sound good. What's wrong?"

"My vase cracked." She heaved a rather dramatic sigh.

"It's going to happen sometimes, sweetie. You can't always tell if they're completely dry. Especially up here. There's a crazy mix of dry mountain air and humidity off the lake. Your last three have been great."

"I know, but this one was special."

Oh? Here was the opening she'd hoped for. "As in for a special person?"

Nicole carried the ruined piece to the trash can marked "Recycle" where they kept broken pottery to be donated to the college for art students to use for mosaics. "Sort of."

Claire waited, but the girl didn't elaborate. This wasn't going well. It wasn't going at all. "Nicole, do you have a boyfriend?"

Nicole stared at her like she'd sprouted antennae and grew one eye in the middle of her forehead. After a second, she dropped the bisque in the can. "No boyfriend."

Sorrow colored her words gray. What could have happened? Claire immediately regretted her words. Blasted tongue got her in more hot water. "Feel like talking about that?"

With a shrug, Nicole turned to clean the area where she'd been working. "Not much to tell, really. Last year I fell in love with a guy, but it hasn't gone anywhere."

Anger welled at a boy she didn't even know. "Why not?"

A small smile tugged at one corner of Nicole's lips. "He ... I'm merely his sister's shadow. A nonentity."

Okay, how could she do this without looking pushy? Did Melissa ever try to intro—whoa. Could it be— "Did 'Lissa ever tell you about her brother Wes?" She glued her eyes to Nicole's, watching for any sign of recognition. The girl glanced at her then quickly away, her mouth working like a goldfish looking for air. Was that a good sign or a bad one? Should she say more or leave it there for now?

She put her hand on Nicole's shoulder and gently turned her around. Cupping her other hand under the girl's chin, she peered into the sweet face. "Is this boy you fell for Wes?"

Two large tears slipped down her face as she nodded. Claire pulled her into a hug. Why in the world didn't Wes see the gem under his nose?

Did she even mention Nicole's name to him?

"I'm so sorry." She rubbed Nicole's back for a moment. As soon as she drew back, Claire released her. "Is that why you wanted to work here?"

"No! I really want to work for you, Claire. Please, I don't want to leave."

"No need for panic. I'm not letting you go, sugar. Why, you're a treasure to me." A wild strand of hair from Nicole's bangs stuck straight up in the air. Claire tamed it. "You know, some boys need an extra push. They don't see the fine work of art right in front of them."

Nicole tilted her head, a slight frown creasing her brows. "You'd do that for me? Why?"

Was her motive wrong? Rescuing Wes from whatever held him prisoner was paramount. Van Gogh's ear. What a revoltin' development this was. Her—Claire Bennett, the queen-of-come-back—didn't have a clue what to say.

The gallery's front door bells jangled. Nicole tossed her cleaning rag into the laundry bin. "I'll get that." She trotted into the display room.

"Nice going." Patsy's disembodied voice rose from behind the largest easel.

Claire screeched. "Don't do that. You scared the fire out of me. And what do you mean 'nice going?'"

Patsy poked out her head from behind her painting. She wore an indulgent smirk and a streak of Benzimida Orange in her bangs. "You—Yenta Claire."

"Hmph. You been talking to Wes?"

"No, why?"

"He called me that, too." Claire pulled out her stack of commissions to see what she needed to work on. "I just know that if he found a girl who captured his interest, he'd quit whatever it is he's doing."

"I thought he was talking again."

After selecting a commissioned platter, she set the other orders back in their tray. She hadn't made a large platter lately and inspiration swelled. "He's talking but still hides behind his computer most of the time. I can't for the life of me figure out what he finds to keep him tethered to it so much. A hundred scenarios have gone through my mind, and none of them are good."

"And you think matching him up with Nicole is the answer?"

"I did, but now I don't know what to do. Apparently 'Lissa introduced

Wes to Nicole, but it didn't take."

"So I heard."

"Maybe all he needs is a little push. After all, love turns many a man's thoughts away from ... whatever he's doing." A memory of Joel rose from the past. She chuckled. "Do you remember when we went to Joel's baseball game our senior year?"

She'd been dating him for a couple of months and was head over heels about him. He wasn't immune to her, either. It was his turn at bat. He loped out of the dugout, checking the stands for her. She waved, he swaggered to the plate, and took his stance. The pitcher fired the ball but missed the mark. Joel tapped the bat on the plate, took his stance again, and glanced up to Claire instead of the pitcher.

Patsy's laughter brought her back to the present. "I remember all right. That pitch broke Joel's nose. You two are a perfectly matched pair. One or the other of you is always—"

"Yeah, yeah. But it illustrates my point. Love sidetracks a man. If Wes gets interested it'll take precedence over his computer obsession. We just need to help him realize Nicole's a lovely girl."

"But, Claire, what if whatever he's doing is something good?"

Chapter 12

The phone lines at Chapel Lake Spa blinked like a Christmas display set to rock music nearly giving Lydia a nervous tick. Sucking in a deep breath, she recorded a facial client in the computer's appointment program, hung up that line, and picked up the next.

"Thank you for holding. How may I help you?" With her free hand, she pushed the hair obscuring her vision behind her ear. She needed a haircut, but the phone wouldn't quit, and no one else was available to answer.

"Yes, ma'am, I can schedule you for a full day package on Thursday. Will that work? Wonderful. I have two of you down for nine o'clock. Thank you."

Averill Kennedy, who worked at the post office, walked in with a woman Lydia didn't recognize but gauged to be in her late fifties, with dyed black hair. Fat sausage curls piled atop her head and rhinestone studded, black cat-eye glasses made her look like she belonged on the set of Saturday Night Live.

Averill took her friend's elbow and brought her to the desk. "Lydia, this is my old college roommate, Sharlene Davis. We'd like massages, manicures, and pedicures. Can you fit us in? Together?"

Lydia checked the appointments, moved one client to another technician so the two friends could be next to each other. "If you're willing to wait a few minutes, we can accommodate you both."

She recorded their desired treatments, printed out the receipts, and called the technicians. "It will be a few minutes, ladies. If you'll have a seat, I'll get you some tea while you wait." The phone rang. "Excuse me."

While she helped the caller, Averill kept fluttering her hand at Lydia while Sharlene tapped her foot. As soon as Lydia hung up, she crossed the room to get the ladies their tea. The phone's insistent chiming began as soon as she put the teabags in the water. Sharlene pinched up her mouth and narrowed her eyes, as Lydia, restraining from rolling hers, turned back to the desk.

While she helped the client, a regular, Averill got up and frowning, stomped across the room, where she retrieved her and Sharlene's teacups. The clink of spoons against the saucers hit Lydia's last nerve. She could just imagine the tale Averill would spread about poor service. What if Olympia gave them the extended massage, gratis? She grabbed another call.

A few minutes later, the lines were finally all dark. Maybe if she didn't breathe or move, she could get a minute respite.

Over their chatter, the metal tap on the toe of Sharlene's high heels beat a rhythm into Lydia's head. Nathan was due in the afternoon and she didn't have the bills ready for him to pay. She had to hire another massage therapist—not that she was ungrateful for the increased business, but she couldn't seem to catch up, no matter how many hours she worked. The toe-tapping started a headache at the back of her skull. *Hurry, Olympia.*

The phone lines lit up again. All of them. So did her nerves. She punched the first one. "Chapel La—oh hey, love." She glanced up and caught Averill, a busybody if there ever was one, leaning closer to the desk.

Lydia turned away as Graham's "hey, baby" sent a delightful shiver up her weary spine. "Oh, honey," she lowered her voice. "I'd love to go out with you, but I'm not going to be able to get away." Averill stared intently at her. Lydia turned her head. "One of the girls called in sick. Why don't you come here and we can at least hole up in my office?"

"Does the door have a lock?"

She blushed and glanced at the ladies. Averill leaned toward Sharlene and whispered something as she stared wide-eyed at Lydia. She just hoped they didn't overhear anything.

She ducked her head. "You're wicked, and I love you for it. That sounds delicious. See you soon."

Oh, dear. Averill's expression resembled a prune. Even her eyes scrunched, and she glowered at Lydia. What was her problem? Sharlene waved her cup for more tea. Good grief. This wasn't a teashop. Praying

Olympia would hurry up and take them into the back, she pasted a smile on her face and refilled their cups.

The phone rang just as Graham arrived bearing a takeout bag from The Krill Grill. Lydia waved and pointed to the receiver. He gave her a circumspect kiss on her cheek, to the delight—or disgust, Lydia wasn't sure—of the women, then headed upstairs to her office. He paused and crooked his finger, wiggling it in a come on motion, then he winked at Averill, who gasped and whispered to Sharlene.

One would think Averill had never—oh wait, she hadn't. She was a spinster. No wonder she had her knickers in a knot. Her face looked like she sucked a lemon. Finally, Olympia came for Averill and her old pal and got them settled into their respective service rooms.

Lydia pulled out the sign she made two days ago that read, "Please take a seat and someone will be with you shortly." She stood it prominently on the top of the reception desk, then headed for the stairs and her waiting husband.

The phone's ring collared her as effectively as a leash. She put her head in her hands. *Calgon, take me away!*

Dutifully, she returned to the front desk and answered it. Before she could hang up that line, another lit up, and then another. Then the door opened and a group of three women entered, chattering so loudly, Lydia had to put a call on hold. She got the ladies settled in the waiting area and returned to the phone.

Loud footsteps descended the stairs, swiveling the heads of the ladies in the waiting area. All chatter stopped as a red-faced Graham approached her, his lips set into a thin white line. Before she could react, he thrust a creased and wrinkled bag at her. With the receiver in one hand and her mouth hung open, she bobbled the bag to keep it from falling.

"Your now-cold food is in there. I ate. You're obviously too busy for me. I'll see you at home tonight—if you can get away."

"C-can you hold a moment, please? Thank you." Resting the handset on her shoulder, she locked eyes with Graham. "Honey, I'm sorry. I—"

He held up his hand, his voice low behind clenched teeth. "I understand, Lydia. I work, too. But I hire enough people to handle the business."

"I'm trying, Graham, but it—"

"Just do what you have to. I'll see you tonight." He walked out.

Her clients hid their faces behind magazines.

Seething, Lydia wadded the crumpled bag and only with extreme discipline, avoided slamming it into the wastebasket. A temper tantrum wouldn't help. She took a deep breath, in and out. Then another. By the fourth, she'd calmed enough to go back to the waiting customer.

"I'm sorry to keep you waiting. Now, how ... hello?" The line was dead. Great. Lydia balled her fists and forced back threatening tears. While they might give her an emotional release, they wouldn't solve anything.

She needed help, but her husband needed an attitude adjustment. How could he be so patient about Kenny quitting his job because his leg or hip or whatever hurt but not understand the spa being busy? Theoretically, Kenny left Joel in the lurch much the same as she had been left with an employee calling in sick. But it was okay in Kenny's case?

Mad settled all over her like bark on a tree. But mad never added one leaf to that tree. She'd better call a temp agency and get a receptionist until she could hire a permanent one. Her foot beat a pattern against the floor as she dialed, but before the number rang, the front door opened. Kenny walked in. She hung up.

Goodness gracious, what was he doing here?

"Hey, Lydia. Dad called and told me you were really in a bind. I'll be glad to help out if you'll let me."

Fabulous. Graham complained to his son. "I appreciate that, Kenny, but you don't know anything about the spa."

"That's easy to rectify in a hurry. I can answer phones and make appointments as well as the next person. Just hand me a list of who does what."

She studied him a moment. He had his dad's eyes and strong chin, but more important, Kenny had Graham's sharp mind. Phones weren't that hard, after all, and the appointment program listed the technician with the service and the hours they were available. "You're right. Pull up a chair and I'll run you through it. And thank you."

Within forty-five minutes, he was handling the phones by himself with Lydia merely watching. She laid her hand on his shoulder when he hung up from a call. "You're a quick study. Did I say thank you, dear? I can't tell you what a help this is."

He tossed her a grin and answered the next line. She went to her office for a few minutes peace and quiet. Her stomach growled, reminding her she hadn't eaten. She pulled an apple from the mini fridge and munched as she gathered her thoughts before she called Graham.

She appreciated him asking Kenny. No, she didn't—not if she were being honest with herself. It was Kenny's help that she appreciated, but she did *not* care for Graham's interference in her business.

Tossing the apple core in the wastebasket, she picked up a pencil and threaded it between her fingers. Graham wasn't her banker. He was her husband, even if he was a slightly neglected one. But come on, it was only two days and both those days she went home and cooked dinner. When she was on her own and worked late, she stopped by one of the town's restaurants. No, Graham's impatience didn't set well with her. Not one itty-bitty bit. The pencil snapped in two. She tossed the pieces in with the apple core.

One of the traits her late husband had was impatience, and it killed her love before the heart attack killed him. When she first met Graham, she noticed that long lines didn't bother him. Neither did slow drivers, and when she took her time in answering a question, he waited for her to think without hurrying her. So why now? What made the change?

Her intercom light blinked. She mashed the button. "Yes?"

"Dad's on line one."

She hoped her mad dissolved enough to talk to him. "Thanks, Kenny." She pressed the waiting line. "Hey."

"Hey, baby. Can you forgive an idiot in love? I honestly don't know what came over me."

Whatever mad had been leftover dissolved like a snow cone in July. "I can and I do." Love butterflies fluttered in her tummy. She hoped that never ended. "I wondered what had happened to the man I married."

"He momentarily turned into a grumpy old caveman. The minute I got outside I knew I'd been wrong. I—"

A knock sounded, followed by a muffled "Hello?"

"Wait a minute, honey. There's someone at my office door. Yes?" The door opened and a huge bouquet of red roses and white calla lilies entered the room, followed by a delivery boy. Her hand flew to cover her gaping mouth. "Oh, my. Graham? Are these ..."

"Yeah. I needed to tell you I was sorry, but I couldn't wait for them to arrive. I had to call. I didn't want you upset."

"Hold on a sec." She took the flowers and thanked the kid. Was she supposed to tip him? She grabbed her wallet out of her purse.

"No, thank you ma'am. The gentleman took care of that."

Of course he did. She picked up the receiver. "Thank you, my love.

They're beautiful."

"I promise I won't go Neanderthal again."

She laughed. "You better not, or I'll find me a club to hit you over the head."

"You being a successful businesswoman was one of the things that drew me to you. I don't want you to change, Lydia."

"Thank you, sweetheart. I love you, too."

"Is Kenny helping?"

"Better than I expected. He picked up the appointment system quicker than I thought he could. I plan to call an agency this afternoon to get a temp. Then when she arrives, we can release Kenny to find a better job for himself. Now, I'd better get to it. I'll see you tonight."

"I'll take you out to dinner."

"That will be very nice and appreciated, love. Bye."

She punched another line, the only one not lit. The phone's lights blinked as one was put on hold and another answered. Kenny seemed to have developed a system that didn't keep anyone on hold for too long. Too bad the job didn't have enough challenge for him. But she could ask him to help train the temporary receptionist.

The temp agency had a girl she'd used before. Arrangements made, Lydia went back down to the main spa floor. Kenny wasn't at the desk but had the feather duster and was attacking the display shelves. He stopped when he saw her.

"You know about Bluetooth, Lydia? Your phone system supports it. A headset would free up your receptionist to dust among other things and still answer the phones."

Why hadn't she thought of that? "Good idea. Do I have to change anything?" She crossed to the desk to look at the phone system. "Where's the connector?"

"No. It's built into the system. No additional equipment required. See that little symbol?" He pointed to the back of the desk unit. "I'm surprised the salesman didn't tell you about that."

"He may have, but I was kind of in over my head at first. Local people started showing up for services before I actually opened." She chuckled, remembering Claire and Patsy's first visit. She only had one massage therapist on site, Olympia, and she wasn't expecting to work that day. But work she had, and she'd given Claire a mud wrap after her massage. None of them realized Claire was allergic to the natural minerals in the mud. Poor thing. Fortunately, the hives went down within a couple of days.

Kenny squatted to search the cabinets below the desk and came up, triumphantly holding a box. "Here it is. Problem solved." He showed her the earpiece, attached a little box and another couple of cords, then programmed something into the desk unit. "This will help a lot. The receptionist can now move around the room at least—get a client tea or whatever and still answer the phone. She'll have to move back to the desk unit to transfer or put the call on hold, but it's still better than the cord chaining her to the desk."

Lydia put her hand on Kenny's shoulder. "You, my dear stepson, are a life-saver."

"Thanks." He glanced at his watch. "If you don't need me for a while, I have a couple of places I want to check out for jobs."

"You go on, dear. You've done a fantastic job here today. I'll be glad to give you a reference."

A party of three entered the door when Kenny left. As she checked them in, Lydia thought about her stepson. Funny that Joel had thought he was too helpful. How could someone be overly helpful? Joel had to be wrong. Kenny merely wanted to please, and she appreciated that.

Chapter 13

*D*ee's 'n' Doughs was filled to capacity when Claire walked in. Local business owners getting their morning coffee and checking their ads in the *Weekly Voice*, chatted with friends before starting the day. It was this way most every weekday morning. This was their time and they cherished it. These were her friends. They shared concerns and triumphs. It's what made Chapel Springs ... *Chapel Springs*.

She grabbed a cup of coffee and stopped to say "hey" to Gloria and Faye. Theirs was an odd friendship. They owned competing B&Bs and given that Gloria's husband, Warren, was Felix's right hip, one would think Faye, who wasn't a big fan of their mayor, would stay away from Gloria. But they'd been friends since the fourth grade when Faye's parents first moved to their little village.

"Are you both still booked up?" Claire asked.

"All the way through New Year's." Faye's wide smile lit the room as much as her bright red hair. "Gloria, too." Faye usually did the talking for Gloria, who—since trained by years of marriage to Warren—didn't say much.

"Glad to hear it." Claire had another question for Faye. What was it? Oh—

She snapped her fingers. "You're on the traffic control committee, right? Have you considered Joel's idea?"

"We love it. It's brilliant. We're negotiating right now with Happy for a price on the land. Whether we buy it or lease from him, it's going to cost a bundle. Lakefront property doesn't come cheap, but commercial lakefront is premium." She frowned. "That's the sticky point with Felix. He wants to charge people to park. In a way, he's right. It would help pay for the land."

Claire chewed that for a moment. "It's all in how we present it. They don't have to pay for gas to get around—a good savings with the price of gas now, plus less wear on their vehicles and looking for a parking spot. And they're getting door-to-door transportation. Maybe we could include the tram service in the parking fee."

Faye laughed. "You sound like a commercial, but I think you're right. It's a great idea, putting tram service in the parking fee. You gave me a different perspective on it. Thanks, Claire. Oh, and here's the book you wanted to borrow." She reached under the table and brought up a paperback.

"Thanks." Claire rubbed her fingers over the worn spine. "I'll get it back to you when I'm done."

"Just pass it on when you're finished. I bought a new copy for guests."

Waggling three fingers on the hand clutching her coffee cup, Claire edged her way toward the table where Patsy sat. "Morning." She set her tote and the book on the table.

Patsy reached for the book. "What are you reading?" She flipped to the back to read the blurb about the story. "'A woman without a past comes face-to-face with a family she didn't know she had.' Sounds interesting. Can I read it after you're finished?"

"Sure." She took a sip of her coffee, then told Patsy about her conversation with Faye and Gloria about the parking. "What do you think would be a reasonable amount?"

"Per day or week?"

"Good question. I guess we could have both a day rate and a weekly discounted one." Claire pulled a pad and pen from her Sak tote, scribbled the suggestion to tell Joel, and slipped it back into her bag. "What's bothering you, girlfriend? That wrinkle between your brows will become permanent if we don't solve whatever's eating at you."

Only one corner of Patsy's lips rose, rendering the half smile sorrowful. "Nathan is going to New York City next week to check out job possibilities." She turned her coffee mug around and around. "Claire, what am I going to do?"

Claire's heart missed a beat. She put her hand over Patsy's to stop her frenetic turning. "I'd hoped the last town meeting would have given him a glimpse of a potential solution in the works."

What would Claire do without Pat-a-cake here? Her sweet friend, who always looked out for her? *What about Patsy?* A twinge of guilt flicked Claire's ear like Great-aunt Lola used to do when she wasn't paying attention. How would Patsy get along without *her* best friend?

Claire squared her shoulders. "I promise, I'll find a solution that will keep Nathan here. I can't let you go off to that bastion of Yankeeism. You'd wither and die up there."

Patsy squeezed back then picked up her cup. "I hope so. I couldn't *not* go with Nathan, but at the same time, how could I leave my home?"

"I can't even imagine—"

"Claire Bennett, have I got hot news for you!" Dale's raspy voice rose above the din in the bakery.

If she knew Dale, and she did, his volume was calculated to draw attention to whatever gossip he had simmering. She measured the distance to the bakery's back room and how far Dale was to her table. Rats. She'd never make it. Next to her, Patsy sat up straight, ready to do battle in her defense. Claire nearly laughed, but it died in her throat when Dale stopped in the middle of the room. With his hands on his hips and a gleeful smile on his weasel-face, he locked eyes with her, his voice echoing off the walls.

"Guess whose son just got married—*secretly* married—in a South American country?"

After Patsy's attempts at the Heimlich maneuver to clear her airway, Claire stormed into the marina. She found Joel in the boat storage, finishing a lift. "Where's your son?"

Joel blinked. "My son. You mean Wes? He's in the office. What's wrong, Claire?"

"Get him out here," she said between clenched teeth.

"Honey," he tied off the rope on a cleat. "Tell me what this is about, first, so I'm not blindsided."

Every muscle in her body was tense, including her jaw, but she managed to spit it out. "Our son is married." She flung up her hands. "Married! Apparently, he lied about Virginia Beach and went to Brazil and married some ... some ... *Brazilian*." She wanted to burst into tears, but the heat of her anger dried them to dust.

With his mouth gaping wide open, Joel looked gobsmacked. Exactly how she felt. She began to pace. "What could he have been thinking? He can't know this girl. She's probably a gold digger, looking for citizenship." She stopped. "Or a drug-runner looking for easier access to the U.S. Oh, Joel, what could he have been thinking?"

Joel followed her. "You said that already."

"I know I said it. I want an answer to it."

"Sweetheart, don't bite my head off. Let me get Wes down here. How do we know Dale isn't making this up?"

Claire stopped so fast, Joel plowed into her backside. He grabbed her shoulders to steady her. She turned back to him, searching his eyes. "Do you think Dale's lying, really? But why would he make something like this up?"

"Who knows with Dale? But I think we owe Wes the chance to explain, don't you?"

Taking a deep breath to help lower her rapidly rising blood pressure, she nodded. She wanted an explanation all right. "Get him."

Joel grabbed his cell phone and activated the direct connect. "Wes, come out to storage, please."

The phone double beeped. "Sure, Dad. Be right there." A chair scraped on the cement floor. "What's up?"

Joel waited for the beeps then pressed a button again on his cell. She and Patsy needed one of those. It'd save time punching in each other's number. "I'll tell you when you get here."

Claire couldn't stand still, waiting. She paced while Joel fiddled with ropes and straightened things, waiting for Wes. That boy had better have a good explanation. Like telling her Dale was full of hot air. She wanted him to pull out a receipt from Virginia Beach. He'd better if he knew—

The door opened with a metal-on-metal screech and Wes stood in the opening. Backlit by the sunlight, her last born—her baby—appeared to have a halo around him. An aura of innocence. She prayed it wasn't misleading.

"Come on in, son." Joel waved him over. There was nowhere to sit in the boat storage building. It felt awkward and confrontational, but that was okay by her, she wanted a confrontation. How much of one depended on his reaction. She glanced at Joel. When he nodded, she let loose both barrels.

"I was in *Dee's 'n' Doughs* this morning with my friends, when Dale announced to the town that you're married."

Wes flinched.

It was true? Her heart broke into hundreds of little pieces. Each shard pierced a memory of her little boy confiding a secret with her, showing her a treasure he unearthed in the garden, the two of them building—okay, blowing up a science project together. What happened to that boy who trusted her? Who shared important decisions with them?

Tears rained down her cheeks and she folded against a sailboat waiting to be lifted to its storage bed. Slowly, she slid down to the floor.

Joel squatted next to her. "Are you okay?"

She'd never be okay. Not now. Wes dropped to his knees in front of her.

"Ma, I'm sorry. I ... I don't know what to say. I didn't want to tell you until Costy was here and you got to meet her."

Costy? Claire groaned. She didn't want to meet her. What kind of name was that anyway? Cost*ly* was probably more like it. Maybe it was an alias. What could Wes know about her anyway? She didn't want some unknown foreigner in her family.

"Does this girl even speak English?"

"Uh-uh, not yet."

Her son married someone he couldn't even talk to? Claire buried her face in her hands. Why couldn't he have listened to her? Chapel Springs had lots of nice *North* American girls for him to choose from.

Joel glared at him. "Hold on. You didn't want to tell us until she was here, but you felt you had to marry her first? Son, what was going through your head? I think we deserve an explanation. Where did you meet her? Who is she? And whatever—"

"I met her online."

Claire wiped her wet face with a used tissue she dug from her pocket. "What do you mean 'online'?"

"In a chat room for singles. On the Internet." He sat back on his heels. Her beautiful man-child, with his sun-bleached hair and golden tan. "It's like a singles bar without the drinking."

She snorted. "And without living flesh. How can you meet someone without seeing them?"

"I saw a picture of her. You can look at the profiles of the people who interest you."

"This was a dating site?"

"No, Dad. Not in the strictest sense of the word. I didn't pay anything."

Too bad. Maybe he could have gotten his money back. Didn't those places have some guarantees? "Well what kind of site is it?" Besides one that conned young men into marrying foreign women looking for U.S.

citizenship.

Wes seemed to search for the right words. "It's a chat room, Ma."

"You said that. How, no, *why* did you go there?" That's what she really needed to know. Why.

"I hadn't met—well, that's not really why. First I went there because one of the guys at the college told me about it."

She knew it. "Who was it? And how do you know you could trust him? Oh, Wes, why some girl from South America? Were drugs involved?"

She clapped her jaws shut. She hadn't meant to say that out loud. Wes's eyes opened so wide, his eyebrows nearly disappeared in a forehead fold.

"No way! Good grief, is that what you thought?"

She lifted one shoulder. "What *was* I to think? Your personality changed, you never talked to us anymore, and you hid out in your room all the time. And your grades slipped."

Wes flopped onto his backside, resting his arms on his bent knees. "Wow, I didn't realize. I'm sorry, Ma. Dad."

Joel soft punched Wes's shoulder. "Go on. Tell us about this girl and what happened."

Claire leaned her head against Joel's shoulder. "Yeah, and I want to know why you lied about Virginia Beach. You've never lied to us before."

"I never said I was going there, Mom. I had planned on bringing Costy up here first, but I couldn't get her into the country without us being married. I knew if I told you beforehand, you'd pitch a hissyie fit about me going to Brazil. So I left that part out."

"It was still a lie, Wes, by omission," Joel said.

Her baby hung his head. "I'm sorry. I really am." He looked like he did when he was four and had broken one of her vases. He hung his head then, too.

After a moment, he raised it again, and his eyes glowed and snapped. "But wait till you meet her. She's beautiful and wonderful."

Another shard pierced her heart. It wasn't like she was trying to keep him her baby. She wanted him to meet a wonderful girl—like Nicole— and get married. Like his brother. Some day. When he grew up. She didn't feel like this when their Charlie announced his engagement to Sandi. She was thrilled. They were thrilled for him. Did this girl—"Did this Costy make you keep it a secret?"

"Costy, Ma. It's short for Costancia. And no, she didn't."

Joel laid his hand on Claire's hand, his thumb caressing. "Let's hear the whole story."

Wes clasped his hands around his bent knees. "She and I both love to hike. That's what the chat room was for, singles who hike. We shared the best trails and hikes from all over the world. Costy and I began to communicate outside the chat room."

She had to ask. "Why?"

Something about Wes's slow smile turned her son into a man. Who was this?

"We had so much in common. She likes all the same things I do."

Claire just bet she did. The man-eater. "Did she have access to your profile thing?"

"Yeah. We all did."

"Did you ever think she could have looked at that and faked it all?"

"No, Ma. You have to give permission to a person to access your profile. We'd already been communicating for a few weeks before I gave her permission."

"Oh."

"Look, we got to know each other over the past year. We shared our hearts. She comes from a good family. She's a believer. Wait, let me finish. I know what you're going to say. She could have faked it all. Well, she didn't. I went down there to be sure. I'm not stupid, you know."

"Son," Joel interrupted. "We know you're not stupid. But you're young and feelings can cloud your judgment."

"I'm the same age as you were when you married, Mom."

Joel grimaced. "I can't argue that."

Claire could and wanted to. Joel had been out on his own for a couple of years before they got married.

He nudged her. "I guess parents tend to see their children as less mature than they were at the same age. Go on. Where did you stay?"

Whose side was he on?

"I stayed at a small hotel—a bed and breakfast kind of home. It turned out her uncle owns it. I met her family. Her dad's a representative in the local government there. She's wonderful. And she loves me and I love her. We got her parents' blessing and got married while I was there."

Another shard. What about her and Joel's blessing? Her heart completely shredded, Claire bit her lip until she tasted blood.

"Okay, so it's done." Joel ran a hand through his hair, tousling it. "Now what?"

"Can it be annulled?"

Wes jumped up. "No, Mom. I won't do that. I love her. There's no way I'll do that. We were married by a priest. That's the same as Pastor Seth marrying us. I'm married. And I'm staying married. Costy will be here in a few weeks. You'll just have to adjust to it."

Joel stood and put his hands on Wes's shoulders. "Calm down, son. Give your mother a chance. This has been hard on her. On both of us. You didn't trust us to talk it over with us. You asked her parents for their blessing but left us out. That hurts, Wes."

With his shoulders slumped, Wes looked at his dad. "For that, I'm truly sorry. Please believe me. I love you, Dad. You and Ma. I'm sorry for hurting you."

But not sorry for what he did. Claire stared up at her husband and son. Wes seemed so young to her, but she and Joel fell in love when they were sixteen. They waited until she finished two years of college before they got married, though. They were twenty and felt so mature back then. Was that how Wes felt? What was she going to do when this girl arrived here?

"How old is your—is she?"

"My *wife* is twenty-six."

Seven years older? Claire winced. He thought he was really in love, but she couldn't help feeling suspicious. Why did this woman go after a kid? And why did it have to be her kid?

Chapter 14

Claire hunched on the edge of the bed, her head in her hands. Her eyes burned, the rims swollen and tender. For two nights, she'd hardly slept, and what little she got was broken by nightmares of drug-runners chasing Wes. She dragged herself to the shower, letting hot water sluice over her, hoping for rejuvenation. With one hand, she rubbed the back of her neck and rotated it to work out the stiffness. Her aching muscles could use one of Olympia's massages. Like that would happen. The spa was overbooked with *tourists*. Like an unwanted credit card application, her world was being reduced to bits in the shredder of life.

Feeling only slightly better after her shower, Claire pulled on a new pair of jeans. Sucking in her stomach at the anticipated squeeze the zipper would apply to her abdomen, she slid up the tongue. With ease. When she let her breath out, there was still a one-inch gap between her and the waistband. She stared at Shiloh, who lay at her feet.

"Who knew the secret to losing weight was a town conundrum compounded by a family fracas?" The mastiff raised his head and cocked it. "I don't recommend it, so don't go telling your friends."

With Patsy gone to New York looking at apartments, and Lydia now married to Graham—Claire couldn't help it, every time she said his name she thought of crackers—she went straight to the gallery, skipping *Dee's 'n' Doughs*. She had no appetite, anyway. Besides, after Dale's public announcement, she wasn't up to answering questions. She groaned. How could Wes humiliate her like this?

When she opened the gallery's door, a fine layer of dust stole the shine from her pottery. No lights illuminated Patsy's paintings. What happened to Nicole? She never allowed a speck of dust to mar the artwork.

Claire hurried to the workroom, dropped her Sak, and grabbed a feather duster, slipping into a smock to cover her clothes. Back in the gallery, she attacked the dust with vigor. If only she could flick away her problems as easily.

The lock clicked and Nicole came in. She looked like Claire had this morning, her eyes red and swollen. When they fixed on the feathers in Claire's hand, they welled with tears. "I couldn't ... I didn't ... I'm sorry."

Claire dropped the duster and pulled the weeping girl into her arms. "What's wrong, sweetie?"

"I heard about Wes get ... get ... getting .. ma ... married." A fresh sob shook her shoulders.

It broke Claire's heart. Here was a girl she'd have loved to embrace as a daughter-in-law. Nicole felt like family. She was close friends with the twins and most of all she loved Wes. Plus, she was already a U.S. citizen.

Nicole pulled away and used her sleeve to blot her face. "It's not like he betrayed me. We never really dated, but when he came to see Megan and Melissa, I was always included on their outings. I couldn't help falling in love, even though he treated me like another sister. But in the past few weeks, he's been friendlier. I started—" a hiccup cut her short. "I started to hope again." Fresh tears spilled down her cheeks.

Claire grabbed a box of tissues from behind the register and thrust it at Nicole. They were both so low they could sit on the curb and still dangle their feet. But that wasn't going to change a thing. "I need to think." She handed over the duster. "If you'll finish up, I'm going to find a way out of this."

Nicole stood in a pool of light from the window, a waif with the feather duster in one hand and a dented box of tissues in the other. What was not to love? She was adorable. Wes had his head screwed on wrong. Stupid kid.

Claire barreled into the workroom and turned on the computer. Determined to get the lowdown on this woman who'd snared her son, she logged on and brought up Google. She typed in Costancia and stopped. Wes didn't tell them her last name. How many Costancias could there be in the world? She hit enter to see. Pages and pages. And some spelled Constancia—with an "n." Could Wes have gotten the spelling wrong? No, he called her Costy, not Consty.

Claire clicked on page two and found a town in Mexico and a street in *New* Mexico. By page ten, she'd discovered most were in Spanish. By page twenty-three, she was cross-eyed and closed the search engine. Without a last name or a translator, she could be here until next week.

Like a lost soul, Nicole wandered into the workroom. Claire felt as bad as she did, if not worse, but they couldn't wallow in a pit of misery. That wouldn't get them anywhere.

Shoving from the chair, she crossed the workroom to slip two fingers under Nicole's chin. "Girl, where's your faith? I don't know what's going to happen, but I do believe God has an answer." Claire just hoped it was the one she wanted.

Squaring her shoulders, Nicole pulled her lips into a semblance of a smile, warming Claire's heart. "You're right. I've got to put it behind me and move on."

Wait—not move on completely, or worse, leave. "Uh, what do you mean exactly?"

"I've got my art. I'll pour my heart into the clay. Create beautiful works through my sorrow."

Claire scratched her nose to hide her smile at Nicole's dramatic flair. Actually, the idea wasn't a bad one. Maybe she should give it a try. What would anger look like in pottery? "You might have something there." She checked the wall clock. "We still have an hour before the gallery opens. Let's create."

Claire closed *The Painted Loon* an hour early and went home. All the kids, with the exception of Adrianna, were coming for dinner. She missed her eldest daughter and wished Nashville weren't such a long drive. That was the only disadvantage of living in Chapel Springs. There weren't any interstates close. At least the twins didn't have any classes tomorrow and would be here soon.

They arrived home shortly after Claire. Charlie and Sandi would get there about five-thirty. Wes was in his room, most likely on Skype again. If she ever needed Patsy, it was now. Claire prayed they didn't find an apartment. *Please?* Maybe that wasn't nice, but she needed her best friend more than New York did.

Megan's chatter filled the kitchen while she and Melissa made dinner. Claire assisted by sitting at the banquette, watching from where they'd placed her. Shiloh lay at her feet, watching "his" girls. Their giggles and practiced kitchen duet almost made Claire wish she could cook. It wasn't like she'd never tried, but God hadn't given her any cooking genes.

Okay, maybe one.

She made a mean Jell-O mold. Once again, she had to thank the Lord for Joel's love of cooking. She didn't want to take that from him, after all.

Soon, the kitchen smelled of garlic and spaghetti sauce. Good old American food.

"Hello? Anybody home?" Her firstborn's voice carried from the front door to the kitchen. It always made her heart catch.

"Charlie's here," Megan shouted and in a race with Shiloh, charged the front door, followed by Melissa. "And Sandi!"

Claire waited for them in the kitchen, letting the twins hog the hugs. You'd think they hadn't seen their brother and sister-in-law for a year, instead of a few weeks. She thought back to their wedding, just a few months ago. She and Joel had been involved in all the plans, but Wes had left them on the outside. It was like he decided he didn't need them or—she sucked in a breath—wasn't part of the family any more. Was that it? Had he divorced them? Just what kind of hold did this Brazil nut have over him?

Only this morning, he announced he'd leased an apartment. It was the second one they'd looked at, the two-bedroom in the center of Pineridge. After he found the washer/dryer hookup in a closet, it had everything on his must-have list. He'd even rented a truck, and Charlie and a couple of buddies were coming to help him move. Tomorrow.

It was too fast. She hadn't gotten used to the idea of him being married. What had she done to make him do this? Had she been too lenient? Joel too strict?

When they sauntered into the kitchen, Sandi glowed and Charlie looked content. This was how it was supposed to be. A long courtship, deep friendship, and an abiding love. Claire patted the bench next to her.

"Sandi, sit beside me, dear." Claire hugged her daughter-in-law.

Charlie joined his wife after kissing Claire's cheek. He grilled the twins on their classes and friends, but she noticed he avoided mentioning any boyfriends. That was odd. But then, the twins didn't mention dating anyone, either. There was an elephant in the room and it wasn't Shiloh. They all tiptoed around it—almost like the twins were making elephant stew and no one wanted to alert the main ingredient.

When Joel walked into the kitchen, the twins attacked him from both sides with hugs and kissed cheeks. Her husband reveled in their welcome. They'd done something right with these kids. So what happened with Wes? On one hand, he was still the same kid. He wasn't in jail or anything. On the other hand, he closed them out. Why? What had she done? She rubbed her temples. Her brain ached from picking through it for answers.

The object of her sorrow entered the fray, his hair wet from the shower. Charlie clapped him on the back. "Congratulations, old man."

Claire glared. *Et tu, Brute?* No lecture from the older brother? Maybe Charlie figured the horse was already out of the barn.

Whoa horsey. How did Charlie—

Sandi glanced at Claire, her lower lip tucked between her teeth and worry all over her pretty face. What was going on? Megan patted Wes's arm while Melissa stood to one side, her lips pinched. Her expression matched Sandi's. Those two were so alike. And Wes? He toed the floor. Joel waved at her over Wes and cocked his head in question. She shook hers and lifted her shoulders. She had no idea what was hap—

Wait a corn-shucking minute. This was no surprise to them. They already knew.

She narrowed her eyes now, zeroing in on the culprit. "Wesley Vincent Bennett. When did you tell your brother and sisters about this?"

Even his ears turned red. Joel frowned, Charlie looked at his feet, and 'Lissa was ready to cry. Only Megan shrugged like it wasn't any big deal. No big deal, eh? Claire would *"deal"* with her later.

Joel turned a dark shade of red. All but his nose. The tip was white. A sure sign of barely contained anger. After a well-aimed "look" silenced Megan, he turned the expression on Wes. "Answer your mother."

"I guess, uh, I mentioned something ... last year."

And none of them thought to tell her and Joel? It boggled her mind and rendered her speechless. And wounded.

"Last year." Joel glanced at Claire and took a deep breath. "I won't say I'm not disappointed, son. We had that discussion already. But why didn't you tell us that your brother and sisters knew?"

Charlie stepped up and put his arm around Joel. "Pop, I already told him he went about it the wrong way. But the point is he's married. It's done."

"Yeah, Daddy," Megan said as she snuggled close to her brother's side. "Besides," she looked to the rest of the kids for support. "We think it's romantic."

"Romantic?" Joel said. "Deceit isn't romantic, Megan Elizabeth."

"Oh, Daddy, people elope all the time. You and Momma need to get over it. Be happy for him."

Claire jerked back as if she'd been slapped. Get over it? Was she so wrong to want to be told of her son's choice of a bride? Didn't she and his daddy deserve to be at the very least, confided in? Didn't his sisters care that—

"Have any of you considered that this woman he married might be using him just to get into the U.S.? What if in a year or so she walks out on him? Then what? That won't be so romantic, will it?" She looked at Wes. He blurred as she stood. "I'm—your daddy and I are only trying to protect him."

She walked out of the kitchen and up the stairs, using all her strength to contain her tears. The moment she shut her bedroom door, sobs racked her body, and she collapsed on the bed as the sharp fragments of her broken heart stirred up a froth of sorrow.

A few minutes later, the door cracked open, and Joel entered the bedroom. "Honey?" He eased onto the side of the bed and rubbed her back. "Tell me again why we had kids?"

She hicupped a wry chuckle. "Whatever were we thinking?"

"Babe," he pulled her up to sit beside him, handing her a tissue. "Somehow, we have to push past our hurt and try to embrace this. Wes is still our son. Charlie is trying hard to smooth things over. He told me he warned Wes this wouldn't go down good. It's only Megan I'd like to turn over my knee. That daughter needs an attitude adjustment."

Claire leaned against her sweet husband and dried her tears. He'd changed so much in the past few months. He still had his moments, but he'd truly become her champion, her heart-mate, her hero. And he even worked at sharing his feelings. That amazed and thrilled her. She knew it wasn't easy for him.

"I'm so glad I married you." She sniffed.

Joel laughed and gave her a squeeze. "Me, too, babe. Let's hope Wes chose as well as I did."

Claire could hope, but she didn't believe it. Not for one cotton-pickin' minute.

The next day while Wes carried the last box to the truck he'd rented for the move, Claire stood in his empty room, trying to keep her heart out of her throat. She walked over to the closet and peeked inside, checking it for the last time. Shiloh looked up at her and whined.

"Me, too, boy. Me too." She stroked his big head.

"Ma?"

She turned. Wes stood in the doorway, looking for all the world like her little boy. She swallowed. His cowlick had even reappeared in the sweat of lifting furniture.

"Thanks for all your help, Ma. I love you. I know this is hard for you."

Hard? He didn't know the half of it. More like impossible. She wanted to lock him in the closet she'd just helped him empty. He had no idea how crazy this ... this modern day mail-order bride idea was. A hundred years ago, those were marriages of convenience, and she suspected this was too. On the *bride's* part.

Wes handed her an envelope. "This is for the spa. It's for a massage." He kissed her cheek. "The guys are waiting. Gotta go. Bye, Ma." He loped out the door and down the stairs.

"Thanks, honey," she called after him.

She'd keep his room for him and not even paint it. He'd need it again. She just knew it.

Chapter 15

Claire plucked a towel from the basket by the entrance to the spa's exercise room and draped it around her neck. She'd put the certificate Wes gave her to good use by burning off some of her frustration on a treadmill—Chapel Springs was too congested for a good power walk.

Next to her, Patsy bent, tying her shoes. "Ready, girl?"

Claire gave her a sharp nod. "Let's get moving."

Inside the spa's small gym, another client pedaled away on a stationary bike. She nodded at them then locked her eyes on the droning overhead TV.

Claire hung her towel over the handlebar of the first treadmill. She turned the machine to speed one, stepped on, and stumbled forward. Phooey, she'd never be graceful on these things. How could her BFF step and turn on the thing at the same time without being clumsy? Her hand-eye coordination was good or she wouldn't be able to manage her pottery wheel. So why not her feet? She stepped back on the moving belt, found her rhythm and moved the speed up to the second line.

Patsy's tread zipped along twice as fast as Claire's. She even pumped her arms as she walked and didn't cling to the sides. Claire dropped her hands off the rails.

"Nicole's eyes were all red and swollen this morning," Patsy said. "You have any idea what's wrong with her?"

"Ohh yeah. Turns out she's been in love with Wes for months."

"What?" Patsy jolted, coming as close to stumbling as Claire had ever seen. "She is? How? I mean when did she meet him?"

"Melissa introduced them when Wes went to visit her and Megan."

"So how did she hear about him getting married?"

Claire stumbled—again. She jumped to the side of the tread and reduced the miles per hour. "I never asked, but I'm guessing it might have been before I did." She rocked a couple of times, trying to syncopate her feet to the moving tread, then stepped back on it. After a moment, she increased the speed and raised the incline two degrees.

Patsy wiped her face with her towel. The tilt on her treadmill was higher than Claire's and her face glowed a healthy pink. "What do you mean before you did?"

"I called you last night, but you hadn't gotten home yet." She held on to the machine's handles and glanced at Patsy. "Tell me y'all didn't find an apartment."

Patsy's arms pumped with her feet. "That's going to be harder than Nathan thought. Do you have any idea the cost of real estate in New York City? Diamonds are cheaper."

"Really?" Finally—a bright spot in her week.

"For half a million dollars, we could buy an apartment the size of our family room. It's unbelievable. The bedroom was miniscule and the bathroom almost wasn't."

Claire chuckled and tried to look sorry, but glee pushed her mouth into a smile instead of something more contrite.

Patsy grinned back. "I know, I'm hoping and praying we can't do this. I reminded Nathan he might make more money, but if living there costs so much more, we don't come out ahead."

"Behind, actually." Claire tripped but caught herself on the cup holder. Why could she run on the street, talk at the same time, and never stumble? What difference did a treadmill make?

"How so?" Patsy continued to run at a graceful lope.

"You know New Yorkers. You'd be eaten alive there."

"Maybe, but think of the culture—the art galleries and the museums."

"Think of the commissions you'd have to pay them." Zing! Score one for Claire. Patsy's sigh immediately stuck a pin in her elation. "I guess I'll keep trying to find all the reasons you shouldn't go. Oh, Pat-a-cake, what will I do without you here?" The lump in her throat made it hard to breathe.

"Keep trying, girlfriend. I can plan a trip to those galleries or ship them my artwork, I don't need to live there. I don't want to move. What am I going to do?"

"Have you talked to Nathan about how you feel?"

"Of course I have. Remember? No secrets allowed in our house."

"Then how come he's still so intent on going?"

"I don't think he truly is, but the possibility of a job offer has him thinking."

"Well, hang in there. I'm working on a plan. Lydia, too. She's planning to add some guest rooms above the spa. That'll help a little bit."

They ran for a couple of minutes in silence, broken only by the whir of treadmills and rhythmic pounding of their feet.

"We got sidetracked with my problem." Patsy adjusted the rise of her tread. "I want to know how Nicole found out about Wes."

"I'm not sure, but I suspect Melissa told her, knowing the cat was about to slip its bag. Can you believe the kids have known about this cradle robber for nearly a year? That none of them told us really sticks in my craw. How could they keep it a secret?" A trickle of sweat trickled down Claire's forehead to her nose. She wiped it with the edge of the towel she'd moved from the handlebar to hang around her neck.

"Of all of them, I'm surprised Megan managed. She usually can't keep a secret longer than a minute. Hey, I wonder if they told Deva, Dane, or Chase."

"I'd be shocked if they didn't. Our offspring are their own tribe."

Patsy laughed. "They are, aren't they? But if mine knew, they never told me."

"At least I wasn't alone, then." Claire needed to run. Increasing the speed past a jog, she took her hands off the rails and pumped her arms. Soon, her breath came in puffs and perspiration dripped off her chin.

"So, how are you going to handle it?"

Claire placed one hand on the railing to balance herself. "Handle what?"

"Wes and what's-her-name? What *is* her name?"

"Costancia. He calls her Costy. I call her Cost*ly* because that's what she's going to be. She'll get her entry to the states, drain his wallet, then break his heart by leaving. Just wait and see."

"I wouldn't say that out loud if I were you, Claire. You'll alienate your son."

"I can't stand by silent, when she's going to bleed him financially and emotionally." Her thoughts darkened with each pounding step. "Somehow she bamboozled him. I don't know how, but I'm gonna find out and expose the little carpetbagger."

"Girl, you're going to dig yourself a hole deeper than that grave you fell into the day of Charlie's wedding. If you attack her, you know Wes will go on the defensive. You learned that when the kids were in high school and brought home friends you didn't like. Remember?"

"This is worse. He married this one."

Patsy slowed her treadmill. "Girlfriend, you'd better bite your tongue and accept this girl. Pray for her and pray for yourself to love her."

Pray for her?

Claire jerked up. Her feet stopped moving, and she flew off the treadmill, slamming into the wall behind her. Her knees buckled and the concrete floor rose to meet her face. Pain exploded in her knee, and she rolled to her side.

The bike-riding woman stood above her, gaping, then ran from the room.

Patsy squatted next to her, the magnetic key from her treadmill clutched in her hand. "You all right?"

"I've been better." Claire's stomach churned like Dee's giant mixer. She clenched her jaw against the pain radiating from her knee down her shin. "I think I heard something pop, but I don't know if it was my knee or my head." She raised her hand and felt her head then checked her fingers. No blood, but a bump had blossomed.

Patsy's face turned a bit green.

"What? I don't have any bones sticking out, do I?" The pain was bad enough to make her queasy, but she couldn't see any blood.

"No, but I think I'd better call my dad or Vince."

"Okay." Stars—or were they bees—swarmed in front of Claire's eyes. "But please don't call 911." She swallowed against the rising nausea and fear that something was broken. "I don't need to advertise this."

Ever so slowly, she tried to straighten her leg. Her knee hurt, but she could move it. So, maybe it was just bruised and not broken. As she stared, it had the audacity to swell in front of her eyes.

At her groan, Patsy whipped out her cell phone and called her dad's clinic. When she told her dad's nurse what happened, Claire dropped her head into her hands. It all sounded so dorky. She could almost see the nurses laughing. *She'd* laugh if she didn't hurt so much.

Patsy slid her phone back into her pocket. "Vince is on his way over."

Claire took shallow breaths. She wanted to keep her cookies inside. "Good."

She leaned her head against the wall and closed her eyes. When Joel's brother went into practice with Patsy's dad, it delighted her whole family. The poor guy needed them. His wife ran off with somebody and broke his heart. He was twelve years younger than Joel, who put Vince through college and med school. Funny, how the elder brother looked up to the younger. One day, she hoped her dear husband could fulfill his dream of going to college. At least all but one of their kids had.

By the time Vince arrived a few minutes later, the pain had reduced to one degree below hurl level. Naturally, he wore a cheeky grin.

"You keep my Starbucks habit alive and well with your accidents."

"No way. I'm simply keeping your skills honed."

"Tell me what happened." His gentle touch probed as she explained. She gave him credit for not laughing out loud.

"Can you move it at all?"

"Yes. What do you think it is, and can I get up now?"

"No. You may have a fractured patella. I don't want you putting any weight on it until I know what we're dealing with. Between us, Patsy and I can help you to my truck. And don't argue," he said before she could open her mouth.

They lifted her to her feet and keeping her leg off the ground, she hobbled between them through the waiting room and the clucking ladies, to Vince's SUV. Lydia followed, wringing her hands. They sat Claire on the edge of the backseat. She couldn't decide which was worse—the mortification or the pain.

"Don't move and keep it straight." Vince jogged around to the passenger's side, put his arms around her waist, and pulled until her leg was all the way inside.

Patsy jumped in front with Vince, and they drove the quarter-mile to her house, where the original guesthouse out back had been converted to a clinic when Doc bought the home forty-five years ago. As little girls, Patsy and Claire loved to peek inside the waiting room to see who was there, and, of course, get candies from the old ladies. Vince pulled up the long driveway to the clinic.

After the X-rays and determining she could lift her leg against gravity, Vince and Doc came into Claire's exam room and clipped the x-ray to a light box. Vince pointed to her kneecap. "You're fortunate. No fracture and not displaced, but it's badly bruised."

Thank the good Lord. She didn't have time to be laid up. "Does that mean I can get up and go?"

Doc snorted. "I don't think your knee would thank you, Clairey-girl. Because I know you, I'm fixing to suggest a brace to remind you not to overuse it. The bruising is deep and into the bone."

Claire glanced at Vince. "Bones bruise?"

"They do indeed," Vince said, "and for two days, I want you to keep it elevated and no weight. That means you don't walk on it. And ice therapy. Then come in here for micro-therapy."

She shifted her weight on the table and stars came out of nowhere again. "I can't be immobile." Her voice came out in a squeak. She tried again. "I've got too much, I mean I'm too busy to be laid up. Wes moved, and I need to help him decorate and with ..." Her stomach really churned now. She dropped her head into her hands. "Felix will have a field day with this."

Patsy got in front of her and pulled her hands away. Her scowl demanded attention. At least she chased away the stars. "Girlfriend, you need to let your pride take a permanent vacation. You worry entirely too much about what people think."

Claire grimaced at her BFF, and then glanced at Doc and Vince, standing behind her. They nodded in agreement. It was a conspiracy. She glared at them.

Then again, maybe hiding out for a couple of days wouldn't be so bad. The gossip would have time to die down a bit. Resigned to her fate, she closed her eyes. "So, um, when does this brace thing go on?"

"In about thirty minutes. Vince will have Helen ice your knee first."

There was nothing she hated worse than sitting still—never mind the ice—watching the clock. Her mind whirled with things that needed doing. "So if I'm good, when will I be able to take it off?"

Her brother-in-law wagged his finger at her. "That's a big 'if,' Claire. If you don't behave and follow instructions, it could get infected."

"How? It isn't even cut."

"No, but it still could develop an infection. Please obey orders."

"Okay, okay." She saluted Vince.

"Will you be okay without me for a bit?" Patsy asked. "I'll run back to the gallery and tell Nicole what's happened. Don't you groan, she has to know. I'll be back in a half-hour. You should be ready by then."

"Oh, I'll be more than ready. I'll be sittin' right here feeling like an iced cocktail." She scowled at Vince, who smirked and left the exam room. Claire snorted.

After the door closed, she reached out and squeezed Patsy's hand. "I'm taking your advice about Wes and his ..." it was hard, but she forced herself to say the words, "his ... wife, Costancia." The name still tasted bad. "I'm praying I can love her. I'm not saying it will work, but I'll try."

God better still be in the miracle business because she'd need one for that to happen.

Chapter 16

Lydia slapped a dab of grease into the frying pan and turned up the heat. When it sizzled, she cracked the eggs and dropped them in, watching the whites until the right moment. When they were ready, she flipped the eggs without breaking their yolks. The mingling aromas of bacon and freshly brewed coffee made her pappy growl in anticipation. It took her back to the farm, before her daddy ran off. He would come up behind Mama while she was cooking and say, "That smells so good it makes me want to slap my pappy." Then he'd rub his stomach. They'd been so isolated out on their small farm she didn't know that was just Southern.

Funny, she'd been thinking about her daddy a lot lately. With the spatula hovering above the pan, she counted off the seconds in her head. Over easy was the family favorite, and fifteen was the magic number for perfection if the flame was set at medium low.

Three. Family favorite. The sound of it filled her with happiness. Her only hesitation was Kenny's age. At twenty-five, he should be out on his own, or at least be a *contributing* member of the household.

Seven. They weren't alone, though. With the economy, a lot of her friends' kids had lost their jobs and moved back home.

But they were at least active in their job search. Kenny hadn't applied for any jobs, and he'd already been here two weeks.

Ten. She didn't mean to be unsympathetic. She understood he couldn't work retail because of his leg or hip or whichever it was that hurt the most, but he hadn't gone to Pineridge to look. Thirteen. It was a shame Claire's son had gotten married.

Fifteen. "Come and get it, y'all." She slid the eggs onto the platter and set it on the table along with the toast, bacon, and fried tomatoes. When Sam had been stationed in England, she learned to love fried tomatoes with her eggs. Graham liked them, but Kenny had so far refused to try one.

After Graham blessed the food and the cook, she passed the platters around the table. Sharing breakfast with her men was nice. She missed having Morgan at home, but her daughter was very independent, a trait Lydia had fostered. She wanted Morgan to be self-reliant and had helped her find her apartment.

Kenny refilled their coffee cups. "I heard Nathan say he was moving to New York."

"When did you hear that?" Lydia knew Nathan was thinking of moving, but as far as she knew, they hadn't made any decisions. She stirred sugar and cream into her coffee. If he moved, who would be her accountant? She supposed she could courier things to him, but that would be an added expense.

"On Sunday. I overheard him tell some man about a job offer he'd received. If he moves, I could take over his clients."

Lydia doubted it. She dipped a triangle of toast into an egg yolk. Local folks were slow to take to newcomers. She didn't think they'd be so quick to release their finances into his hands.

Graham blew on his coffee, then took a tentative sip. "That's a good idea. You'll have to ask him for a referral." He folded a slice of toast and mopped up the egg yolk left on his plate. "Say, did you get your certification?"

"I took the exam but didn't pass. I can take it again, though. Can I have the bacon, please?"

Why didn't he pass?

As if he heard her thoughts, Kenny smiled. "Only about five percent pass on the first try."

Heat rose in her cheeks. She hoped he didn't think she condemned him for not passing.

Graham handed him the plate of bacon. "What if you talked to Nathan about a job with his firm? It could be the in you need, and you could help him with audits."

Lydia's spoon clinked against the side of her cup as she stirred her coffee. "But, love, if he's thinking of moving, he probably isn't hiring."

"She's right, Dad." Kenny slid down in his chair. "And with so many people out of work, jobs are scarce."

He'd been so helpful to her at the spa, maybe she should hire Kenny. That would help others see him as part of the community, too. She could make him a—what? Certainly not a janitor, she had a cleaning service. She squinted, eyeing his physique. Too bad he didn't have the training. He'd make a good massage therapist.

"I've been trying to think of what I could have you do at the spa. Have you ever thought about becoming a masseur?"

"Can't say I have." He glanced at his dad. "What is it?"

Graham laughed. "It's a massage therapist."

Kenny seemed to chew on the thought for a moment along with his toast. "That's kind of cool. They have those at gyms, too. What's involved?"

Having to keep up on her employees' training, Lydia knew the requirements by heart. "Georgia requires 500 hours of training at a board approved school and passing the state board exam. Plus an additional twenty-four hours of training every two years."

Kenny sat up straight. "I might like that. The schooling would take about sixteen weeks. That's not too long. I could get a part-time job to help out here if you'd let me stay for now."

That cinched it. "I'll hire you at the spa, dear." She glanced at Graham for his approval. He beamed. Her gaze returned to Kenny. "Until you get the massage license, I'm not sure what all I can have you do, but we'll work it out."

He stood and carried his dishes to the sink then came back and kissed her cheek. "Thank you, Lydia. I think this may be the career move I've needed."

She patted his hand. "Do you really think you'll like being a masseur?"

"Yeah, I do. It's professional, and I don't imagine there is a slew of them hanging around."

"You're right about that. I've had a hard time hiring one. You might well be the answer to *my* problem."

Graham clapped Kenny on the back, then slid his arm around his son's shoulder and gave him a one-armed hug. "It's the perfect answer. Has Kenny met Morgan?"

"Not yet, sugah. It was her day off when he was there."

"Who's Morgan?" Kenny asked.

"My daughter." Lydia picked up the remaining plates and carried them to the sink. "She used to be a teller at the bank with your dad. She left a couple of months ago to come work at the spa."

"Is she a massage therapist, too?"

"Morgan's in training to manage the spa, but first she has to become proficient in all the various services we offer." She turned on the hot water. "Even I took the massage training and got certified." She rinsed a plate and put it in the dishwasher. "That's how I know if my employees are doing things right."

Kenny was part of her family now. He needed to know her plans. She turned the water off and leaned her back against the counter as she dried her hands. "I have a dream for the spa. I'd like to become certified for medical therapy, too. Hire a physical therapist and a dietician." She glanced between her husband and stepson. "There's room for you in this business, Kenny, as well as Morgan, if you're willing to learn."

Her stepson closed the space between them and hugged her. "Thank you. I promise I won't disappoint you for believing in me."

"I'm sure you won't, dear." She pulled away. "Now I need to finish loading the dishwasher and get to work myself."

Kenny pushed between her and the counter. "I'll finish them. Then I'll come to the spa to get your help in enrolling in school."

"Thank you, dear." She gave him the dripping sponge.

Graham pulled out his wallet and handed Kenny two twenties and a blank check. "The check is for your tuition."

Kenny hesitated then took them. "Thanks, Dad. I'll pay you back."

"Morgan, he's your stepbrother and part of our family now. He'll be an employee, sugah, like any other, even after he gets his massage certification." Lydia stood toe to toe with her daughter—an exact replica of herself, except for her eyes. She had her father's blue-grays, a startling contrast to her brown hair. She reached out her hand and ran it along Morgan's cheek. "Sweetheart, if you're worried about your inheritance, don't be. You're my heart, and I'm building all of this for you."

Morgan leaned into Lydia's hand. "I'm sorry, Mama. That was really the brattiest outburst, wasn't it?" She scrunched her lips and nose. As a little girl, she did that when she found something distasteful.

"I'll welcome Kenny and treat him like ... like a brother." She sniggered. "Just kidding."

Lydia gave her a playful swat. "I know I can depend on you. Now, let's get down to business. Have you gotten all the requirements we need to implement for medical certification?"

Like she'd flipped a switch, Morgan became all business. She tapped her finger a few times on her iPad. "I just sent it to your computer. The list is complete, so now you can concentrate on checking things off. The most important is the physical therapist. We have to have a board certified and licensed PT on staff."

She tapped her tablet some more. "From what I've learned, the PT oversees all treatment and works in conjunction with the patient's doctor. Then, if we hire a PT technician, between the two, I think we can handle any and all patients we'd get for a while."

"What about equipment?"

"That part's easy—expensive but easy, and to be a step above any competition, we could put Dr. Vince on retainer. With his office a couple of doors away, it would work."

Vince Bennett was a brilliant idea. She pulled one corner of her lower lip between her teeth. How much would his retainer be, though? Maybe Claire would have an idea before she approached him. Lydia didn't want to insult him with too low an offer, yet they couldn't afford too much in the beginning.

"And the dietician? I want to begin offering safe diet plans and support for our clients."

"I've found one already." Morgan slid her finger down the tablet. "She worked at a spa in Palm Springs, California. Her husband was transferred to the hospital in Pineridge and that brought her here. She's anxious to get back to work. I've scheduled an interview with her." Morgan turned the tablet to show Lydia her calendar. "Tomorrow at one."

Morgan had also gotten her father's logic gene. She had a keen mind. Lydia swelled with pride. Morgan rolled her eyes.

"Mother, you're looking at me like I just discovered gravity."

"Can I help it if I admire my daughter's brilliance?"

"Can I admire it, too?"

Lydia jumped and Morgan turned around. Kenny stood in the doorway, grinning. Lydia motioned him in.

"Kenny, this is my daughter, Morgan. She'll be your supervisor when you're finished with your training. Sugah, this is your stepbrother, Kenny."

Kenny thrust out his hand. Morgan hesitated only a fraction of a second then shook it. "I met your daddy before he and Momma got married. They forgot to tell me about you." She smiled at him.

"Same on my side." He smiled back.

"Where did you go to school?"

"UGA. You?"

"University of Richmond."

It was like watching a fencing match. They circled, verbally taking each other's measure.

Morgan thrust. "What did you study?"

Kenny parried. "Accounting. You?"

"Business major. Did you do any work in your field?"

Ooh, Lydia winced at Morgan's score. Kenny slapped his hand to his chest like he'd been wounded.

"Not in this economy."

Morgan's smile lit up the room. "Not to worry. You'll soon be the spa's most requested masseur. Actually, you'll be the only masseur, but you know what I mean."

Kenny glanced at Lydia. "And that's what I'm here for. Where do I apply to school?"

Morgan took him to her desk, logged onto her computer, then stepped back, motioning for him to sit. "We have a list of the schools by region. We use it for hiring. Just look for the closest one."

They didn't need her anymore, so Lydia moved to the door. "I'm going to make rounds and see how the temp is doing. Kenny, if you'll relieve her at dinner—I mean lunch, I'd appreciate it. And Morgan, help him find a good school as close as possible."

Lydia walked the hallways of the old home-turned-spa. The elegant mansion had converted beautifully—almost as if the original architect had known she'd buy it one day. It was large with ten bedrooms, which made wonderful massage facilities. The downstairs had been turned into more public service areas, with the foyer as a reception area. The dining room became the hair salon after they tied the plumbing into the adjoining kitchen, which they kept as the employee lounge. They used the front parlor for manicures and pedicures, and she'd turned the former maids' quarters into linen closets. Lydia had the downstairs bathroom expanded into the sunroom, surpassing code by adding six stalls for the toilets and four shower enclosures, as well as lockers for clients' clothing. She had so few male clients—and then only for massages, so she added a simple two-two-and-two restroom/shower for them next to the women's.

In the foyer, the temp was serving tea to three ladies as they labored over the services menu together. Lydia straightened the magazine selection and waited for the temp to finish her task. The last temp didn't stay more than a week. This girl, Lydia hadn't caught her name since Morgan trained her when she arrived this morning, talked easily with the clients. She pointed to a few items on the service menu, then returned to the front desk.

Lydia introduced herself. "How are things going?" she asked the girl.

"Very well. Your system is logical, so I had no problem picking it up. Morgan is a great mentor. Oh, and I'm Hannah Tucker."

"Thank you, Hannah. I'm Lydia. Kenny will relieve you for lunch. I'll be available if you have any problems."

"Thank you."

Clients' happy chatter rang out behind her as Lydia walked away satisfied with Hannah's manners. She would check on her a few more times, but if the girl could handle the heavy phones as well as she did the customers, she would offer her the job permanently at the end of the week.

Her heels clicked cheerfully on the wood floors. One more item checked off her list.

Chapter 17

"**B**uoy nose die us."

That didn't sound right. Claire wrinkled *her* nose and stared at the blackboard. The classroom smelled of chalk and old paper. Copying the phrase into her notebook, she straightened her braced leg, sticking it out in the aisle. Her knee started to ache if she kept it bent for too long.

She'd lucked out when finding a night course in conversational Spanish that started this week at the high school. Her only other choice of classes had been at the college, which didn't start until next semester. That would have meant she wouldn't be able to welcome her daughter-in-law in her own language.

"Try again, Claire. And the 'i' is pronounced like an 'a.'"

"Buoy nose dee us?"

A snicker sneaked from the back of the room.

"Soften the 'oo,'" Mrs. Sanchez, their teacher, said. "More like 'buh-way.'" Mrs. Sanchez, her teacher, looked past her, focusing her gaze on the owner of the snicker. "And if you're so amused and obviously an expert, how about you try this one, Mr. Riley." She scribbled on the board *Usted es una persona grosera.*

Riley? Claire came close to whiplash, snapping her neck to see the last row. What was Dale doing here? Why did he need to learn Spanish? It wasn't his kid who married a foreigner.

"Us ted is un ah person ah gross era."

A snort bubbled up in Claire's throat, even though she knew she couldn't have done any better. She came close to feeling sorry for Dale. Close ... but not quite. Why was he here? It seemed like she saw him everywhere she went, almost like he was stalking her.

Mrs. Sanchez crossed her arms. "From now on, let's not laugh at each other. It's rude, which is what that phrase means."

"Okay, okay. I'm sorry."

Dale's apology sounded more embarrassed than sorry. Claire turned back to her papers. The handout had twenty pages of common phrases, and Mrs. Sanchez was teaching them the pronunciations.

"Let's try again, but all together this time."

Claire strained to hear the teacher's inflections. The "ooo" was shorter than she said. "Buh-oo-ay-nos dee-ez."

"Very good, Claire. That was better. When you speed up and don't separate the syllables, it will blend together and sound right."

Speed up. Okay, she could do that. She hoped. This was a one-week crash course. She'd get the basics. That was all she needed, right? After that, a dictionary could be her companion and help her get by conversing with Costly—uh, Costy. She hoped. A lot rode on her hoping.

"Remember, class, this is your first night, so don't be too hard on yourselves. Let's take a moment and introduce ourselves and tell why you're learning Spanish. Ms. McPherson, will you go first, please?"

A mouse of a woman, who looked like a twelve-year-old, fingered an earring. "I'm Sally. My husband's been out of work for two years, and to make ends meet, I'm cleaning houses. I got a job at the Spanish consulate's home. That's why I'm here so I can speak with my employer."

The irony wasn't lost on Claire. The next student was a young man who couldn't be more than Wes's age.

"Hey, y'all. I'm Wade. I took French in high school because I thought it would impress the girls. It didn't help." He laughed at himself. "When I graduated and got a summer job in construction, I found I loved it. Most of my fellow workers are Hispanic, and I'm learning some of the language on the job, but I thought this would help speed me up so I could become a foreman sooner."

That seemed to be the common tale. When it came her turn, Claire didn't quite know what to say. She took French in high school, too, because she thought it was the language of art. That would work, but it didn't really tell *why* she wanted to learn Spanish.

Tell the truth.

She took a breath. "Like Wade, I took French. Unfortunately, I don't seem to have an ear for languages. I barely skated by. Now, I'm getting a daughter-in-law who speaks Spanish. I want to be able to communicate."

As long as no one asked how they met, she was fine. And if Dale said anything about it, she'd be arrested for verbal assault. When it came his turn, she held her breath.

"I'm Dale Riley, brother of Chapel Springs' mayor." He paused.

What was he waiting for? Applause? Claire rolled her eyes.

"I'm going to be working with Hispanic laborers, too." Dale nodded at Wade. "It's been a lot of years since I took Spanish. All I remember is enough to order at a Mexican restaurant." He grinned and didn't say anything. Probably waiting for a laugh. Wait a minute—didn't Felix tell him he was off the restoration project?

"All right. So most of you took another language. How did you do in those classes?"

There were more red faces there than at the beach in the middle of July. Apparently they were more like her than she thought. That was encouraging. Or were they all doomed to failure? Could a person gain an aptitude for languages over time?

"Some of you will learn easily, others not so much." Mrs. Sanchez looked at Claire. Did the teacher think she was a lost cause? Claire set her mouth and sat straighter. She'd show them what determination looked like.

While Mrs. Sanchez wrote more phrases on the board, Claire studied the pronunciation tip sheet. Apparently, a "j" was pronounced like a "y." How silly. They have a "y" in their alphabet, so why did both sound the same? And what's with having "n" in twice? What did the little squiggle over one mean? At the bottom of the page, there were some Internet links on the page for homework help. Homework? Ack! It had been years since she had homework.

"All right, everyone. Let's look at these. Here are some basic phrases. Can you sound them out? When you're finished, translate them. Claire, you're first this time." She pointed to the first phrase.

Claire studied it. That word *buenos* meant good. *Noches*. She thought it was spelled with an "a." She'd have to look at the menu again at the Taco Bell. Maybe they spelled it wrong.

"Boo-ay-nos naw-choz. Uh, good chips?"

Joining the snickerers, Mrs. Sanchez laughed then quickly clapped her hand over her mouth. Claire was confused. Sure her pronunciation was probably off, but after getting on Dale, why did the teacher laugh at her?

"Uh, not chips, Claire. That's spelled n-a-c-h-o-s and actually, that's not the translation for chips. Nachos is the same in English and Spanish. Noches is night. Good night. And forgive me for laughing, please."

"Oh, sure." She was used to it. Even when it hurt. Why was she doing this again?

They spent the next ninety minutes working on the twenty phrases. Claire's knee ached, her brain hurt, even her ears hurt. She couldn't make her tongue trill on the letter "r" like her teacher, but despite her setbacks, she learned the phrases, even if her pronunciation wasn't great.

Mrs. Sanchez pointed to another one. While the next student pronounced it, Claire tried, silently. It wasn't even close. Who was she trying to kid? She couldn't do this.

Love the Lord your God and love one another.

Yeah, yeah, she heard. Okay, once more. Comb-o es-taw ooze-ted. Hey! That sounded the same, well almost the same, as the teacher. She got it. All right, maybe she could do this. Her accent wasn't great. Hmm, did the people in south Brazil speak with a Southern accent? If so, she might be okay.

The ache in her knee radiated up to her hip. She shifted her weight and slid her leg out in front of her as much as possible, hoping it would be better by the time Costly—er, Costancia arrived. She wanted to go to the airport with Wes.

"Claire, it's your turn." This time, Dale only snorted, earning him a glare from Ms. Sanchez. "Try the next one."

Claire read the words on the board, sounding them out. "Ez-toy be-en, much-us grass-see-us?"

Claire sank onto the guest bed with a weary sigh. Every muscle rebelled. "Who knew this bruise thing would make the rest of me hurt, too? Vince wasn't kidding about it being deep."

Joel, bless his heart, lifted her leg and slid it onto the mattress for her. "You're depending on other muscles more than normal. Give it another week, and it won't be so hard."

"I'll be out of the brace by then." She chuckled and caught his hand before he turned. "I appreciate you, honey."

And she did. The night she got hurt, they stood at the foot of the stairs and looked up at its length. There was no way she could get up and back down without subjecting herself to mortal danger. Joel had suggested the guest room and made four trips up and back collecting clothes, cosmetics, and anything else he thought she might need. Then he got into his PJs and joined her in the guest room. Even Shiloh, once he got over his confusion, joined them.

They'd shared the room since. Now, Joel slipped under the covers and snuggled up, smelling like citrus soap.

"How did your class go?"

"You'll never guess who was there."

"Since I'll never guess, tell me."

She elbowed him. "Dale Riley."

"Why was he there?"

"My question exactly. He *said* it's because of the work on the springs, but I don't believe him. Besides, he's off that project. It's like he's following me."

She felt his muscles tense. "What do you mean?"

"Everywhere I am, he turns up like a bad cliché."

Joel's low chuckle rumbled in his chest. "That could be said of everyone in Chapel Springs."

"I suppose you're right. I'm probably making more out of it than there is."

"Tell me what you learned."

Claire turned her head and kissed his cheek. She still couldn't believe how much Joel had changed. He was really trying to show her he loved her. Her heart filled with thankfulness.

"Just a few phrases so far. She's trying to drill some pronunciation into us."

"In one week? How'd you do?"

"Don't ask. My only hope is that Costancia will appreciate the effort even if she doesn't recognize any words with the way I murder her language."

"She'd better appreciate it."

She kissed her hero's cheek again. "Do you know how much I love you?"

He pulled her close. "I love you, too, babe. When I think that I almost lost you ..." He squeezed her and kissed her temple. "I'd love to show you right now how much I love you."

"Mmm, I'd love to see." She gave him a come-hither look and he hithered.

Later, Joel fell asleep with her head cradled on his shoulder. His reference to a few months ago when she was so stupid to think he wasn't God's choice for her, made her glad she realized in time that the grass in her own yard was the greenest. Joel's soft snores soothed her, and her eyes grew heavy.

Too soon, his noises were drowned out by Shiloh from the floor at the end of the bed, where he slept. She'd forgotten about how loud that dog snored.

Chapter 18

"Claire, I'm worried about Nicole. Her face is longer than a Basset hound's. She's clouded up and ready to let go a gullywusher."

Claire lowered her dog-eared catalog and peered over her readers at Patsy. "I know. She needs something to take her mind off Wes. I've tried everything I can think of. You got any new ideas?" Her leg itched. She unlatched the brace and scratched.

"I might." Patsy dabbed her brush on her palette and made sweeping strokes across her canvas. "I was thinking of introducing her to Chase."

Claire dropped the brace on the floor and slid her readers to the top of her head. "I thought he had a girlfriend."

"They broke up about a month ago. He called last night to ask if I had Debby Jo's email address. I had to tell him the Greins moved." Patsy grimaced. As usual, she'd gotten paint on herself—this time on her front tooth. An attractive viridian green. "Then he asked if a cute girl had moved into their house."

Now that stuck in Claire's craw. "How come your kid asks for your opinion on girls and mine gets a mail-order bride? And wipe your front tooth." Patsy swiped at her teeth. "No the other side." She wiped again and bared her teeth at Claire. "Got it."

"Chase wasn't asking my opinion about a specific girl. He merely asked if there were any new girls in town, and I casually mentioned our new assistant."

"Did he bite?"

"Nibbled. I think he already knew about her through the tribe."

Claire set the catalog aside—she'd order later—latched her knee brace, and went to her paint table. "That figures."

She picked up a bowl and turned it. Lifting her arm, she studied each round side, looking for its essence, that once found, would dictate the colors she used. The undulations of this bowl's form reminded her of the Northern Lights. Where was that photo Bev sent to her from her Alaskan vacation? She set the bowl down and pawed through a drawer.

"Voila!" Extracting it from the mess, she held up the photo and waved the image at Patsy. She then reached for paints that once fired, would give her all the swirling colors of the Northern lights. "So, what's wrong with the girls he works with?"

"He doesn't like to date them. Too much tension if it doesn't work out, and *we* know from experience, they usually don't."

Claire laughed. "Oh, my word, I can still see the stockholder's reports Wayne had worked on so hard, shredded into a pile on his desk." They both had worked at the same company their first summer in college. "That Marsha was one vindictive girl."

With her wrist, Patsy pushed her bangs out of her eyes, then stuck out her lower lip and blew upward at a strand that refused to comply. "I need a haircut. So, whatever happened to Marsha?"

"She got fired, and the boss said no more interoffice dating."

"Ah well, if Chase won't date anyone at his work, maybe Wes can give him a push toward Nicole."

"We need to be careful, Claire."

A half-inch of blue blended with white on her palette. "I know how to be subtle."

"Right, you're about as subtle as a tsunami."

Claire snorted. "Subtle's overrated. So, when is Chase coming around to meet her?"

Patsy hid behind her easel. "I'm not sure. Next week sometime."

"I see. And how did Ms. Subtlety manage that?"

Patsy quirked her mouth in a cheeky grin. "I told him I had another painting for his office and to come pick it up here."

Claire dropped her brush. "And you call me conniving?" She shook her head. "You're goofy, Pat-a-cake, but I adore Nicole and would love to keep her."

Claire slid the back onto one earring. "Joel? Are you almost ready?"

"Just have to find my shoes. Have you seen them?"

With Herculean discipline Joel would be proud of if he knew about—

but wouldn't find out from her—Claire refrained from rolling her eyes. "You took them off in the den. They're probably still down there." Last week, she'd had enough of the guest room. A streetlight shined directly into its window. Why hadn't they ever realized that? None of their guests had ever complained, but she cringed at their discomfort. Now that she managed the stairs just fine if she was careful, it was worth the slower pace to sleep in her own bed.

Joel's impudent smirk still had the power to diffuse any annoyance she might have felt. "Thanks, babe. That's why I need you."

"Uh-huh." She slid the back onto her other earring and picked up her pocketbook. "I don't want to be late. Lydia's bringing ... oh, whatshisname—you know ... Cracker's, er Graham's son, Kenny, to church."

"You better stop thinking that. You'll say it and someone will think you're calling him poor white trash. Graham Sanders is anything but."

"I know, but I can't help what I think, and when I hear his name, I think crackers."

Joel bounded down the stairs. She followed but at a slower pace. Her knee was finally healing, and she had ditched the brace with Doc and Vince's okay two days ago.

"Graham is a normal name. Didn't you ever hear of the Galloping Gourmet, Graham Kerr?"

"No. But it fits a chef. This cracker's a banker."

Using his foot, Joel maneuvered his shoes from under the coffee table. As he slid one foot into the first, he stopped, reached inside and pulled out a Milkbone biscuit. "Shiloh, do you have to hide these in my shoes?" The mastiff raised his head. Joel tossed him the bone, then he slipped on his shoes sans biscuit.

Joel turned and kissed the end of Claire's nose. "You're a goose. Come on. We don't want to be late." He swatted her backside as she passed.

They managed, no thanks to Shiloh, who had to go out at the last minute, to arrive at church on time. Joel liked to sit in the back, but Claire spotted Lydia in the fourth row, sitting between her husband and his son. "Honey, do you mind if we go up by Lydia?"

"Why? You can't talk during the service. Let's sit back here. We can go with them to lunch after church."

She couldn't argue with that, so she gave in, grudgingly. There were too many people in the way to watch Kenny from the back, and she wanted to observe him undetected from behind her hymnal.

Joel surprised her when, moving past the back row, he went about halfway before stepping into a pew. After settling, she craned her neck to the right and forward just a bit. Bingo. She could see a quarter-profile of Kenny and the back of Lydia's head. He leaned over and whispered something to Lydia, making her chuckle. Cracked crockery, she'd like to know what he said.

Joel poked her ribs, tickling her, just as Lester Gordon handed them a bulletin. "Morning, folks. Good to see you."

Joel nodded and shook Lester's hand. "Are you entering the winter bass contest?"

"Sure am and plan on beating you this year." He grinned and moved to the next pew.

Joel handed her the bulletin and motioned for her to scoot down. Happy Drayton, followed by Ellie Grant, joined them.

Claire hadn't seen Ellie in church for weeks. Her mother couldn't get out anymore, and Ellie, her sole caretaker ever since her sisters moved away twenty-five years ago, was often stuck at home. As far as Claire could tell, her sisters cut all ties when they left. It was a crying shame. Especially since Ellie's former fiancé got tired of waiting for her mother to get well. He broke Ellie's heart when he married someone else. She never showed any interest in another man as she spent her life caring for her mom.

"How's your mother, Ellie?"

"She's about the same. The county nurse is sitting with her so I could come to church."

Claire couldn't help but wonder what if Costy's mother—no, she stopped the thought. She'd vowed to accept her son's marriage. No more what if's or too bad's. Not one. Pastor Seth and JoAnn's daughter, Cynthia, walked past the pew. Well, maybe a teensy one—Wes used to date Cynthia. Too bad ... Claire sighed.

The music director came onto the platform and the service began. Soon, caught up in the praise music, Claire didn't have time to watch Kenny or Ellie. Her voice might not be that good, but she made a joyful noise. Joel, however, could sing the birds out of the trees but didn't open his mouth. While she wished he'd at least try, it was an argument she wasn't willing to start.

Unlike the previous weeks, Joel actually stayed awake during the sermon. The few sidelong glances she risked, he appeared deep in concentrated thought. Her hope soared, but when Seth gave the invitation, Joel sat like the proverbial knot on a limb, ignoring it. He plucked the bulletin from her hands and read the announcements with great interest.

With the service over, Claire grabbed her pocketbook and Bible and waved at Lydia, who worked her way toward them, Graham and Kenny in tow.

"Hey, y'all. Beautiful morning, isn't it? I'd like y'all to meet Graham's son, Kenny." Lydia gestured to each as she introduced them. "This is Happy Drayton, who owns *The Happy Hooker Bait Shop* and the hobby shop. Ellie Grant is our head librarian. Joel, y'all know already, and this is his wife, Claire. She's a renowned potter."

Kenny leaned in and shook hands with the men. "I'm taking my dad and lovely stepmother to lunch. Would you care to join us?"

After Lydia's nod, Claire agreed. "We'd love to." Kenny seemed sincere, but was it an act? Joel seemed to think it was. Maybe it was his choice of words. They seemed too grown up or formal or ... something.

"Ellie?" Happy peered down at the diminutive librarian, who actually fluttered her eyelashes as she nodded acceptance. Claire had never seen Ellie act so ... so unlibrarian like. Her usual no-nonsense demeanor had flown the coop and let the door bang shut. Could it be she was finally interested in someone? In Happy? *Well, shut my mouth.*

"Lydia chose Jake's Krill Grill. Shall we?" Graham held out his arm for Lydia, then laid his hand over hers. Kenny trotted behind them.

That was so sweet. It filled Claire with longing. After high school, public displays of affection still embarrassed Joel.

Lacey's husband, Jake, met them at the door of the Krill Grill. He always went to the early service and usually alone. Ten years younger than Claire and Joel, she'd babysat him when he was a little boy. Seeing him as a business owner and married to Lacey made Claire feel old. The feeling quickly vanished, though, when Joel caught her eye and winked at her, making her heart jump.

"You're not old."

She blushed. He may not display affection in public, but he sure could read her.

Once seated and orders given, Happy gave Graham a frank stare. "You a fisherman, Graham?"

"I've caught my share. Never competed though. Kenny tells me that you and Joel are the champs hereabouts."

As the men discussed fishing and told Graham about the upcoming winter fishing contest, she studied Kenny and his dad. Kenny's hair, like his dad's, was the color of sand, except his hadn't begun to recede, yet. She examined Joel's hairline. It receded some, but not as much. Graham had a youthful look, but trustworthy. That was good in a banker. He reminded her slightly of that retired football player, Joe Montana. She wondered if Joel noticed the resemblance.

"I guess you and Lydia's sister have a lot in common," Claire said.

"Even more, now." Graham grinned at Lydia.

Lydia's cheeks filled with the newlywed blush. "He's bein' modest. He was just named branch manager."

Graham colored slightly. So, he balanced pride in accomplishment with a humble attitude. That raised him up a notch in Claire's book. He would have let them think he meant because he was married to Lydia.

"Congratulations." Joel raised his water glass in a salute.

Graham clinked glasses with him. "Thanks."

"Will you stay in Lydia's house or buy a new one?" Ellie asked. "I know a good real estate agent if you need one." She fished in her pocketbook. "I have one of her cards somewhere in here. Ah." She held up the card like a prize. "Here it is."

Graham pocketed the card. "We hadn't thought about that, yet."

"Up until recently, there wasn't anything available here, anyway," Happy said. "But now there are a few properties on the market."

"That's what Lydia told me." Graham looked at each of them. "What's the general feeling about this high-rise she mentioned?"

Everyone spoke at once.

"We're against it."

"It would ruin our town."

"It's a dumb idea."

"If we wanted that, we'd live in Miami."

"We have all we can handle now without adding more."

Graham nodded, his lips compressed in a thin line. What was he thinking? Did he know something—?

Joel leaned forward. "Do you know anything about this?"

"I might. What I'm interested in most is what it would do to property values. It has the potential to raise or lower them, depending on the amenities."

Lydia's brows dipped. She leaned back. "What exactly do you mean by amenities?"

Before he could answer, Kenny jumped in. "If it's a first class hotel, they'll have a day spa, weight room, pool, five-star restaurant ... the works."

Lydia's face lost its rosy glow. "That would ruin me." Her words were barely audible. "Everything I have is sunk into my spa."

Graham frowned at Kenny and put his arm around her. "Then, we'll have to stop it. But we need to look at this with open eyes. Much will depend on what the investors have in mind. If they only plan on rooms with minimal amenities, it could lower property values."

"The whole thing is a Catch 22. So, how do we find that out?" Joel leaned back for the waiter to set his plate down.

Graham waited until all had been served. Happy asked the blessing, and they started to eat.

"You asked how you'd find out about the hotel. To start with, the builder will have to present the plans to get a permit. Who's on that committee?"

Happy stuck up his hand while he swallowed a fried shrimp. "I am." He wiped his mouth on his napkin. "They aren't on the schedule for this month's meeting." He picked up another shrimp and dragged it through Jake's special horseradish cocktail sauce.

Graham paused, his fork halfway to his mouth. "Does the committee ever consider requests not on the schedule?"

"We haven't in the past," Happy said. "But there's no rule against it that I know of."

Claire's fork fell from her hand, hit the tartar sauce, splattering it onto Joel, and clattered against her plate. She grabbed her napkin and wiped the white blob from his arm.

"That's what they're going to do. I just know it. That way, no one can protest." She put her hands on the table and pushed herself halfway to her feet. "Tell everyone to be at that meeting. We've got to stop them!"

Chapter 19

C laire followed Patsy's son into the gallery, then locked the door behind them, waving at a few early morning tourists through the glass. "Thanks, Chase. Just set it over there by the register."

Bending his knees, he lowered the heavy box to the floor. "What's in that thing, Aunt Claire?"

"Some of my old textbooks for Nicole and a few of my early 'mistakes.' She thinks I've always been good at this." Chase wore the cutest grin whenever he was about to make a snarky remark. She headed him off by shaking her finger. "Don't you dare. Now, come pick up the painting your mama has for you. You can meet Nicole, too. Under comfortable circumstances."

He glanced at his watch. "Okay, I've got a few minutes before I need to be at the dentist's office."

She led him into the workroom, where they found Nicole, wet clay up to her elbows, concentrating at the wheel. Claire turned to caution Chase to be quiet so they didn't startle her, but his expression stopped her tongue. She returned her gaze to Nicole to see what he saw, but while adorable, her assistant wasn't exactly a vision of loveliness. Not today. With her hair frizzy and flying, and a splotch of dried clay clinging to her cheek, what exactly was Chase seeing? She glanced back at him. Whatever, he was enchanted.

Okay, Cupid, it's all yours. Claire took a step back, but her heel hit the riser going up into the gallery, and she lost her balance, plopping down hard on her rear. Both Nicole and Chase jumped. *So much for that romantic moment.*

Nicole's cheeks infused with a becoming rosy blush at the sight of

Chase, and she gulped. "Oh!" She brought the pottery wheel to a stop. "I didn't know anyone was here."

At least she didn't try to smooth her hair.

Chase grabbed Claire's hand and pulled her up. "You okay?"

"I'm fine." She brushed off her rear and turned to Nicole. "Sugar, I know you've met Dane and Deva, but this is Patsy's other son, Chase. Sweetie, this is Nicole."

Nicole stuck her hand out then quickly withdrew it. "Oh, sorry. I ... uh, really get into my work." Her giggle sounded like tinkling bells.

Chase grinned but not his impertinent smirk. This was a smile Claire hadn't seen before. For a young man who wasn't excited to meet their assistant, she had a feeling he was about to miss his dental appointment. Now if he could win Nicole over so she forgot about Wes's marriage ...

Claire slipped out of the workroom. Grabbing the feather duster, she started on the shelf of whimsy vases. She could easily occupy herself in the gallery for a few minutes. Too bad she couldn't have sidetracked Wes as easily. Lord, why did that boy have to be so stubborn? He and his dad were just alike in some ways.

As she dusted, she mentally checked off her inventory of commissions and stock pieces until she was satisfied she could complete them by five o'clock. The last thing on her day's agenda was tonight's council meeting. She grimaced and stuffed the feather duster behind the counter. She had to find a way to stop this high-rise mess.

Boone banged the gavel and brought the council meeting to order. After Ellie read the minutes from last month, he asked for old business. When Joel raised his hand and Boone acknowledged him, Claire nearly popped her buttons with pride. He'd done a terrific job in pulling together all the figures and projecting costs for parking and the trams.

"What I propose," Joel said as he passed out the paperwork containing all the stats. "With Happy in agreement, is to lease the land for the parking lot, which lowers the initial outlay of cash for the town. With the cost of an annual lease and the price of the trams, offset by the revenues from the parking of ten dollars per day or fifty per week, including subtracting monies spent annually on infrastructure repairs, *and* if the tourist business continues as it is, we should see a profit within two years."

For someone without a college degree, her Joel was one smart man. Even Felix looked impressed.

"Two years? How's that possible?" Boone asked.

Just you wait and see. She bit her lip. She didn't want to embarrass Joel by blabbing that out loud.

He flipped to another page in his notes. "I've studied parking costs from residential to commercial across the Southeast. In some areas, residential runs an average of a hundred dollars a month. We're a resort, so I doubled that. It's not a cost visitors are going to be paying on an annual basis and figuring in the high price of gas, it's reasonable. However, I've also included a lower cost for a whole-summer resident vehicle pass."

The town knew Joel didn't go to college, and sometimes that lack made him uncomfortable, but tonight her hubby surprised them all. Claire fairly wiggled with glee.

"Happy, how much do you propose for the lease?"

Her hackles rose at the insinuation in Felix's tone. "Happy loves this town, Felix. He isn't going to rape the coffers." *And you'd better not mess with my Joel's idea.*

Joel pulled on his nose, sending her their private signal to settle down and watch. Although still fuming, she crossed her arms and sat back, letting him fight this battle. He could probably do it better than her anyway.

"Happy has agreed to fifteen-hundred per month, which is very generous, considering what the town's income will be from this. Chapel Springs will take on the cost of resurfacing the lot and painting the parking slots."

"And is that figured into your cost analysis?" Boone asked.

"It is."

The mad melted off her like chocolate in the sun. Her Joel had all his facts laid out perfectly. She nudged Doc. "Will you make the motion?" she whispered. "It would look bad if I did."

He donned his best doctoral persona. Boone asked if there were any more questions. When no one spoke, he called for the motion.

Doc raised his hand. "Given the fiscal facts and acknowledging the work Joel has put into this, not to mention Happy's generosity, I move we accept the proposal to go forward with this venture."

Tom Fowler raised his hand. "I second."

Noting the motion and second, Boone called for the vote. "The ayes have it. Ellie make a note to have our attorney draw up a lease with Happy for the land. Now, who is going to oversee the project?"

It was times like this where Claire almost wished they were big enough to have a hired city manager. But they weren't. So, like with the warm springs restoration, one of them would have to volunteer.

"I'll do it," Doc Benson said. "I'm semi-retired now and, to be frank, I need something to do. It'll keep me out of Cooper's hair."

The sweet old phony. He was thrilled when Patsy's mom, being in the early stages of Alzheimer's, had responded well to the medications and supplements. Her depression lifted, she was painting again, and according to Doc, giving him a long "honey-do" list.

"I think you'd be perfect for it, Doc." Claire patted his arm.

"Any other old business before we move to the new?" Boone asked.

"I have an item," Felix said. "I heard today that the Muldoon Investments group found out that Howie Newlander's family owns that land north of Ollie Katz's place. They're trying to locate Howie to make him an offer."

Van Gogh's ear! How could she have forgotten to get to Granny Newlander? Her stomach churned over the implications. From the audience, Joel raised an eyebrow at her in question. As surreptitiously as she could, she shook her head. He frowned, and she shrugged one shoulder, pointing to her leg. He nodded and gave her a half smile. At least he understood. Her knee and Wes had completely upended her world, and she'd forgotten a lot of things.

She could hardly concentrate on the rest of the meeting. First thing in the morning, she'd drive out to the assisted living facility where Granny lived. She was Howie's great-grandmother and had to be ninety by now, maybe ninety-one. Claire hoped she was still alive and had all her faculties.

The next morning, Claire left instructions for Nicole and said she'd be back by noon. *Sunny Meadows* was halfway around the lake, and Claire arrived midmorning. She approached the reception desk.

"Is Granny, uh, Celia Newlander here?"

"She is. Are you family?"

"No, but her son and I were friends years ago. I spent a lot of time at his house and knew Granny well. She used to tell us stories about her youth." Why was she telling this woman all that? "May I see her?"

"Of course. Let me get someone to take you to her. She'll be in the garden now, tending her flowers. She'll welcome a visitor." She pressed a button on her phone and asked for an attendant. "So will the flowers."

The woman rolled her eyes.

Granny had always been feisty. What could be strange about her tending a garden?

A young male attendant rounded the corner. "If you'll follow me?" He turned his muscular self and headed down a hallway.

"There's a path around the outside of the lawn area. Be sure to use that," the girl called after them.

Claire followed the fellow out onto the patio. She could see where they got the name *Sunny Meadows*. The grassy acreage sprawled behind the building. Carved out of the forest and dappled in sunlight, the surrounding flower gardens made it a paradise. Lounge chairs protected by large umbrellas dotted the meadow.

When the young man stopped and pointed to the right, Claire shaded her eyes and turned. About fifty yards away, a tiny woman bent over the flowers. Wearing an old-fashioned sunbonnet, she looked like someone out of *Little House on the Prairie*. But the path the receptionist told her about was on the opposite side of the meadow and led only to the back where the lounge chairs were. There wasn't one anywhere near Granny. Claire turned to ask the young man about it but found herself alone.

With a shrug, she decided she'd try a shorter way across the lawn. Her knee was still a bit stiff, so maneuvering down the patio steps to the meadow was slow and somewhat jarring. Thankfully, the deep grass was more forgiving than the cement.

She began her schlep. About halfway there, the center lawn sprinklers came on. Claire shrieked and scooted to the edge of the grass, getting half drenched. It didn't do her knee much good either. Pain radiated around it and up her thigh.

Skirting the sprinklers, she closed in on Granny, stopping a few yards away. She blinked, not sure she believed what she saw.

Granny systematically clipped the bloom from each flower, letting them fall to the ground.

Claire called softly, not wanting to startle the old woman. "Granny?" When she didn't raise her head, Claire called again.

"No need to holler, child. I heard you the first time. I was just placing the voice. I've got a lot of memory files to look through." She stood up. "I'm delighted to see you, Claire."

Claire widened her eyes then swiped her brow clear of water droplets. "You remember me?"

"Of course I do, child." The old lady winked. "You were the only one who ever listened to my stories. Now come greet me proper, and give me some sugar."

Claire gave her a warm hug and kissed the weathered cheek. Her own grandmother had died before she was born. Granny Newlander filled that empty place in her heart and life. Plus, she'd been a close friend of Great-aunt Lola's. Why had Claire stayed away for so long?

"Will you forgive me for not coming to see you sooner?"

Granny waved her apology away. "You young people have a life to live. I've lived mine. I'm happiest here in my garden, communing with the Lord. He's working on my mansion, don'cha know."

She pulled off her garden gloves and led Claire to a path—the path she hadn't seen in the long grass—that led to the lounge chairs. "Now, I know you didn't come to jaw about the past, and you've heard all my stories. So what can I tell you? And then you can explain why you're dripping water all over."

After settling themselves, Claire admitted she disobeyed the receptionist and got caught by the sprinklers, laughing when Granny said the woman was worthless.

"Walking on the lawn is what God intended grass for. It's good exercise and it inspires the grass to grow, don'cha know. They should leave the watering to the Lord."

Granny didn't say anything about why she beheaded her flowers and Claire wasn't about to ask.

"So what brings you here, dear?"

Claire related the town's conundrum and their proposed solution for the traffic. "But our main problem is stopping this group from building a high-rise hotel. They discovered the land they want belongs to your family and have started looking for Howie to make him an offer."

"Who's Howie?"

Uh-oh. Was Granny getting senile? "He's your great-grandson."

"Ah, yes. Howard. It seems I remember a scrawny kid hanging around." She turned a sharp eye on Claire. "That's my great-grandson, you say?"

She gently patted the old woman's hand. "Yes, Granny. He's your grandson's only child."

"Well, I still own that land, sugar, not someone named Howie." Granny leaned closer until she was almost nose-to-nose with Claire. "You sure *you're* not my great-grandchild?"

She shook her head. "No, dear, though I always wished I was."

"Well, now ain't that a hoot." Granny cackled and rocked back and forth. Then a coughing spasm hit her, and she alternately laughed and coughed. Claire offered her a bottle of water she had tucked in her tote. Granny drank and when the spasm ended, she turned twinkly blue eyes on Claire.

"Don't worry your pretty head about that Howie. It'll never happen."

"That's a relief, Granny, but how can you be so sure?"

She looked around, pulled Claire closer, and whispered in her ear. "I lopped his head off." Granny pointed an arthritis-gnarled finger to the bare stems in the garden and hooted.

Claire startled. Oh, dear. Their only hope to stop the hotel was to stop the land purchase, and Granny's cheese had slid clean off her cracker. She thought Howie was a flower. Wide-eyed, she watched as Granny gleefully snipped the air with her scissors.

Now what?

Chapter 20

"So let me get this straight, Lacey. The bank wants *me* to sit on its board of directors?" Claire sipped her coffee as Lacey nodded. They were the first ones in *Dee's 'n' Doughs* this morning. When Lacey called last night and asked her to meet early, Claire couldn't imagine why. Now she knew—and wondered if the board had lost their ever-lovin' minds.

"That couldn't be construed as any kind of conflict of interest, could it?"

Lacey shook her head.

"But why me?"

"You're a council member. A business owner. You've got the credentials." She paused, a hint of a grin dancing on her lips. "And Pastor Seth put your name up."

She had credentials? "Has someone vacated their seat?"

Again, Lacey nodded. Claire wished she'd speak up more. Pulling information from her was harder than yanking the stubborn weeds in her garden.

"Who?"

"Madison Grein, when they moved."

"Oh." Their move upset her kids and now it was messing with Claire's life. She was too busy for this. Spinning the coffee stirrer in her fingers, a few errant drops splattered onto the table and her blouse. She dabbed at them with a napkin. "I don't know, Lacey. I've got a lot going on right now."

"Please consider it. We really need you. For a number of reasons." Lacey got up and went to the coffee bar for a refill.

Claire pursed her lips. What reasons? Okay, the bank had vested interest in a number of the businesses, and she was on the council but was there something else? And what made Seth think of her? She couldn't even keep her checkbook balanced. Joel had to do it, and Nathan took care of the gallery's books. She frowned and tapped her lips. It didn't make any sense.

Before she could question Lacey further, Lydia and Patsy arrived, followed by a gaggle of tourists. Behind them, Nancy Vaughn breezed in as bright and chipper as her shop's name. *SunsSpots,* being the sole boutique in Chapel Springs, kept her hopping. The tourist trade added a frenzied inventory turnover, so much so, she didn't often join them anymore. Lacey pulled a chair from a neighboring table for her.

"How did you manage to get away this morning?" Claire asked.

"I've moved up in the world." She placed a napkin in her saucer to soak up the spillover, then with the flair of a game show host, announced, "I finally hired an assistant. A lovely girl who just graduated with degrees in merchandising and fashion design."

At the word "lovely," Claire shared a glance with Patsy. Hopefully, Chase wouldn't notice this new girl. "How'd she manage a double major and where did you find her?"

"Her name ... are you ready?" She laid both hands on the table and leaned forward. "It's Chartreaux Katz." Her head bobbed up and down. "Yes! Ollie's daughter."

"The bank board president Ollie?" Claire blinked. Was this a weird coincidence or a sign?

"I remember Chartreaux," Patsy said. "She designed Deva's prom dress. She used to make all her dolls' clothes when she was a little girl. I'm so glad she achieved her dream."

Claire frowned. She wouldn't go so far as to call *Sunspots*—even if it was her favorite boutique—the pinnacle of a designer's dreams. Surely the girl had goals beyond Chapel Springs.

Nancy stirred her latte, destroying its foam design. "She got her BFA from American InterContinental University in Buckhead. My old college roomie called me about her. We still have dinner once a month and I'd been moaning about needing help." Nancy's eyes could have rivaled the night sky for twinkling. "I snapped her up before anyone else could. If we keep growing at this rate, *Sunspots* could offer haute couture."

"That's not such a far stretch." Claire eyed Nancy with a new respect.

"Word has spread since the Nashville music folks and some Hollywood stars discovered us. We even had a Broadway diva in the gallery last week."

The Painted Loon had become a hot ticket among the stars who collected art, and Chapel Springs the hottest resort for stargazers, and—oh, no. Nancy could switch sides on them—vote for the hotel. The thought churned the coffee in Claire's stomach like one of those high-speed stick blenders.

She shot a glance at Patsy, who nodded ever so slightly. Thank goodness. Pat-a-cake, as usual, caught her thoughts. She could ask much better than Claire could.

"Nancy," Patsy twirled her coffee stirrer in her cup. "I'm thrilled for you. But tell me you'll still offer the wonderfully eclectic variety you do now. I mean if this hotel gets built, they'll surely have a dress shop."

Oh, Patsy was good.

"Of course, I will." Nancy reached over and patted Claire's hand. "And don't you worry, Claire. I'll never agree to that hotel. Goodness, like Patsy said they'd have their own boutique and steal business from me."

Claire gave her a weak smile. "Was I that obvious?"

Nancy's chuckle took the heat off her. "I know you too well, dear. You'd never make a poker player. Every thought is like a neon sign on your face."

"Terrific." Claire thought she'd perfected a neutral expression, but one glance at Patsy affirmed Nancy was right. They both laughed at her. Rats. Gathering her tote and to-go cup, Claire rose.

"It's time to go to work, ladies."

Patsy grabbed her coffee and followed.

The bells on *The Painted Loon's* door jingled, bringing Nicole from the workroom as Claire and Patsy entered the gallery. Claire searched the girl's face for any sign of misery, but unless she'd become an accomplished actor overnight, her entire little self was an animated bundle of joy.

Look what Wes gave up.

Claire headed to the front desk to check the receipts from yesterday. On the other hand, as much as she wanted it, maybe it wasn't meant to be given how quickly Nicole recovered.

Sharing a grin, Patsy and Nicole watched her. Claire laid her tote next to the cash register, then curiosity got the best of her. "What's got y'all so chipper this morning?"

Nicole blushed and glanced at Patsy, whose kisser sported a self-satisfied grin. She knew?

"I had a date with Chase last night." Nicole dropped her gaze to the floor, where she found something mesmerizing and rubbed her toe over it. "And one tonight."

Claire came around the register and pulled her into a hug. "I'm happy for you, sweetie." She leaned back and searched her assistant's eyes. "You like him, then?"

"Yes. He's a lot like Wes in many ways, and yet completely different." She squeezed Claire then bounced back into the workroom. "I'll clean up then come out front again," she hollered from the back.

Patsy shook her head. "Ah, the resilience of young love. I wonder how many more hearts will be broken before she settles on one boy."

Claire frowned. "You're not worried Chase might *not* be 'the one'?"

"Goodness, no. They just met, they're young, and they'll both get over it if it doesn't work out."

"How can you be so sure? It's your son's happiness you're gambling."

"Trust, my dear, trust. Both these kids are Christians who love Jesus and are following him. Remember what Melissa told you about praying for a future spouse last year?"

Claire waved that away. "Of course I do, but what about Wes? He loves God, and yet he went and married that Brazilian—a girl nobody knows. She could be the original Bridezilla for all we know."

The side of Patsy's mouth twitched.

Claire couldn't believe her best friend would betray her like this. She narrowed her eyes. "You don't think he did the wrong thing, do you?"

"That's not what I'm saying at all. I agree he went about this the wrong way. But are you sure, really sure deep down, that he didn't seek God in his decision? What if this *is* God's will?"

"I don't like it, not one bit." But if Patsy was right ... Wes told them he'd prayed and felt it was God's will. Claire just wished God had told her about it or had at least asked her opinion.

Patsy stood with her arms crossed, watching her—probably knew what she was thinking, too. Claire grimaced and nodded. She'd promised Patsy—and God—that she'd welcome Costancia. Okay, okay. *And* try to show her love. But God was going to have to throw some heavenly Miracle-Gro on her.

They went to the workroom. "Do you ever get tired of being right?"

Patsy picked up her palette. "I'm not always right, but I am in this, Clairey-girl."

Clairey-girl. The nickname took her back to her childhood, the movie Georgie-girl, and its title song. When Claire was in elementary school, the kids used to call her Clairey-girl because she was awkward. It hurt then, but like the movie's heroine, she'd blossomed after she met Joel.

Claire tossed a small blob of clay at Patsy. It flew over her shoulder and landed on her canvas.

"Hmm, a new dimension to my art—a blend of pottery and oil paint. We'll call it Part." She laughed and picked off the clay.

They settled into work. Claire pulled out a large lump of clay from the barrel, kneaded it, and when it was pliable, got her wheel turning. Before she could let her thoughts wander, she had to get a new bowl shaped. She moved her hands, molding and stretching the clay.

Kind of like you stretch me, huh, Lord? It was one of life's little ironies, God making her a potter. Finally, with the bowl holding the contour she wanted, she could share her and Lacey's conversation with Patsy.

"I've been asked to sit on the bank's board of directors."

"I know. Dad told me Pastor Seth presented your name."

"He did? Why didn't you tell me?"

"No chance. I only heard last night. Are you going to do it?"

"I don't know. I'm so busy, and all this stuff with Wes makes it hard to focus, let alone take on new commitments."

Patsy peered at her from around the edge of her easel. "Why?"

Claire's hands jerked. The bowl flopped. "Oh, fer the love o' Van Gogh." She gathered the mess into a ball. "What do you mean why?" Adding a bit of water to remoisten the clay, she started all over.

"I mean why, if you've decided to love Costancia, are you still stewing over it? Let it go, girl, and get on with business."

"I'm trying, but it isn't as easy as you make it sound." It wasn't easy at all. It wasn't what she had planned for her youngest son. She wished things were like the old days when parents chose their kids' spouses. Well, almost. She wouldn't be married to Joel if that had been the case. With a sigh, she shaped the blob of clay back into a half-flattened round. Oh, why did life have to be so complicated?

"It isn't," Patsy said. "And you wouldn't really want to choose Wes's wife. The first fight they had you'd be filled with guilt and think it was your fault."

"How come you can always read my mind?"

"It's like Nancy said this morning. Your face is a window to your brain. I can almost see your thoughts tripping over each other in there."

"Terrific. I'm going to start wearing a mask."

Patsy chuckled and disappeared behind her easel. Claire restarted her wheel, shaping the clay upward and outward—again. Its shape grew taller and wider, and when it thinned to where she wanted, she stopped the wheel and added waves to the sides. It reminded her of an upside down garden hat.

"So, are you or aren't you?"

"Am I or aren't I what?" She slid the wire beneath the bowl, releasing it from the wheel. Using both hands, she carried it to the drying shelf.

"Are you going to take the seat on the board?"

"I don't know. I have to talk to Joel first. Do you think I should?"

"I do. You're a force all by yourself, and you can mobilize people like no one else I know."

Claire frowned. "What does that have to do with the bank's board?" She ran a finger down her inventory list then pulled another chunk of clay from the barrel, large enough for a fat-bottomed pitcher.

"Dad only hinted, but the impression I got is some of the people from the bank's Atlanta headquarters don't think like we do up here. They need a strong personality on the board, someone, who has the ability to change minds and get people to agree. That's you."

Did people really see her like that? "I thought they needed comedic relief."

"Oh, Claire. Felix and Dale are the only ones who view you like that. And I'm not convinced that Felix isn't secretly envious."

"Come on. Everyone laughs at me." She didn't try to be funny. Just the opposite. She wanted the respect of her community, but things always seemed to go wrong for her. She'd give her eyeteeth to be graceful like Patsy and not so clumsy.

"Honey, you're the sunshine in all our lives. Sunshine makes people feel good and laugh in delight."

Claire rolled her eyes. "Boy, are you the drama queen today."

"It's true."

"Have I ever told you I'm glad you're my BFF?" She started her pottery wheel. "I'll talk to Joel tonight."

Joel handed Claire a small bowl of popcorn and settled into the chair next to her, holding his own bowl. She opened her mouth and tossed in a couple of kernels. This was the good life. A cheery fire in the hearth and a bowl of buttered popcorn—both made by her husband. Shiloh even had a bowlful, minus the butter, which he gobbled then eyed hers.

Joel turned his attention to the UGA football game. "What did I miss?"

"No score yet and not even an exciting play. The half is about to end."

She'd tell him about the bank's offer during halftime. They hadn't had a chance to talk since he got home. Wes stopped by with a couple of friends, and Joel invited them all to stay for supper. They always had a good time with their kids' friends. Then as soon as the dishes were cleared, the game started, and the boys all stayed to watch. They left for Wes's apartment just before the end of the first quarter, armed with popcorn.

Joel cheered when the Bulldogs scored a touchdown with seconds left in the half. Kernels of popcorn bounced out of his bowl. He gave her a smirk and picked them up, tossing them to Shiloh, who made short work of them.

"Cheeky devil."

Joel smirked and set his now empty bowl on the floor beside his chair. "How was your day?"

"Good. I got two-dozen pieces formed." She worked her tongue to pull a hull off her eyetooth. "Honey, Lacey brought me an offer from the bank to sit on the board of directors." She definitely had his attention. His brows knit together. "Uh, what do you think?"

He didn't answer right away. The wrinkle on his brow indicated he was lining up words like letters on a Scrabble tray. Was that good or bad? While she loved the changes in Joel, she wasn't always sure what his silence meant. She picked a hangnail.

"Did she say why they asked you?"

She told him the reasons both Lacey and Patsy gave her. "I'm divided. I like the idea of it, but I'm not sure what I can really offer. You know I'm not good with financial stuff."

He chuckled. "That you're not. But I have to agree with Patsy's thinking about your ability to bring people together."

"With the exception of Felix, Dale, and their sidekick, Warren."

That got another laugh. "None of them sits on that board. But you'd bring the heart of Chapel Springs to them."

"Doesn't Doc do that? And Pastor Seth?"

"Sure, but you bring a women's intuition, and most men, while they may joke about it, don't discount that. Y'all have been proven right too many times."

The man melted her heart. "And you don't think it will take too much time?"

"Sweetheart, our nest is empty. You don't have that much to do here. There aren't a bunch of little feet dragging in dirt. We only have to vacuum twice a week now instead of twice a day. Even the washing machine is lonely. Take the seat."

"The extra money would be nice. Maybe we can take a cruise next year." She almost laughed out loud at Joel's expression of pure horror. Unless that cruise was on a lake and involved fishing, he wasn't interested. "Okay, maybe not a cruise, but how about renting a big RV and touring a couple of national parks?"

Oh, yeah. He brightened at that one. Her fit of giggles earned a thrown pillow, which deserved retaliation, which started a pillow fight until halftime was over. He moved faster since her knee was still slightly stiff and slowed her down, and he took full advantage of it. Exhausted by laughing, she was glad when the game started again.

With the snap of the football, her strange conversation with Granny popped into her mind. She wondered what Joel would make of the old woman's peculiar behavior and her last comment. The attendant had come to collect Granny just before Claire had a chance to question her further. Too bad she said she wasn't family. They might have shared Granny's medical prognosis.

When the game ended, Joel pointed the remote at the TV and clicked it off. "All right, you've been cackling over there for the last hour. What's up?"

Claire turned sideways in her chair. "Wait till you hear about my visit with Granny."

Chapter 21

Claire swung into the bank's marble lobby, her footsteps echoing in the cavernous space. The bank had been a fixture in Chapel Springs for as long as she could remember, a century-old institution of financial stability. Even through economic downturns, their bank remained solid.

She climbed the stairs to the boardroom and took a deep breath. With trembling fingers on the door handle, she hesitated. She'd never been inside what she considered "hallowed halls." Her place had always been on the outside of the teller's cage, handing over her money.

Please, don't let me make a fool of myself.

Taking one more breath for courage, she pushed down on the handle and against the door. It didn't budge. She tried again. Had they changed their mind and locked her out? She jiggled the handle the other way. Nothing. Frowning, she looked up and down the thankfully empty hallway, then back at the door.

And the sign.

The sign positioned at eye level.

The one that read, "Knock for entry."

Oh. *Good start, Bennett, a really stellar beginning.* She lifted her hand to knock, but the door opened and she rapped her knuckles on Doc's nose.

"Ow."

"Oh!" She jumped back. "Sorry, Doc. I told Lacey this wouldn't work." She turned to leave.

Doc grabbed her wrist. "Get in here, you goofy girl. Nobody's here yet but me." He tweaked his offended nose. "See? No damage." He wiggled his ears.

That made her laugh and she followed him into the room. After moving a couple of name placards around, he placed her next to him. "I'll keep you safe. Now, how's the knee feeling?"

Claire kissed his cheek. "Pretty good. I'm glad to be rid of the brace, though. My knee thought it had a life sentence." She puffed out her cheeks and released the air. "Doc, I'm so nervous I can hardly think straight." She set her tote on the floor beside the chair and sat. "You realize your son-in-law does all our accounting, don't you? And Joel has to balance my checkbook."

When Doc smiled, his eyes crinkled until they nearly disappeared. "You already know that's not why we wanted you. So quit thinking that way. In fact, whatever you do, don't try to think—" he lifted his fingers and curved them into air quotes. "—financial."

Van Gogh's ear, he'd adopted Joel's saucy grin. She swatted his arm then took a moment to acclimate to the inner sanctum. A huge mahogany table dominated its center. Ten chairs surrounded it, giving each person ample elbowroom. Woven linen-draped windows let in light at one end of the long room. The only wall without windows or cabinets was painted in eggshell white. How boring. There wasn't a bit of artwork except portraits. Whose were they? When she spied one of Doc, she blinked. Good grief, did that mean her portrait would hang there someday? The thought made her laugh.

"What's so funny?"

"If my likeness ever graces that wall, somebody will surely draw a mustache on me."

He waggled Groucho Marx eyebrows, only Doc's were white like his mustache.

"So what should I expect?"

"The suits will arrive soon. Very pompous and very sure of themselves. There's the CEO & CFO from Atlanta—I forget their names—the bank President you know. Ollie Katz. Mark Nicholson is the V. P. from Atlanta. He's here a lot because he's on the loan committee, too. He wears a double-breasted on board day." Doc chuckled. "He wants them to take him seriously. I think he has an eye on the CEO's spot when he retires. That's it for the suits. The others you know."

Claire made notes while Doc recited. "What about Lacey? And Graham? I thought he was the branch manager?"

"Lacey's on the loan committee but not the board. Since y'all meet

ANE MULLIGAN

every day, Ollie asked her to relay the offer. And yes, Graham is the manager, but he doesn't sit on the board, either."

So, did that make her Graham's boss? She sure didn't understand banking hierarchy. One loud rap resounded on the door before she could consider any more questions. Doc rose and opened it.

The "suits" marched in one after the other. Each wore a dark pinstriped suit—designer she bet—the prerequisite monogrammed white shirts, blue-and-gold-striped silk ties, and carried brown leather briefcases. All they needed were top hats and a key in their backs to look like mechanical wind-up dolls—or penguins.

Doc caught her eye and winked. A fit of giggles threatened to erupt, forcing her to look away, suck in her lips, and bite down. The "trio of suits" sat at one end of the table. A moment later, Barbara Roche, the mortgage officer entered, followed by Wendy. She was the board's non-voting secretary, according to Doc. They found their placards on the side of the CEO, and Wendy took over the door duty in between getting coffee for everyone.

Claire sipped on hers, fascinated by the Atlanta trio. These men were the banking world's stars. She'd seen their type in the gallery. They had to be sure what they owned was original, and that no other copies were owned by anyone, anywhere. One Hollywood producer she remembered insisted on seeing the other items she'd made, to check for similarities. He finally bought a vase, after asking her to destroy the other two. He paid for them, quite generously, so she did. While he watched.

Did these three have any inkling what made Chapel Springs the close-knit village it was? How the villagers thought? How they did business? She shifted in her seat. This could be interesting after all, and she was beginning to get a sense of her position on the board. She was known for speaking her mind, and no suit would intimidate her. She sat straighter.

Another knock brought Wendy to her feet. "That will be Seth. We can start now." She opened the door.

"Sorry to be late. An emergency hospital visit." Seth slid into his seat and nodded to the CEO. Wendy returned to hers and set her laptop on the table. She opened it, positioning her fingers on the keyboard.

The CEO folded his hands over his pile of papers. "Before we begin, Seth, please introduce the newest board member, and Wendy, get Ms. Bennett a board policy and procedures book." He gave Claire a well-

153

rehearsed corporate smile. "It has all the bank's policies and procedures you'll need to know."

Seth nodded toward her. "Claire Bennett is a local business owner and renowned pottery artist. She represents the heart of Chapel Springs and a number of our entrepreneurs, especially the women. She's known for her honesty ... and for speaking her mind. I'm pleased to welcome her to the board."

That was laying it on a bit thick. As for speaking her mind, more often than not that included sticking her foot in her mouth. Her smile felt weak at the light smattering of applause, but the urge to roll her eyes was so strong a headache started from her restraint. Thankfully, the CEO asked Wendy to read the minutes of the last meeting.

While listening to Wendy drone took the spotlight off Claire, it added more strain on her head as she tried to take in the foreign language of finance. Now her eyes wanted to cross. Were all the meetings going to be like this?

When she finished reading the minutes, Wendy moved to a side table, pulled out a notebook, and gave it to Claire. The thing was a good two inches thick and had to weigh five pounds. The others had theirs open to the second section, so she flipped hers to that divider, but she couldn't understand the legalese—or was that financialese? Her knee began to ache, and she moved it around under the table, searching for a more comfortable position.

Thirty completely confusing minutes later, the CEO—she couldn't begin to remember his name—asked for new business. Ollie Katz shuffled some papers in the stack in front of him.

"At the last council meeting, a new proposal was passed for restricted vehicular usage in town."

Was that what they did? Coming from Ollie, it sounded like a dumb thing to do. But then, he was a real pessimist.

"Why should we want to restrict driving in town?" The CEO shook his head. "That could affect banking."

Claire glared at Ollie. "It isn't quite like that. Local residents will be issued permits to drive anywhere in town. It's the visitors we want to restrict. They cruise up and down Sandy Shores Drive, causing so much congestion *we're* losing depositors." She mentally high-fived herself for that last brilliant tidbit.

"What?" The CFO scowled. "Why haven't I heard about this? Why are we losing them?"

Why did he think? "Because they're moving away. What we proposed is a tram to drive the tourists all over town, including to the bank, grocery store, library, and well, everywhere. The town's small enough so the tram can make a circuit every fifteen minutes."

He leaned to the side in his chair and tapped the arm of the suit on his left. "That's a good idea. I noticed the excess of traffic. It made me late to our last meeting, and it doesn't seem to have diminished any, today."

Doc winked at her. Maybe she did have a spot on this board. But Doc could have presented the voice of reason. So why was hers different? She still couldn't figure that out.

"Will the town finance this venture?" The CFO asked.

Doc nodded. After explaining the details, he said, "Felix wanted to propose a bond initiative, but it's only a quarter-million that's needed for the first tram and surfacing the lot. We may look into a second tram after a few months. Joel Bennett, Claire's husband, ran the numbers and shows a profit after two years."

The suits eyed her with new appreciation. They went on to discuss some new ideas for increasing deposits and offering junk for opening new accounts. The department heads gave reports, and Claire was soon struggling to keep her eyes open. They droned on for another hour.

"All those in favor, say aye."

What? In favor of what? She cast a panicked glance at Doc. He nodded slightly, so she "ayed" with the rest. What had she just agreed to? Doc scribbled a note and slid it to her. Oh. The vote was to end the meeting.

Everyone rose and began to chat as they gathered up their papers and briefcases. The suits glanced at her, smiled and nodded, but didn't come to chat.

"I must be the chopped meat at this banquet."

Seth picked up her notebook and handed it to her. "Don't pay them any mind. They're a breed unto themselves. I'm glad you accepted the seat, Claire."

"I'm just praying I don't embarrass y'all. I guess I should thank you for putting in my name, but—"

Seth laughed as they exited the boardroom. He waved goodbye when she stopped to make the gallery's deposit.

"Claire?" Lacey appeared at her elbow. Her eyes darted to each side and her brow furrowed. "When you finish, can I talk to you for a minute?"

"Sure."

"Come to my office when you're done."

Claire accepted the deposit slip from the teller and stuffed it in her tote. "I'm done now. What's up?"

"Shh." Lacey shook her head and looked over her shoulder. "In my office," she whispered.

Claire, feeling more CSI than was comfortable, followed Lacey, whose loafers squeaked in contrast to Claire's clacking heels on the marble floor.

The minute Lacey closed her office door she handed Claire a file. "Look at this."

It was a commercial loan application. "What am I looking for?"

Lacey pointed to line number nine. "Look at the property address."

Claire stared at the paper as her heart skipped a beat. "That's the Newlander property."

"Right. And this investment group has a signed agreement with Howard B. Newlander to purchase the property."

"But they don't have a permit to build a hotel."

Lacey folded her arms and leaned one hip against the corner of her desk. "Apparently they don't think that will be a problem."

"But—" What about Granny? She was still alive and the legal owner. "Howie's bypassing his great-grandmother? Can he do that?" Claire frowned at the paper and glanced at Lacey. "Who is in this investment group? Do we know?"

Lacey raised one expressive eyebrow. "That is the sixty-four-thousand-dollar question."

An idea popped into Claire's head. "Would you share this with Nathan?"

"Why him?"

"Because if we can find a connection here and blow this wide open, he and Patsy will stay in Chapel Springs. I'm trying to slow down his apartment search in New York. To do that, I want to involve him in finding out who's in this group. I have an idea we'll discover someone very close to home."

"I'm afraid I can't do that, Claire." Lacey reached for the loan application.

Claire pulled her hand back out of reach. "Wait a minute. Ask yourself this. Why is an investment group applying for a loan? Don't they usually finance their own ventures? They invest their own money, not borrow it. Something isn't right about this, Lacey."

Lacey pulled on her nose, then turned her back. "I always keep a second copy of loan apps, in case one is lost," she said over her shoulder as she exited her office.

Left alone with a smile and a prayer for forgiveness, Claire slipped the folder into her tote and sauntered out of the bank. On the sidewalk, she stopped, fished out her cell phone and dialed Nathan. "Are you in your home office?"

"Good afternoon to you, too, Claire."

"Sorry, but this is really important. Are you home?"

"Yes, why?"

"I need to talk to you in private. I'll be there in a few minutes."

"I'll be waiting."

Claire swiped her phone off and swung along as quickly as her knee allowed. Fourteen minutes later, she stood in Nathan's home office, huffing and puffing.

"I feel like the big bad wolf." She handed him the paperwork and paced the Oriental rug as she caught her breath.

He perused the application, glancing up at her a couple of times. "Are you sure about all this, Claire?"

"Yes." She explained what Granny said about still owning the land. "Maybe she's senile ... I don't know. She appears sharp as a tack. I mean, she remembered me and all, but she did and said some odd things, like claiming she's lopped off Howie's head. What could she have meant? Was it senility talking?"

"I don't know, but none of that is as strange as why this group is applying for a loan."

"Exactly what I said to Lacey." Claire put her hand on his arm. "If we can find out something illegal or at least unethical and expose it, you and Patsy won't have to move."

Nathan lowered the papers. "I got an offer from a firm in the city, Claire. I'm considering it." He held up his hand to stop her protest. "If this proves to be what you think, and you figure out a solution to the congestion, I won't take it. We'll stay here. Now, is this a copy I can keep? And don't tell me how you got it. I don't want to know."

She left the papers with him and made her way home. A snail sped past her on the sidewalk, as she used the time to think. She suspected skullduggery was afoot, and the trail pointed to the Riley brothers. If

Felix was part of this group, and she was positive he was, considering how hard he'd pushed for the hotel, granting the permit would be a conflict of interest.

If Nathan could expose it, she would blow it wide open. She'd finally gain some respect, and all would be well in Chapel Springs again. Then all she had left to worry about was her son and his bride. The yogurt she ate at noon curdled with that thought.

Chapter 22

Lydia zipped her jacket against the early morning chill. The sun hadn't broken over the mountains and in the predawn light, painted the sky deep purple to dusky rose on the horizon. She drank in its beauty as she walked down the hill toward town to check the day's appointments and go over the supply inventory before she met her friends at *Dee's 'n' Doughs*. Kenny had taken on the task of inventory control, and until she was sure he had a good idea of the client to product ratio, she planned to keep an eye on him. And on Morgan. After all, she was still learning the business and could easily overlook something.

At the corner of Hill and Park, the fall colors on the trees drew her to cut through the woods to the spa's rear entrance. It was light enough now, and she loved the crunch of leaves underfoot and the smell of pine in the air. The North Georgia Mountains were a blend of evergreens and deciduous trees, turning the forest into an artist's palette with varying shades of orange, red, gold, and green with browns as the frame. Claire and Patsy could probably name all the different shades of green.

Lydia inhaled the heady earthiness of it before she emerged from the trees and onto the spa's rear parking area. Pushing up her sleeve, she glanced at her watch. Six-forty-five. That was a speedy stroll through the woods. She unlocked the door and flipped on the lights. Hannah should arrive at seven. Morgan, if Lydia knew her daughter at all, would already be in her office.

In the reception area, she turned on the lights for Hannah, glad she had trusted her instinct and hired her permanently at the end of her first two weeks. She still had to serve out her six-week contract period with the temp agency, but Lydia already gave her a key.

Instead of going upstairs to see Morgan, Lydia opened the supply cabinet and studied its contents, pleased with what she saw. Not too much but enough to cover four days. She had told Kenny their supplier could get them anything within three days. He used his head.

She moved to the linen closet, which was actually a small room and contained towel supplies for three days. The linen turnaround was two days, so they didn't need three days' worth. They had a washer and dryer in case they ran out. She pulled out her cell phone and sent Morgan a text message. She could pass that along to Kenny.

Finished at the spa for now, Lydia walked to the bakery. Its cheery light spilled through the window and onto the street, drawing her in, and if that hadn't, the warmth of friendship inside would. Spying her friends, Lydia waved then poured her second cup of coffee for the day and selected a small raspberry Danish resisting the sugary frosting of Dee's large ooey gooey cinnamon buns.

"What's new in the blushing bride's life?" Claire asked, scooting her chair over as Lydia joined them.

"Kenny started school and he's working for me part-time."

Patsy handed Claire a napkin, pointing to her cheek. "He's industrious."

"He's that for sure. Every once in a while, I remember what Joel said and wonder if it's real, but Kenny hasn't done anything to make me think otherwise."

Claire wiped her cheek and glanced at the napkin. "Joel's used to high school kids working for him. Most don't have the greatest work ethic yet." She spread a thin layer of cream cheese on the second half of her bagel.

Lydia pushed her Danish away. It had lost its appeal. "My main concern right now is the hotel." She twisted her napkin. "They'd be stupid not to have their own spa, and I'm sure stupidity isn't a job requirement for hotel management."

"You're not alone, Lydia." Claire laid her knife down on a napkin. "A lot of us are scared. There aren't many whose businesses wouldn't be hurt. The only ones pushing for this are the Rileys and Warren."

Lydia pulled a new napkin from the holder. The other one lay in shreds. "Can we petition to stop the building permit?" A hotel spa would have unlimited funds. Her stomach churned as she visualized a for sale sign in front of her spa—and no buyers.

"I'm not sure," Patsy said. "There's an even split on that committee."

She moved the salt and pepper shakers in line with the napkin holder. "If only we could stop the sale of the land." She looked at Claire. "Have you found Howie?"

Claire shook her head. "I can't even find a phone number for him. I asked Granny, but her answer was lost in dementia, I'm afraid. She said she lopped off his head."

Lydia startled and coffee sloshed over the top of her cup. "She said what?" That didn't sound normal, even for someone with dementia.

"She'd been cutting the blooms off each flower in the garden when I went to see her. I think she mixed Howie up with the geraniums."

Lydia had to ask. "You don't suppose the dementia's an act and she actually murdered Howie do you?"

"No way." Claire held up her hand and ticked off her fingers. "First of all, she's been in assisted living for the past ten years. And secondly, she's a tiny little thing. Not growing up here, you wouldn't know, but Howie was a fullback on the football team."

Oh. Still ... "Those little old ladies are the ones who wind up poisoning people. When was the last time anyone heard from this Howie?" Lydia knew she was grasping at straws, but if she lost the spa, she'd lose everything she had. She wouldn't have anything of her *own*.

Claire shook her head. "Lydia, that's ridiculous. Besides, the Muldoon group has been in touch with Howie, isn't that right, Lacey?"

Lydia glanced at her sister. Did Lacey know something she hadn't told her?

Lacey nodded.

"When was that?" Lydia searched her sister's eyes.

Lacey returned her stare. "I'm not allowed to say."

Claire thunked her coffee mug on the table. "Well, I am. This group has made an offer to Howie. They haven't had any trouble finding him."

Patsy frowned. "How do you know that?"

Lydia leaned forward. That's exactly what she wanted—*needed*—to know. She took a deep breath to stop her hands from shaking.

"Don't ask," Claire said, glancing at Lacey. "But it kills your murder theory. Unfortunately. Not that I wish Howie any ill, but that would have made our life easier."

"Not necessarily."

Unused to her sister speaking, they all turned their heads to Lacey. She glanced between them then shrugged. "There are other heirs."

"Who?" Lydia hadn't heard of any. Of course, she didn't know the

Newlander's family history, being the "newcomer" in Chapel Springs.

Claire counted off on her fingers. "One sister, three cousins, and a couple of nieces and nephews. And, of course, Granny."

Lydia's spirits fell. What would she do? Graham made a good living, but he didn't have much savings. He admitted to helping his kids more than he probably should, especially his daughter, whose husband hadn't worked in a year and wasn't even looking. Graham really needed to tell them no next time they asked for a handout. His excuse was his grandbaby. She understood his desire to help, but it wasn't like they were unable to work.

Lacey shoved back her chair, pulling Lydia from her thoughts. "Can you keep us alerted to any progress?" *Please?*

Lacey shook her head. "I've already done more than I should." She gave Lydia a sad little smile and left.

Glancing between Claire and Patsy, Lydia shared their despair. If Nathan moved to New York City, she'd lose her CPA, too. "Claire, you've got to help us."

"I'm trying. Your sister left me alone with some papers. God forgive me, I took them and gave them to, uh … someone. They're looking into the investment group. But that's all I can say."

Lydia sighed. "I guess we'll have to leave this in God's hands, then." She pushed her chair back. "I need to go, too. See y'all tomorrow."

Her walk back to the spa lacked the buoyancy she felt earlier. She tried to have faith, but a black cloud of fear hovered over her. She'd been so sure the spa was God's answer to her financial stability, but now it seemed like he was about to yank it out from under her. Where would she land? Without its income … poor Graham. He married a woman on the brink of bankruptcy. And he didn't have the savings to bale her out.

Lydia timed the roast to come out of the oven when Graham got home. It needed to sit for twenty minutes before carving and that gave him time to change and relax. She checked the timer. Ten minutes left. Enough time to put the vegetables on and make a salad. She opened the refrigerator door and her cell phone rang. She pulled out the lettuce and snatched her phone off the counter. Graham's name popped up in the caller I.D. window.

She smiled. "Hey, sugah."

"Kenny called me, babe. His car's broken down. I've got to go to Pineridge and get him."

There went the roast and all her preparation. It wasn't Graham's fault, though. She sighed and swallowed her annoyance. "Okay. I'll hold supper."

Turning off the burner beneath the peas, she slid the pan to a cool spot on the stove's surface and returned the lettuce to the fridge. On second thought, she'd skipped lunch and was hungry. A salad would tide her over. She dug out the salad fixings from the fridge.

Two hours later, her bedraggled and hungry husband and stepson walked through the front door. She greeted Graham with a kiss. "Your dinner's ready whenever you are, sweetheart."

He ran his hand over his five o'clock shadow. "If you can stand the way I look, Kenny and I are both starved."

As long as they were home safe and sound, she was happy. After setting their plates on the table, she sat to join them.

Graham frowned at her empty placemat. "You're not eating?"

"I ate earlier." She waited until they wolfed down a few bites. "How's the car?"

"The transmission's gone. It's time for a new car."

Years ago, when her car's tranny went out, Sam had it replaced. "Why not just get a new transmission?"

Graham reached for the peppershaker. "It's not a sound financial decision. The car isn't worth the investment."

"Oh."

Kenny averted his eyes and shoveled meat into his mouth.

"So what's the next step?" she asked.

"I'll co-sign a loan for him in the morning." Graham picked up his water glass. "He can use my car until we get the new one. That is if you don't mind loaning me yours." He downed half the water in one gulp.

Lydia didn't know what to say. If she said she needed her car, she'd sound selfish. Maybe it would only be for a day or so. "Kenny, will you shop for groceries if I give you a list?"

"Sure, no problem."

Graham's pleasure beamed on her. "Thanks, babe." The peas rolled off his fork.

She laughed when he chased one across the table and Kenny scooped it up first. "So what kind of car are you going to look for?"

Kenny deposited the pea on the side of his plate, glancing at his dad. "Well, I know what I'd like, but I guess I need to be practical for now."

"What would you like, son?"

Kenny could have posed for a dental ad. His orthodontist had done a good job, but the tiny gap between his eyetooth and the next one was enough for a sliver of meat to wedge in.

"A Beemer." He held up his hand against his dad's protest. "I know, not practical, too expensive, and all that. But you asked what I'd like." His smile turned boyish. "I'll settle for an SUV, maybe a Jeep. I like Mrs. Bennett's."

Lydia frowned. That wasn't much of a settle in her way of thinking. What would Graham say to that? While he chewed one bite, he cut another piece of meat and speared it with his fork.

"Well, if that's what will make you happy, son, then a new Jeep Cherokee is what we'll get."

Make *him* happy? What about what he could afford? She paid Kenny's wages, and he didn't make enough to cover that. Her house and car were paid for, thank goodness. She and Graham didn't have any loans, and he made a good salary as the bank manager, but they needed to save for retirement and—she had to speak her mind.

"With Kenny in school, wouldn't buying something used be a smarter choice?"

A cloud darkened Kenny's expression then cleared as quickly as it appeared, making her wonder if she'd imagined it. Graham harrumphed.

"Not sound. You inherit someone else's problems. There's a reason they traded it in. Like Kenny's car. Some used lot will throw in a rebuilt tranny and sell it to an unsuspecting chump."

"Do they really do that?"

Kenny nodded. "Yeah, they do. If they can make a dollar, they'll hide all kinds of things."

"But I thought they had that car facts thing that tells you the vehicle's history."

Graham patted her hand. "I've just always been more comfortable with a new vehicle. Probably because I'm a banker instead of a mechanic."

Well, that made sense, still ... she nibbled her lip. "What about the money a car loses the minute you drive it off the lot? Wouldn't a low-mileage pre-owned car be smarter? With the economy, a lot of people have had to sell."

Graham considered it for a moment. "You know, I hadn't thought about that. If we can find one with low enough mileage."

Kenny's gaze went back and forth between them. "But why would someone have turned in a car with low mileage?"

Lydia had the advantage now. "If they've been laid off they can't afford the payments any longer. Or it could be an older person whose spouse died or lost their driver's license. A teenager, who had theirs taken away. That happened to a client of mine. Her daughter got caught driving under the influence and they sold her car."

Kenny stuck his lips out, then quirked his mouth to one side, and after a moment nodded. "I'll look around."

She got up and took their plates to the sink. At least she had them thinking a bit more conservatively. They needed to be careful. If that hotel got built and she lost the spa, her stepson would be out of a job, too. She didn't like how quick Graham was to dole out money to Kenny.

Chapter 23

Joel sat across from Claire in the kitchen as they lingered over their coffee. She swapped Saturdays with Patsy so she could stay home today. Costly—oops. Costy. She had to stop thinking "costly" or she'd say it out loud.

Costy was due to arrive this afternoon. Claire's stomach twisted and she pushed her cup away.

Joel turned down the corner of the sports section and studied her over its top. "Something wrong?" Shiloh stretched out on the floor, and taking up a good chunk of kitchen real estate, snored loudly.

She wrinkled her nose. "I'm just nervous about meeting Costy."

"Are you still wanting us all to go to the airport? Don't you think Wes should go alone? After all, it's been more than a month since he's seen his wife."

Wife. She hated that word when it was associated with her youngest child. She waved his objection away. "If it were me, I'd want to feel welcomed. Wes can meet her right outside customs. We'll wait at baggage claim."

"Can he actually meet her there?"

"I don't know. Why wouldn't he?"

"Security." He flipped up the corner of his paper and went back to reading.

To be honest, Claire wasn't sure how she felt about going. Curious. Anxious to meet this girl—woman. On the other hand, if she had her druthers, this wouldn't be happening.

The front door opened. "Mom? Dad?"

"In here," she called.

Wes, handsome in jeans and a short-sleeved blue shirt, sauntered into the kitchen, bent and kissed her cheek. Shiloh's tail thumped hard against the floor, so he greeted him next, then poured a cup of coffee, and slid onto the banquette bench. Her son wore a new aftershave—one she didn't recognize.

Claire sniffed again, trying to place it. "What aftershave are you wearing?"

"You like it?" He grinned at her. "Costy bought it for me."

No wonder she didn't like it. Her nose twitched. "It's ... different." Joel gave her the evil eye. "Uh, what time does she arrive?"

"She just landed in Miami. Her next flight will take off in ninety minutes. We need to get moving." He took the lid off the sugar bowl and lifted out a heaping spoonful, then stirred it into his cup. "Thanks for the help getting the apartment ready, Ma."

"I didn't do that much, other than advise."

"That's what I needed. I don't have any idea of style. I'm like Pop."

Joel peeked over his paper and scowled. Claire snickered. His sense of style was embodied in a mounted fish. *High* style was one that moved and sang when anyone got near it. As if reading her thoughts, Joel cocked an eyebrow then disappeared once more.

"So, are you ready?" She pushed a plate of bagels and a container of cream cheese to Wes.

"Yeah. It still doesn't feel real. I guess it won't for a while."

Boy howdy, he wasn't alone. "I suppose not. I certainly can't believe it yet." That was an understatement if there ever was one.

Wes's mouth turned down. "I'm sorry, Ma, but I'm hoping—no, I *know* you'll love Costy. She's fun-loving, caring, sweet, intelligent, beautiful, and ..." he put his hand on his chest and lifted his chin in a dramatic gesture. "She loves me."

Claire laughed at his theatrics despite her doubts. Still, she'd made a vow to try. "Well then, I'm sure I will. What time are we leaving for the airport?"

"In ten minutes. Better get a move on." He looked her up and down, his forehead creased.

She surveyed her old jeans and comfy flannel shirt. "Is there something wrong with the way I'm dressed?"

"I guess not, but I've told Costy a lot about you, how artistic you are. I was thinking one of your long skirts would match the image I gave her."

When had Wes become a fashionista? For that matter, when had he become a snob? He never used to think she was underdressed. She didn't want to change, but he looked so hopeful.

"All right, but I hope your bride doesn't judge people by their clothing."

To his credit, Wes's ears turned red.

Twelve minutes later, she was redressed and they headed out. The airport was a good three-hour drive if they hit any traffic, and in Atlanta, traffic was inevitable. From the backseat, she leaned forward and tapped her finger on Wes's shoulder. "Why didn't you have her get a connecting flight to Charlotte? That way, it would only be a ninety-minute drive."

Wes caught her eye in the rearview mirror. "I didn't want her to try to navigate Hartsfield alone. And ... and her English is very basic."

She'd been right. The girl was going to be needy. "How basic?"

"Oh ... pretty much non-existent. She's been taking classes though."

At least Claire would be able to impress her with her Spanish. She had kept that a secret, hoping to please Wes with her efforts. Joel winked at her from the passenger seat. She sat back and watched the scenery pass by.

Traffic was brutal even though it was Saturday. "Is there a game on or something, Joel?"

"I think it's people leaving town for the holiday."

"Van Gogh's ear, I'd forgotten next week's Thanksgiving."

Wes cast his dad a quick look. "We're having all the traditional stuff aren't we? I've told Costy about it."

"Sure," Joel said. "Why would we change now?"

Claire would like to implement one change right now. She'd like to refuse entry to this cradle robber.

You made a promise to pray for her.

Claire rolled her eyes then whispered, "All right."

Wes caught her eye in the rearview mirror. "Whose house is it this year?"

"Ours. Patsy offered to do it again because of my accident, but my knee's fine. Besides, my part isn't that big. I've done most of the shopping." Although, with her mind so preoccupied with everything else, she could have goofed and gotten moose or maybe a goose instead of a turkey. Except they had goose at Christmas, which was right around the corner. Thinking of all she had to do scrambled her brains. She laid her head back and closed her eyes. Soon, Wes and Joel's voices became a receding hum.

"Claire, we're here, honey." Joel's voice pulled her from a dream where she'd been dipping leaves in gold and hawking them on the street—probably triggered by the new necklace Melissa showed her. She wanted to look into the art form, maybe make some herself. Funny, what sparked dreams.

Wes was already out of the car and jogging toward the terminal. She shook the cobwebs out of her head as Joel helped her from the car. They took a slower path toward the parking lot's exit to the terminal.

"I told Wes we'd meet him at baggage claim. He's over by the escalator so she'll see him as she comes up from the tram."

"What about going through customs?"

"She did that in Miami."

Taking care to avoid any oil spots, she trailed along beside him. "Oh. I'm pretty nervous about meeting her, Joel. What if I can't like her?"

"Honey, I can't imagine you not liking someone. You like everyone. For that matter, everyone loves you."

She blinked, the sunshine blinding her after the dark subterranean parking facility. "I don't like Dale Riley. And I'm not too fond of his brother."

The signal changed and they started across the street.

"Baloney. I'm convinced that you and Felix enjoy sniping at each other."

"What have you been smoking?" Claire's right foot hit the lip of a small pothole, throwing her toward the ground and twisting her knee. "Yeowch!"

Joel caught her before she hit the pavement, and traffic came to a halt. A policeman started for them but stopped when a rude driver blasted his horn.

"Is she all right?" the cop asked, after glaring at the limo driver.

"I think so. Honey?"

The sharp pain receded, leaving a dull ache. "I'm okay. My bad knee twisted. Let's get out of the street." She was afraid the smile she aimed at the policeman came off as a grimace. He tipped his hat and waited for them to finish crossing, then he motioned the traffic to move on.

As they approached the curb, Joel stopped. Claire raised her eyes from the pavement. Standing on the sidewalk beside two large suitcases, were Wes and his bride.

Who looked down her patrician nose at Claire.

Whose mouth twisted in a smirk.

Oh, great. She must have seen her new mother-in-law make a spectacle of herself in the middle of the street. Heat rose in Claire's cheeks. She wanted the pavement to open up and swallow her, but she pulled up a smile from somewhere.

"Costy, wel—"

"Costancia."

What? Claire stared at the cold eyes boring into hers. She blinked. Where was the sweet girl Wes told her about? She glanced at her son. His brows made a slight dip then he smiled and mouthed "nervous." Nervous huh? Well, so was she, but she wasn't an iceberg. For her son's sake, she tried again, searching her mind for the Spanish phrase for welcome.

"Ben-vee-need-o uh Georgia ee noo-es-truh family-ah."

Wes's eyes bugged and his jaw dropped, but his wife laughed. Out loud. Claire knew laughter and this was not a laughing-with-anyone type. Maybe if she understood that Claire took the classes just for her sake ... She tried again.

"Apre-hend-ee ez-pan-yol tan yo poh-dree-uh hah-blar cone uze-ted."

Costancia frowned. "*Español?*" She laughed again. "*Não falo espanhol. Em Brasil falamos português.*"

Huh? Claire glanced at Wes. He'd finally recovered and was grinning. To his bride, he blathered off some words Claire couldn't understand. Now she knew what he'd been doing all those months of sitting at his computer.

"Ma, Costy speaks Portuguese, not Spanish."

Claire blinked again, hoping that would help clear up this fiasco. She bit back the retort she wanted to make and forced a smile. "Well, I guess the joke's on me."

Her throat felt thick and the back of her eyes stung. She turned and started back across the street, trying to watch for potholes, but the pavement blurred. Joel's hand on her upper arm gave her the strength to keep moving.

"That was unbelievably rude," he whispered through clenched teeth.

What? "I was rude?"

"No, babe. Not you. Costy. I'm going to put it down to nerves and try to forget it."

Claire sniffled. "That's probably a good idea. I remember I was immobilized meeting your dad for the first time."

"But you weren't rude."

"No. But that's my Southern upbringing. Maybe they're different in Brazil."

"Somehow, I don't think so. Manners are manners, no matter where you live. I'm trying to see the girl Wes fell in love with. This was not a good first impression."

"It's going to take time. She made it pretty clear I wasn't to call her Costy, though."

Wes and *Costancia* caught up with them so Claire couldn't say anything else. Not that she wanted to. Okay, not true, she did, but she wouldn't say what she'd like to. And why, for the love of Van Gogh, had her new daughter-in-law taken a dislike to her?

Joel helped Wes get the suitcases in the back, assisted Claire to get settled in the backseat, and slipped in beside her. Costancia chattered and giggled with Wes in the front and didn't give a glance at the backseat. Claire had been around some arrogant people before, but never one who radiated icicles. Or such strong disdain.

After they'd been driving for about an hour, she caught Costancia peeking sidelong at her, a sneer marring her pretty mouth. Did Wes see it? It disappeared instantly when he glanced toward her. Claire didn't know what to make of it, but it was going to be a long ride home.

Joel fell asleep, his head back and his mouth open, snoring. Costancia turned around and stared at him, an indulgent smile on her face this time. Her gaze swept past Claire as if she weren't in the car. She jabbered to Wes, who laughed.

Claire caught the word "papa."

"She said Dad reminds her of her father."

Well, wasn't that sweet. Claire opened her mouth then shut it again and simply smiled at Wes through the rearview mirror. He pointed to their apartment building as they drove through Pineridge, and Costancia twisted in her seat to look at it. When they finally entered Chapel Springs, she again looked around with interest. At least the town garnered some approval.

Wes pulled into the driveway. Claire was never so glad to see home. How was she going to love this girl? At that moment, it looked like a Mount Everest impossibility.

Joel woke up with a snort, sending Costancia into giggles. The laugh-with kind. Wes said something to her and she got out of the car.

Once Joel helped Claire out, he turned to Wes.

"I'm sure you kids want to get on to your apartment, so we'll see you tomorrow."

Costancia stepped up to him, stood on her tiptoes, and kissed his cheek. Joel looked uncomfortable. Maybe she was regretting her attitude. Ready to forgive, Claire moved forward. Her daughter-in-law turned her back and climbed into the car. Wes waved a hand and joined her.

That did *not* just happen. When they backed out of the driveway, Claire didn't move. Why did her son ignore the snub, and what did this girl have against her? Examining her own behavior, she couldn't find any fault. Okay, she got Costancia's language wrong, but was that reason enough for scorn?

Scorn nothing. That was a declaration of war.

Chapter 24

"I tell you, Patsy, the girl hates me, and I have no idea why." Claire kept her voice low. Their husbands flanked them on the pew, and she didn't want them or anyone else to hear. With the musical prelude, people getting settled and greeting others, she was safe enough.

"Sure you aren't overreacting?" Patsy whispered behind her bulletin.

Claire shook her head and relayed every detail. "Even Joel noticed it. I doubt Wes did, his eyes were too filled with stars."

Patsy stared at her. "That's awful! I can't believe she was so rude."

Her words cascaded over Claire like a soothing balm. She'd been afraid of getting a lecture about loving her daughter-in-law. That girl was not loveable. No way, no how. And Patsy agreed. Okay, maybe not agreed, but at least she didn't think Claire was nuts.

She leaned forward slightly so she could see her son on the other side of Joel. Wes had his arm around Costancia, and she looked a bit lost. Unsure of herself. Her son, however, wore the contented look of a man in love and pleased with himself, complete.

Claire sighed deeply. She promised to love this girl. How could she do that when Costancia hated her?

Love her.

Claire rolled her eyes heavenward. Yeah, yeah, okay, she'd try. But it would take more than her strength to accomplish it.

Then let Me love her through you.

She lifted her bulletin and whispered to Patsy, "It could have just been nerves and jetlag. I'm going to give her the benefit of the doubt." She sighed at Patsy's raised brows. "Oh, quit looking at me like that. I haven't lost all my marbles. Just a few."

Patsy snickered, earning her a scowl from Nathan. She sucked in her lips and stared straight ahead. Claire received an elbow tap in the ribs from Joel. The service was starting.

An hour later, they stood outside the church as Wes introduced his wife to Pastor Seth and JoAnn. Claire focused her attention on Costancia's reaction to JoAnn. Maybe she disliked women in general. But no, her daughter-in-law's body language was open and even her eyes smiled at JoAnn. Claire's spirits sank.

"Ma?" Wes tapped her shoulder. "If you don't mind, we're going home. Costy's still jetlagged."

Claire patted his hand and smiled. For his sake, she'd do what she had to. "I understand, dear. Tell her I hope she feels better soon."

"Do me a favor?"

"Sure, what?" As soon as the words popped out, Claire regretted them. Things had changed. He was no longer just her son. He was now somebody's husband, and his words took on different meaning.

"Take her with you when you go to Henderson's tomorrow. I don't have some of the things she wants to cook."

She glanced at the clouds floating in lazy streams across the sky. *Thanks a lot.* "Are you sure she wants to go with me?"

Wes's forehead puckered. "What do you mean? Of course she does."

Oh, was he in a lover's fog. "All right. I'll pick her up around one."

And she'd bring reinforcements. It hadn't gone unnoticed that the twins got in the car with Costancia and Wes. Apparently, she could abide them, and Claire was happy about it. She *was*. She didn't want discord in her family. If she took Megan with them tomorrow, her happy chatter would help cover things.

It was a good thing the twins had learned some Portuguese. Too bad none of them told her about it. Or mentioned Costancia. Or Wes's marriage.

Well, what was done was done. So, would Costancia take it wrong if Claire bought her one of those computer lessons to learn English? Probably. But if Wes or the twins gave it to her...

Claire tested her knee's strength as Vince and Doc watched. "It feels okay. I was afraid I'd reinjured it when I twisted it at the airport the other day."

"You still need to be easy with it, Claire. Walk carefully, okay? And no treadmills for a while."

She stuck her tongue out at him.

"He's right, girlie," Doc said. "Just because he's family—"

"Oh, I'm listening, Doc. But Vince doesn't have a woman in his life right now, so it's up to me to give him a hard time." She winked at Doc and grabbed her tote from the examining room floor. "Now, I've got to get going. I'm taking my newest daughter-in-law grocery shopping."

Doc gave her a hug and went to see another patient. Vince leaned against the wall and folded his arms. "How's that going, Claire?"

She reached for a Kleenex from a box next to the Dixie cup dispenser. "Honestly? Not well." She blew her nose.

"Joel told me about what happened at the airport."

"Well, I'm hoping it was jetlag and nerves."

Her brother-in-law didn't say anything for a moment. She wadded the tissue and tossed it into the wastebasket.

"You're a good woman, Claire. Too bad there isn't another one of you out there."

She placed her hand on his shoulder. "Oh, honey, you'll find someone. And you wouldn't want the aggravation of another me."

She hugged him goodbye and left him laughing, exactly what she wanted. She adored her husband's younger brother. She sent up a quick prayer for God to send him someone to love.

Claire's decision to take Megan with them to Henderson's was a good one. The girls chattered in a mixture of Portuguese and Pidgin English. When she tried to speak to Costancia, she stared at Claire with a blank expression on her face. Megan had the same Southern accent she did, so why could Wes's wife understand her sister-in-law and not her?

Alone in the front seat and feeling a bit like a chauffeur, Claire glanced in the rearview mirror at the girls. A pair of dark brown eyes stared boldly back at her. She smiled, but Costancia looked away.

Was it some form of rebellion that made Wes marry a girl from a foreign country? Claire didn't understand any of it. Her eldest son chose a girl she loved and welcomed to the family. She was as close to Sandi as her own daughters. If Wes had listened to her, she wouldn't be in this predicament.

Costancia's eyes widened as they pulled into the parking lot at Henderson's. She said something to Megan. Claire waited for her daughter to translate.

"She said it's a lot bigger than any market she's ever seen. They shop in an outdoor market in her village."

What if her father was the Brazilian Juan Valdez and trying to get his beans into America? Maybe they'd researched to find some young gullible kid. If so, could she have truly lured Wes into marrying her? Still, Wes *said* he'd prayed. Claire groaned.

"Momma? You all right?"

"What? Oh, I'm fine, Meg." Claire pulled up a bright smile. "Let's go shopping, girls."

Depending on which direction you faced, the air inside Henderson's Market carried scents of fresh sweet fruits, earthy vegetables, and pungent meats cooking at the food bar. Costancia's eyes remained wide as she took it in.

Claire panned the store for any of the managers who'd been present the night she set their second-floor cooking school on fire. She didn't see any. This was her first foray back into the store since then. However, by the time they saw her that night, she'd been covered in Halon foam, so maybe no one would recognize her.

After testing the wheels, she chose a grocery cart. "Ask Costancia if she'd like to try something to eat here."

Megan babbled and pointed to the various kiosks where chefs chopped and cooked. Costancia nodded a wordless consent and pointed to the seafood station.

Claire pushed her cart toward the vegetables. "Tell her we'll do the produce and non-perishables first, eat, then finish our shopping. And don't you *dare* tell her about the fire."

"I wouldn't do that to you, Momma." Megan grabbed a buggy for Costancia, and they followed.

Claire carefully chose the tomatoes, celery, and the other produce Joel had put on her list. She kept close watch on her daughter-in-law as she selected some things. Should she tell her Wes didn't like leeks? No, Costancia would think she was interfering. Besides, Wes might change his mind if she was a good cook.

Claire stopped at the sweet potatoes. Thinking about how Joel made them pureed with orange zest and served inside orange halves, her mouth watered. She licked her lips. Costancia looked over the potatoes and wrinkled her nose and shook her head as Megan said something to her. What was that all about? Megan moved over to bag some Brussels sprouts.

Since Claire promised Wes she would help his wife, she selected a nice fat sweet potato and handed it to her daughter-in-law. Costancia took it, turned it over in her hand, then sniffed and tossed it back on the pile. She locked gazes with Claire, tilted her head, and raised one haughty eyebrow.

"Costy, come here, *venha cá.*"

Costancia walked away without a backwards glance. Claire picked up the sweet potato and took aim. She moved her hand back and forth a couple of times, visualizing Costancia with orange potato flesh splattered over her.

"Momma, what are you doing?" Megan laughed. "You look like you're about to throw a pass."

Her fantasy broken, Claire dropped the potato into her bag. "Guessing the weight."

"You're such a hoot. Let's get moving. I'm hungry."

Megan pushed the cart up another aisle and missed the glare Costancia sent Claire, before following her sister-in-law. Letting the girls go their own way, she said she'd meet them at the seafood kiosk in twenty minutes.

This costly little import of Wes's needed an attitude adjustment. Claire glanced at her list and threw a bag of walnuts in her cart. If only she hadn't promised Patsy she'd play nice. Pressing her lips together, she marshaled some apples into a bag. She tossed one up and down in her hand. What she'd like to do with that ... she added it to its companions. She was getting tired of trying to be nice. How many times did she have to forgive the insulting behavior?

Seventy times seven.

Oh, Lord. This is really hard. Harder than anything I've ever done.

It will be worth it, you'll see.

It had better be. Wes had better appreciate what she was subjected to for his sake.

She checked her list again. Pumpkin—she'd forgotten the pumpkin. She went back and found a good specimen. She might not be able to cook, but she'd learned to choose the best and freshest produce. When they were first married, she'd accompanied Joel when he grocery shopped. He took the time to explain what he looked for and how to tell a good melon from an unripe one. After a few months, he left her a list and she did the shopping. It helped her assuage her guilt over not knowing how to cook.

Girls nowadays didn't have that guilt, but she was from an era where the woman did the cooking. Not only did Claire not learn how, she failed home economics in school. She had zero aptitude when it came to things culinary. Thankfully, her family didn't mind, since Joel felt right at home in the kitchen. He really was the perfect husband for her. Why in the world had she ever doubted that?

Checking her heaped cart, she ticked off her list. She had everything except the turkey, dairy, and frozen items. It was time to meet the girls and eat. The thought of sitting with her daughter-in-law curdled her stomach. Clenching and unclenching her fists, she took a deep breath and prepared herself for battle. On the way to the seafood station, she practiced biting her lips ... and praying.

Megan and Costancia were already seated when Claire wheeled her cart over. She parked hers next to Costancia's and took a seat. "Have you ordered?"

Megan nodded. "I got you the blackened tilapia. I know how much you like it."

Costancia had her head down, opening her packet of plastic ware. "Thank you, sweetie. What did you and Costancia get?"

Her daughter-in-law startled at the sound of her name. Two sharp lines formed between her brows. Those would become permanent if she weren't careful. Smile lines were more becoming than grooves from frowning.

Megan said something to Costancia and her frown disappeared. Claire didn't know what her daughter said, but she got no more glares, at least as long as Megan was present.

Claire managed to enjoy her fish, letting the girls do the talking. She didn't mind being excluded from the conversation. That way she wouldn't have to mutilate her lips.

Chapter 25

With Nicole and 'Lissa covering the gallery, Claire and Patsy took advantage of the rare downtime and strolled along the boardwalk. The late afternoon sun hung low over the lake, and curls of aromatic smoke rose from large oil drums-turned-incinerators in neighboring yards. Claire took an appreciative sniff of one of her favorite scents—leaves burning in the autumn air.

"Remember how we'd jump into the piles of leaves my dad or Doc raked?"

"I still can't believe how patient they were."

They strolled in silence for a moment, the kind best friends can share without discomfort. Kelly Appling waved at them from the beach where she supervised a group of children, feeding the ducks. She should invite Kelly and Earl to join them for Thanksgiving ... next year, maybe.

"You and Nathan are joining us tomorrow, aren't you?"

Patsy kicked a small pile of leaves on the sidewalk, smiling as they scattered. "We're looking forward to it. I haven't seen Adriana since Charlie's wedding."

"She loves her life in Nashville so much she rarely comes home anymore."

"I think the four of us should plan a trip to see her and take in a show at the Grand Old Opry."

"That's hard to do. If we're slow, Nathan's in tax season." Claire gestured to the lake. "Then fishing season opens. And really the gallery is busy year round now. Yikes! We do need a vacation. And more than just an afternoon walk." She slid her hands into her pockets.

Sandy Shores Drive sparkled in the softened sunlight of the late fall afternoon. Glints reflecting off the lake bounced on the shop windows. Claire's whimsy pots—grandfather clocks at the antique store, playful bunnies ready to eat the contents of their pot at the boutique, and jumping fish and loons—stood as colorful sentinels, flanking the entrance of each store. The shopkeepers had replaced the summer flowers with mums, salvia, and pansies. Even the lampposts all along the Drive held pansies in every color. Chapel Springs was adorned in her fancy fall duds.

It was Claire's favorite time of year. Family time. Thoughts of tomorrow being wrapped in tension dampened her spirits. She shook it off as best she could. No use borrowing trouble for today.

Wearing a colorful apron as bright as the flowers, Nancy Vaughn swept the boardwalk in front of *Sunspots*. She labored at one particular crack between two boards but looked up as Claire and Patsy approached.

"Happy Thanksgiving, ladies."

"What's new?" Patsy asked.

Claire zeroed in on the crevice Nancy had been harassing, but she stopped her sweeping and leaned on the broom. "Several things." Her eyes danced merrily as she eyed Claire's frayed jeans. "I just received a shipment of hand-painted broomstick skirts you'll love. And they have coordinated tops by the same artist. They aren't unpacked yet. I'm bringing them out on Friday for the sale."

Claire forgot about the boardwalk with this bit of news. Her girls forced her out of her favorite long denim skirts. At least they approved of broomstick skirts. Sometimes, they were simply more comfortable than pants. "So, who is it?" She knew most of the state's artists.

"The designs are Chartreux's. She sent them off to a friend from school, Delaine Devore."

Claire loved to help new artists. "You can count on me being here." If the designs and artwork were as good as Nancy inferred, she'd buy a couple of them. Her kids paraded through her mind. Adriana would love one. The twins, too. Would Costancia appreciate one? That's what she could get all the girls for Christmas.

"Can I count on your help with the community theatre's spring play, too? Lacey's written a delicious murder mystery."

Nancy was the community theatre's stage manager. Claire had managed to avoid the last play by her treadmill debacle. However, there was no way she'd get out of helping this time.

"Sure, I'll help, Nancy. When do you start?" She'd have to be sure to avoid Eileen Carlson for a while. She tried to grab Claire every year to play a role but the very idea of learning lines and being on stage gave her hives.

"We'll hold the initial planning meeting right after Thanksgiving. I'll call you."

Nancy resumed her sweeping once they moved on. Just as they passed the *Gifted Gifter*, Patsy stopped suddenly and grabbed Claire's arm, pulling her tight against the storefront.

"Shh." She lifted a finger to her lips. "Listen."

Claire held her breath. Mumbled voices reached her ears. Focusing all her attention, she listened.

"... in Buckhead and Virginia Highlands. Don't forget Charlotte and Ashville."

That was Dale's voice. Who was he talking to and why were they hiding in the narrow walkway between the buildings? She glanced at Patsy, then leaned forward and peeked. Dale had his back to the street. She couldn't see the person he was talking to. She ducked into the shadows.

"Does Felix know?" A man's deep voice. This was no romantic rendezvous.

"Nope. Quit worrying about him. He trusts me."

"We have to be sure. There's a lot of money at stake."

Claire exchanged a glance with Patsy and frowned.

"And I'm telling you it's in the bag. My brother will do what I tell him."

The voices grew softer. They must have gone through the walkway to restaurant row. Claire grabbed Patsy's hand. "Come on. I want to know who that other person is."

"What do you think this is all about?"

"What else? The hotel. Dale's been yapping about this to Felix every chance he gets. He wants it and I want to know why."

Employing stealth, Claire tiptoed around the dumpster and down the alleyway with Patsy on her heels. At the end, she peeked into the parking lot of restaurant row. Not seeing Dale or his companion, Claire stepped out from between the buildings and stopped beside *The Pasta Bowl*. "Where do you think they went?"

"I'm no clairvoyant."

"I guess we'll start here, then."

"Wait. Think. It's a little after four, too early for supper, too late for dinner. And there isn't a bar at *The Pasta Bowl*."

As usual, Patsy was right. Claire passed *The Burger Gourmet*. "*The Rib Cage* and *The Krill Grill* are the only places that serve drinks. We'll check *Rib Cage* first."

"Hold on, Claire. Think about what you're doing. You can't just barge in there to look for Dale. If he's there, he'll see you."

"I'll simply tell the *maitre 'd* I'm looking for someone. And don't roll those eyes at me." Claire opened the door and sauntered in. No one greeted her. All the better. Standing in the entryway a moment, her eyes adjusted to the dark interior. Dinner preparations must be under way because she could smell roasting meat.

Facing the door was a half wall, and on top of it a planter. Had she ever noticed that before? She peered right and left. Nobody was around. It would have been bad for business if she'd been a customer, but good for her mission. Two steps forward brought her to the wall and its top hat of greenery. Crouching slightly to keep her head below the tangled mass of variegated leaves, she reached up and stuck her hands into the foliage to make a peephole for herself.

"May I help you?"

Claire jumped back. Thankfully, she didn't recognize the girl. Probably a college student from Pineridge or somewhere. "Uh, I'm waiting for a friend. I was, uh, looking to see if she was already here. I wanted to surprise her if she was." That must have sounded reasonable, because the girl nodded, turned around, and left Claire alone.

She returned to her stealth, parting the leaves. The front door opened. She whirled and faced Patsy. "Good grief, you scared me," she whispered. "Watch out for me." She turned back to her post.

"What are you doing?"

"Shh. I'm checking out who's here." Through her peephole, she had a good view of the room. Her gaze swept from the left side of the room to the right—wait. Was that—

"I see Dale."

Her whispers brought Patsy to her side.

"Where?" Now Patsy had her own peephole through the plants. Claire swallowed a giggle. If this weren't so serious, she'd have let it out.

"Over there by the far window on the right. In the corner."

Patsy moved her head around then gasped. "That's Nathan with them! And he saw me."

Claire grabbed her hand and pulled her outside the restaurant. "Are you sure?" They moved to the corner of the building.

"Yes. Why is he with Dale and whoever that other man is?"

"I asked Nathan for his help. He must be on the case. I told him what I suspected and asked him to help find out who all was in the investment group. I think that's what he's doing. And I almost blew it. When will I learn?"

"What? Bulldozer Claire worry?" Patsy snorted. "Honey, you've got to learn to put your brain in gear before putting the gas to your feet."

"All I could think of was Dale. He's behind this and that flat flummoxed me. He's not smart enough to be involved. Or is he? Could his dumb and dumber be an act?"

Patsy started laughing. "Do you have any idea how silly that sounds? You'd think we were private detectives or something."

Silly maybe, but Claire wasn't about to admit that. "In a way, we are. We've got to get to the bottom of this, Patsy. Nathan said if we can solve this dilemma in town, he wouldn't accept that job in New York."

Patsy stopped laughing. Her face lost its color. That wasn't good.

Claire took her hand. "Pat-a-cake, what's wrong?"

"What job in New York?"

Uh-oh. "Nathan didn't tell you?"

"No. Apparently my dear husband has already forgotten what happens when he keeps secrets."

Poor Patsy. The last time Nathan kept a secret from her, she thought he was involved in an affair. Turned out he wasn't, but it took weeks of heartbreak before she uncovered the truth. And Nathan had promised her no more secrets.

"Honey, I don't know why he hasn't told you. When I approached him about helping, he said he'd just gotten the offer. Maybe he's hoping to refuse it before he has to worry you."

"That's not the point, Claire. He should have told me. When did you talk to him?"

Claire stuck her hands in her pockets. "Last Wednesday. He didn't say not to tell you. I'm really sorry, Patsy. I wish I'd kept my mouth shut for once."

"And for once I'm glad you didn't."

What did she mean by that? "What do you mean 'for once'?" Was her BFF mad at her?

"This isn't about you, honey. It's about me and Nathan."

"Okay. Well, tell him—no never mind. This hotel thing has us all discombobulated."

Patsy sighed. "I guess you're right. I'm going to talk to him, though. I'm not some child he has to shelter."

"I know, but you have to admit, it's kind of sweet." Claire pulled a loose thread on her sweater button, which promptly dropped to the ground. She tried to stomp her foot on it, but her knee wouldn't move fast enough. She missed and it rolled toward a crack. Patsy dove for it, but it fell through and disappeared beneath the boardwalk.

"Brussels sprouts! Now I'll have to replace all the buttons."

"Better buttons than replacing your best friend. Or Nathan replacing a wife if he can't learn to share." Patsy patted Claire's shoulder. "Close your mouth, girl. I wouldn't leave him. But I might threaten him if he doesn't learn."

"Just don't get too mad at him, remember, it—" The restaurant door opened. Claire grabbed Patsy's hand and pulled her around the side of the building and into the alleyway just as the men exited. Muffled voices carried around the corner, but Claire couldn't make anything out.

"You can come out now, they're gone."

She and Patsy jumped as Nathan sauntered into the alley. Claire swatted his arm. "Don't do that. You scared ten years off my life. What did you find out?"

Patsy crossed her arms and tapped her foot. Nathan glanced at her and suddenly looked very unsure. "Not much yet, but Dale said he'd talk to his partners about me maybe becoming an investor."

Patsy shied back. Claire's voice and hers blended into one, "Investor?"

Nathan shrugged. "It was the only way I could think to get close enough to know who was involved. But I convinced Dale I was interested. He gave me enough info to find what I need without investing." He took Patsy's hand. "I should have an answer within a week. Ten days at the most."

"Great. Now, I have to get moving. I have a ton of prep work to do for Joel for tomorrow. See you about two o'clock."

"I'll bring the cranberry relish and the fried Brussels sprouts."

"Yum. I love those sprouts with the walnuts."

Claire crossed the parking lot of restaurant row to Sandy Shores. Poor Nathan. Patsy would give him grief for keeping another secret. She waved at Tom Fowler, the pharmacist, through the window of the drug store. Scuffling through small clusters of leaves along the boardwalk, she passed the ice cream parlor. The sun, close to setting, sat low and large over the lake. How thankful she was to live here in Chapel Springs. She couldn't think of another place on earth she'd rather live—tourists or no tourists.

Voices caught her attention in the alley between the *Gifted Gifter* and the *Tome Tomb* as she passed. A young woman's back looked vaguely familiar. She was in conversation with Dale Riley. That man was involved in more skullduggeries. What could this one be?

Claire kept moving, but the image stayed with her all the way home. She'd just stuck her key in the front door lock when it hit her.

Dale had been talking to Costancia.

Chapter 26

Claire dried her hands on her apron and glanced at the to-do list taped to the kitchen counter. The aroma of cooked sausage filled the room. She snitched a tidbit and popped it into her mouth as she checked off her list. The celery, Vidalia onions, and mushrooms were all chopped and waiting for Joel to turn them, along with the sausage—if she could stay out of it—into his fabulous dressing. The sweet potatoes were peeled and in boiling water. The turkey was brined and ready for the deep fryer.

All she had left to do was halve the oranges and scoop them out. Her mouth watered as her knife sliced through the first orange, releasing a citrusy cloud of nose-tingling goodness. Joel's sweet potatoes served in orange halves were always a hit and a good alternative to the gooey marshmallow-topped casserole everyone served.

She untied her apron and hung it on a drawer knob, then checked the oven's timer. After Wes and Costancia arrived, the whole family would finally be together under one roof again. Adriana had flown in last night. How Claire had missed her eldest daughter. Her heart swelled with love as she cocked an ear to the stirrings upstairs. Adrianna would be down soon wanting coffee.

Charlie and Sandi had arrived with the sun and that sweet daughter-in-law had been a huge help with preparations. Those two were all about family. Maybe Costancia would learn something from Sandi.

"Happy Thanksgiving, y'all!"

Wes's voice bellowed from the entryway. Costancia squealed. She must have met Shiloh. Claire dropped her knife and with her apron, wiped the orange juice from her elbows as she hurried to the door.

Wes grabbed her in a bear hug. Sweet boy. Anyone would think he hadn't seen his momma for a month instead of a week. She turned to Costancia, who took a step backwards and pointed to her arm where a stubborn piece of orange clung. Claire grimaced. Oh, good grief. Who's afraid of Virginia Pulp? She refused to allow Costancia to ruin the holiday. It was time to punt.

"Welcome and happy Thanksgiving, dear." She slipped her other arm through Costancia's and pulled her toward the kitchen, ignoring her balking. "It's a Bennett family tradition. The newest bride has to help prepare dinner." She winked at Sandi, who looked like Sylvester Puddytat hiding Tweety bird in his mouth.

Costancia turned her head toward Wes, but he must have liked his momma's idea because he babbled something to her and disappeared into the family room where the men had the TV blaring. In the kitchen, Claire handed her daughter-in-law a knife and pointed to the stack of oranges, then took one and demonstrated what she wanted.

Spying Costancia's dark expression, Claire was glad Megan and Melissa popped into the kitchen just then or she might have been halved instead of an orange.

"Hey, sleepyheads. 'Lissa will you help Costancia scoop out the oranges? And don't lose the juice. Megan, you're down for making the rolls." Claire kissed each twin on the cheek then turned back to her task of combining all the ingredients for the dressing. When done, she left them in a covered bowl for Joel to cook.

Costancia kept one eye on the dog, who'd taken up residence under the table, and one on her knife as she slowly sliced the first orange. She asked Megan something. After answering, Megan said, "She wanted to know what you were making. And if Shiloh was part horse." She giggled. "Where's Daddy?"

"With the men. He'll be in here soon, then y'all can scram." Claire checked to see how Melissa and Costancia were doing with the oranges. Sandi had come in and stood by the girls, chatting. 'Lissa helped translate using a combination of English and Portuguese. Whatever the girls said, by Costancia's expression, it appeared she didn't believe what she was hearing.

"Now that's a welcoming sight." Joel stood in the doorway. "Never has a chef had so many lovely assistants."

All the girls surrounded him and kissed his cheeks. *All* of them. Their newest daughter-in-law had no problems with him, it seemed.

Claire replayed every moment since Costancia walked into their midst, searching for something she'd done to offend the girl. She couldn't believe it was the simple act of getting the language wrong. Shouldn't the trouble she'd gone to take classes to learn a second—albeit wrong—language carry some value? If someone had done that for her, she'd have thought it was sweet.

Joel shooed the girls back to their posts. After a few minutes, the twins left. Sandi continued to work without being told what to do. She wiped counters, counted out silverware, and put potato peelings in the plastic bag for the compost pile. On her way out to the backyard with the peelings, Claire stopped her and pulled her into a quick hug.

"Have I told you lately how much I love you and appreciate you?"

"You have, Mom, in more ways than you realize. I don't understand her." She tilted her head toward Costancia, who hung over Joel's shoulder. "You welcomed her like you did me. This isn't the girl Wes introduced us to online."

Claire snapped her attention back to Sandi. "What do you mean? Surely she's not an imposter."

"No, no, I didn't mean that, but online, she was so sweet and embraced us all."

"All but me." That hurt. "Do you suppose she wondered why Joel and I weren't told about her? Maybe that's why she hates me." Except, that didn't compute. Costancia didn't hate Joel. Claire walked outside with Sandi. A breath of fresh air might clear up her perspective.

"I have no idea. I've given up trying. Once she recognized my relationship with you, she started freezing me out, too."

"Did Charlie say anything?"

Sandi lifted the lid on the compost bin and shook the peelings out of the bag onto the pile. She shook her head. "I don't think he's noticed, and I haven't said anything. I'm trying to follow your example."

Hers? Was she, Claire Bennett, suddenly a good example? Or was she leading Sandi astray? Claire took the now-empty bag from Sandi. "What do you mean?"

"You haven't retaliated even once." She nudged Claire with an amused grin. "And don't think I don't know your tongue is sore from biting it." She brushed her hands together. "I'm done here. I'm going to find my husband and engage him in a game of chess."

Sandi disappeared into the house, and Claire walked over to the old river birch. She leaned against one of its three fat trunks and turned her gaze upward through leafless branches. Large clouds gathered themselves into towering thunderheads. A storm brewed up there that would lash out at them later today. But right now, she'd been handed a moment of respite from the boiling waters brewing inside her living room. "How about that. I'm a good example. Your wonders never cease, Lord. Thanks for that."

Back in the kitchen, Costancia and Megan giggled on either side of Joel. Her spirits buoyed from her conversation with Sandi, Claire wandered to the stove. "What can I do?"

Joel leaned over and kissed the tip of her nose. "What you do best at this point. Go sit at the table and look gorgeous."

Shaking her head at his silliness, she checked the counters first. Everything was clean so she sat in the breakfast banquette. Megan had translated for Costancia, who now gave Claire a withering sneer and babbled something. Megan stiffened and frowned, glanced at her dad and back to Claire. Whatever Costancia said hadn't pleased Megan. Joel, intent on his cooking, didn't notice.

It was time for her to vacate the kitchen. Claire was thankful for the chiming of the doorbell and Patsy's voice in the foyer. That woman had the world's greatest timing. Claire tripped on the kitchen threshold in her haste to greet her. A derisive giggle erupted behind her, stabbing her in the back.

"Reinforcements are here." Patsy, dressed in comfy looking slacks and a dark green sweater, handed her the cranberries and took the Brussels sprouts from Nathan, who made a beeline for the family room.

"How are things going?"

Claire debated what to tell her and decided to let her form her own opinion. "Just fine."

"And why don't I believe that? Did the bumfuzzle fairy make an appearance this morning?"

"I'm not confused. I've decided to take control of my reactions." She just hoped she could stick to it. Sometimes her tongue had a mind of its own. And Sandi was right about the little traitor getting sore from biting it. It was almost as sore as her heart.

They walked to the kitchen together. Joel greeted Patsy—rather he greeted her Brussels sprouts with an appreciative sniff. As an afterthought, he bussed her cheek.

Costancia eyed the dish with suspicion. Maybe she'd cho—no, for Wes's sake, Claire wouldn't go there. She didn't truly want that. She wasn't sure what she wanted, other than a peaceful holiday right now.

A headache tattooed the base of her skull. Rolling her shoulders didn't do much to work out the tension from her neck. Instead, she opened the fridge with one hand and slid the cranberry relish onto the shelf. The timer dinged, signaling Joel to dunk the turkey into the boiling oil. As he headed to the backyard with the bird, Patsy took over stirring the gravy. The sweet potatoes were in their cups and ready for a final glaze under the broiler when the turkey was done. There was nothing for Claire to do but wait.

"How about a cup of coffee?" Patsy suggested.

Caffeine might help her headache. "Good idea." While she scooped grounds into the machine, Claire could feel eyes boring into her back. She didn't mean to, but she whirled around.

"What?"

Megan's brows knit and her forehead wrinkled. She glanced at Costancia, whose mug wore a smug sneer. Megan opened her mouth then closed it and walked out.

Costancia moved closer to Claire. "You no cook," she whispered then followed Megan.

Claire couldn't move. The repugnance in that whisper dealt a fatal blow to her self-esteem—and the holiday.

After Charlie asked the blessing, plates passed as each person had responsibility for adding a helping of the dish in front of them onto each plate. Costancia, having the sweet potato cups, managed to upend Sandi's and Claire's. The words she babbled and the apologetic face she presented didn't reach her eyes as she handed Claire her plate. Joel frowned and opened his mouth, but Claire gave a small shake of her head and he closed it.

Thank goodness for Patsy and Nathan. They kept the conversation flowing and soon, laughter accompanied the chatter.

"Sandi's playing Mary this year in the Christmas pageant," Charlie announced with pride swelling his chest.

Claire flapped her napkin and laid it in her lap. "How fun! I didn't know you liked to act, sweetheart."

Sandi glanced sideways at Charlie and blushed. "Well, my acting ability isn't why they chose me."

Charlie's ears turned red as well. "No, Ma. It's because, like Mary, Sandi's expecting."

Claire's heart leapt with joy. Like Elizabeth's in the Bible. Tears of happiness stung her eyes, and she blubbered and laughed. She couldn't keep her seat but jumped up and scurried around the table to hug the mother-to-be and her firstborn son. Her happy Thanksgiving restored, whatever Costancia slung at her faded into the background. God was good, indeed.

While they all hugged and Wes slapped his brother on the back, Costancia sat staring at her plate and pushed vegetables around. Her expression tugged at Claire's happy heart. She went to her newest daughter-in-law and patted her own tummy. "Bambino," she said, hoping that word crossed all the Latin languages. Then she thought of the French she'd tried to learn in high school. "*Bebe.*"

This time Costancia's eyes registered and she nodded, then stared at Claire, her eyes searching. For what? Was this an opening finally? But after a moment, the door slammed again. Costancia looked down at her plate. She took a tentative bite of Joel's sweet potatoes, smiled and told Wes something then took another bite.

"She loves your sweet potatoes, Dad, and the turkey."

Claire noticed her finicky daughter-in-law pushed the dressing aside and wrinkled her nose. None of her other food had been touched. What was wrong with this girl?

"Wes, tell your wife she ought to at least try everything."

"I did, but she says she doesn't recognize a lot of it and she's afraid to."

Claire couldn't help the snort—it snuck out on its own. "When y'all were little, I made you try at least one bite. You were allowed to spit it out, but you had to try it."

Charlie laughed. "I remember that." He looked toward Costancia. "It's what makes me open to trying new foods now. And I'm sure glad y'all raised us that way, Momma." He patted his stomach. "When I think of what I might have missed—"

Everyone laughed.

Wes translated for Costancia, who eyed Charlie. A slow smile pulled at her lips, and she took a Brussels sprout with a piece of walnut clinging to it and placed it in her mouth, holding it there for a moment. Her eyes widened and she chewed. She speared another.

"See?" Oops. Claire stuffed a Brussels sprout into her mouth before it could betray her again.

Costancia's face darkened. She leaned closer to Wes, who scowled at

Claire. "Ma, give her a break. This is a lot of new stuff for her to absorb."

The dining room went silent. Joel's knife and fork didn't break their stride, but between bites, he said, "Son, that wasn't called for. Your mother's remark wasn't a challenge but a revelation."

"Sorry, Ma. Guess I reacted instead of listening."

He didn't avoid eye contact with her, and he sounded sincere.

She reached over and patted his hand. "Accepted, dear. I understand." Not. For some reason he couldn't see that his wife had it in for her. But why? It made no sense.

Chapter 27

Claire sat at the kitchen banquette, hoping the tension would drain away. Thanks to Patsy and Sandi, the dishwasher hummed and the pots drained in the dish rack. Claire heaved a deep sigh and took another sip of spiced chai, letting the aroma of cloves, cinnamon, and cardamom penetrate her senses.

Slipping her bare toes beneath Shiloh, who lay under the table, she sighed again. Every nerve and fiber were strung tight—any tighter and she wouldn't be able to control what happened. She'd probably take out everyone within a twenty-yard radius. She could see them now, falling like dominoes until nobody was left standing.

Sitting cattycorner from her, Patsy set her mug of tea on the table, reached over, and squeezed Claire's hand. "I'm glad Joel defended you. At least he sees what's going on. When she fawned over him while he was cooking, I wanted to slap her into tomorrow and him to Saturday."

The only thing better than a hubby who ran to her defense was a BFF who did. She chuckled. "Whoa girl. He isn't taken in by her."

"Lucky for him."

"Hey, I had to hold him back. He said he almost choked when Wes excused her behavior. You didn't see me kick his ankle under the table."

Melissa sauntered into the kitchen and joined them. Claire moved over and patted the bench next to her. 'Lissa was her soul mate child, the one most like her. And something was bothering her.

"What's up, sweetie?"

She glanced between Patsy and Claire. "I heard Costancia telling Wes she wanted to go home, and she didn't mean the apartment."

Leaving? Wes's face appeared in Claire's mind, and any warmth she'd gained from the tea turned to ice. "She's leaving him?"

'Lissa shook her head. "No, she's trying to talk him into moving to Brazil. She says none of us love her and she misses her family."

A fissure opened in the middle of Claire's heart and split her in two. "What did your brother say?"

"He tried to tell her she was wrong, that we want to love her but it takes time. She's impatient, though, and wants to feel it now."

Patsy's mug thunked against the table. "To be loved, one needs to act lovable."

"Aunt Patsy, you nailed it. But how can we tell her that without alienating Wes?"

Claire inhaled a deep breath, letting it out slowly. There was only one thing to do. "Prayer, sweetie, and lots of it."

Wes sauntered into the kitchen. "Ma? We're leaving now." He bent down and kissed her cheek. "Thanks for a wonderful Thanksgiving."

"You're welcome, dear. I hope Costancia enjoyed it."

From the doorway, an angry glare shot Claire's way.

The next morning while the girls hit the pre-Christmas sales in Pineridge, Claire donned a slicker against the misty rain and schlogged through the woods behind the park. The crushed leaves beneath her feet sent up a musty-earth scent. Did broken hearts send up an aroma of sorrow to God?

A few minutes stroll took her deep into the woods. She squatted, sifting through a pile of leaves, looking for specimens. Not just any old leaves, but ones pretty and small enough to be dipped in Dahlonega gold—if she could get any—and worn as jewelry. She'd picked a few tiny Japanese maple leaves from her front yard but wanted other specimens from Chapel Springs. Seedlings or full-grown didn't matter as long as they were small enough for a necklace or Christmas tree ornament.

She rose, dusting off her hands. The pile there yielded nothing. Walking with her eyes down, she searched both sides of the path. On the right amid the pine needles, a small three-leaved plant thrust itself toward the light. That was pretty. It wasn't alone, either. She didn't recognize it, but then she wasn't a gardener. After picking a few, she zipped them into a baggie. They were the perfect size to make a delicate pendant.

Deeper in the woods, she came to a clearing and what appeared to be a small farm. Whoever did the planning wasn't a practiced farmer, though, because the rows weren't straight. Not by any stretch of the imagination. And what about sunlight? Claire raised her eyes to the tree cover, but it wasn't that thick, so when the sun shone, the plants would receive light. It was a strange place to plant a garden unless it was to feed wild animals. That made her laugh, but her laughter rang out against the stillness and raised goose bumps on her arms.

Something was weird about this, but the leaves were pretty and she didn't think anyone would mind if she plucked a few little ones. She turned one over in her hand. Maybe it was tea. She'd never seen tea growing, though, so how would she know? After bagging them and making a note of where she found them in case she wanted more, she headed back to the gallery.

"What have you got there?" Nicole asked.

"Leaves for a new project." Claire shrugged out of her slicker and hung it on the coat tree. "I plan to cover them with gold and make them into pendants."

"I've seen those. Some lady came in here last week with one that I admired. How do you do that? Cover them with gold I mean?"

"At first I thought they were dipped in it, but now I'm not so sure. The heat of liquid gold would burn them up. Anyway, I'm researching that now. I picked some leaves for inspiration." She didn't tell Nicole she hoped to please Costancia with one. Her assistant would call it a lost cause, and Claire wasn't quite ready to give up. Yet.

It didn't take her long to discover her rethink had been right. The leaves weren't dipped *in gold* but painted with a copper based paint then electroplated. Then they were dipped in a solution to dissolve the fleshy parts and leave the veins and stems intact. She could do the first part and the last part easy enough. But the electroplating needed an expert.

"Hey, Patsy, didn't Max over at Artistic Expressions tell us about an artist who electroplated stuff?"

Patsy's head popped out from behind her easel. "I remember that. Wasn't it ..." " She scratched her ear with the bottom end of her paintbrush, "Unity Jones, the metal sculptor. She has a workshop over in Hiawassee."

"That's the one. Your memory is better than mine for names."

"Yours would be if you slowed down when you met people, but you're so anxious to learn their story, you start firing questions at them."

Claire flipped through her art association address book. "You're probably right, but—ah, here she is." She stabbed her finger next to the listing. "I'm going to see if she can do that part for me."

"That part of what?"

"Didn't I tell you?" Claire pulled out the leaves. "These are going to become jewelry."

Patsy eyed them suspiciously. "What kind of leaves are those?"

"How should I know? I'm no botanist, but they'll look pretty covered in gold, don't you think?" Claire laid one against her chest just below the hollow beneath her neck.

"Hmm, very." Patsy disappeared back behind her easel.

Claire emailed Unity, placed an order with Max for the copper based paint, then got busy making another platter. She had three plus four vases, and one large whimsy urn to make that afternoon.

Three hours later, Claire stretched the kinks from her back and set the last vase of the day on the drying shelf next to the platters. The urn rested on the floor beneath the bottom shelf. She'd fire them in the kiln on Monday. "Patsy?"

"She left about an hour ago, Claire," Nicole called from the gallery.

"Oh, thanks." Claire hadn't heard her leave, but that was often the case. She checked her email one last time and was tickled to see a note from Unity.

I've done several. Come up any time. Bring your leaves.

Claire shot back an answer saying she'd come next Monday. "Nicole, are you okay closing up? I'm done for."

"Sure. I want to try out a couple of new things, so I'll lock the front door and then work for a bit in back."

"I thought you had a date with Chase?"

"I do. He's coming around six to pick me up. I'll work till then."

Kids. She used to spend an hour agonizing over what to wear when she and Joel were dating. Now it's "accept me for who I am." She wondered if her generation could have learned a thing or two from this one. Probably so. They might have been able to bypass some junk. On the other hand, that time spent agonizing—trading clothes with Patsy and giggling—was *fun*.

Claire pulled on her slicker, waved goodbye, and slipped out the door. The haunting wail of a loon echoed through the mist. The boardwalk along Sandy Shores was quiet for once, empty of visitors and residents alike. Pulling her raincoat tighter across her chest, she didn't hurry. Odd as it might seem, this was her favorite type of weather to walk in. The mist wrapped her in its cocoon and the loons' tremolos kept her company.

The first signs of Christmas dotted Sandy Shores Drive. The lampposts sported bright red bows and poinsettias had replaced mums. Tomorrow, she'd pull out the gallery's decorations and let Nicole have at it. If Claire could get these leaves done, maybe she could make some to hang on the Christmas tree. Better, perhaps these leaves would be the key to her new daughter-in-law's heart.

The next morning, Claire took the car and stopped by the gallery to see if they needed anything from the art supply store. Patsy handed her a list.

"I called ahead so Max will have everything ready."

"Thanks, that'll save me some time." Claire pointed out the boxes to Nicole. "If you'll go through the Christmas decorations and toss out anything broken or sorry looking, we'll decorate this afternoon."

Patsy leaned against a display case, her arms crossed. "I can't wait to put the tree up."

"You are such a kid when it comes to Christmas." Claire reached in her pocket and pulled out her keys.

"Oh? And you're not? My *kid*-brain seems to recall an incident from the not too distant past." Patsy turned to Nicole. "It was only a few short years ago—okay maybe ten, but who's counting? Chase was almost ten, and at the age where he had big questions about Santa Claus. Auntie Claire couldn't stand the idea of the last of my chicks giving up the belief. Christmas Eve at about eleven o'clock, Nathan and I woke up to hear tapping on our roof." Patsy started to giggle. "It got louder—" She stopped to draw a breath. "And louder. Then we heard bells jingling. We couldn't figure out what was going on. Then we heard a whoop and a crash." She doubled over, laughing.

"It started out so much fun," Claire said, "but ice on the roof was my undoing." She sniffed and grimaced. "Patsy loves to tell that story."

"We ran outside to see Claire, hanging from the corner of the roof. Fortunately for her, the gutter was very secure in that spot. Nathan grabbed a ladder and rescued her."

Nicole's mouth hung halfway to her chest. She stared wide-eyed at Claire. "What were you doing?"

Patsy's laughter had the best of her. Claire shrugged. "I was giving Chase one more year to believe. In the morning, he told us all he heard

Santa and his reindeer on the roof that night. I'll never forget his delight that Christmas."

"That's a hoot." Nicole chortled. "I can see you hanging from that roof, Miss Claire."

Claire put her hands on her hips. "Now wait a cotton-pickin' minute—"

Patsy pushed her toward the door. "Don't you have an errand to run?"

Just before the door closed, she heard Patsy say, "I can tell you some other stories about Christmas past—"

A chuckle bubbled from Claire's throat. They did have some funny stories. There was the time she decided to make a Christmas pudding and hide money inside for the kids. It was one of the traditions Great-aunt Lola always held to when Claire was a kid. That was long after her career as a silent film star was over. If she'd realized Aunt Lola was going to die that summer, she would've asked the secret to the pudding. But what kid of nine thinks about death? Claire's pudding was a disaster—like most of her culinary attempts.

She started the car's engine and headed to *Artistic Expressions*. At least she was good as a potter. It was her one redeeming value. Now, she'd expand that talent to jewelry. It was, if nothing else, a nice deviation from clay. Not that she could ever stop being a potter. Something about her hands, covered in wet clay, creating beauty from the earth, satisfied her—made her feel complete. Pastor Seth said it was because she was called to be a potter. Was that true? Was her talent a gift from God?

"Have I said thank you?"

Claire heard a chuckle. Or was it her imagination? She glanced in the rearview mirror, but, of course, the car was empty. Then, it was more a quickening—like the first flutter an expectant mother feels early in her pregnancy—she knew she was welcomed.

"I suppose you're laughing at me, too." Somehow, the Lord's laughter didn't sting but warmed her soul.

Two-dozen leaves hung drying from a line strung over Claire's workbench. Some looked like little stars, and a few brought to mind the Bethlehem star. A bit oddly shaped, but stars nonetheless, and they were delicate and would catch the lights on the Christmas tree. Once dry, she'd slip wire through the stem and make a loop for hanging. Then after electroplating, the loop could be attached to either an ornament hanger or a chain for a necklace.

"Those look good, Claire." Patsy stood behind her. She pointed to one. "That leaf looks familiar." She pulled her mouth to one side. "Uh-oh."

"What?"

"I think that's poison ivy."

Claire craned her neck to look up at her. "I don't think so. I picked that one a couple of days ago and haven't had any itching." She glanced down at her rash-free chest where she had touched the leaf to her bare skin. "If you remember my last encounter with poison ivy, I broke out the same day."

"That's right. Whew, I was worried for a minute there. Are all these," Patsy waved at the collection, "for Christmas ornaments or jewelry?" She pointed to the third one on the left. "I love that one. Can I buy it?"

"I'll give it to you for Christmas, and they can be for either. I'm making the loop large enough for an ornament hook or to slide a fine chain through."

"Clever. You said they could be gold, bronze or silver. Can mine be bronze?"

"Absolutely. I'm making a silver one for Costancia. I was thinking I'd make one for a necklace and then two teensy leaves for earrings. What do you think?"

"I think she'll love them. That just might be the ticket to her accepting you."

Claire hoped so, but she wasn't as sure as Pat-a-cake. Things never seemed to work out for her like she planned.

Chapter 28

Lydia handed Morgan a stack of folded terry towels, then reached into the dryer for the robes. The spa's signature-scent of pear and lavender from her specialty dryer sheets engulfed her.

"Mom, I appreciate your help, but why are you here today?" Morgan paused in her folding and lifted one beautifully arched eyebrow. "You haven't worked a Saturday since you got married."

"The guys are car shopping, and someone has to cover Kenny's morning shift." Lydia frowned and reached for more towels. "To be honest, I don't know why he couldn't have waited until after work."

She and Graham could have enjoyed a quiet Saturday morning, but he didn't even put up an argument. He caved to Kenny's request. Again. The same way he did when his daughter, Sherry, called for more money last night.

"They should be back soon, I imagine." Morgan grabbed the armful of towels, turned, and set them on the shelf. "Then Kenny can finish the laundry."

Lydia folded the first robe and stacked it on the table next to the dryer. It had been Morgan's idea to combine the laundry room and linen closet. It saved them all a lot of time. Her daughter was one clever gal.

Morgan twisted a loose thread on one of the towels and broke it off. "What's Kenny looking for?" She dropped the thread ball in the trash.

"He wants a new Jeep Cherokee."

"He's a bit picky, isn't he? Wheels are wheels." Morgan picked up a stack of facial towels and put them on the shelf above the terries.

"They're men. What can I say?"

Laughing, Morgan plucked a piece of lint from Lydia's shoulder. "I suppose, and maybe I shouldn't get involved, Mom, but it bothers me the way he thinks his dad's wallet should always be open to him. After dinner on Thanksgiving, he told Graham that he wanted some weights to strengthen his forearms. It really surprised me when his dad handed over his credit card."

Sticking out her lower lip, Lydia blew her bangs up off her forehead. "I know. I've noticed it more since he started school. I wonder if it's simply a result of the economy. Millions of people are out of work. This has to be going on in more than just our family."

Morgan hoisted herself up onto the folding table. "I don't know. There's something about the way he asks—like it's his due. Why can't he buy a used car like the rest of us?"

"In their defense, neither of them pretends to be mechanical. Graham feels it's borrowing trouble, but I did get him to agree to look for a low mileage one over at Baffi Motors." She folded the last spa wrap and handed the warm stack to Morgan.

Her daughter hopped off the table and set the wraps on a shelf. "Being unmarried, I'm no expert, and I'm your daughter not your mother, but I think you should talk to Graham about Kenny. Maybe he doesn't realize what he's doing."

Morgan had been sixteen when Sam died. For so long it was just the two of them and as she grew up, her daughter became her confidant. Lydia slipped her arm through Morgan's as they left the linen closet. "I think you're right, sweet pea."

Morgan went to relieve Hannah on the phones so she could go eat. Lydia returned to her office to get the bills ready for Nathan to pay. She pulled out her file of invoices and another of signed receivers and began to match them, checking the items against the purchase requests her employees gave her. She planned for Kenny to take over this job. It would give him an idea of the costs of running a business.

An hour later she stapled the last one and put them all in a large envelope for Nathan when he returned. He should be back in time to get them paid. Rotating her neck to work out the kinks, she caught sight of the wall clock. How did it get to be two-fifteen already? Kenny and Graham were probably home by now.

Downstairs, clients murmured in the foyer—one of them Dee Lindstrom. Strange. She rarely got out of the bakery. On either side of her sat Patsy and Claire, who all looked up at her approach. "Dee, I'm surprised and delighted to see you here. Did these two kidnap you?"

"They did. They said I had enough help that I could get away. Besides," she grinned, "it's my birthday present from them."

Lydia took Dee's outstretched service card. "Then today, the mani-pedi is on the house." She held up her hand to stop Dee's protest. "They can pay for the massage. It's my spa, and I have a birthday rule for friends."

"How come *you're* here today?" Claire asked.

Lydia shrugged, weighing how much to say. "Kenny needs a new car. He and his dad are out looking for one. I'm covering for him until he gets back."

"How's he working out?" Claire tilted her head. The sunlight through the window glinted off the dark blonde lowlights in her hair.

Lydia tucked up a stray wisp of her own, wishing she were blonde. Maybe she should look into streaks. "Better than I expected, except for not being here this morning."

One of the massage therapists called Claire's name, then Dee's. Lydia spoke with her for a moment, and then waved at Morgan. "Call me if you need anything."

Lydia ambled up the hill toward home. She hadn't heard from Graham yet. What was keeping them? As she topped the crest and the house came into view, Graham and Kenny were on either side of a sparkling red Camaro, poking, polishing, and examining. When she got to the driveway, she saw the year on the dealer sticker still in the window. A new car? What happened to their agreement?

Graham bounded toward her. "Hey, sweetheart. Come see Kenny's new car. I know we agreed on a used one, but there weren't any that had low enough mileage, and this one was such a great deal. Come on, get in. Sit in the driver's seat. Come on. Look at all the things it has—G.P.S., a dock for his cell phone that overrides the CD player. It's got it all. Come on, Kenny, let's take her for a ride."

Lydia's jaw muscles tightened. It seemed they already had. "I don't need to sit in it. I won't be the one driving it." She walked around him to the house and opened the front door. "I'll be inside."

In the kitchen, she jerked chicken breasts from the freezer for supper. Fuming as she was, she could probably defrost the chicken just by holding it. Didn't Graham see he gave his son whatever he asked for—without reserve? She dropped the meat in the sink.

Graham's hands turned her around. "Honey? I know you're upset. We need to talk. I sent Kenny on to the spa."

She hadn't heard him come in. "You're right. On both counts." She blew her bangs out of her eyes. "Let me get us some sweet tea and we'll sit down."

She filled two glasses with ice and poured the tea. "Graham, this is a difficult position for me. We're married now, and I need to know what we're going to do about financial decisions."

She brought the glasses to the table and sat across from him. "Are we keeping our finances separate? Is it going to be your money and my money? Or is it ours?"

Graham's brows dipped together. "It's ours. That's what we decided before we got married, darlin'. Other than the spa itself which will one day go to Morgan, the income from it, like mine, is ours."

Lydia leaned forward. "Then why did you let Kenny talk you into a *new* car when we'd decided as a family he'd get a used one?"

Graham stared at her for a long moment then lowered his gaze. His normally smiling eyes were hooded, like window awnings to hide his thoughts. It was the guilt again. How could she help him get past that?

She put her hand over his. "Honey?"

He raised his gaze to meet hers. "I'm sorry, Lydia. This isn't fair to you."

"That's not what I'm concerned about. It's you. Honey, I love you. The guilt you're carrying isn't healthy."

"I've spent years trying to make up for their mother's death." A muscle in his cheek twitched. "It was my fault." His voice was heavy with sorrow. He believed a lie. A lie his children had perpetuated for years to get their way on everything.

That made her so mad. If it weren't unladylike she'd spit. "No, Graham, it wasn't. Haleigh could have said no—made you go into that store. You didn't pull that trigger. It isn't your fault."

"But I was a stubborn so-and-so, too lazy to go myself."

"Graham, did you physically abuse Haleigh? Hit her so she was afraid of you?"

"What? No! I never raised a hand to her or any woman. I'm not like that."

Lydia squeezed his hand. "I know you're not, so don't you see? Haleigh wasn't afraid of you. She could have refused to go and made you."

His eyes filled with doubt. It was like he wanted to believe her, but a little imp on his shoulder kept whispering in his ear.

"Honey, I know you've heard the expression 'tough love'. That's what Kenny and Sherry both need. They may get mad and not like it, but you don't need to say yes to everything for them to love you."

"I didn't realize that's what I was doing, but you're right." His voice cracked and he cleared his throat. "I don't know what I did to deserve getting you, but I thank the good Lord I did something right." He came around the table and pulled her into his arms. "I love you, Lydia. More than I ever could have believed."

His kiss was sweet and filled with promise. When he ended it, the smile that had won her heart was in place. He rotated his shoulders. "Now I just have to find the backbone to enforce it."

"I'll be praying for you, my love." He disappeared through the kitchen door.

With the refrigerator door open, she peered into its depths for what to serve with the chicken and prayed for Graham. Give him strength, Lord, and resolve.

Are you so different from Graham?

What? She wasn't riddled with guilt nor did she believe a lie.

No?

Did she?

You strive for approval from everyone, when all you need is my acceptance.

She did, if she was honest, and always had. Was it the same as Graham? Did she believe a lie? A memory rose of her dad, gazing at her mother like Graham looked at her. As a child, she idolized her daddy, but he never had time for her. She did everything she could to gain his praise, but it never happened. And then his final betrayal—he left her. She hadn't been good enough to gain his love or make him stay. But she'd blamed Lacey instead of placing it where it belonged—on her immature father.

She thought she'd put that to rest. Apparently, once a lie took up residence, it was hard to evict. Like Graham's, hers had been ingrained and she'd lived with it so long, it was part of her. It was time to kick the habit. She yanked out a bottle of capers and shut the fridge door. They both needed to look to God for strength and see themselves as he saw them.

The basement door slammed, and the house shuddered. Graham walked into the kitchen, his face dark but resolute. He folded some papers and slid them into an envelope.

"It wasn't pretty, and he's mad as a hornet, but," he held up the envelope, "I'm taking the car back. We're going to look for a used one like we agreed." He sighed. "I hadn't realized how spoiled he's become."

Lydia put her hand on his cheek. "You're doing the right thing, love. Kenny will get over it, and if he doesn't, it's his problem. He's all grown up now." She kissed him. "Would you like company on this trip?"

Chapter 29

The moment Claire walked into the cavernous old barn, even before the coppery scent of burning metal tingled her nostrils or she caught sight of the artist, she spotted a leaping bass captured in bronze. It was perfect for Joel—her toughest-buy Christmas recipient. Her only problem now was where to stow it until she could get a box big enough.

She rubbed her nose against the ozone-like smell permeating the barn and wrote a check for the amount on the invoice.

"Thanks, Unity. I really appreciate you carving out time for me. Let me put these in the car and come back for the sculpture."

Once she got it all loaded in the Cherokee, she called Patsy. "I need to hide Joel's present at your house. Can I bring it by?"

The line crackled. "Sure ... get ... big?"

"You're breaking up. I'll see you—" The line went dead. Cell service was sketchy in the mountains, so Claire laid her phone in the cup holder and headed for Chapel Springs.

The electroplated leaves turned out as wonderful as hoped. Some were filigreed and others solid, but each displayed its own beauty. One of them she planned on making into a necklace—a Christmas gift to herself. It reminded her of an abstract star with one longer beam pointing down, like the star of Bethlehem.

The sun had climbed high enough to burn off the worst of the frosty chill. Claire opened her window a bit to let in the smell of the forest. Pine, fir, and the earthy aroma of the mulched floor filled her nostrils as she took a deep breath. She couldn't live without this. It was the scent of home.

When she'd wondered what her new daughter-in-law thought about these beloved mountains, Wes said she came from a large city, *Belo Horizonte*, surrounded by a high range. He also told them she laughed at theirs, saying Georgia had hills compared to Brazil. Claire didn't know about that, but she knew Costancia had a chip on her shoulder for some reason, and someone needed to knock it off.

"Lord, why couldn't Wes have listened to me? Don't I know him best? Know his strengths and sensitivities? The moment I met Sandi I knew the girl was perfect for Charlie, just as I'm certain Costancia isn't right for Wes."

She always wanted a close relationship with both her sons' wives. Why had Wes done this? Meeting an American girl on the Internet would have been weird enough, in her opinion, but to choose his wife that way? And then one who couldn't even speak his language?

She snorted. "It's like shopping for a car online and then buying it without even turning on the engine." Not to mention the fact he was too young to have good sense about choosing a wife.

God was silent. She shivered. The air temperature dropped, forcing her to close her window, shutting her off from the forest. Now in a hurry to get home, she pressed her foot harder against the accelerator.

Forty minutes later, the last curve before entering Chapel Springs came into view. She drove to Patsy's house, let herself in the back door, and took the sculpture down to the basement. Nathan had made sure the space was dry and airtight since Patsy needed a place to store some of her paintings. The bronze fish would be safe here. Claire set it in a corner, found an old blanket, and covered it. Hopefully, Nathan wouldn't find it.

After parking in the garage at home, she grabbed the box of golden leaves and walked over to the gallery. She slipped in the back door, startling Patsy.

"Sorry about that. I left Joel's present beside your washing machine. I figured that was a safe place for Nathan not to find it."

"It is. Good thinking." Patsy wiped her hands on a rag and came over to where Claire was laying out the leaves on an empty worktable. The overhead lights sparkled off the shiny metals. "Oh my, they're beautiful."

Holding up one, Claire slipped an ornament hanger through the gold loop at the end of its stem. "These will be perfect for Christmas. I love that they look like abstract stars. And I have smaller ones for necklaces."

Patsy scrunched her mouth to one side and pointed. "The middle leaf on those is longer than the side ones. That's one uneven star."

Claire waved her criticism away. "Like I said, abstract in a metaphorical sort of way." She pulled a slender gold chain from a drawer, slipped it through the loop, and fastened it around her neck. Turning around, she laid her hand against the pendant on her breastbone. "Is this chain the right length?"

Patsy tilted her head. "I think it's perfect. This was a great idea, Claire. These are beauties and tourists should snap them up. Especially if you put a sign by the display stating they're from Chapel Lake forest." She looked over the selection. "Where's my bronze one?"

"Put away for Christmas, so don't get nosy. Now, help me slip some ornament hooks in these and we'll get to decorating."

"Oh, Claire!" Nicole tripped over to her, pointing to the necklace. "That's beautiful. Oh! Oh, my." Her eyes widened and she raised her eyes to Claire's.

"What?" Claire fingered the necklace. "What's wrong?"

Nicole stared at her, opened her mouth, then closed it and shook her head. "Nothing." Her forehead wrinkled then cleared. One corner of her lips twitched. "Uhm, Christmas Decoration Day has officially begun. The others are all outside. Decorating. Shouldn't we get a move on?" She picked up a box of decorations and left the workroom.

Whatever Nicole was thinking flew over Claire's head without stopping to roost. She glanced in the mirror at the delicate gold leaf resting on her chest. It sparkled in the light. Touching its dainty points, she shrugged.

Patsy had already taken a box of garland and joined the others out on the Drive. Claire picked up the last tub of decorations and headed outside. Skirting the ladder, Nicole sat atop stringing lights on the awning, Claire maneuvered around it and onto the boardwalk.

It was a perfect day for Christmas decorating. The air was filled with the scent of pine. The street rang with laughter and good cheer. Even some tourists—those who rented cottages for the month—lent a hand in the festivities. The temperature had dropped and clouds drifted overhead. Colorful hats and neck scarves added to the kaleidoscope of Christmas.

Claire set the box on the bench beside the door and went back for her jacket. The mountains might get snow soon. A white Christmas would be welcomed. They didn't always get one, but when they did, Chapel Springs turned into the quintessential Christmas wonderland.

She hurried back outside to join the fun, taking a scarf along for Patsy. After tying it around her BFF's neck, Claire moved to the edge of the boardwalk and surveyed the decorating progress. The streetlights already wore bright red bows. Traditionally, those and the poinsettias were in place for Thanksgiving, but they held off the rest of the Christmas decorating for the weekend following turkey day. Red, green, gold, and silver were the predominant colors.

Inspired, Claire opened the first box and lifted the gallery's door wreath carefully. She and Patsy had made it years ago from nuts and seedpods. They'd left it in the natural colors but highlighted the edges of the pods with gold leaf and threaded lacy gold ribbon through it, tied into a large bow at the bottom.

With the wreath in place, Claire outlined the door with white twinkle lights. Patsy entwined matching lights in the topiaries beside the door, residing in two of Claire's whimsy pots. The large urns were bunnies surrounding the plants, each holding a knife and fork, ready to devour the pot's content. Patsy wrapped small winter scarves around each bunny's neck and slipped on miniature stocking hats.

Claire clapped her hands. "They look adorable, Patsy. I love them. When did you think of the caps and scarves? And where did you get them?"

Patsy stood back, eyed her handiwork, then adjusted one hat. "I made them."

"And here I thought you were knitting for somebody's baby."

"Fooled you." She waggled her eyebrows. "I wanted to surprise you. I looked at them last week when the temperature started dropping and thought they looked cold."

"You made four scarves and hats in a week?" Claire reached down to examine one of the scarves. They were as meticulously knit as the one Patsy made for her.

"They only took a short time. I worked while Nathan and I watched TV."

Claire stared at the pots. "Maybe we should put a little wrapped present under the trees."

Nicole climbed down the ladder and blew on her hands. "That's a terrific idea, and I've got some itty-bitty boxes. I'll wrap them after we get the rest of the decorations done."

Eileen Carlson walked over and handed Claire a box of small red balls. "For your topiaries. I had them left over."

"Thank you, Eileen." Claire followed her next door to see what she'd done this year. Eileen had an odd but creative bent for decorating. This year, she borrowed a window mannequin from *Sunspots* and dressed it as The Grinch. Claire laughed. "You're a hoot." She wrapped an arm around Eileen's shoulder. "Your window always makes me laugh."

"That's my goal." She picked up a large roll of red ribbon. "Now I'm off to help Happy decorate his hobby shop. Ellie was helping him, but they both have the flair of a dead trout."

Still chuckling, Claire rejoined Patsy and Nicole as they painted the gallery windows with a snowy forest scene, foreground to the ceramic village that would go inside. When she finished her part of the windows, Claire planned to set up the tree inside and add a few of her new gold leaves to its ornamentation. She could hardly wait for tonight. Happy chatter and laughter bubbled from both sides of the street. Shoppers sidestepped them to enter the gallery, then after coming out stopped to watch them paint the window. For today, at least, they were part of the community.

"Can you stop for a second? I found a vase I can't leave without."

Claire looked over her shoulder. It was Motorcycle Mama.

"Of course." She set her brush down and went inside. The woman made her as nervous as a long-tailed cat in a room full of rocking chairs. Dressed in faded Levis with holes in the knees, a leather vest that had seen better days a decade ago, and a gray long-sleeved T-shirt with a grease spot on the front, she wasn't sure this woman could afford the price of the vase.

Motor-Mama pointed to a mid-level shelf and a cross-eyed raccoon. "It reminds me of Oscar."

Oscar? Her riding buddy? Was he worth two hundred and fifty dollars? He must've been because Motor-Mom didn't blink an eye and paid her in cash. She just hoped it wasn't stolen. Turning her back to grab some bubble wrap, she surreptitiously checked the bills for counterfeit.

"A Christmas present?" Claire wrapped the vase first in the plastic bubbles then newspaper for protection.

The woman nodded, so she called Nicole in to box and Christmas wrap it for her, then went back to her window painting. A few moments later, Motorcycle Mama walked past her, carrying the bow-bedecked package like it was a baby.

Patsy raised an eyebrow. "What did she buy?"

"Rocky Raccoon."

"Aww, the shelf will seem bare without him. Will you make another?"

"I don't think so. He was unique." She wondered what those two would do with the vase. Probably use it to store their drugs. "I'll make another raccoon, though, just not cross-eyed."

Nicole took a step back to study the window. "I can hardly wait to see all the others once it's all lit up. How does this parade work?"

Claire pointed to the far end of town. "After dark, we'll all congregate at the north end of town, starting with Chapel Lake Inn. Then everyone strolls along Sandy Shores Drive, looks at all the decorations, and chooses the annual winner. Cora Lee Rice started the tradition with Granny Newlander, during the Great Depression, to help keep the villagers' spirits up. When things got better, it died out. Then, my Great-aunt Lola retired and came home, and she and the gals reinstated it."

New York could have its Thanksgiving Day parade. Here it was the Boardwalk Window Parade and Claire preferred their version.

"I think it's a wonderful tradition," Nicole said. "It's homey and personal. I hope it never dies out."

Patsy put her arm around the girl's shoulders. "After the parade, the young folks pile into Pastor Seth's horse drawn wagon to go Christmas caroling to any shut-ins. You and Chase would have fun. They end up back at the church for a party."

Dipping a feather-tip brush in a can of white paint, Claire studied the window for inspiration. Her contribution was the snowflakes. She'd start with the ones at eye level, painting each one with lacy delicacy, and gradually move up to pinpoints near the top of the window. Her brush, steadied by her other hand, moved with rhythm, leaving tiny snowflakes in its wake. Patsy worked beside her.

Stepping back, Claire surveyed her handiwork then added one more to the quadrant she was working on. "Wes said he and Costancia are coming tonight."

"I wonder what she'll think of it."

"I don't know. She presents a sophistication that's so opposite of Wes." Claire continued painting in silence. How Costancia managed to snag his attention was a mystery.

Patsy nudged her. "What has you frowning?"

"Trying to figure out what Wes sees in her."

"I have to admit she's completely different from anyone he ever dated. Maybe that's what attracted him."

"I've tried to figure it out, but I come up blank every time. I'm just praying she doesn't succeed in persuading him to move to Brazil."

Claire finished the snowflakes and left Patsy to complete the ground scene beneath it while she went inside to dress the window. Soon, she had the pottery village in place. She'd made them—each a perfect model of its real Chapel Springs shop—the year they opened the gallery. Now, she strung lights through them to show through the windows. In the center of the scene, she put a two-foot tree and decorated it with tiny red and green balls. Then she added her gold leaf ornaments. They looked beautiful, sparkling in the lights.

Patsy tapped on the window and gave her a thumbs-up. Nicole waved at her to come out and see. Claire joined them and was pleased with the results. The finished window resembled Sandy Shores Drive in miniature, and Patsy's snow scene drew the eye into the village.

Claire nudged her. "Maybe we'll win this year. Your idea to paint the outside of the window added a third dimension to the display. I love it. Nicole, do you have enough tiny boxes to add some under the tree inside as well?"

"Sure do. I'm finished out here. I'll do them now."

Claire checked her watch. "Joel's meeting me at *The Rib Cage* for dinner. You're welcome to join us, Nicole."

She shook her head. "Thanks, but Chase is bringing me dinner. I want to be sure I get these finished before the parade begins." She held up one of the miniscule boxes to be wrapped. "I found some teeny bows for these. They're going to be adorable." She disappeared inside, taking a few empty boxes with her.

"She's a treasure." Patsy gathered up tissue and newspaper, stuffing it in an empty box.

"She's growing into an outstanding creative talent."

"And you're okay with her and Chase?"

Claire gave her a half smile. "Yeah. I'd rather Wes had fallen for her, but I'm fine with it. Do you think they're getting serious already?"

Patsy brought the last box inside and shut the door, shivering. "I think we might get snow tonight. It sure feels like it. And no, they aren't serious ... yet. But I think it's heading that way."

"Well, if it does, you'll be happy, won't you?"

"Definitely. She's open and lovable like Sandi."

And how Claire wished Costancia would be. She sighed. No use in empty wishes. She slid the boxes into the storage closet. "Are you ready? Is Nathan meeting us there?"

Patsy slid into her jacket. "Yes to both. Let's go."

When they exited the restaurant, the sun was below the horizon, and the temperature had dropped further. In the twilight, Chapel Springs appeared to be a fairyland of twinkle lights. The crowd swelled far beyond the normal residents this year, and Claire had to admit the visitors added to the festive atmosphere. She spied Motorcycle Mama and her "old man" and quickly looked the other way. Even though she'd become a customer, and though they hadn't caused any trouble, they still made her nervous.

She took Joel's hand and pulled him along. When they joined everyone outside Chapel Lake Inn, he let go of her. Why he thought anyone would see him holding her hand in this crowd, she didn't know. Still, he tried though it went against his nature. With a soft chuckle, she slid her hands into her coat pockets.

Felix welcomed the crowd, telling them to pick up a ballot from Ellie as they began the tour. Then he gave the signal to light the lampposts. That was the official start to the Parade. A soft golden glow fell over the street and lit up the village and—Claire looked up. Snow! Gentle flakes floated down, catching the light.

Joel nudged her and pointed over her shoulder. "Look. Wes is here."

She turned. He and Costancia stood a few yards behind them. Wes loved Christmas and the Boardwalk Window Parade. It seemed Costancia wasn't immune to its appeal if her wide-eyed, smiling face was any indication. She turned and kissed Wes then laughed. He stuck out his tongue to catch snowflakes. She did the same and caught one. As she laughed, she turned and froze, the delight sliding off her face as fast as a kid down a snowy hill when she locked gazes with Claire. She turned her back, took Wes's hand and pulled him toward the Inn.

Wes, oblivious to what had taken place, followed his wife. Claire's heart hurt from the snub. Beside her, Joel stiffened and Patsy gasped. Even the unflappable Nathan frowned.

Joel took a step in their son's direction. "It's time I took that boy aside and had a talk with him about his wife's behavior."

Claire grabbed his arm. "Let it go, honey. I don't want to put a wedge between him and us. And I don't want to spoil our fun tonight."

Joel's facial muscles twitched as he worked to control his anger. He took a deep breath. "Okay, but only because you asked. Let's get our ballot."

Strolling through lazy snowflakes, they picked up their voting slips from Ellie. The setup of a small table and a thermos beside her was typical, efficient Ellie. "Hot chocolate. Since I can't walk, I need something to keep me warm." She winked and giggled.

Claire eyed the thermos. Could their little librarian have something more than just hot chocolate in there? She took her ballot, and they went to look in the Inn's windows. This year, they depicted another inn from the first Christmas. With his guests leaning out the windows, a miniature innkeeper pointed to a stable across a field, where a small crowd of shepherds gathered. A star, hanging from the window's top corner, shone down on the scene, and through a speaker, Christmas carols played. Claire fingered the star on her necklace.

Next on the route was Lydia's spa, resplendent with a gorgeous display. The window, which was bedecked with green boughs, gold balls, and tiny twinkle lights, served as a frame to a huge Christmas tree covered in rose and gold glass balls and golden bows. Lydia and Graham, and all the employees stood at the entrance with trays, bearing cups of hot, spiced cider for everyone.

"I think the spa may be our winner this year," Claire whispered to her as they passed. "I sincerely hope so. It's a spectacular display, my friend."

Lydia gave her a one-armed hug as she balanced the tray against her hip. "Thank you, Claire. That means a lot to me."

Joel stared at her. "What did you say to Lydia that made her so happy?"

"That I hope she wins this year."

"But what about you and Patsy?"

Claire shrugged. "I love our window, but Lydia's is elegant. It's breathtaking."

He cocked his head. "I suppose, but it's a bit too frou-frou for me."

"I'm with you, buddy." Nathan scratched his chin. "Too pink."

They strolled on to the drugstore, where Tom Fowler had brought his trains from home and had them chugging through a mountain scene. Santa and his bag of toys sat atop the coal car. The lower part of the window was smeared with fingerprints. It was a big hit with the kids.

As they sauntered down the Drive, Claire stopped in front of the

Tome Tomb. The bookstore's window depicted the nativity scene but not the typical one. A cradle, nestled in a bed of hay, instead of a baby, an unfurled scroll lay in it, stamped "PAID IN FULL".

In the bottom corner of the window was a sign:

He came to pay a debt he did not owe

Because we owed a debt we could not pay

Beside her, Joel didn't pull her on but stood silent and contemplative. She searched his profile. A muscle twitched near his eye, and he swallowed. Still he didn't move. After a long moment, he looked at her, his eyes searching deep into hers. She didn't know what to say or *if* to say anything. It felt like a holy moment, but what was going through his mind?

Finally, one side of his mouth quirked up in a half smile, and he tugged on her sleeve. "We're stopping traffic."

They moved on, but Claire savored that moment in her heart, hoping its significance remained with him. They crossed the side street and stopped at *The Painted Loon*.

Nathan pointed to two of the figures on the miniature boardwalk. "Is that me and Joel?"

"What made you guess that?"

"The fishing poles."

Claire laughed. "I hoped you two would get that." She'd worked hard on getting their stances right. They moved on to *The Halls of Time* with its 1940s display. Wes and Costancia were behind them in the tour. Wanting to invite them over for dessert after they finished, Claire turned to find them.

They stood in front of *The Painted Loon*, viewing Claire and Patsy's work. Costancia pointed to something in the window. Wes threw his head back and laughed, but Costancia turned her head and pinned Claire with a look of shock on her face. Her eyes bugged then narrowed, and her lips thinned into a hate-filled glare. There was no mistaking her intent.

If looks could maim, Claire would be dripping blood. Next to her, Joel stiffened, his lips a thin line.

"Enough's enough." He took a step forward.

Chapter 30

S unlight streamed through Lydia's office window and across the resumes for physical therapists she considered good candidates. When she flipped through the stack the first time, she'd set those requesting moving expenses into a "no" pile. That simply wasn't in her budget.

Twisting a strand of hair as soothing strains from an Enya CD played in the background, she studied the resumes left in front of her. Three candidates looked promising. Two were from an adjoining state, and the other lived in Georgia. That avoided any problem with a cross-country move. She folded the corner on a resume from a woman in North Carolina. She'd worked in a spa before, giving her an edge over the other two. She'd talk to Morgan and get her opinion.

The phone rang. Graham's name blinked from the caller ID. Lydia picked up the receiver. "Hey, love. How's your day going?"

"Fine until a minute ago."

The edge in his voice sent her heart into her throat. "What's wrong?"

"One of the women who clears checks brought me three that bounced. They're from the Spa's account. What's going on?"

"Bounced? That can't be, Graham. Hold on. I'm sure it's a mistake." Lydia brought up her accounting software to look at her balance. "According to my books, I've got more than enough for this month's payables. And there's a little over sixty-three thousand dollars in the savings account. They always transfer if I'm a bit short."

"Lydia ..." Graham's voice strangled and caught. "There's one hundred dollars in your savings account. And the checking account is overdrawn by several thousand."

Her breath came faster and her head felt light. "That can't be. I need to call Nathan."

"Are you sure it isn't him?"

Could it be? No. Of that, she was sure. "No way. Nathan has been my accountant since I opened, Graham, and the accounts have always balanced with my software. That's what we set up, an accountability system. It was *his* idea." Her voice rose to a squeak. She took a breath. "It's a ridiculous question. There's some other answer."

"Call him. I'll be right there."

She hung up and dialed Nathan. She wasn't sure how to broach the subject. Did one just blurt something like this out? His phone rang and rang. Finally, he picked up.

"Nathan? This is Lydia."

"Yes?"

Why did he sound so reserved? Guarded. "Um, I've got a problem with some checks. Can you come over and help me straighten it out?"

"Lydia, I don't work for you anymore."

What? "Of course you do. I sent you this month's bills and you paid them." Something made her pause. Her heart stopped with her tongue. "Didn't you?" It came out in a breathless whisper.

"No, I haven't been there since last month. Your stepson made it clear that my services were no longer required."

"Kenny?" Her voice cracked. Her account, with big zeroes all over it, rose in her mind's eye. "Nathan, I never gave any such directive. Nor did he have the authority to tell you that. Can you come to the spa? Quickly?" Her head spun, feeling like it was filled with Co-cola.

Nathan's former reserve vanished. "Oh, my. I'm sorry, Lydia. I guess I should have checked with you, but Kenny was quite convincing, citing family and all. I'm on my way. Give me a few minutes."

Her dreams to expand the spa dried up and blew away like dandelion dust. Some other spa would be the recipient of the publicity the TV show *Losing* would have brought her. She dropped her head into her hands.

What now, Lord?

Ten minutes later, Graham walked into her office.

Nathan trailed him and tapped him on the shoulder. "Graham, what's going on? Lydia said there's a problem. I explained to her that Kenny fired me a month ago. Said I wasn't needed any longer, that he'd be doing all the accounting for the spa."

The color drained from Graham's face. He groaned and put one hand to his forehead. The other reached out to the desk as his knees buckled.

"Graham!" Lydia grabbed his arm and Nathan helped him into a wingback chair. "Are you all right? Do I need to call 911?"

"No." He put out a hand. "I'm all right. I just—Lydia, I'm ... I'm afraid it was ... it must have been Kenny. He's the one who cleared out the Spa's accounts."

She stared at him. "Cleared out? How?"

"Electronically. He must have hacked your computer to get your password. There've been two large withdrawals from the savings, and another from checking, virtually wiping them out. He was clever, though. He left a hundred in the savings account so it didn't generate an automatic notification of a closed account."

"May I look at your computer?" Nathan asked.

"You were never fired, Nathan. Go ahead."

She held her breath and moved aside to let Nathan sit. None of this seemed real. How could a member of her own family steal from her? Granted he hadn't been her stepson long, but she thought he cared for her, or at the very least accepted her.

Nathan looked up from the computer screen. "Kenny listed all these invoices as paid and cleared. You wouldn't have any reason to question your accounting software." He continued to scroll through the accounts. "I have to say he was clever with it."

Graham sank further into the chair. "This is all my fault."

He seemed to shrink before her eyes. Her heart went out to him, and she knelt in front of him. "No. Graham, this is *not* your fault. There are a lot of spoiled kids in the world who don't embezzle."

He blanched.

Lord, help us.

Graham had just started to realize he needed to be tougher with Kenny and now this. She squeezed his fingers. "Honey? Look at me, please?" She waited until his gaze—haunted and hollow—met hers. "I love you. This doesn't change that one bitty bit."

He searched her eyes for a long moment. "I'm so sorry." His voice held hope.

"It's not your fault. Do you believe me? I don't hold you accountable."

"I don't deserve you." He dropped his chin to his chest.

"Of course you don't."

His eyes popped open. Good. She wanted to shock him into actually hearing her.

"Graham, no one 'deserves' love. Real love is unconditional—like God's love for us. We can't earn it. It just *is*. I love you unconditionally."

Graham glanced at Nathan, but he was focused on the computer. Her husband stood, pulled her into his arms, and held her tight. "I love you, too," he whispered. "You mean more to me than anything."

"You, too." She kissed him. His color had returned. *Thank you, Lord.*

"We'll confront Kenny tonight." Graham released her, set her in the chair, then went to Nathan. "What can we do?"

"I'm running a quick audit. It's not as bad as it looks, as far as the bills go. This week's revenues will cover most of them. Since we never pay late, I can work with a couple of your suppliers to delay payment another month. It won't hurt your credit."

Graham began to pace. While Nathan got on the phone, she joined him. "Sugah? What are you thinking? You can't still be blaming yourself."

"No, but if I—"

"No buts. Kenny's old enough to know right from wrong. He's responsible, not you."

"Will you press charges against him?"

"He deserves it, but no. This is family. He can replace the money or pay it back."

Nathan tapped the monitor screen. "Looks like Kenny played around until he figured out your password, then he changed it at the bank a couple of days ago."

Graham's shoulders slumped. "When we told him he couldn't keep the new car."

Her heart broke for him. The retaliation wounded him deeply.

He looked down at her. "I feel a bit like David when his son Absalom betrayed him."

She laid her head against his chest. "We'll get through this, love. I'm praying it will wake Kenny up to his childish selfishness."

"If it doesn't, then he's on his own. No more bail-outs."

Nathan handed her a pad and pencil. "Figure out a new password. Use upper and lowercase letters, random numbers—no birthdates or addresses, and add a punctuation mark. That will make it nearly impossible to hack."

She wrote out the password and handed it to Nathan. "Keep a copy until I get it memorized."

"Lydia, if you wipe that counter again, you'll take the sealant off the granite."

She put the cloth down, joined Graham at the breakfast bar, and cupped her chin in her hands. "When do you suppose Kenny will be home?"

"He should be along any minute, although the way he's been acting the last couple of days, I'm not sure of anything about him."

She got back up and started a pot of coffee, wiping up the drops of water she splattered on the counter. The coffee canister had a light film of coffee dust on it. She wiped it off, then picked up the one containing sugar and cleaned it. Graham's hand stayed hers, and he took the dishrag from her, tossing it into the sink.

"Hushpuppy, you're strung as tight as a bass fiddle."

She reached for the lotion bottle next to the sink and squirted some into her hands. "I know. I can't help it. I'm mad at Kenny, but I hate confrontation. I know we have to do it, but I wish it were over already." She massaged the cream into her cuticles.

"Let's go turn on the TV and see if we can find a movie to take our minds off this for a little while."

She followed him to the couch. He'd spent some time this afternoon alone in prayer, and now he was calm. And, though she had lost her dream, the Lord filled her with peace about the loss. She didn't understand it, but she was certain they'd get through this. She just hated the anticipation of it.

Scrolling through the movie options, Graham stopped on *A Walk to Remember*. "What about this one?"

"I love that movie." It would help as she mourned the loss of her dream. While the movie rolled, her tears fell. At least she could blame them on the film's story. She hated to make Graham feel worse than he already had. She curled into his side as they watched.

But when the movie credits rolled, Kenny still hadn't come home.

"I'm going up to check his room." Graham stomped down the stairs.

She straightened the magazines on the coffee table. A moment later, he came back up. "His room's cleaned out. He's gone."

Lydia wasn't sure how she felt about that—glad to have avoided the confrontation or sorry to have missed the chance to let him have it. She leaned against the sofa's arm. "Now what?"

Determination settled over her husband like snow on the lawn, growing into a thick blanket. "It's time to make a change. I set up accounts for Kenny and Sherry when they were small, and added a little each year. I'm closing Kenny's tomorrow and putting that money into your account. It's not as much. It's only about forty-eight thousand, but it's a start. And if he comes home, I'll tell him he stole his own inheritance."

And if Kenny slunk home apologetic, her sweet husband might regret this later. She picked up a throw pillow and fluffed it before setting it down. "Maybe you should leave it and pray he becomes like the prodigal son. He may wake up one day."

Graham shook his head emphatically. "No. Even if he does come home, he still has to face the consequences of his actions. You've given him grace by not pressing charges. We don't know yet if the bank will or not. Either way, that account gets closed. If he comes to his senses, he'll agree it was the right decision."

"And you won't feel guilty?"

"Not anymore. It's proven to be a destructive emotion."

Chapter 31

Claire handed Joel a steaming mug of coffee and joined him on the couch to watch the football game. She snuggled beside him and pulled an afghan over their legs. The phone rang. Whoever it was had lousy timing. With a sigh, she tossed the blanket aside and answered it.

"I found some information." Nathan's voice blasted a double-barreled load of disgust.

"What?"

"What you asked me to."

"Oh, right. So, what did you find?"

"Not on the phone. Can you and Joel come over?"

"Give us five minutes." She hung up. "Joel, Nathan's learned something. We need to go over there."

"What do you mean 'learned something'?"

"About the high-rise or the investment group. I don't know exactly." She grabbed his arm and pulled him off the sofa. "Come on."

After bundling up against the cold, they jogged over to Patsy and Nathan's. A nice three-inch layer of snow blanketed the front yard and the warm light from the windows was inviting after the two-block sprint.

"Come on in." Patsy held the door open then took their coats and scarves. "Nathan's in the kitchen."

The kitchen, large but cozy was Claire's favorite room in Patsy's house, built in the 1920s. The original family had eight children and designed it to accommodate them all. Patsy had painted the walls a light sand color and decorated with dark green and brick red. A long farm table sat at one end of the room, flanked by a single bench where Nathan sat. Ladder back chairs lined the other side. A file folder lay on the table in front of him.

Claire dropped into a chair across from him. "What did you find?"

He opened the folder. "This same group, Muldoon Investments, has funded buildings in several towns around the Southeast. Every time, they've gotten the mayor or a member of the town council to expedite the permits with little or no public hearings. I had a private investigator dig further. In each case, either the town official was an investor or there was a payoff."

"I knew it. I felt it in my bones. Felix needs to be exposed for the shyster he is."

"Hold on, babe." Joel's hand stopped her. "We don't have any evidence of that. Do we, Nathan?"

"No. Felix isn't an investor."

How could that be? "Could he have used a different name?"

"No."

She tapped a finger on the open folder. "Are you sure? Do you need to dig deeper?"

"He's not an investor, Claire. I'm sure of that."

"If not Felix, then who?" Joel asked.

Nathan closed the file. "Dale Riley."

"Impossible!" *Dale?* "That country hick? He's dumber than a box of rocks. I can't believe he has the brains to do this."

Joel reached for the folder. "What I'd like to know is where he got the money. Something is mighty fishy. Dale hasn't held a full-time job since he got out of the army, and he never rose above the rank of sergeant, so his pay wasn't great. From what I know, he never invested any money. Or saved any. Every time he came to town before he lived here, he looked for a handout from anyone he could find. He rented real dives until he moved in with Felix."

Claire stared at him. "How do you know where he lived?"

"I went to see him a couple of times."

"What for?"

Joel shrugged. "Felix asked me to. He and Dale were on the outs for a few years, but Felix still loves his brother. If I was going to a tournament at a lake near Dale, Felix asked me to look in on him."

Claire had trouble computing the information. "You never told me."

Again with the shoulder. "It wasn't a big thing." He pulled on a corner of the folder. "Can I see this?"

Nathan held his hand over the folder. "Can't let you. Better for you not to know, anyway. The point is Dale's the investor. And it's a large amount." He picked up his cup and took a long swallow of coffee. "If this is what Chapel Springs has come to, it makes me want to accept the New York job."

Joel looked like he'd been punched. Claire shook her head. "No. It's not going to happen, Nathan. And we're going to make sure of it. I'm calling an emergency council meeting. Tonight. We can meet in the church basement." She turned to Patsy, who had come into the kitchen to make fresh coffee. "Pat-a-cake, call your dad. Nathan, you call Tom and Boone. Joel, you call Seth and ask if he'll unlock the church basement for us. I'll call Nancy and Ellie."

"Wait. What do we tell them?" Nathan asked.

"Tell them we've uncovered a conspiracy regarding the high-rise—a potential conflict of interest. Tell them confidentiality is of the utmost importance."

Claire bounced her leg while Boone called the meeting to order. As soon as he finished, she pushed Nathan's sealed file folder to the middle of the table. "We've uncovered—well, Nathan has—a potential conflict of interest with Muldoon Investments."

"Just who is Muldoon?" Tom Fowler asked.

"A Nashville-based investment group." Nathan tapped the folder. "From what I've found, they've pulled this scheme before. And Dale Riley is one of the investors."

"What?" Faye shook her head. "How is that possible? He doesn't have two nickels to rub together."

Claire pointed at her. "Bingo. That's what I intend to find out."

"It's in our list of questions," Nathan said. "There's also the conflict of interest. Felix is using his influence to urge the zoning committee to grant the permit. With his brother an investor, it's definitely a problem and quite possibly a felony."

Everyone spoke at once.

"What can we do?"

"How do we stop it?"

"It's preposterous!"

"They'll ruin this town."

"Felix needs to be impeached."

"Quiet down!" Boone banged his gavel, making Claire jump.

It was time to make some decisions. She grabbed a pencil and a piece of paper from Nathan's folder. "Does anyone have a suggestion? Because *I* suggest we confront Felix on this and avoid a scandal."

Boone nodded. "That's good, Claire. It just might stop the whole thing."

Doc shook his head. "I'm not so sure."

"What do you mean?" Ellie scribbled furiously on her notepad. "If Felix understands the potential for a media frenzy over this, why wouldn't he cave?"

"Because right now, Howie is meeting with the people of Muldoon Investments to accept an offer for the land."

"How do you know that, Doc?" Boone asked.

"Because I saw them together in town. With what you have told us, I put two and two together and came up with Benedict Arnold."

"But ... but ..." Claire couldn't get her tongue to work or her brain to wrap around the notion of Howie selling out his hometown. All she could see was the back of a moving van setting off for New York City and Patsy and Nathan following it. Her eyes narrowed and she grit her teeth. "Where are they?" She jumped up.

"Sit down, babe." Joel put his hand on her arm, pulling her back to her seat. "We can't charge in and stop them. Howie can sell to whomever he wants."

"But ... but ..."

"You already said that."

She swatted Joel's hand on her arm. "I'm frustrated beyond words."

"Hang on, Joel." Boone pulled on the little tuft of hair beneath his lower lip. "Claire has a good idea."

"Whoa." Doc motioned for them to sit. "Everyone sit for just a minute. Ask yourself why the Muldoon group is so positive about getting the permit? Could it be Felix already granted it?"

Ellie gasped. "He wouldn't dare. We didn't vote on it."

Claire frowned. "Felix is a lot of things, but I honestly can't imagine him doing that. He knows that dog wouldn't hunt." They were back to where they started. She tossed the pencil on the table. "Now what?"

Boone rose. "I say we put Claire's plan into action. We go see Felix."

When he answered his door, Claire studied Felix's body language. He appeared surprised to see them but not nervous. She'd half expected to see guilt stamped on his forehead or at least beads of sweat rolling down his temples.

"Come on in. What can I do for y'all?"

A bachelor, Felix's living room was small and unimaginative in its décor. The white walls didn't have a single piece of art to add any color. Newspapers covered the coffee table and a dirty plate and cup sat on the floor. Men never noticed those things. Ellie crossed to a lamp and straightened its skewed shade. Joel pushed the cat off the sofa. With eight people in the room, it seemed to shrink to miniscule.

Felix motioned for them to sit and took the remaining place on the couch. It sank beneath his weight, making Ellie lean against him. He shifted with an apologetic smile. "Now, what's the occasion?"

Boone stood by the fireplace. "Felix, we have a conflict of interest brewing."

A frown pulled Felix's brows together. "I'm not sure I like those words, Boone." He flicked his glare to Claire then back to Boone. "How about you explain this."

Boone threw a stare on him like a wrestler threw a headlock. "Did you know your brother is an investor with the Muldoon Group?"

Felix stared at Boone, slack-jawed. As the implication sank in, the color drained from his face. Claire had never seen him speechless. She couldn't remember him ever not having some comeback.

"Are ..." His voice broke, and he cleared his throat. "Are you sure about this?"

Nathan handed him a page from his folder. Felix scanned it and his face turned purple. "That imbecile!" Tiny drops of spit flew from his lips. "What does he think he's doing? This could ruin me."

"Not to mention Chapel Springs."

Felix's glare fell off his face at Claire's words. He blanched. "You're right, and no matter what you think of me, Claire, I wouldn't have that."

In her heart of hearts, she knew he spoke the truth. At the core, they both loved this town. "I know that," she admitted softly. "Oh, I suspected you, but I wondered why."

Doc slid his sleeve up and checked his watch. "Felix, do you have any thoughts of where your brother might have gotten the money to invest in this? He's ... well, he's never been known to have any spare change. He's always hitting folks up for a loan."

As Felix's gaze roved from one face to another, his face turned gray. "None." He scratched behind his ear. "You don't suppose—"

Newspapers flew off the coffee table with a sweep of his arm. Beneath them sat his laptop. He tapped on the keyboard, stared at the screen, and slammed the lid shut in disgust. "He got into my account, the dirty dawg. I didn't have as much as that paper of Nathan's showed, though, so he got the rest somewhere else."

The memory of Dale following Wes upstairs to take a computer lesson crossed Claire's mind. She glanced at Joel. He looked at her and grimaced. Yeah, he was thinking the same thing. But Wes couldn't have known what Dale would do.

Nathan nodded. "That's happened a lot lately. "I've tried to tell people about secure passwords. Let me guess. You used your birthday."

Felix nodded and Nathan shook his head.

"I think we need to find this meeting," Boone said.

Felix sat up. "What meeting?"

"Howie and the investment group are completing the property sale tonight. They're over at *The Rib Cage*." He turned to the others. "Jake called me on the way over here."

Felix stood. "Then how about we go there now?" A wicked gleam twinkled in his eye. "Tell them they ain't about to get no permit. See what my brother has to say then."

Because of the cold and expediency of time, they piled into Felix and Boone's cars. Within moments, they pulled into the parking lot at *The Rib Cage*. Jake met them at the door and pointed out the group in a secluded corner of the restaurant. Claire didn't recognize any of the three men at the table except Howie. Dale wasn't there. She glanced back at Jake and raised an eyebrow in question. He cocked his head toward the restroom.

Howie spotted them approaching. A muscle in his face twitched, and he glanced at the paperwork on the table. He closed a folder in front of him.

A large man with bushy eyebrows and massive shoulders sat across from Howie. He scowled. "What's going on here?" He glanced from the council to Howie. "Who are these people?"

Felix pushed to the front. "I'm mayor of Chapel Springs and—"

A door slamming on the other side of the restaurant interrupted him. Claire turned but didn't see anything.

"This permit isn't going to happen," Felix continued.

Mr. Shoulders rolled his cigar to the other side of his mouth. He leaned back and sneered. "We'll take it to court, of course. With our resources, we'll win. Now if y'all are cooperative, the town can see some nice revenues."

Felix sputtered. "You realize what the media will do with this?"

Another cigar-smoking man to Howie's right, frowned. "Why should they be interested?"

"For one, my brother is one of your investors."

Shoulders looked to his companion, whose grin spread. "Sure enough is. But that's their problem, not ours. Speaking of brothers, where is Dale? How long does it take to wash his hands?"

"I'll go get him," Felix said. "I'll bring him back too if I don't kill him first."

"While Felix is gone, I'd like to ask a question." Claire stared straight at cigar-man. "Why Chapel Springs?"

He shrugged. "Why not?"

Claire opened her mouth, but Joel nudged her and nodded toward Boone, who had some of Nathan's research in his hands.

Boone presented the paper to Howie and the two men. "What about this? You've done this in other towns before. We'll use it in court if you persist."

Shoulders shrugged again. "All speculation and innuendo. It won't hold up."

"Dale's not in the restroom." Felix dropped into a chair. "Apparently he saw us arrive and skipped out. I'll deal with him later. Right now—"

A tall, skeletal man with tufts of gray hair approached the table, huffing and puffing. Hat in hand, he paused to catch his breath. Claire stared at him, hoping he didn't expire before they knew who he was and what he wanted. He directed his question to the men seated at the table.

"Which one of you is Howard Newlander?"

Howie looked askance at him. "I am, why?"

"I'm Mortimer Kotkiewicz, your grandmother's attorney. The assisted living manager called me when she couldn't reach you. I called your office, and they told me where you were. I got here as quickly as I could. I'm sorry to inform you that your grandmother passed away yesterday."

Claire's eyes filled. She adored Granny Newlander. Howie's face worked. He swallowed and compressed his lips. At least he showed some sorrow. She knew the old gal loved him.

Mr. Kot-whatever-his-name-was put his hand on Howie's shoulder. "Son, I have the will with me." He glanced at the men assembled around the table. "If you'd like to step over here, we can dispense with this rather quickly." He winked at Claire. Now, what was that about?

Mr. Shoulders grinned and rolled his cigar to the other side of his mouth. "Go ahead, Newlander. That will make our business go smoother. As her heir and owner of the land, you're on better ground than with just her power of attorney."

Mr. Kots-itz tilted his aged head to the side, his scraggly gray brows dipping till the hairs interlocked. Then he took Howie's arm and directed him to a table a few feet away. They sat and Kotzie opened his briefcase with the methodical movements of an octogenarian. The papers came out in slow motion. Then, they put their heads together.

Howie's eyes went back and forth, following Kotzie's finger. Without warning, Howie's head popped up, and he stared at the attorney, his jaw slack. The old man nodded. Howie turned his head toward the Muldoon men and swallowed. Then Kotzie turned to another page, tapped a gnarled finger midway down the page and said something else. Claire tried to read his lips. It looked like he said grandfather. Howie's face turned a mottled red. She took a step closer. Joel pulled on her arm and shook his head. Rats. She wanted to know what the old man said that had Howie so upset.

Finally, Kotzie slid the papers back into his briefcase. He rose and shook hands with Howie. "I'll file these with the state tomorrow. I imagine you'll want to tell the mayor yourself."

At "mayor," Felix turned his head. Howie nodded, shook the old man's hand and watched him leave before he returned to the table. Once again, Kotzie winked at Claire and made scissor motions with his fingers. Claire couldn't wait to hear what Kotzie had told him.

"What happened?" she asked.

He looked at her, then Shoulders. His mouth worked but nothing came out. He took a deep breath and tried again. "Granny—" He sucked his lips in until they all but disappeared. His nostrils flared as the air flew in and out. A purple vein on his neck stood out, igniting a flare of smaller vessels on his cheek.

Howie was hyperventilating.

Chapter 32

Claire wanted to shake Howie. "Spit it out! Granny *what*?"

His eyes bulged, his face turned pink, then ruddy, and finally red. His words sputtered through clenched teeth. "Granddad. Not Granny—Granddad. He willed the land—upon Granny's death—to the town. For a park." The last word exploded from his mouth.

The hotel was done for. It took all her strength, but Claire managed to keep herself from dancing a jig. Her knees, however, quivered. Nathan grinned, and Joel clapped him on the back. Now, he and Patsy would stay in Chapel Springs.

Shoulders jumped up. "I'll sue!" Spittle flew and landed on the contract.

Cigar-man used his napkin to blot the mess then slid the document into his briefcase. "Even better, we'll contest the will." He raised his head, leveling his gaze at Howie. "The old man is dead. How do you know he was in his right mind?"

Of all the nerve. Claire stepped inches from Cigar-man's face. "Howie's granddaddy had all his wits even in his nineties. He was sharp as fox teeth. If this gets contested, I'll testify against it."

"You're a bunch of backwoods fools." Shoulders stormed out, his companions trailing him like a pack of mongrels.

Howie scowled at the retreating men then looked down at Claire and roared, "You did this. You were always butting in with Granny and Granddad." He clenched his fists.

Joel moved between her and Howie. "Back off, Newlander." He took another step, moving Claire behind him and putting distance between them.

Felix shouldered up beside Joel. "You left town. Claire spent the time you should have with your grandparents. She stepped up when you flaked out."

Claire blinked. Joel's defense she expected but did Felix realize what he was doing? Laughter bubbled inside her throat at the irony.

Howie slapped his hat against his pant leg. "Bah. You're all crazy. I'm out of here." Howie grabbed his coat, slung it over his shoulder. "Don't think you've heard the last of this." He stormed out of the restaurant.

For a moment, no one said a word. A pan clanged and crashed in the kitchen, resounding in the silence. Then Nathan and Joel high-fived each other.

"It's done." Joel put his hand on Claire's shoulder. "And you did it, Clairey-girl."

She shook her head. "It was Nathan who found the evidence."

"On *your* insistence," Ellie said. "But now that we've rid ourselves of the blight, what should we do about more room for the tourists?"

What would they do? The obvious answer would be to—"Build!" Claire blurted. "Add onto the existing inns. Faye, you've talked about expanding. I know the bank would approve a loan now because of the increased tourism. It's a good risk."

"For years, I dreamed about it. Before, we didn't have enough guests to warrant it." Her feet stomped a little victory dance. "But we sure do now. You really think the bank would make the loans?

Claire nodded. "Lacey brought up that possibility at loan committee last month. Everyone there loved the idea. Commercial loans in town are good for everyone."

Faye grabbed her handbag. "I'm going to get Paul and head to the bank."

Claire put her hand on Faye's arm, chuckling. "You should probably wait until tomorrow, Faye. No one's there at this hour."

The next morning, gathered around a table at *Dee's 'n' Doughs*, Claire filled Patsy in on the details Nathan had left out. Now she realized what Granny meant by lopping off Howie's head. "Granny made sure with her attorney shortly before she died." She told them about Kotzie's scissor motions. "If y'all could have seen Howie's face. I swanney, he was fixing to have a stroke."

"I can well imagine. I remember his temper."

"Granny'd jump on him like a duck on a June bug when he got a pout on." Claire chuckled. "She was a feisty old gal."

"I've always wondered how Howie got so spoiled."

"His daddy, Theo, was weak. I remember Granny talking when she didn't know some of us kids were close enough to hear. She didn't care much for her daughter-in-law's ways, either. That woman kept Howie's daddy hopping."

"Yet she spoiled Howie."

Claire shrugged. "I think Howie's mother had bigger plans for Theo than he had. When the family wouldn't fall in with her schemes, she put all her hope in her son. She was a social climber, although where she thought she'd climb to in Chapel Springs, I have no idea."

Dee escaped the kitchen and joined them. She slid her hairnet off and stuffed it in her pocket. "Congratulations, Claire. I hear you're the town heroine."

Claire rolled her eyes. "Until they remember it was my idea to revive the town, which started this mess."

Lydia and Lacey arrived together, followed by Faye and Gloria Jenkins.

"Faye told me about her expansion plans." Gloria pulled out a chair next to Lacey and dropped into it. "How soon can I come in and apply for a building loan?"

"As soon as the bank opens this morning."

Faye pulled a napkin from the canister on the table. "Here's what I plan to do." She sketched a couple of squares on the paper napkin. "I can easily double the size of the inn."

Gloria studied what Faye had drawn. "I'll have to go out the back to get enough room to expand. Our lot's not as wide as yours, but we have plenty of land behind *Sweet Dreams*."

"Well, don't take that," Dee pointed to the napkin, "into the bank. You'll need an architect's plans to get the loan, surely." She glanced at Lacey. "Won't she?"

"She can start the initial paperwork without plans. It won't hurt to take her drawing along."

Faye smoothed her napkin. "Do we know any architects? Claire, do you?"

"Not a one." She nudged Patsy. "Does Nathan have any as clients?"

"I can ask."

While they nattered about plans, Claire let her thoughts wander to Granny. Did the old gal know about her husband's will? Most likely.

Granny was no pushover. A true steel magnolia, she would have steered him like a car to do what she wanted. As sweet as Southern tea, she could get a weeping willow to stand up straight. And in this case, she probably wanted to make sure her daughter-in-law didn't get her Yankee hands on the family land. Howie's mama would have subdivided it or built a country club or something equally unfitting to Chapel Springs—like a high-rise hotel. Howie didn't fall far from his mama's tree.

"Where are you?" Patsy tapped her arm.

"What?" They were alone at the table. Claire blinked. "Where did everyone go?"

Patsy laughed. "To work. Where we need to be. What had you in a foggy bog?"

"Thinking about Granny. She used to tell me how she and Miss Cora Lee were best friends when they were girls. Though she was older, they invited Great Aunt Lola into their friendship. For all their differences, they were a lot alike. They kind of remind me of Faye and Gloria."

"Now that's a strange friendship."

Claire slipped her arm through Patsy's as they left the bakery. "I wonder if people say that about us?"

"Most likely." She laughed. "Either that or we're loony."

"Speaking of loony," Claire opened the gallery door. "Where do you think Dale got the money to invest with the Muldoon Investments group? It wasn't all from Felix's coffers."

Chapter 33

Claire fastened the chain around her neck and in the mirror, admired the way the star-leaf sat just below her collarbone. There were only a couple of weeks left until Christmas and she had sold out of her gold leaves—the star ones being the most popular. In a rush of gathering and Unity electroplating, she had a new batch ready to sell. Some people had an odd reaction to them, eyeing her with suspicion, while others wore delighted grins and winked. She couldn't understand it, but maybe the frowners were tree huggers who thought it was sacrilege to use real leaves. Whatever.

Tugging her boots up over her skinny jeans, she realized she hadn't actually pointed them out to Joel during the Boardwalk Window Parade. She was interested in his take. Well, she'd show him a couple of them tonight.

She shoved her foot all the way into the boot. Something stopped her. What in tarnation? After yanking it off, she thrust her hand inside and felt the round end of a dog biscuit.

"Well, shut my mouth. Shiloh!" The mastiff, snoozing in the doorway, raised his head from his paws. His eyes brightened when he saw the Milkbone that Claire shook at him.

"Why do you have to hide your cookies? There are no other dogs in this house to steal them." The big goof doggy-smiled at her and lumbered over to take the treat from her hand. The large biscuit stuck straight out of his mouth like a cigar, making her laugh. "You look like Winston Churchill."

The boot was much easier to slip on now that it was empty of Shiloh's treasure. She snatched a jacket off its hanger then bent to pat the dog's massive head.

"Be a good boy. I'll see you later. Eew, wipe your chops, Shiloh." She laid one of the ever-present doggie towels across his paws. He dutifully wiped his face against it, then nibbled his front teeth on it. Crazy dog thought he was brushing them.

She jogged down the stairs and out the door. The snow they got on Friday already melted. Later in the season, they'd probably get another snowfall that would stick for a while, and she looked forward to it. If they got more than three inches, Joel loved to bring out the toboggan. That was always fun. Patsy and Nathan usually joined them and the men's competitiveness ended in loads of laughter and turned over toboggans.

She rounded the corner and went straight for *The Painted Loon*, foregoing *Dee's 'n' Doughs* this morning. She was late and with the Christmas rush, everyone was probably already at work. "Morning," she called as she entered.

In one corner of the gallery, Nicole removed a painting from its easel for a customer. It was one of Patsy's Lake & Loon scenes. The tourists loved them, but most bought the more affordable giclée prints, which looked like originals but were in actuality, prints on canvas. This one was an original. The customer looked vaguely familiar. She nodded hello and moved closer. It was Karen Rice, Miss Cora Lee's great-granddaughter. The last time she had been in Chapel Springs was years ago—she'd still been a teenager. No, she was here once since then, but Claire couldn't remember when.

"Karen?"

The woman turned and after a second, recognition lit her eyes. "Miss Claire, how are you?" She pointed to the display rack of whimsy pots. "Are these yours? My husband bought a unicorn pot and my little boy has loved it. He thinks it's magical."

"How delightful. I'd love to meet him. How old is he?" She tried to think how old Karen would be. Thirty, maybe. She looked even younger, with her smooth olive complexion. Her brown hair had both golden and auburn highlights, so well done, they appeared natural. Were they?

"He's six. Rick brought the pot home when JJ was three."

"I suppose he's over at your Nana's. Nicole, I'll take care of Karen. Go tell Patsy to come see who's here, but don't tell her." Claire turned back to Karen. "So, look at you, all grown up. How is your Nana? I was by to see her last week, but she wasn't there."

"She's beginning to fail, I'm afraid. I haven't seen her as much as I should since JJ was born. I'm having to move her into assisted living this weekend."

Claire patted her hand. "I know she understands, Karen. She's kept us all up to date on your career. She's very proud of you and rightly so. Is she objecting to the assisted living?"

"Not really. She used to visit Granny Newlander at Sunny Meadows, so that's where I'm taking her."

"You do know Granny passed away, don't you?"

Karen's wistful smile tugged Claire's heartstrings. "Yes, but she has other friends there, so she's not against the move. She knows I'm too far away to care for her. I offered to have her with us, but she flat refused to move to Atlanta."

That would finish off the poor old dear. Mountain folk don't do well in big cities, and Miss Cora Lee was mountain folk.

"Karen Ja—Rice!" Patsy's squeal turned heads. It was a good thing she caught herself or they'd have had a mob on their hands. Several of Karen's books had made the New York Times bestseller list, and people knew the name, Jardine.

Patsy took the painting from her, thrust it at Claire, and hugged Karen. "We don't see you enough in Chapel Springs. How's your little boy?"

Patsy knew about him? How come she didn't? She took the painting Karen had chosen to the register for Nicole to wrap. Patsy finished visiting with Karen and went back to her work.

Karen paid for the painting and started to leave. She turned back at the door. "It was nice to see you again, Miss Claire. Say hello to Adrianna for me."

"I'd forgotten you two were friends. I'll be sure to." Claire wandered back to the workroom.

Patsy's head popped out from behind her easel. "It was nice seeing Karen, wasn't it?"

"It was, but I'm reminded how life keeps marching on. She's putting Miss Cora Lee in Sunny Meadows this weekend. Now the old house will be empty. I wonder what they'll do with it."

"Maybe Karen and her husband will keep it for a weekend place."

"Maybe." Claire extracted her reading glasses from her pocket and picked up her commissioned orders list. She had a dozen more pieces to make for Christmas. The first—and a fun one—was for a chocolate-chip-cookie cookie jar. Hmm, that gave her an idea for a set of canisters made to look like what they held—a coffee bean, a penne pasta, hmm, what would be best for the flour one? After jotting a couple of notes about the canister set, she donned her work apron and pulled a large lump of clay from the barrel.

The wet clay took shape beneath her hands as she lifted and smoothed. When it reached the right point, she began to hollow it out, pushing and pulling, manipulating its form. She wet her fingers in the bucket of cool water beside her and applied it to the clay's surface to keep it pliable. Like God did to her. If she grew brittle with trials, he rained blessings on her to keep her pliable. And, she supposed, the opposite.

Is that what you do, Lord? Send a trial when I get so confident I take over?

After the second pull, the cookie jar had reached the dimensions she wanted. She slowed the wheel and slid the wire beneath it, releasing the jar from its hold on the wheel head. Now, she needed to add the "chocolate chips." Judging the size of the cookie jar, she'd need a good six-dozen.

Patsy popped her head around the easel. "What has you chuckling?"

"Was I? I didn't realize."

"So, what was it?"

"Wes would love one of these cookie jars—filled with the cookie it represents."

"Good idea."

"I'm not so sure now that I've said it out loud. Costancia might take it wrong." Claire pulled out a second smaller lump of clay. She rolled it into a long snake and pinched off a small piece the size of a chocolate chip. She then pulled a teeny bit upward to form the chip's tip. One down and seventy-one to go.

Patsy stood and stretched. "You can't keep worrying about offending her. That girl's piqued by you merely taking a breath."

"Why do you think that is? Really? I've tried and tried to think of what I could have done to offend her. I even called the Spanish teacher and asked if something I said in Spanish might have been an insult in Portuguese."

"And?"

"The answer was no. I'm weary from the stress of it. I don't know what to do."

"Then let God do it."

"I'm trying, but I miss seeing Wes. She hardly ever lets him come over, and we haven't been invited to their place."

"Claire?" Nicole's voice quavered.

"What's wrong, sugar?" Claire wiped her hands on her apron.

"Uh, the pol—"

"Claire Bennett?"

"Jim Bob?" The new sheriff filled the doorway. When the town burgeoned with tourists and celebrities, it had become apparent Chapel Springs needed their own police department, especially after the college crowd decided their little village was the perfect party town. They ran a special election and Jim Bob Taylor won. A bit of a yahoo, he'd hired his cousin, Farley, as deputy, and to their credit, the two of them managed to keep the peace.

"What are you doing here?"

"Claire Bennett, you're under arrest."

Chapter 34

Patsy's palette fell on the floor with a loud clatter, startling Claire from her stool. She jumped to her feet and faced Jim Bob squarely. "What are you talking about? Arrested for *what*?"

"Drug trafficking—marijuana to be specific." He pulled out a business-sized card from his breast pocket and began reading. "You have the right to remain silent. Anything you—"

"Me? Drugs? You're crazy. This has to be some kind of mistake." Or a nightmare from which she'd awake any minute now. Farley appeared from behind the sheriff.

"—say can and will be used against you in a court of law—"

This was nuts.

Patsy stomped forward. "Jim Bob, Claire wouldn't even know what marijuana looks like. Neither would I. How could she—"

"Step aside, Patsy. Don't interfere." He cleared his throat. "You have the right to an attorney. If you cannot afford an attorney, one will be appointed for you. Do you understand your rights?"

Candid Camera. It had to be. She thought that show went off the air, but this had to be—

She scanned the room. "Jim Bob, is this a joke?"

"No, ma'am. Now please turn around."

"What for?"

"So Farley can handcuff you."

"What?" Patsy shoved between the deputy and Claire. "Don't you lay a hand on her."

Farley hesitated and Jim Bob shook his finger in Patsy's face. "Unless you want to join her in jail for obstruction of justice, kindly move aside.

It's standard treatment of a drug trafficker."

Farley moved toward Claire.

Patsy didn't back down. "Claire is no druggie, and you know it."

Farley backed up.

Jim Bob glared at Patsy. "That doesn't mean she wouldn't sell them."

Farley moved in again and turned Claire around, clapping the cuffs on her. Suddenly this felt very real, and she was scared spitless.

"Patsy." Claire's voice squeaked out. "Get Joel." Tears spilled over and down her cheeks. "This ... it has to be some kind of misunderstanding."

Patsy stood her ground. "I'm not letting him take you out of here in handcuffs." She turned on Jim Bob and sidled closer.

He backed up a bit. "Now, Patsy—"

"Don't you Patsy me, you puffed up possum." Her finger jabbed at his chest with each word. "Claire is on the town council, for pity's sake."

"That doesn't give her immunity. Just the opposite, to my way of thinking. She should have thought about her standing in the community before she got involved in this."

God, where are you? Claire could hardly catch her breath. Fear sucked it right out of her. As Patsy pounced closer and backed the sheriff up against the drying shelves, a vision rose from a few months ago of the sarcastic art critic being backed into a display shelf and clobbered by her turkey sculpture.

"Patsy, stop!"

Her warning came too late. The shelving rattled and a large vase on the top—right above the sheriff's head—wobbled.

Patsy stood still as a statue, her eyes wide and her mouth gaping. Claire stopped trying to breathe.

Then it toppled.

Claire shoved her shoulder into Jim Bob, knocking him aside.

The sheriff drew his gun on his way down.

Farley gaped.

Patsy screamed.

Nicole screamed.

Claire dove.

A gun went off. Pain exploded and the lights went out.

Cold. Wet.

Water dribbled into her ear. Something cold and wet was lying on her face.

"She's coming around." Patsy had her hand on Claire's shoulder. "Don't move, honey. You've got a nasty cut on your head and may have a concussion or even a skull fracture."

Claire opened her eyes. Patsy was glaring at someone over her shoulder. Claire couldn't see that far. It hurt to look. She shut her eyes again. Who ... or what ... hit her?

"She's not getting out of going to jail."

Claire blinked, this time squinting. Above her, Jim Bob glowered. What was the sheriff doing here?

"You idiot!" Patsy screeched. "She saved you from getting beaned."

Blood ran into Claire's eye. She raised her hand, but Patsy stopped her. "Don't touch it."

"I thought she was trying to get away."

Get away? From who? Why? What—?

"Jim Bob, you're pathetic." Patsy's voice dripped disgust. "She took that vase for you, buster. You can forget another term."

Vase?

Farley moved next to Patsy and put his hand on Claire's head, applying pressure to the wound. "Call an ambulance."

"I called Doc." Nicole stood over her with her cell phone at her ear.

Patsy glared at Farley and pushed him out of the way. "Leave her alone. I'll do that." Her face hovered above Claire. Nicole's voice grew faint. Patsy's mouth moved. What was she saying? Something about Joel.

She hoped he hurried.

"Claire? Honey?"

Joel. Claire struggled to open her eyes. They felt like they were glued shut. Was she dead, then? They put pennies on dead people's eyes to keep them shut. Did she have pennies on hers? But how could she hear Joel if she were dead?

"Claire, baby, it's me."

She wanted to answer him, but her mouth was glued as tight as her eyelids. Did the sheriff do that so she couldn't talk? But why? Finally, she shoved her tongue between her lips and managed to mouth, "Water."

"She's coming to. She passed out when she first got hit and then again a few minutes ago." Patsy turned to Doc. When did he get here? "Does that mean she has a concussion or her skull's fractured?"

"Not necessarily, but judging by the size of that vase, I wouldn't rule it out, although Claire's pretty hard-headed. I remember when she fell out of a shopping cart at the hardware store. She was about two and she landed on her head. Cracked the concrete floor, but she was fine."

Patsy swatted her dad's arm. "That's not true and you know it."

"It is. Okay, she didn't crack the concrete but she was fine. And once I stitch this up, I think she'll be okay."

Jim Bob arrested her, the vase fell, and ... it all came back to her now. "Can I get up now? This floor's cold and hard."

"See?" Doc said. "Told you she'd be fine." He turned to Jim Bob. "Joel and I are taking her over to the clinic to stitch her up and X-ray her."

Jim Bob stuck his hand up. "Hold it. No way. She's under arrest."

Doc and Joel both turned on him, but Doc stopped Joel, whose fists were clenched. "You want to be responsible for her not getting medical attention? What if, as my daughter pointed out, her skull is, in fact, fractured? That would make a great news story, and I think," he stretched his neck to see through to the gallery showroom, "I see Boone in the doorway. Word travels fast in Chapel Springs."

Jim Bob blanched and coughed. "I guess I can wait until you're done."

Joel bent and picked her up, cradling her close to his chest. Worry pinched his brow. His eyes searched hers. "When Nicole called me about the sheriff, I ran over here. I was just outside when I heard the gunshot." He glared at Jim Bob. "You could have killed her."

"When that vase hit me, I thought I *was* a goner," Claire moaned.

Doc patted her back. "You need stitches. And that X-ray. Come on."

"I'm coming with you." Jim Bob's voice echoed in the room. "I don't trust any of you not to help her escape."

In the shape she was in? Good grief. What a doofus.

Joel turned toward the door where the sheriff stood. "You pompous bag of wind. We already explained this to you. She had no idea those leaves were marijuana."

"And Farley already searched the gallery," Patsy said. "There aren't any plants here. Besides, Claire couldn't keep a houseplant alive."

Her hubby and Pat-a-cake always came to her rescue. Claire looked over Joel's shoulder. Patsy stood by her worktable, ready to attack. Claire aimed a little smile at her. But she still couldn't understand what they were all talking about.

"What marijuana?"

"Well, until she can prove where they came from, she's under arrest."

Nobody paid any attention to her.

"You can come with us," Doc said. "I hope you're good with the sight of blood."

A little while later after being X-rayed and ruling out a skull fracture, Claire laid on the table back in one of the exam rooms. Her brother-in-law, Vince, lifted the cloth from her forehead. "That's a nasty cut, Claire. Good thing you wear bangs." He wet a gauze pad with alcohol and wiped the wound.

"Yeowch." Her whole body jerked. "That stings."

"You make lethal vases. Be thankful it didn't take you out." He picked up a straight razor.

"What's that for? Please tell me you aren't going to shave my head." *Please!*

"I'm sorry, Claire, but I have to."

"Then cut it off first and save the hair for me."

"What?" Vince stared at her. His brows dipped so far they rested on the bridge of his nose.

"Just humor her," Joel said to his brother as he squeezed her hand.

She sent him a thankful glance.

"We don't know what's going on in that head of hers, but it got a hard knock. So save the hair." A cheeky grin stretched across his face.

So much for sympathy. Something stung her scalp. "Ouch."

"That will numb it so we can stitch." Vince glared over his shoulder at Jim Bob, who stood blocking the doorway. "You'll be getting quite a few stitches."

She winced and Joel squeezed her hand again. "I remember another time when you got stitches." He elbowed Doc, who stood next to Vince, observing. "Remember that, Doc? We'd just bought the house and she decided to store some things in the attic. She shoved that heavy box up the ladder."

Doc chuckled. "I remember the box didn't want to be up there and came back down the ladder. But that time it was her shoulder that took the brunt of it."

Even if it did make Joel relax, they were having too much fun at her expense. "Hey, I'm here, remember? Stop telling stories about me."

Vince handed Joel a baggie and took his scissors to a swatch of her hair. He handed it to Joel, who laid it in the baggie, sealed it, and gave it to Claire.

"Thank you."

"I'm dying to know what you have planned for that."

"Never you mind." She'd learned a thing or two helping with the community plays, one being how to use spirit gum to glue hair on an actor's face for a beard. The same trick should work on heads.

A sharp intake of breath came from the doorway. Claire couldn't move her head, but she rolled her eyes in that direction. Jim Bob's eyes widened as Vince made the first stitch, and he lost all his color. He flicked his gaze off her to the ceiling. As Vince sewed the next stitch, he made a small scratching noise with his tongue.

Jim Bob crumpled in the doorway.

She looked at her brother-in-law and giggled. "Some big bad sheriff."

Joel grinned. "Think I should help him up?"

"Naw," Vince said as he inserted another stitch. "He wanted to make sure she doesn't escape, and we wouldn't want to take him away from his duty."

Vince continued to work on her and banter with Joel. Doc took a call on his cell phone. It all seemed so normal, but as she lay there, she realized she was going to jail. She'd never been inside the jail. What would happen to her? What if she were tossed in with some hardcore criminals? What if they cornered her?

"Claire? Am I hurting you? You're hyperventilating."

"Hurt? No. I'm thinking ... what—" She glanced at Joel. "What's going to happen to me in jail?" It came out in a whisper.

"I wouldn't worry too much," Doc said, shaking his head. "Apparently you aren't going to be there alone."

"What do you mean?"

"My daughter just got herself arrested."

"What?"

"Claire! Hold still." Vince put his hand on her shoulder and shoved her back down. "I only have a few more stitches to put in."

She raised her hand to feel, but he swatted it away.

"How many am I getting?" she asked.

"Eighteen. It wasn't a straight cut. It sort of resembles one of your whimsy pieces."

It pulled when she frowned. "Ouch. What are you talking about?"

"It's loosely shaped like a turkey come home to roost." He chuckled.

"Oh, great." Like the one that clobbered the art critic. "Like I need a reminder of that episode?"

Jim Bob moaned from the doorway.

That reminded her—"Doc, what happened with Patsy?"

"Farley decided to search your backyard while we were mending you. Without a warrant, I might add. So, she let Shiloh out. Need I say more?"

Claire bit her lower lip to keep from giggling since that hurt her head. "What happened?"

"Shiloh chased him up a tree and Patsy refused to call him off."

Joel laughed. "She didn't tell him Shiloh's bark is all he's got?"

"Not if I know my daughter, she didn't. He's still up there from what I gathered. She told me he said once he got down, she was under arrest. And my guess is until Joel goes home, Farley's still up that tree."

Shiloh deserved an extra cookie for that.

Vince finally put the last stitch in her head and laid a bandage over it. After telling Joel about the care and cleaning of her wound, he patted her shoulder. "I'll bake you a file in a cake, big sister, and bring it to you tonight."

Claire tried, but with her head hurting and fear of what was coming, instead of a witty comeback, all she could conjure up was the vision of a line of hardened criminals backing her into a wall. When she needed it most, her funny bone had deserted her. The traitor.

Chapter 35

The steel door clanged shut, making Claire jump and starting a whole new throbbing in her head. A set of narrow bunk beds stood against each wall of the small cell, and a toilet sat out in the open against the back wall. She stared at it in the dim light. Was she expected to do her business in front of everyone? Her eyes darted around. Who else was here? Her stomach tried to crawl out her throat.

"You okay?" Patsy's voice drifted out of the shadows from a corner of the cell behind a bunk bed.

Claire jumped, sure she was hearing things. Then her BFF stepped forward. Relief weakened her knees. Pat-a-cake wrapped an arm around her shoulders and helped her sit on the closest lower bunk.

"Except for my head." Now that her eyes were adjusted to the low light, she studied her surroundings. On the upper bunk across from her, someone snored. Loudly. She glanced at Patsy, whose mouth twitched.

"Have you met our cellmate?"

Patsy shook her head. "I haven't been here more than ten minutes. I hid in that corner until you arrived." She kept her voice low.

Claire didn't blame her for hiding. But with her best friend at her side, her fear wasn't as overwhelming.

"Tell me what happened with Farley." She put her hand up to the bandage that covered her wound. The Novocain was wearing off and the pain pills were starting to take effect. The sting on her head was less, but now she had to concentrate not to drool. With each heartbeat, her brain went zub zub.

Patsy's lip twitched some more. "He really goofed. He didn't have a search warrant. I couldn't believe he wanted to get in your yard without one. But I wanted to be a good citizen, so I said I'd let him in."

Holding her head, Claire shook with silent laughter. Patsy was the best BFF in the world. "I wish I could have seen him when Shiloh appeared."

Patsy leaned into her. "He came through that doggie door like a bullet. Farley was about to go into your shed when he heard the first woof." She stopped and looked at the other bunk, then took a deep breath to control her laughter. "He barely made it up the tree before Shiloh reached him. I swear I saw a dark stain on the back of his trousers."

"I suppose you didn't tell him that Shiloh wouldn't have bitten him, that he just wanted to play?"

Patsy crossed her arms and slowly shook her head. "Nope. No way. He was conducting an illegal search and deserved everything he got."

Footsteps echoed in the passageway between the four cells. Claire turned toward the sound. Jim Bob opened the door and pushed in a girl who had more holes in her than Swiss cheese. Goth-girl must have had five pounds of jewelry in her nose, eyebrows and lips. Claire had never seen so many piercings. She looked too slight to hold all that extra weight. Added to the jewelry, black hair, and black lipstick, dark tattoos ran from the side of her face, down her neck and adorned both arms. When she snapped at the sheriff, a white ball in her tongue flashed in the dim light. Eew.

Jim Bob removed her cuffs, then he stepped back and closed the door. The lock clanked. The girl rubbed her wrists and looked around. Her gaze fell on Claire and Patsy. Her face hardened and she glared.

"What're you two starin' at?" Her voice, harsh and challenging, rang out in the silence.

Claire and Patsy shrank back, shaking their heads. In the top bunk across the cell, a face appeared. Vague recognition niggled Claire's mind. Who was she?

"Keep it down, will ya?"

Claire blinked. *Motorcycle Mama?* She glanced at Patsy, who was shaking and Claire was sure it wasn't with laughter. What had they gotten themselves into? It was her fault poor Pat-a-cake was here.

Goth-girl whirled around. "Shut-up."

Uh-oh. Claire pulled her feet up and scooted to the dark corner of the lower bunk, pulling Patsy with her.

Motorcycle Mama threw her legs over the edge of the bunk and slid to the floor. Her bleached blonde hair bore the distinct style of booze-induced dreams. More than a head taller than Goth-girl, Motor-mom faced off with her, looking down her nose. Goth-girl scrunched hers, curling her upper lip, and like two cats they circled, taking each other's measure.

Claire didn't know whether to call out for Jim Bob or stay in the shadows. Patsy clung to her like a leech, squeezing her arm. Then the two stopped circling. Goth-girl must have decided Motorcycle Mama had too much height and weight on her. She shrugged, then flopped onto the lower bunk across the cell and rolled over to face the wall.

Claire's heart pounded as Motor-mom bent over, hands on her hips, and peered in at her and Patsy, cowering in the shadows. Then the dark rooted blonde's eyes widened and she barked a harsh, smoker's laugh, which made Claire's head pound in counter sync to her heart. She scootched back against the wall, wishing she could stop her knees from shaking.

Motor-mom took a step closer. "Well, lookey what we have here. What did you two do? Frame a duck?" She threw her head back, screeching a cackle at her own joke.

"Keep it down in there!" Jim Bob's voice echoed in the cell.

Goth-girl rolled over and sat up with interest. "Who framed who?"

"It's the loon lady and her sidekick."

Goth-girl jumped up. "Whatta ya mean 'loon lady?' Is she crazy? I ain't stayin' with no crazies."

Motor-mom turned around and told her about Claire's pottery. "The other one's not a bad artist, either."

Not bad? Patsy was—Claire snorted and her knees stopped their shaking. "She's the best in the South and better than any you've ever had the privilege of seeing."

She pushed forward and stood. The cell walls spun. Uh-oh. That wasn't such a smart move. She reached a hand back to the bunk's frame and took a breath. That helped. The last thing she needed was to give over to weakness. A scene from a movie where the hero's cellmates beat him up rolled across her mind's screen. Seeing herself and Patsy at the bottom of a cell brawl, she swallowed. If she didn't want to get beaten to a pulp—or worse—she had to stand up to them.

Um, how did she do that? She released her hold on the bunk. Motor-mama stood across from her, her hands on hips. Claire put hers on her hips and stood tall. Yeah, that looked good. Then she stuck out her chin and narrowed her eyes. Raising one side of her lip, she hoped it looked intimidating.

Claire inhaled, trying to look bigger. Her five-foot-seven wasn't short by any stretch of the imagination, but Motor-mom had two inches on her. And fifty pounds. She stared at her arms and flexed, hoping the woman saw her strength. Too bad the only muscles she had were her forearms. She looked like Popeye for pity's sake.

Motor-mama burst out laughing. She bent over, hands on her knees, and cackled. That was *not* the reaction Claire wanted.

Goth-girl stared at her a moment then rolled her eyes. "Loonies. I'm locked up with a bunch of loonies."

Motor-mama gasped for breath. "Naw, just a couple of local art types. They're nuts, all right, but harmless." She stuck out her hand to Claire. "I'm *Hazel* Jones, from Cucamonga, California."

Cucamonga? Claire always thought that was an old comedian's joke.

When she didn't move, Hazel grabbed her hand, pumping it with bone-rattling vigor. When she let go, she plopped down on Goth-girl's bunk, shoving her over and receiving a glare for her efforts.

Claire's shoulder ached from the handshake. She rubbed it. It must have gotten bruised when she dove to push the sheriff out of the way. By tomorrow, she probably wouldn't be able to move.

She eyed their two cellmates. "So, what put you in here?"

"We're on a cross-country motorcycle run. We partied too hard last night, and the sheriff tossed us both in the hoosegow."

Beside her, Patsy finally quit shaking. "It's nice to meet you, Hazel."

"Nice?" Goth-girl snorted. "Y'all sound like yer at a ladies tea. You're in jail, in case ya didn't notice." She raised her hand like she held a teacup with her pinkie extended. "Ya don't have tea parties in here."

"Really?"

Patsy kicked Claire's ankle. Okay, maybe sarcasm wasn't the smartest thing in this situation, but she couldn't help it.

Goth-girl pinned her with a lip-curled stare, but Claire hadn't lived through five teenagers without gaining a few smarts. This kid was harmless in spite of her rough exterior.

She took a chance. "I'm in for drug-running. What about you?"

"You? Running drugs?" Goth-girl hooted.

Claire didn't know whether to be relieved or insulted. "Well, I didn't really do anything. I just gold plated some leaves I found in the forest. They make pretty necklaces. How was I to know they were marijuana?"

That stopped Goth-girl's giggles, and even Hazel stared at her. "You never saw a marijuana leaf? Where you been, girl, under a rock?"

Claire shared a glance with Patsy, who was losing the battle at hiding her amusement. "I guess I've lived a fairly sheltered life."

"Ya think?" The sharp edge to Goth-girl's sarcasm had dulled. She shook her head. "My granny wouldn't have known one either."

"Granny? Now just a—"

"Back off, Claire." Patsy elbowed her. "I'm sure she didn't mean anything by it."

With her head tilted to the side, the kid did look awfully young. "Just how old are you?" Claire asked.

"A hundred and four."

Okay, so her sarcasm was still kicking. "You carry it well."

Hazel cackled again. "Kid, whattcher name?"

Goth-girl rolled those huge eyes. Her lips moved.

"What?" Hazel knocked her right thigh against hers. "Speak up."

"Mel."

"Mel? What kind—" Claire blinked. "Oh. Melanie."

Nobody laughed. It was simply too unbelievable. Not some hippie name, or hard biker-chick name, but Melanie. A huge grin spread itself across Claire's face.

Mel jumped up, ready to fight. "Ya wanna make somethin' of it?"

Claire would probably regret this, but—she grabbed Mel in a hug. "Nah. It's hard going through life defending yourself." She pushed Mel back, holding her at arm's length. "I've had to defend myself all my life."

"You?" Her face twisted with disbelief. "What for?"

Claire shrugged. "I'm kind of a magnet for disaster."

Patsy chuckled and patted her shoulder. "Things just happen to Claire. Like this." She gestured around the cell. "She's an innocent who moves much too fast. The same thing happens with her mouth." She winked at Mel.

A smile spread across the kid's face. "Yeah. I had a friend like that, once. She ended up in the slammer, too."

Oh, great. "So, um, how do you spend your time in here?"

Mel and Hazel grinned at each other. "Waiting to get out." Their words overlapped each other, and the subsequent laughter echoed in the cell.

"Okay, *ladies*, pipe down," the sheriff's voice bellowed again. He hadn't shut the door between the back cells and the outer office or whatever you call the public part of the police station.

The pain meds had kicked in hard. Feeling woozy, Claire laid down on the bunk while the others talked amongst themselves. Patsy was telling them something, but her voice became indistinguishable from Motor-mom's, uh, Hazel's. Right. Their words grew softer until—

"Claire?"

"Mmmm?" Why wouldn't Joel let her sleep?

Wait a minute. She was in jail. Had he been arrested too? Or was this a drug-induced dream? She cracked one eye open. Nope. It was Joel.

"What did you get arrested for?"

He chuckled, his laugh bouncing around the cell. "Nothing, babe. It's morning. You're sprung." He helped her sit up. "How's the head?"

She assessed the pain level against the woozies. "Better. I'm a bit fuzzy-brained, though." And she had to use the restroom. Thank goodness Joel got her out. "So, how come I'm sprung? Did you manage to get the truth through Jim Bob's stubborn, thick head?"

"Shh, honey, he's standing behind me."

"Oh. Well—" She rolled to the side to look around Joel and glared at the sheriff. "You should have known I wouldn't do what you accused me of."

"Yeah, well, you have to admit the evidence looked bad, Claire." At least Jim Bob had the grace to blush. A long string, hanging from his back pocket, swayed as he walked out of the cell. He left the door open.

"Come on, babe. Nathan's here for Patsy, and you can both leave." He helped her off the bunk.

"What about Hazel and Mel?"

Joel glanced at the other ladies, and shrugged. "I'm sorry, I don't know."

"That's okay, Claire. My old man will have me out soon enough. Mel? What about you, kid?"

"My stepmother's coming."

Claire studied her. The girl had a story that she wanted to know. She laid a hand on Joel's arm and gave a slight gesture with her head. His eyes widened then he raised one brow in reluctant acceptance. Claire leaned over and kissed his cheek, then turned back to the teenager.

"Mel, when you get out of here, come by *The Painted Loon*. I'd like to talk to you some more."

She stared at Claire for a long moment, then shrugged. "Maybe."

Claire would have to be satisfied with that. She took Joel and Patsy's arms and they walked out.

They didn't get far before Jim Bob stopped them in the office.

"Claire, we need you to show us where you got those leaves. From what you have said, someone is farming it."

"I can do that now if you want. I'd like to find out who got me into this mess."

A laugh sneaked out of Joel's nose. She elbowed his ribs. "Let me rephrase that. I'd like to know whose farm it is, too."

After a quick stop by the house for her to freshen up, Joel helped Claire into her ski jacket, and they met Jim Bob and Farley in the driveway. Her muscles were stiff and sore but not as bad as she expected. Once they left the yard and started into the woods, the temperature dropped further. The anemic sun didn't make it through the tree cover and it was breath-fogging cold. Dry leaves crunched beneath her feet, releasing the earthy aroma of mulch into the air. A blue jay squawked at them as it flew low over their heads, and a woodpecker applied his beak to a nearby trunk, the mini jackhammer echoing through the trees.

With Joel beside her and Jim Bob and Farley following, she led them to the clearing where she'd found the leaves. When she came to the field, she stopped at its edge. This time, instead of seeing a few rows of plants, she saw a field of illegal activity. Other places may have voted marijuana legal for medical purposes, but it was still against the law here, and it violated the forest.

With a sweep of her arm, she pointed. "There it is. I don't know how big it is, I didn't go into it, just picked some leaves from the outer plants."

Jim Bob reached out his hand to Farley, who slapped a pair of binoculars into it. Jim Bob raised them to his eyes and scanned from left to right and back again.

"What are you looking for?" Joel pulled off his cap and scratched the back of his head.

"I know these woods like my own backyard." Jim Bob handed the binoculars back to Farley. "On the far side of this field and another fifty yards, is Felix Riley's land."

"Felix?" She stared at Joel and Jim Bob. "The mayor may be a sour pickle, but he's no criminal. It has to be Dale. I don't believe Felix knows anything about this, but now we know where his brother got the rest of the money he needed to invest in the hotel group."

Nodding, Jim Bob pulled out a scrubby little notebook and scribbled in it. "You're probably right, Claire, but I still have to talk to Felix."

"You know Dale skipped town, don't you?"

"Yeah, I heard y'all uncovered that hotel business. Good job." His grudging respect came a bit late for her. He folded the notebook in half and shoved it into his back pocket, catching its edge. That's probably how it got so frayed. "But we'll find him. Come on, Farley. Let's go talk to Felix."

Claire grabbed his arm and stopped him. "Don't you dare tell him I accused him of this. I'll never hear the end of it."

The gap between Jim Bob's front teeth always made her stare when he grinned. How was she supposed to ignore something like that? She forced her eyes to his.

"Don't worry, Claire. I'll be sure to tell him you defended his honor."

She wasn't sure how to take that. He disappeared into the trees, Farley waving over his shoulder.

"Well, kid, you're exonerated." Joel hugged her and rested his chin on the unwounded side of her head. She'd always loved that he was a head taller than her. They fit so well together. "I wonder what you'll get into next?"

She slapped his backside. "I'm sticking to my pottery. I'm tired of leaves anyway."

He leaned back and grinned. "Until a new whim catches your fancy. Aw, Clairey-girl, I love you just the way you are."

He looked around then kissed her. Then they strolled back towards home. Overhead, the same blue jay—she was sure of it—squawked at them. They'd invaded its territory. She wished she could capture this moment. Heaven must be like this, beautiful and peaceful. Her heart clenched. It wouldn't be so wonderful if Joel weren't there. If only …

They reached home and Joel opened the front door. "Put a pot of coffee on, will you? We need to talk to Wes and Costancia."

"Oh? Why?"

"Because it was Costancia who called the sheriff."

Chapter 36

"**W**hy, Joel?" Claire blinked to clear his blurred image, but tears continued to fill her eyes. Of all that Costancia threw her way, the verbal jabs and insults, this hurt the worse. This went beyond words to destruction.

"I could have gone to prison. Our family would have been devastated by the embarrassment."

Only by the grace of God, Jim Bob realized it wasn't true, finally. But what had driven her daughter-in-law to carry out such a vindictive act?

"What would she have gained by it, Joel?"

Determination thinned his lips. "That's what I intend to find out. Some things can be ignored, but not this."

Claire went to the kitchen, filled the pot with water, then reached for the ibuprofen bottle on the top shelf next to the fridge. The pain pills Vince gave her were too strong. She needed her wits about her for the coming confrontation.

Tomorrow was Christmas Eve. She scooped fresh grounds into the filter basket. Could they get this behind them and have a merry Christmas or would the holiday be ruined?

Please, Lord? Help me understand.

In a still, quiet corner of her heart, she heard, *"Wait on me."*

As soon as the coffee was ready, she took Joel a mug. He smiled his thanks and took a sip, then punched in a number on the phone. That one was to Happy, asking him to relieve Wes at the marina. Happy was always glad for an excuse to be there. His hobby shop ran itself with the help of a couple of teens, so he could easily accommodate Joel's request. The next call was to Wes.

Claire slipped back into the kitchen. She needed more time. Confronting Costancia was worse than facing the sheriff—or even Motor-mama for that matter. She'd always gotten by with sarcasm or witty remarks to cover for her discomfort. Okay, she could admit she stuck her foot in her mouth a lot, voicing her thoughts. But God had made it clear she couldn't do that with Costancia. As much as she wanted to sling a zinger or two, she had to keep her mouth shut.

"It's been so hard, Lord," she whispered. "Remind me why I'm doing this."

For my glory.

Van Gogh's ear. She couldn't argue with that. She'd just have to trust that God had a good reason. Joel joined her in the kitchen and refreshed his coffee then poured her one.

"Wes will be here shortly. He's picking up Costancia then coming right here."

"You sure we couldn't have talked to Wes by himself?"

"You can't avoid this, honey. Don't try to deny that you don't want to confront her. I understand that, but our relationship with Wesley is on the line here."

She could barely swallow around the lump in her throat.

Fifteen agonizing minutes later, the front door opened. She cast a panicked glance at Joel. He took her hand. "In here, son."

Costancia's eyes were rimmed in red, and Wes slumped. When she saw Claire's bandaged head, Costancia gasped and burst into tears. Wes put his arm around her and led her over to a seat at the banquette.

"Ma, I'm sorry, so very sorry about this." Moisture glistened in his eyes. "Are you okay?"

"My head will be fine. I'm not so sure about my heart, love, but I need to know why."

Joel set mugs of coffee in front of Wes and Costancia. A small, sad smile lifted one corner of her mouth. She whispered something to Wes. He nodded. She took a sip then a deep breath.

"*Dona Claire, sinto, tão arrependido,* sorry. So sorry. I not—" she glanced at Wes for help.

"Understand?"

She shook her head. "No. Not understand." She pointed to her head.

"Know?" Claire said, venturing a guess.

"*Sim,* know. I not know what I do."

"But, Wes, how could she not know?" Claire wanted to understand her daughter-in-law. She wanted to love her. Right now, she felt sorry for her, but what about tomorrow? Would the girl go back to hating her?

Joel squeezed her hand. "Son, Mom and I need to understand why your wife has been filled with hatred for your mother. And she has, you know, not to mention the ridicule."

Wes swallowed. "I know. I didn't see it before, but 'Lissa called me and opened my eyes. I questioned Costy as soon as 'Lissa told me about what happened. She told me about her grandmother—her father's mother. She was a possessive, bitter woman, who hated Costy's mother for marrying her son. This grandmother made her mother's life miserable. Then her maternal grandmother said that *her* mother-in-law had been the same. They told Costy all mothers hate their son's wives, and you would be the same. Loosely translated, they said the only way to make it was to 'give before she got.'"

Joel leaned forward. "But, didn't she see when she got here that your mother wasn't like that? How could she *not* see the way your mom tried to be nice to her?"

"She believed it was all an act. Then, Dale Riley told her you were going to have her arrested for drug running and deported."

"What?" Claire and Joel's words came out as one.

Costancia jumped. Shaking, tears filled her eyes again. Claire saw a frightened young woman, clinging to her husband. One who was in a world she didn't understand, where they spoke a language she didn't know. All she knew was what her mother told her. She scooted down the bench to where Costancia sat on the other side and took both her hands in her own. Claire waited until Costancia looked her in the eye.

"*Perdôo-te.* I forgive you." Claire raised one shoulder at her son and husband's gaping jaws. "I looked it up online and have been practicing."

Joel continued to stare at her like he didn't know her. "But you didn't know about Dale and her calling the police."

"I know, but I kept believing I'd find a way through to her so she'd realize I cared."

When Wes translated, the look of wonder on Costancia's face was worth every insult and barb. Then, her daughter-in-law buried her head in her hands and sobbed. For being seven years older than Wes, she sure seemed young. Maybe naïve was a better word.

Wes cradled her against his chest. Her son had matured into a man. A man with a wife he adored. Pride swelled Claire's chest, making it difficult to breathe. She glanced at Joel. He wasn't looking at them but still stared at her. Did she have coffee dripping off her chin or what? She brushed her hand under it, but it was dry.

Costancia babbled something, and Wes smiled for the first time since he arrived. He nodded. She licked her lips then stood and stepped in front of Claire, reaching for her hand as if to shake it.

She *did* shake it. "*Olá, Mãe Bennett.* Hello, Mother Bennett. I *contente*—pleased to meet you."

Now, her daughter-in-law blurred in front of her. Then she laughed. She stood and pulled Costancia into her arms. "Me, too, sweetheart, me too."

Thank you, Lord.

I told you.

Indeed you did. Oh, it was going to be a good Christmas—that was if Joel would close his mouth and quit staring at her like she was an alien. Over Costancia's shoulder, Claire tapped two fingers to the bottom of her jaw. He clamped his shut.

Christmas morning was all Claire had hoped it would be. Costancia laughed over her star leaf necklace and hugged Claire. Years from now, they would tell their children how their momma had their Nana thrown in jail. Amazing how much wrong love could cover. Sandi, Megan, and Melissa loved their necklaces as well. But Melissa's favorite gift had been the CD Claire gave her of loon calls.

Now the room was a sea of colorful wrapping paper, and she was one contented woman.

"Mom." Sandi stood before her with Charlie just behind her. She held out a small package. "I—we wanted to wait until everyone had finished. This is for both you and Dad."

Claire shifted her eyes to Joel, but he looked as mystified as she was.

"Go ahead, open it." Charlie's chest puffed as he put his arm around Sandi.

Intrigued, Claire couldn't rip the paper off the box fast enough. She opened it, and inside laid two tiny pair of booties. One pink and one blue. Claire threw the box in the air with a shriek and jumped up to hug Sandi. Joel caught the box and one of the booties as they flew. After setting them on the coffee table, he clapped Charlie on the back. "Congratulations, son."

"Twins!" Claire gasped. "I'm going to be a grandmother twice over. I can't wait till May."

Sandi laughed.

Wes translated the news to Costy—as Claire had been instructed to call her—who blushed and gave Sandi a shy hug. They'd learned Costy's family was not demonstrative, so she was still shy about hugging, but overcoming that endeared her more to Claire. She nodded her approval to Costy, who beamed back at her.

Once again, Claire caught Joel assessing her. What was going on inside that man's head? She didn't have time to ask, though, before he rose and went to the kitchen. It was time for their Christmas breakfast, Joel's personal gift to them. Each year he always made something new and special for Christmas brunch.

This year it was seafood crepes in a glorious gravy. Claire cut into hers and discovered baby shrimp, scallops and—""What's the white fish?"

"Pangasius and surimi." He spooned more gravy over hers.

"Hmm, it's heavenly. You outdid yourself this year, chef. What's on top of it?"

"I know, Mom." Sandi jumped in. She'd been taking lessons from Joel. "It's one of the four 'mother sauces' called velouté sauce."

Oops, so it wasn't gravy. Good thing she didn't say that out loud.

Costy tasted hers and pronounced it "Oommy." She hadn't quite gotten a handle on some pronunciations, but she just grinned when they all laughed. She told Wes she'd finally realized their teasing was what she called verbal love. In Portuguese, of course.

The day passed warm and wonderful. Claire couldn't recall a more perfect Christmas unless it was one when the kids were all little. But now, she glanced at Sandi and Charlie sitting with Wes and Costy and Adrianna and her new friend—what was his name? Andrew—by the fire, playing cards. Soon now, she and Joel would have twin grandbabies to play Santa for.

Joel came up behind her and put his arm around her waist. He kissed her cheek. Together, they watched the card game. Wes reached over and helped Costy with a play, and she rewarded him with a quick cheek busing. All six laughed.

Love and laughter. Christmas joy.

Claire laid her head against Joel's shoulder. "Wes really loves her, doesn't he?"

"Yeah. It took us a while, but I think we're finally seeing the girl he fell in love with. Want to go for a walk? Look at the lights?"

She nodded. "Sounds good."

They put Shiloh's new Christmas collar and leash on him, told the kids they were leaving, and slipped on their coats. Their breath fogged as they walked and it smelled like snow. The town glowed. Even the air seemed to sparkle from the lights decorating every house in Chapel Springs. She wondered how it looked—

"Wouldn't it be wonderful to see this from the air?"

Joel pulled on the dog's leash to bring him to heel. "That could be arranged. What would really be fun would be a hot air balloon."

Claire stopped. Shiloh took the opportunity to investigate a neighbor's fence. "That's a great idea." She put her hand on his arm. "Can you really arrange it?"

"I have a new slip rental. He's a balloon enthusiast." He tugged on the dog's lead. "He already offered to take us up."

Shiloh whined so they started walking again. "That's on my bucket list, you know, the hot air balloon ride."

"I know."

They strolled for a few minutes, looking at the lights. Claire pointed to Seth and JoAnn's house with its display of a miniature—if you could call six-feet tall miniature—Ferris wheel with stuffed animals in the chairs.

"This Christmas night felt different," she said. "I'm not sure why, though. Megan and Melissa have dates. That's new for Christmas, but not unexpected. They're growing up." For the first time, Adrianna brought someone home for Christmas. Claire figured that would mean another wedding in the not too distant future. "What do you think of Adrianna's young man?"

Joel turned his collar up around his neck. "He seems to have a good head on his shoulders."

She had to ask. "What do you think of her with a preacher?" Claire waved at Ellie, who opened her door to let her cat in.

"That part surprised me, but only because I always thought she'd go for another techie."

And his answer surprised her. "It won't bother you having a preacher in the family?"

"Nope. I'd like that."

He would? "You would?"

"Yep."

"Oh." Claire waited, but he walked in silence. Then he started to whistle, another of his many talents. She couldn't whistle a recognizable tune if she tried. The only whistle she ever learned was the two-fingered kind to hail a cab or get everyone's attention. But Joel could rival the birds.

Wait a minute. That sounded like—

"What song is that?"

"Don't you recognize it?"

"I thought I did, but then I wasn't sure." It couldn't be. "It sounds like one of the hymns we sing at church."

Joel stopped and put his hands on her shoulders. Shiloh flopped down at his feet. Her husband's eyes crinkled, his smile shy, as he gazed steadily into hers. "It is, babe. It's Amazing Grace."

What was he telling her? Peace radiated from him. Her heart beat faster. "What ..."

"It means I talked to Seth yesterday."

It couldn't be. Could it? She tried to swallow the clump of tears staging a sit-in in her throat. "And?"

Joel's eyes did a kind of slow blink. "And I prayed with him."

Of all the times for her mouth to refuse to work. Her tongue stuck to the roof of her mouth, but in her soul, a symphony played. Tears filled her eyes so she couldn't see Joel clearly, but her heart—oh, how her heart sang. And it was on key.

God had told her to wait and she'd see his glory. Boy, did she!

Thank you, Lord.

Joel held her close for a moment, then nudged her and they started walking again. She blinked away her happy tears and patted Shiloh when he wiggled his way between them. Overhead, the sky let loose gentle snowflakes. She raised her collar against the cold, glancing at Joel. She had to know.

"What made you finally believe? What did Pastor Seth say?"

"Any number of good things that made me think." Joel stopped again. Poor Shiloh gave them an exasperated look and sat. "But it was you, Claire. Seeing you helped me believe."

She turned to him and poked her index finger to her chest. "Me? What did I do?"

"You loved."

What did he mean? "Loved who?"

He shoved his hands in his pockets and shrugged one shoulder. "You were determined to love Costy and didn't give up. I knew her insults hurt your feelings, but you never retaliated. You kept showing her love and didn't say one unkind word." One half of his mouth rose. "I realized only one thing could have caused that change in you. And that's what opened my eyes to a very real God, who cares for us."

It didn't matter that they were on the street. In that moment, she received her heart's desire. She threw her arms around him and kissed him. Right there on Sandy Shores Drive—in public.

And he kissed her back.

The End

Joel's Sausage & Oyster Stuffing

Serves 8 – 12

- 1-2 packages of seasoned stuffing mix (I prefer Pepperidge Farm)
- 8 oz butter (1 stick)
- 1 8 oz pkg sausage links (you'll use the grease and the meat from 4 links)
- 2 C diced onions
- 1-2 Tbls minced garlic
- 2-3 celery ribs, diced (dice some of the leaves)
- 1 C mushrooms, chopped
- 1 8 oz can whole oysters, chopped and reserve liquid
- 1 tsp sage
- 1 32 oz container of chicken stock
- salt and pepper to taste

Preheat the oven to 350° F.

Dice all the vegetables. In a large skillet, cook the sausage. When done, remove the sausage and set aside. When cool, chop into pieces.

In the same skillet, caramelize the onion and garlic. Add the celery and mushrooms, and sauté until the celery is clear. Add the chopped sausage and oysters. Stir to blend. Add salt, pepper, and sage to taste.

In a large bowl, combine stuffing mix, and vegetable mixture, tossing to mix well. Add the reserved oyster liquid and enough chicken broth* to make the dressing hold together.

*If you are going to stuff a turkey to roast, use less liquid as it will absorb liquid from the bird. Refrigerate until cold before stuffing the turkey.

Put dressing in a covered casserole dish and bake at 350° F for 45 minutes.

Sweet Potatoes in Orange Halves

Serves 8

- 7 large sweet potatoes, about 3 lbs
- 4 large oranges, halved
- 1 stick unsalted butter
- 1/2 cup light brown sugar
- 3 large eggs
- 3/4 cup fresh orange juice
- 1/2 cup heavy cream
- 1/4 cup brandy*
- 1 teaspoon ground cinnamon
- 1/2 teaspoon ground nutmeg
- 1/2 teaspoon salt

Bake potatoes at 400° until tender (about 1 hour). Remove from the oven and let rest until cool enough to handle. Reduce oven temp to 350° F.

Scoop out the pulp from the orange halves, leaving only the shell. Set the shells aside to be filled later.

While still warm, either peel the potatoes or scoop out the pulp and place it in a large bowl. Toss the skins and stringy fibers. Add butter and beat out lumps with an electric mixer. Add sugar, eggs, orange juice, heavy cream, and brandy, and mix until smooth. Finally, add the cinnamon, nutmeg, and salt. Mix well, and add more seasoning if needed.

Spoon the sweet potato mixture into the orange halves, rounding off and smoothing the top. Bake until puffed and slightly golden, about 20 minutes.

*If you're a Southern Baptist or a teetotaler, you can skip the brandy. Tillie Payne's late husband was a Baptist preacher. But when he learned that the alcohol baked out, and he could safely indulge in these delectable sweet taters, he became Tillie's biggest fan.

Avocado Potato Salad

Serves 8

Ingredients
- 2 lbs. small red potatoes, cleaned
- 2 ripe, Fresh California Avocados, peeled, seeded and mashed
- 2 cloves garlic, minced
- 2 green onions, whites only, finely chopped
- ½ tsp. salt, or to taste

Boil potatoes until a fork slides in with gentle resistance, drain and refrigerate until cold. Cut potatoes in bite-sized pieces and place in a salad bowl.

Just before serving, stir in remaining ingredients*, adjust salt to taste and serve immediately.

*If desired, you can combine all ingredients ahead of time except the avocado, adding it just before serving. Or if made ahead of time with avocado added, sprinkle generously with lemon juice, then place plastic wrap right on the surface of the salad and refrigerate. Before serving, taste and add additional mashed avocado if needed.

Discussion questions

1. Claire felt betrayed when her son kept his marriage a secret until he could get his bride into the U.S. Have you ever had an adult child keep a secret from you? Is it ever right? How did you feel?

2. Claire's husband, Joel, tells his son he lied by omission. Did you agree with him? How do you handle a situation like that with an adult child?

3. Were Claire's suspicions about her son's bride illogical or justified?

4. Before Claire's new daughter-in-law arrives, Claire wants to boot her out. But Patsy tells her she'd better pray for the girl if she didn't want to alienate Wes. Have you ever had to pray for someone who was your enemy?

5. In what ways did Graham's son cause problems for his new marriage?

6. Lydia saw how her new husband couldn't say "no" to his adult children. Have you ever known someone who was like that? Why were they?

7. Graham is carrying a heavy load of guilt, even though he has a strong faith. Why?

8. What happens when Graham finally applies tough love?

9. Costy was given bad advice by her mother. Why? Have you ever received bad advice from someone you trusted?

10. What convinced Joel that God was real? Do you know the Scripture reference for that? Claire didn't realize that was what she was doing, but she believed God's promises.

Author's note

When writing this story, I had a completely different idea of how it would play out. Claire was going to dislike Costy, yet it would be through her daughter-in-law that Joel got saved, giving Claire the desire of her heart. However, God had a different idea, and as always, His is best.

Claire tried to love this girl, and through her actions, Joel saw the light. 1 Peter 3:1 says ... *Then if some refuse the Good News, your godly lives will speak to them without words. They will be won over by observing your pure and reverent lives.* NLT

Chapel Springs Survival
sponsored by these fine books:

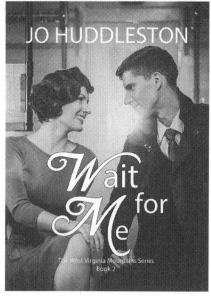

Made in the USA
Las Vegas, NV
01 November 2020

10480757R00164